QUEER FISH
VOLUME 2

QUEER FISH
VOLUME 2
AN ECLECTIC ANTHOLOGY OF GAY FICTION

EDITED BY
MARGARITA BEZDOMNYA
AND ROSE MAMBERT

PINK NARCISSUS PRESS

This is a work of fiction. All the characters and events portrayed in this book are fictitious or are used fictitiously.

QUEER FISH: *An Eclectic Anthology of Gay Fiction (Volume Two)*
© 2012 Pink Narcissus Press

Individual stories © their respective authors.

"The Mark That's Left" © 2009 by John Dimes. Originally published in *Dark Portals*, Spec Fic World. Reprinted by permission of the author.

"The Souk of Dreams" © 2010 by Keyan Bowes. Originally published in *Cabinet des Feés, Issue 11*. Reprinted by permission of the author.

"The Succession of Knoorikios Khnum" © 2009 by Zachary Jernigan. Originally published in *Wired Hard 4: Erotica for a Gay Universe*, Circlet Press. Reprinted by permission of the author.

All rights reserved. No part of this book may be reproduced in any form or by any means without the prior written consent of the Publisher, excepting brief quotes used in reviews.

Cover illustration © P.L. Nunn
Design by Rose Mambert

Published by Pink Narcissus Press
P.O. Box 303
Auburn, MA 01501
pinknarc.com

Library of Congress Control Number: 2011916069

ISBN: 978-0-9829913-9-8

First Trade Paperback: October 2012

CONTENTS

Brian's World
Dan Hart..9

Male Nude and Mango Tree
Eduardo A. Febles...................................20

Cut
Nghi Vo..…..42

Lost at Sea
J. Lannan…..........................…..............50

The Keys to the City Invisible
Willow Fagan...............................…......65

The Souk of Dreams
Keyan Bowes...............….....................74

The Mark That's Left
John Dimes.............................…..........88

The Succession of Knoorikios Khnum
Zachary Jernigan...........................…....111

Lovebites & Razorlines
J. Daniel Stone....................................127

The Clockwork Menagerie
Brian Bobowski.................…...........…..142

Farther Than That
Therese Arkenberg.............…...........162

Renovations
Gregory A. Carter.......................…...171

Apple Pie a la Mode with Just a Smidge of Human Sacrifice
    Nathan Sims......................................182

Cherry Blossom Rhapsody
    Rose Mambert...............................…....206

Camera Obscura: Two Ghosts
    Jeannelle Ferreira................….………....224

Realms
    Michael C. Thompson.........................232

Let Down Your Hair
    Jason Andrew.................….…………...248

What Everybody Sees
    Michael Penkas...............................…....257

The Boy on McGee Street
    Warren Rochelle................…..………….265

Out of Body
    Patricia J. Esposito...........................…...286

"You have some queer friends, Dorothy," she said.
"The queerness doesn't matter, so long as they're friends," was the answer.

–L. Frank Baum, *The Road to Oz*

BRIAN'S WORLD
DAN HART

When he was nine, Brian learned that if he tried really, really hard, he could change the world. He'd returned his pet tabby back to life—continued her life, he supposed, since nobody remembered her squishing into a pavement patty anymore. Nobody ever remembered his changes.

Except Dax, who now grinned at him with the same smirk as the evil cat that lived next door. Brian tried to change reality so the sophomore boy wasn't there, but it didn't work.

"I know about your secret," Dax said. "I know what you can do." Dax's grin softened to a warm, upturned smile, dimpled in the exact way Brian had always liked. "So maybe you should come over some time and hang out."

Brian clenched his fists, furious at his knotted tongue. As a high school freshman, he expected sophomores and juniors to taunt him. But this felt different, and he struggled not to panic.

Dax patted him on his back and walked away. Brian clenched his teeth, gripping his backpack, and didn't move until the first period bell had rung.

Was it possible Dax actually knew?

Brian was skeptical. He hadn't even known his own secret until five years ago, and had only risked a few large-scale changes since then.

He'd changed the cruel sixth grade geezer teacher with old growth forests sprouting from his nose into a handsome blonde who never assigned homework.

He'd changed the species of trees while hiking, elongating their leaves and creating jagged finger edges. The more contrived the look in his imagination, the more effort it took to make it. He found his changes were equally difficult to revert, so he didn't. They were just trees, nothing important.

But he returned to a far more elegant house that afternoon. The art deco carvings had changed. Variations of the leaf pattern he'd created were carved into doorframes and chairs, like a new fractal theme had defined an organic aesthetic.

Pancakes didn't have maple syrup anymore.

So he'd stopped changing things—*most* things. He didn't think anyone knew his secret. Not even Kyle.

He'd tried to tell his best friend once, two years ago in seventh grade after they'd stumbled upon a documentary which introduced the Many Worlds theory of quantum physics. Kyle found the idea of other realities stupid.

Brian thought it explained his power. If he were directly changing the world, why didn't anyone notice? Many Worlds said alternate realities branched off whenever a quantum wave collapsed; that all possible realities exist. Somehow, Brian had the ability to navigate between them.

"I can prove other realities exist," he said, smiling wide enough to hurt.

"Oh, really?"

Kyle's skeptical smirk irritated him. "Yes, really. I'll take you with me. Watch." He clenched his jaw. *Come with me, please!*

A pink cake with yellow candy flowers materialized on the floor. Kyle seemed undisturbed.

"Why's there a cake?" Brian asked. "It's neither of our birthdays." He dabbed a lick of frosting with his finger. "So why's there a cake?" It tasted good.

"Uh, because it's Thursday?"

"Thursday?"

"Cake day? Mom always bakes us cake on Thursday."

Brian suddenly felt chubbier than usual. Since blinking, Kyle's cheeks had put on over an inch of chipmunk fat. Brian felt a disturbing, compelling urge to roll his round friend down a hill. He closed his eyes, bit his lip, and clenched his thoughts to banish both cake and fat.

"So, how you gonna prove it?" Kyle asked.

∞

Brian walked behind Dax in silence the entire way to his house, and even then said nothing until they were alone in Dax's room. A giant plasma television hung off the wall, multiple gaming systems sat beneath it, and Dax's lavish bed was mahogany. "What do you know?" Brian asked, crossing his arms.

"Would you like something to eat?" Dax swept his hand in a wide offering. A box of donuts appeared on the floor.

Brian said nothing but his face burned with alarm. He plucked at stray threads sprouting from his sweater. He wondered if he hadn't changed things himself, subconsciously —but that seemed impossible. Shifting realities took considerable effort. "Who are you?" he asked. "How can you do that?"

"See, that's odd," Dax said. "Most people don't even notice. Do you know why?"

"They don't shift with you—" Brian pursed his lips, wishing he hadn't blurted that.

"So, you know what I can do. We're linked. I've never been able to link to someone before. Can you make drinks?"

"I can get some," Brian said. He feared Dax had an ulterior motive. What if he was with the FBI?

"You know what I mean. Do it."

Brian's racing heart unsteadied his voice. "Do what?"

Dax's smirk tore through his act. Brian sighed, and nodded. A chilled two-liter fruit punch materialized between them.

Dax clapped, beaming. "I knew it! How much have you changed?"

"How should I know? I try not to change much."

"Why not?"

"Unexpected consequences. What about you?"

"Lots. Do you remember North Korea?"

"Yeah."

"Remember what happened?"

Brian did—he'd always thought it was a side effect of his own meddling. It seemed odd that France had invaded North

Korea without provocation. Odder still how little outrage broke out in response.

Dax puffed his chest. "That was all me. It's kind of like a super power, isn't it?"

"Yeah." Brian hoped Dax wouldn't continue the thought. If Dax did something stupid, like summon a meteor, Brian would suffer Armageddon as well.

"So." Dax closed his eyes. The walls changed—fantastical posters of alien worlds and abstract colors now wallpapered them. "How awesome can we be, together?"

∞

That night Brian stayed over at Kyle's. He had only very slightly modified his best friend's room over the years. Kyle hadn't had a trundle bed before, and, until Brian had changed her, Kyle's mom had rarely picked up his clothes. That and the PS3.

"I need to talk to you about something," Brian said.

"Yeah? What?"

"It's secret, OK? I tried to tell you before, but—"

"Aw, shit, this isn't your coming out, is it? Everyone already knows, 'kay?"

"No, not that. It's about—wait, everyone?" Brian bit his lip and frowned. He wasn't out—he'd been careful to choose his realities. His face heated as a slight panic gripped him. He struggled to concentrate on undoing the change.

Kyle patted Brian's knee, interrupting his effort. "Everyone."

Brian shook his head and tried to resume focus. He closed his eyes and wondered how many people he would need to make forget.

"Don't worry about it. I think it's cool."

"Yeah?" Brian smiled. He could deal with his outing tomorrow. He had a bigger concern tonight. "It's not about that."

"So, what? Oh wait—is it about that sophomore you've been hanging out with? I get it! He's your boyfriend, right? I'm right, aren't I?"

"What?" Brian's eyebrows rose in horror. "No!" He

hadn't even considered Dax like that. Well, not really. He was cute, and smart. Maybe *kind of* considered. "It's not like that."
"But you like him, right?"
"He makes me nervous."
"Why?"
"Like, he has this Magneto sort of vibe," Brian said.
Kyle rolled his eyes. "Super-villain, huh? That sounds cute. You're probably just nervous because you're in love." He batted his lashes and giggled.
"This isn't about him. Look, I can blink between realities, OK? Make it so things are different."
"What?"
Brian clenched his teeth. He strained until he could feel the pressure behind his eyes, visualizing Kyle blinking to the next reality with him. A purple cake now sat on the night stand. "Why's there a cake there?"
"Because it's Cake Wednesday?"
"It was Cake Thursday last time!"
"It's always been Wednesday."
"There are too many realities where your mom enjoys baking cake," Brian said in spite, massaging his strained temples. "You just have to believe me, OK? Please?"
"OK," Kyle said. "I believe you. So what?"
"Doesn't that scare you?"
"I dunno. I guess not?"
"Why not?"
"Why would it?"
"What if I blinked us to a reality where Nazis were in charge? Or where McDonalds served cat burgers?"
"You're creeping me out." Kyle bit his lower lip, and Brian knew he was pushing too far.
"Never mind, it's just a joke."
∞
"Why'd you out me?" Brian said, pushing Dax against the lockers at school the next day. Two nearby sophomore girls covered their mouths and giggled. Brian blinked to a reality where they were out of earshot.
"How do you know I did it?" Dax asked, smirking. He

twisted his shoulders and yawned.

"Because *I* didn't."

Dax nodded, smiling proud. "So you turn to the only other person who can change the world."

Brian released him. "So did you?"

"Yeah." Dax straightened his shirt. "Like you said, who else could?"

"You can't just change things."

"Why not? You do. It's better this way. Now you won't be afraid to date me."

Brian loathed Dax's teasing smirk—even more the excitement it caused in his cheeks. He slammed his palm against the lockers and stormed off to his next class. Dax wouldn't listen unless forced to.

Brian imagined the worst possible teacher he could for Dax. In response, a brutal, bald man with a yardstick now led Brian's chemistry class. The man liked to hit things with his stick.

Brian thought to reverse the changes. His mind strained, fighting resistance that had never been there before. He imagined the fire alarms going off instead. Water erupted from the ceiling.

In a blink, things were dry again. Brian closed his eyes and struggled harder, returning to the alarming, drenched reality. He imagined himself anchored here.

He could feel Dax struggling against him. Then his mind was yanked in a different direction.

The school actually was on fire now. In a panic, Brian reimagined himself in the yardstick man's fire-free class.

His heart rate slowed. His peers sat at their desks, oblivious to the burning reality not so far away. He inhaled deeply through his nose. Thankfully, there were no further changes that day.

He caught up to Dax walking home after school. "Why'd you do that?" he asked.

"You started it, remember?" Dax tugged on his backpack straps and grinned.

"Did not."

"Think about it. Look, I like you. You're interesting, and that's rare. Your ability makes you more interesting than anyone. You're selfish, but that's to be expected. Although I never imagined you'd be such a coward."

Brian snorted, wrinkling his nose. "I'm not a coward. I just don't want you changing things. You can't just mess with my life, OK?"

"Like you don't mess with other people's lives?"

"That's different."

"Why?"

Brian didn't have an answer, but he was sure there was one.

"Don't be such a prude. Don't you want to have fun?"

"Yes, but—"

Dax pushed his finger to Brian's lips. "It's OK. I've waited this long. I'll be patient a little longer. Think about it, OK?"

∞

Brian saw Dax's influence on the news, nightly. Repercussions that couldn't possibly come from Brian's own blinking: stock market reversals, sudden shifts of political power, niche toys obtaining unwarranted research and development. He confronted Dax after an insufferable change had been made.

"Make it ice cream!" Brian said in the school cafeteria before school. He wanted it to have ice cream on Fridays, not brownies.

"I like brownies better." Dax elbowed him, which caused a ticklish laugh. Brian enjoyed the warmth of the contact enough to lean into it. "If you like ice cream so much, why not change things back?"

Brian fumed; of course he'd tried. "You're stronger than me. Don't you think you do too much?"

Dax laughed, shaking his head. "I barely do anything."

"What about all the comedians who've been elected?"

Dax shrugged. "They're funny. And probably better, don't you think?"

"How can you be so cocky about it? Aren't you ever

scared?"

"Nope. I've practiced a lot, probably since before I can remember."

"You've always been able to?"

Dax shrugged again and nodded. "I guess so." He walked closer to Brian, until their wrists touched. "I couldn't read until I was nine because I didn't care, so made my teachers not care, either."

Brian leaned against Dax. "I was a normal kid, until my cat died. Then un-died."

"I had lots of pets, but I was always lonely." They weaved around other students as they walked through the crowded hall. "I just wanted a friend who was like me, you know? More than anything."

Brian didn't like the cunning way Dax grinned. He shoved away—too roughly—and fell off-balance into a girl. She screamed and fell backward onto her arm, which made a sound like plastic snapping.

And then he hadn't shoved away at all. He felt a hole in his mind where memories burned away. Then even this feeling faded.

Dax winked at the girl he'd saved. She shuddered and avoided eye contact.

Brian panicked, his muscles coiled. He sprinted down the hall three classrooms before calming to a walk. Dax had reached into Brian's past and changed a conscious decision he'd made. Brian could feel the knowledge slipping away, and feared he would forget completely. He wondered if Dax had done this to him before.

It didn't matter—today was enough. Dax couldn't be his boyfriend, no matter how cute he was. He was a dangerous rival. How much had he changed?

The best approach would be to blink to a reality where Dax had no powers. Brian tried until his head throbbed and he was exhausted. He couldn't visualize it clearly enough; the reality was too far removed.

"Playing hard to get?" Dax asked after school.

"No," Brian said.

"So why've you been avoiding me?" Dax draped his arm over Brian's shoulder.

Brian shoved it off. "It's not gonna work, OK?"

"Why not?" Dax grimaced. "I don't understand why you don't like me."

"I don't want you to change me."

"I won't."

"You did! I shoved you, then you made me not."

"But you broke Jessica's arm."

Brian's face reddened, with embarrassment this time. "You just make me feel uncomfortable. You're so arrogant. But what if you mess things up?"

"I won't. I've practiced too much." Dax grinned, and spread his arms.

The building was no longer there—had never been there. They stood in the grassy valley where their city had been. A breeze rippled through weedy fields.

Dax faced the wind head-on. His hair and loose-fitting shirt fluttered, glowing against the blue sky. "I come here every day. It's easy."

"Isn't this a bit far?" Brian asked. He gazed at the primal landscape, feeling as if he were dangling off a cliff. How many realities removed was this? He'd once tried to blink to a reality without humans—he'd been terrified, but had wanted to push his limits. In his nightmares he'd succeeded.

"This isn't even close to how far I can go." Dax closed his eyes and clenched his fists. His cocky, sublime smile persisted as his head bobbed and rolled. Brian held his breath, fighting fearful dizziness.

The mountains turned into spouting volcanoes. A crimson sky hung overhead, thick with ash and dust. Heat scorched them. Monstrous shadows cast by giant birds speckled the ground.

Then the sky turned a clear, turquoise blue. The volcanoes gone and the valley rife with marigolds, roses, and flowers Brian had never imagined before. Birds chirped a beautiful melody.

Dax took his hand. "You've never come this far, right?

Never traced the possibilities back this far? I had to reshape continental plates for the volcanoes. Cool, right?"

No matter how hard Brian clenched his mind he knew he'd never be able to blink back to a sane reality on his own. "I just wanna go home," he said.

Dax squeezed Brian's hand. "Don't worry, we can." They shifted back into the classroom hallway. "See?"

The normality comforted Brian. But before he could relax, Dax blinked them to a frigid summer day in a tundra valley. The mountains were vaguely familiar rocky skeletons, eerily naked. Frozen stumps of icy, near-dead trees sparkled like crystal spires. Brian's neck grew goose bumps. He'd never breathed air so crisp.

"The atmosphere has more oxygen," Dax said. "It's invigorating, right? If we go even further away from our reality, different forms of life branch off. Entirely different evolutionary trees. Alien geology and chemistry. Biology you can't even imagine. Don't you want to see, together? If we combined imaginations, just think of what we could find."

Brian's stomach bubbled queasy air pockets and he felt dizzy. His knees quaked and he stumbled, but maintained his balance. He found he couldn't meet Dax's eyes. "I want to," he said. But what if he lost his anchor to reality? What if they shifted to a reality without oxygen and passed out? Or too much and a static shock from his sweater ignited the atmosphere? "But I can't."

"Why not?"

Brian didn't want to admit his cowardice, so he lied instead. "Because I don't like you."

"Not true. You have to."

Too many thoughts crowded Brian's mind. He needed time to think. "Find someone else, OK?"

Dax shook his head. "I want you."

"Just let me think about it," Brian said. His throat was dry. "Let me think about it in the real world."

"What real—"

"My real world!" He clenched his teeth. "Please."

"OK. If that's really what you want." They blinked back.

Brian ditched the rest of school. He faked illness and lay on his bed, staring at the glowing stars on his ceiling.

Dax was so powerful. Brian wouldn't be able to resist if Dax decided to drag him to some perverse or horrifying reality. Dax wanted him, and it was probably only a matter of time before Dax would force his will. Brian tried to keep his eyes open but sleep hunted him. Each heavy blink flashed visions of nightmare realities.

There was only one escape, he concluded. He hadn't been able to drag Kyle with him. He bet Dax couldn't drag normal people along, either. If he abandoned his powers, wouldn't Dax leave him alone?

He shed a selfish tear and struggled harder than he'd ever struggled before, to imagine a world where he didn't have his ability. Where his cat was dead and he never got what he wanted. He fell asleep trying.

∞

Dax tapped his shoulder at school the next day. Brian couldn't remember why the sophomore held interest in him. He was glad, though, because he thought Dax was cute.

"You did something rash, didn't you?" Dax asked.

"What?" Brian felt time slow between heartbeats. Had he done something foolish? He checked his shoes to make sure toilet paper wasn't trailing.

"I could undo it, you know." Dax grinned, but it didn't seem like a grin. It reminded Brian of the evil cat next door. "I could make you interesting, again."

"What?" Brian blinked, uncomprehending.

"Don't worry, there'll be others. So I'll respect your choice."

Dax wasn't making sense, but Brian nodded eagerly. "Wanna do something together?" he asked. He hoped Dax would say yes.

"Nah," Dax said. "You're boring."

MALE NUDE AND MANGO TREE
EDUARDO A. FEBLES

My twin brother's name was Òjó Ikú.

I killed him with the umbilical cord while still in my mother's womb.

Mami and Papi never mentioned my twin brother, but I knew they hated me for what I had done. Killing him was like killing them, like killing myself. So I was born in the dead sea of my twin brother. At times I feel as if I have been amputated right down to my soul, as though someone has chopped up half of my being, and it is running around somewhere, like a lizard's tail severed from its body.

And then, there are the shadows from the mango tree.

At night, especially when the moon is out, I can see the little boy hanging there from one of the branches, the noose around his neck, his listless legs swinging to and fro with the wind. The aluminum blinds cut horizontal shadows, the moon casting them onto the blades of the fan above me, dismembering the body into sections as it spins and spins and spins and spins above me. There goes the head. There goes a finger. There goes the...

I go to the window, trembling with fear, and see the little boy out there and I know it's Òjó Ikú with his *ojo* staring at me, as if I were staring back at myself in a mirror, as if my consciousness had been disembodied and it was hanging out there on the tree. I close the blinds, stifling inside, the heavy humid air in the room despite the spinning fan, but to no avail: the shadow remains on the wall, the listless legs, the noose, the to and fro. The blades keep on spinning, and the body keeps on fragmenting. I lie down and close my eyes as hard as I can, but the shadow persists in the back of the screen of my head, the legs, the noose, all is there, I know it's my identical twin, I know it's myself, I know I am guilty.

∞

Miami, Florida
August 1992

Blankness.
The red light, the smell, the blank sheet of paper, the vast potentiality of nothingness. Mo loved putting the paper in the developer and waiting for the image to emerge. From a confused hue of gray, shapes began to make sense, like memories. Shadows grew into perception, producing depth. Here, the bark of the tree. There the ass of Aché. Here the dangling feet. There the scarlet scar. Or was it a birthmark? Right there, you can clearly see it, on the buttock. How did he miss it while shooting him? As soon as Mo saw the scar, he understood Aché was the long lost one.

Earlier that month, Mo had placed an ad in Miami's Spanish newspaper, looking for a male model to do a photo shoot. Aché was the first to answer. He apparently needed the money. Mo invited him over to the house and asked him to strip down so that he could evaluate the man's physique. Mo proceeded to cut him into pieces with a piercing eye. Aché's coffee-tainted face had been nicely roasted by a Cuban sun, eyebrows smiling backwards, dark eyes darting forth confidently, a somewhat flattened nose extending the wings of its nostrils. His well-developed upper body was symmetrically divided by a straight line, accentuating his pectorals and washboard abs. His broad upper back was aesthetically echoed by his curvaceous, tightly flexed buttocks. His somewhat limp, uncut penis proudly hung in the pubic area, surrounded by wild wisps of straw-like hair.

"It'll do."

Aché thought for a moment and seemed to acquiesce with small, nodding movements as he pulled up his underwear.

"How much will you pay me?"

"Fifty bucks a session."

"To do what?"

"Do you see that mango tree out there?"

Mo pointed to the mango tree out in the yard. It was a child of the tree that haunted Mo's childhood with shadows of its branches creeping inside his room.

"What about it?"

"I want to shoot you naked next to it. It's for a series of photographs entitled: 'Male Nude and Mango Tree.'"

It was a magnificent tree. Its branches extended over a large area of the yard though it had grown somewhat lopsidedly, the left side being lusher than the right, giving the impression the tree could topple over from the weight of its foliage. In January, it was covered with tiny, pink promises, blossoms of future delights. At the beginning of the hurricane season, the mangoes were already ripe and exquisite, lazily hanging from branches, waiting to tumble under their weight, to be picked by an impatient hand, to be pecked by the beak of a bird. As a child, Mo remembers savagely devouring the yellowish-orange flesh, biting into its pulp, covering his face as his mouth desperately sucked the seed to clean it completely, threads of fruit lodged between his teeth. But he also remembers the shadows.

"What's your name?"

"Aché."

Like the silent letter H in Spanish, which you only pronounce when spelling it. Like "ache" in English, but not like pain, more like a sneeze, like "achoo" but with an "e" at the end. Like "hache" in French, meaning ax, but with an accent aigu, like "haché." So chop me off already, will you?

∞

The night had not cooled off the steamy heat from the day before. Mo stepped out of a cold shower drenched in sweat. The heat was unbearable, tenaciously sticking to his body like salt after a swim in the sea, like wind-swept sand from a faraway desert. In the fogged-up mirror, Mo captured a glimpse of the tree crying with morning dew. A low-hanging branch was heavy with a pair of mangoes, and from this angle they looked like testicles. He framed a reflection of his own body, drops adorning stray hairs from his underarms, nipples nestled in a forest of darkness, trailing down his stomach to his full-balled flaccidness.

His frustration over the photo shoot had not subsided. It had been a fiasco, what with the erections and all. He'd ripped up all the photos of Aché, strewn them around the floor, stamping on them, *pisoteándolas* with rage and tears streaming from his eyes. He picked up the pieces and taped them to the wall haphazardly, here the ass of Aché, there the bark of the tree. He noticed the dangling feet. He noticed the scar. The blades started spinning again above his head.

Because Mo had wanted to take advantage of the soft morning light, Aché had shown up early the day before. He was wearing a tight, green A-shirt, a puddle of sweat already forming on his chest, jeans accentuating his ass. As of yet, Mo had but a vague idea of his artistic vision. He wanted a naked black man standing next to the mango tree.

"*Desnúdate.* Take your clothes off," Mo ordered.

They went outside in the heat. The tree was waiting, branches extended in a welcoming embrace, rivers of water flowing through the brown cracks of its bark, drops of dew desperately clinging to the green leaves.

"What do you want me to do?"

"Nothing, just stand next to the tree. Don't pose, just stand there with your arms down."

The roughness of the bark contrasted nicely with the smoothness of Aché's skin; the complexity of the branches with the simplicity of his symmetrical body; the straightness of the trunk with the limp penis. Mo took a first picture, and the sound of the click triggered something down there.

"Aché, what's going on? No hard-ons."

Aché looked a bit flustered.

"I don't know. Can't help it."

"What do you mean? I just took one picture, and your penis shot right up."

"Sorry, I guess it got me excited to be in front of the camera."

They waited for his cock to go limp. Mo slowly raised

his camera to frame Aché, and he sensed the tension rising, the erection coming on again. Aché's penis was as magnificent as the tree, the foreskin slowly receding as it grew with expectation, revealing the fullness of the smooth head. Mo thought of eating his mangoes, and the threads lodged in his teeth, and mango goo smeared all over his mouth and, yes, the thought crossed his mind as he looked at the penis rising in its glory.

The thought crossed my mind.

"Listen, why don't you turn around? I don't need a frontal shot just now. Lean against the tree, let your body lean against the trunk."

Mo took a couple of pictures, framing the buttocks and part of the trunk. Frustrated, he paid Aché the $50.00 and told him never to come again.

"Don't ever come back. We're done."

Aché apologized as if he had done something wrong.

∞

Upon seeing the scarlet scar, fragments of memories assaulted Mo's consciousness, firing off like fireworks against the backdrop of a moonless night sky. He recognized it as his own, as the scar of history screaming with the voice of hatred. Mo examined the picture with a magnifying glass, and the scar started to burn, drops of blood irrigating the surface of Aché's buttocks. The wind came in, and the ashes blew and exploded into a fine dusting of confusion.

∞

Puerto Rico
Summer 1979
The story of Mo

I was fifteen years old in 1979, the year in which three storms visited the island in succession: Claudette, David, and Frederic. On Wednesday, July 18th, tropical storm Claudette traversed the island with 35 mph sustained winds. Frederic assaulted the island on Tuesday, September 4th, with 50 mph winds. Of the three, however, David was potentially the most dangerous and the scariest. A Goliath of a storm, David was a category 5 hurricane packing winds of over 150 mph. It would go on to kill over 2000 people and destroy part of the Dominican Republic.

On August 29th, all indications pointed to a direct hit, slamming into the island on the south, where we lived. We proceeded to complete the quasi-religious, ritualistic shenanigans that accompanied every threat of a major hurricane. In fact, hurricanes remain to this day some of my most intense memories of childhood: boiling water, lighting candles, boarding up windows, cleaning the yard. The large glass doors dividing the living room from the dining room were marked by a giant, masking tape X, from top to bottom, to keep it from shattering into shards. We went to bed that night only to awake to the calm before the storm.

Nothing had changed about its predicted path, and the hurricane had only intensified in strength. As night set, we gathered in the living room, waiting in the tense atmosphere of anticipation, waiting for it to begin. Papi was watching the TV weatherman rambling on and on, Mami's already wrinkled hands moved swiftly from bead to bead as her lips monotoned each prayer of the rosary. Next to our panting dog, my sister was dreaming, her pink panties showing innocently through her pajamas. Once in a while, a thump from a tumbling mango added a discordant note to the barely audible symphony being written against the backdrop of the storm. I was lying down on the cold tile floor of the living room and still could not wash away the heat clinging to my skin.

In my memory, hurricanes always struck at night, usually after midnight. The voice of the weatherman rambled on until the lights flickered convulsively, gasping for air as the barometric pressure plummeted, and quietly went out, as if tired of waiting. Darkness fell. An unbearable silence permeated the room, a sheet of gauze hardly scratched by the incessant tick-tock of my grandfather's grandfather clock.

Mami had fled Cuba in 1963 inside the entrails of that clock. She was pregnant with Òjó Ikú and me. Her sister Tata stuffed her inside of it, she had to press on the belly to close the glass door, and I remember the unbearable pressure on my body. It was my first memory. Tata launched the clock onto the sea just as Hurricane Flora was visiting the island. Afefé picked us up and took us all the way to Key West. When we landed in Cayo Hueso, Mami was floating in a wretched sea of death for I had strangled Òjó Ikú with the umbilical cord inside of her right before my birth. His silent wails were carried all the way across the sea by gigantic waves, tsunamis of pain crashing against the shore of Cuba, hitting Tata on the face. She recognized it as the truth and understood that Òjó Ikú had died. She understood she would never see her sister again.

The acute smell of stale air invaded the house, crawled into its corners, hid beneath the furniture, penetrated our imagination. Suddenly, I heard the muffled voice of Òjó Ikú and I approached the window of the living room overlooking the mango tree in our backyard. As night stretched out into an infinite canvas of nothingness, the sky became blue-black with ominous clouds. At first, the branches were eerily still, holding a proud pose against the oncoming storm. The dog's ears perked up, sensing before any of us the slight breeze traveling from the horizon across the Caribbean Sea. His panting became more regular and he stood up and walked to the window, sitting next to me and looking at the mango tree. The branches were imperceptibly moving now; the leaves trembled at the stem, a melodious sound emanating as the wind caressed the strings of their veins.

I pointed with my index finger at my twin brother, and my mother, father and sister all joined me at the window. I told them Òjó Ikú was out there all alone, swinging back and forth as the wind became more powerful.

"*No hay nadie, mijo.* Òjó Ikú does not exist."

That was my mother, but I knew she saw him out there, and my father and my sister did also. Even the dog barked upon hearing the screeching, squeaking, creaking of the rope rubbing against the branch of the tree, as the body moved to and fro, ever faster as the wind intensified in force, like the pendulum of the heirloom clock. The accusatory shadow grew enormously, creeping slowly into the living room, invading the walls, the floor, the ceiling, until we were all engulfed by it, inside of a woman's cavernous womb. As the squalls intensified, Òjó Ikú let out acute squealing screams just like the ones he had spilled forth on the day I killed him with the umbilical cord. The sound of the rustling leaves ceased to be melodious as the thumping of falling mangoes accelerated the tempo of the infernal symphony. The never-ending tick-tock of the clock kept the beat. The dog wailed a long, drawn-out, lonely howl. My mother's lips murmured prayers at dizzying speeds. I thought she was accusing me of the murder, resentful of what I'd done, regretting her long lost son.

My father shut the blinds, but I stood there by the closed window, listening intently to my dead brother's suffering. The shadow remained.

∞

Papi brought out the candles, and the living room was suddenly transformed into a chapel. I knelt and confessed my sins. I used to like the confessional because it had two sections, and you were separated from the priest by a wooden mesh, so you really couldn't tell who was on the other side though you could see the color of his cassock and the movements of his hands as he raised and lowered them. I started going to confession when I was seven years old to prepare for my first communion. When Padre B. asked me if I had sinned, I told him I had. He recognized my voice and told me to trust him.

I trust you.

Come around to this side, my son.

I hesitated a bit because I did not know if that was allowed, so I asked him.

Of course it's allowed. As a priest, I'd never tell you to do something that's not allowed, my son. So, what's on your mind?

Forgive me Father, for I have sinned. I killed my twin brother Òjó Ikú. I strangled him with the umbilical cord when I was in my mother's womb.

Padre B. wasn't expecting this from a child. He put his hand on my head and told me this sin was very grave indeed, that it was a mortal sin, that I could go to hell, and that my mother would be very upset if I went to hell. His hand lingered

on my head as I was kneeling down in front of him and my knees started to itch, and the odor from his cassock was a bit foul, so I wished I were still on the other side of the divider. His hand lingered on my head and he touched my left cheek, my right cheek, my lips.
 You don't want to go to hell, right, my son?
 No, Father, I don't want to go to hell.
 He asked me to sit on his lap, that it would be more comfortable than kneeling down. So I stood up and did not understand what was happening when I sat on his lap. He told me I was going to hell unless I did exactly as told. The sin could be erased, but it would take a long time to heal. I was to come to confession every week and I had to do as told but never to speak to anyone about it.
 That would make it even worse, that would send you to hell instantly, you will die if you ever tell anyone.
 Not even Mami?
 Especially not your mother, my son. She is never to know what transpires here in confession. You promise, my son?
 His hand touched my cheeks and my nest. I did not know if that was allowed. I felt ashamed because I felt pleasure.
 I promised.
 I promise.
 It's OK, my son.
 But I killed my brother, Father.
 It's OK. God forgives you, and so do I.
 At that point my heart was pounding as hard as the ticktock of the clock in the living room, to the rhythm of the little boy's dead body swinging to and fro in the wind, hung from the mango tree. I was small then, very short, so Padre B. basically covered me under his soutane, whiteness around me, spinning like a hurricane and the Òjó in the middle. I felt like vomiting from the stench. He told me God liked it.
 God likes it, my son.

∞

 At the exact moment that my grandfather's grandfather clock chimed midnight, the house started to shake with the wind, the roof stubbornly clinging to the walls like the roots of a powerful tree. The door came asunder, opening with a thrash as loud as thunder, letting the wind invade our abode. The clock was swept up, flying through the living room and hitting my mother in the face with truth. Yet, she did not recognize it as such, crept back inside it like when she fled from Cuba, and fell asleep.

Papi told us to go to our rooms and to remain there until he came to get us.

So I'm in my bedroom, the one at the end of the hall next to my parents' room. The one with four sets of windows letting all the shadows in through the aluminum blinds even though they are shut tight, even though there is no light. The heat is unbearable, and the sound of the tips of the branches scratching at the aluminum shutters like nails on an empty blackboard shatters my nerves. The motionless blades of the fan above me still reflect fragments of my twin brother. I pull two candles from under my pillow and, with a set of matches that I'd stolen, light them and place them on the floor. The flames flicker with the wind penetrating every fissure of the house, and the shadow of the hanged boy grows ominously larger. The impatient branches tear apart the blinds, crawl into the room, the roots rattle as they glide across the floor. The branches creep up my leg and slowly entangle my limbs, my limb. They creep up my chest and slowly entangle my back. They creep up my face and slowly coil around my thoughts. They find my boyish nest and nestle there uncomfortably like Father B.'s prurient dick. I become one with the tree.

The mattress catches fire as the wind fans the flames. They spin like the blades of the fan and engulf the bed, the tree, my body. The ashes blow around and swirl into a fine dusting of confusion. The door of my room comes asunder with a loud explosion, the clock flies across the room and crashes in on me. I finally understand.

I AM Òjó Ikú.

$$\infty$$

Miami, Florida
August 1992

Mo called Aché, asking for forgiveness, telling him he had to see him again, that it was urgent, very important.

He came the next morning and Mo showed him the picture.

"What do you think of the feet?"

Mo could perfectly see the feet of a small boy hanging above Aché's ass.

"What feet?"

"The ones dangling from the mango tree."

Mo showed him the feet on the picture.

"I don't know what you're talking about."

"What do you see in this picture, Aché?"

"I see my ass and the trunk of that damn tree."

"No feet?"

"I think it's just a shadow."

"What about this scar on your ass?"

"What about it?"

"How did you get it?"

The scar adorned the left buttock, traversing the whole cheek from the darkness of his manly nest to the edge of the hip, a raised red fleshy protuberance in the form of the island of Cuba.

"I was born with it. Granma told me it was because of my slave ancestors, who were branded by their masters. Somehow it got into our genes, passed down from generation to generation."

Mo started to take off his pants.

"What are you doing?"

"I need to show you something."

He lowered his pants and part of his underwear and revealed the very same scar on his right buttock, but a sunken mirror image of Aché's Cuba. If they were to stand back to back, buttocks touching, Aché's scar would fill in Mo's.

Aché looked at Mo's scar and began to caress it instinctively. His fingers penetrated the ravine, slowly moving back and forth from left to right and then back. The desire was too strong, so he kneeled in front of Mo's ass and kissed the gorge. His tongue found its way into the crevasse, and he licked it back and forth from left to right and then back. Aché revealed his scar and Mo proceeded in the same way, reading it as if a text in braille holding the secret of their past. And he kissed it and licked it.

We tore into the skin of ripe mangoes and reached the flesh and smeared it all over our faces. The juice dripped onto our shirts, staining them, making them feel sticky to our body, so we took them off. And then the juice dripped onto our pants, and it felt sticky, so we took them off, sitting there in our underwear, eating mangoes, smeared with globs of mango goo, threads of mango sticking out of our mouths, caught between our teeth. It stained our underwear and we took them off. And we kept on eating and smearing and smiling. Under the dying sky, the light made it look like we were smeared in blood, cave dwellers coming from a hunt, bathed in blood. We couldn't satisfy our hunger and we kept on eating, tearing, biting. The juice dripped all the way to our cocks and cracks. It felt good down there. We tore into each other, as we couldn't help it. Our bodies slipped and slithered into each other, the juice working as a lubricant, allowing it to slide in and out. The taste was fresh. The white, pearly sex juice contrasted with the carmine blood: it was religious, a true communion, the flesh and the blood of Aché, the flesh and the blood of Mo. When the sun came up, we were still entangled together, covered in mango juice, limbs twisting every which way, knotted together like branches from a mango tree.

We WERE the mango tree.

∞

"What's the rope for?" Aché asked.

"I have a new idea for the photo shoot. I want to take pictures of you with the rope."

So Mo made a noose out of the rope and told Aché to hold it and kiss it.

"It's for play only. Kiss the rope."

Mo took a picture and asked Aché to tie the rope to the tree. As if to hang someone.

"It's for play. Don't worry."

Mo took a picture of the lonely noose. Of the potentiality

of the noose.

"Can you pretend you are being hung? It's just for play. Yeah, like that, Aché. Like that. Let me take another picture. Beautiful."

Click, click, click, Mo took pictures of Aché, dangling from the tree, pretending to have been hanged naked, listless like Òjó Ikú, listless like his slave ancestor in Cuba.

∞

The collage of photos adorned his wall. They were all broken up, pieces of Aché's body and pieces of the mango tree. Nothing made sense. Here his hand next to a limb, the limb like hands, as if the tree had hands, open, ready to embrace. There the ass of Aché with the scar of the Island of Cuba, here the trunk of the tree, like if the tree were, yeah, fucking him. A horrific image. There the neck and the rope, the rope yeah, as though he had been hanged before, far away, in Cuba. And the noose, the solitary noose grabbing desperately at the tree, grabbing desperately at the neck.

∞

Cuba
May 1980
The story of Aché

My mother died at childbirth.
At least that's what Granma told me.
I grew up in a bordello named Paraíso at the corner of Independencia and Revolución in Havana. Granma was the nickname of "Grande Madame," the obese ex-slave, who ran the house of ill-repute. After the hurricane of '32 destroyed her establishment in Santa Cruz del Sur, she moved it to Havana where she'd been ever since. The sultry smell still permeated every crevice of the house, but the crucifix had been replaced by a picture of the Comandante whose lascivious eye now bore witness to the orgiastic rituals of Paraíso. All the efforts by the Party to cleanse the Island of prostitution were for naught: the oldest profession in the world, like capitalist weeds, always found a way of sprouting anew in the interstices of socialist purity. The *milicianos* and party officials had replaced the

bourgeois, respectable men of the past, as the largest clientele of the bordello, thus offering it a certain protection from political vicissitudes.

How I came to land there is still a mystery. But, in a way, it was a saving grace. The *putitas* became my surrogate mothers and sheltered me from the ugliness that had invaded the Island. Paraíso was an oasis of liberty in an otherwise desert of tyranny. Granma tells me they'd found me one morning in a basket outside, like a little Moses on the door of a convent. She liked this comparison, and laughed her raucous smoky laugh. *Las putas son como las monjas*, she would say, prostitutes are just like nuns.

They named me Aché, meaning "Let it be" in ancient Yoruba. Since I was never officially registered with the government, I was a nonperson, I did not exist, possibly one of the best things that could happen to any citizen. Of all the *putitas* in the bordello, one in particular took me under her wing. Tata was the daughter of Estrella, Granma's star prostitute while in Santa Cruz del Sur, who ran away with her lover just before the hurricane of '32. In a previous life, Tata had been a Discalced Carmelite in the Convent of the Precious Blood. In her closet, she kept her old habit next to a statuette of Yemayá illuminated by three votive candles, one silver, one blue and the last one white. Tata would leave her various offerings: white roses, ripe melons and papayas, a little *tinajón* containing rain water mixed with tears of frustration and tinted with blue ink.

She was popular for her enormous breasts, two huge *fruta bombas,* which men liked to caress and bury their face in. Whenever a client came by, she would ask me to wait in the closet and, through the cracks of the door, I and Yemayá would watch silently as she lay nonchalantly in bed, a politician or a *miliciano* fucking her, moaning and groaning upon reaching ecstasy. Rivers of sadness would flow forth from Yemayá's lustrous eyes. After having satisfied his needs, he would pay and bid her good night, and she would stay in bed staring blankly at the ceiling fan, thinking about her sister, who had fled to Florida, thinking about her child that could have been.

She would then put me in her bed still warm from the bodies of men who had used her and I would get aroused from the sensuous smells staining the sultry air above us. She would press me hard against the fatty flesh of her breasts and, when I was about to drown in her jars of tainted water, I would come up and gasp for air, climbing out of the *mogotes* of her corporal geography. She would then tell me stories, about her mother Estrella, about Santa Cruz del Sur and the hurricane of '32, about her sister who fled to Florida, about her father Don Pedro Ceballos, who became one of the party leaders. After so many years together, we forgot we were not related, and I started calling her Mami, because she was the only mother I'd ever known.

Since I didn't officially exist, it was easy to change identities, to role play different realms of possibilities in an otherwise stark existence. Shortly after I hit puberty, I started dressing like a woman. My very first dress was the Carmelita's habit that Tata kept in her closet. I would also steal Tata's *tacones*, her high heels, and paint my face with her make-up, and glue false eyelashes to my eyelids. I loved putting carmine lipstick on my mouth and kissing my image in the mirror. I soon realized I wanted to be just like Tata, a *puta* working for Granma. I adopted a female alter-ego named Titi, just like Tata but with i's instead of a's. That's when we started working together, so to speak, combing through the debris scattered in the nostalgic streets of the capital for potential customers. We were the last vestiges of capitalism incarnate. We would stand in line for hours at Coppelia for an ice cream, and the men would stare at us knowingly as our bottoms invitingly swayed back and forth. Little did they know I was a false woman, an illusion luring them into damnation.

While waiting in line to order a strawberry and chocolate ice cream one afternoon in 1980, Tata pressed my hand and told me we needed to get back to Paraíso, that she was feeling ill. Her *fruta bombas* fell sadly over her barren, bulbaceous stomach, and the past slapped her in the face when she caught a glimpse of Vladimir standing near Coppelia with a machine gun in his hands and an ammunition belt sashed around his lean body. He had hardly changed since she had last seen him on the *Nochevieja* of that year, when he had dragged her out of seclusion from the cloister of the Precious Blood and brutally raped her at midnight. When the child that might have been was conceived out of a violent encounter between religious and revolutionary purity. She hurried along, not wanting to be seen, but it was hard to run with the *tacones* and the *calor*. Sweat adorned our foreheads and the rouge in our cheeks became a clump of dirty clay caked to our faces like terracotta tears streaming from the eyes of sad clowns. Under the thin mustache on Vladimir's upper-lip, an etching of a sadistic smile betrayed his revelation. He walked behind us, we could feel his foul breath down our necks, as Tata tried to escape once again from Vladimir. It was the same breath, it was the same mustache, it was the same sadistic smile. A *tacón* gave out and I fell to the ground, almost losing my wig and breaking part of my nose. It was too late.

When Granma saw us entering Paraíso, she understood we were in trouble and she laughed her raucous laugh and said "Aché," let it be. Tata ran upstairs to her room and opened her closet. She lit the votive candles around Yemayá, put the offerings around her and invoked her help, but to no avail. Vladimir entered the bordello with his machine gun and asked Granma where Tata was. He had come for her and this time he wouldn't let her go. Tata told me to hide in the closet next to Yemayá. What I saw next through the cracks of the closet door has forever been branded in my memories, like the scarlet scar on my butt cheek; it filled me with a kind of hatred I didn't know existed, a ball of pure fire burning the edges of my soul and flowing like molten lava through my body.

Vladimir was reputed to be the biggest *cabrón* to have ever tread the face of the earth. He was known outside Paraíso for his ruthlessness and lack of compassion. He had been the head of the *Unidades Militares de Ayuda a la Producción*, the state-sponsored forced labor camps for homosexuals and priests in the province of Camagüey during the 1960s, and reveled in torturing the prisoners, tearing their fingernails off with pliers, using baseball bats to smash shins, making them suck his gun and then sticking it down there to play Russian roulette. A moment's bad luck left entrails shattered. He brought his torture techniques and sadist ways into our house, inflicting so much pain onto Tata that she would have to bite her tongue lest he kill her right then and there. Her silent screams invaded the house, reverberating throughout the conscience of history, creating concentric waves of terror, which shook the very foundation of the Island.

Vladimir's visits were frequent during the early part of 1980, and he continued to exert his terror upon Tata. Shortly after Palm Sunday, however, rumors started to spread, murmurs running through the streets like prayers from a whirling dervish in trance. Could it be true? Had someone scratched the uniform surface of the ideological mirror? Hector Sanyustiz drove his bus into the Peruvian embassy on Fifth Avenue on April 1st. A swarm of people followed his lead, invading the grounds, swelling to the impossible number of 10,000 by Easter Sunday, demanding political asylum. Tata saw her chance: it was now or never. She took her habit out and dressed up as the Discalced Carmelite she'd once been and headed towards Miramar in the north side of the city. From afar she heard the grumblings coming from the Embassy, she followed them through the streets, her mouth tasting future freedom. She thought about joining her sister over there, on the other side. She had crossed over the River Almendares and had already reached 7th Avenue. The streets were deserted, an ominous silence hovering above the neighborhood. She started to skip and jump and run, as if in prescience that something might go wrong. You can see Tata there, running through the streets of Havana, evoking Yemayá, asking for her help. She is running so fast, her heart is beating so loudly, she wants to take off, her feet don't touch the ground, she is flying away, she feels her body lifting ever so slowly, floating, soaring. She sees the island of Cuba becoming smaller and smaller, disappearing in the distance.

"*Compañera, ¿adónde vas?*"

She recognizes the voice of Vladimir, standing with a group of soldiers.

He understood that Tata was trying to flee, and the

sadistic smile flashed before her, and she knew then she was doomed. She understood that she would never leave, that she was condemned to stay, that she would never again see her sister. She fell back to Cuba with a loud thump, like a mango falling from a tree during a hurricane.

"*Vamos, Hermana Sor Tata. Llegas demasiado tarde.*" It was too late. The government had sealed the perimeter of the Embassy, and no one was allowed to approach it. Certainly she was going to be arrested as part of the *escoria*, the dregs of society, trying to escape. But Vladimir had other thoughts and told the soldiers to leave her to him. "*Yo me encargo.*" And he did. Again. Like before. History has a sad way of always repeating itself.

Tata entered Paraíso a defeated woman. Her habit had been torn in various places and was red from the blood, white from the sperm. Her face was covered in bruises, her lip broken from the violence, her eyes bloodshot from centuries of accumulated desperation. I was waiting for her in the closet with the quiet statue of Yemayá. I heard her coming up the stairs. She told me to come out of the closet.

"*Prométeme dos cosas.* Promise me these two things. First, you will kill Vladimir. Then, you will leave this Island. *¿Me lo prometes?*"

They were her last wishes, so of course I acquiesced.

She took the *tinajón* from the closet and threw the tinted water from the balcony as if it were *Nochevieja*. The whole Island shook as Tata fell to the ground. She was no more than a splattered bit of fruit on the street. Granma brought the corpse inside, and we took off her habit and hung it in the closet with the stains and all. After her cremation, we placed her ashes on the *tinajón* and offered them to Yemayá. I knew I had to avenge her death, to kill the *hijo de puta* that had killed my Mami and then to find a way to leave the Island behind.

The *cabrón* had the gall to come back to Paraíso towards the middle of May looking for Tata. He didn't know she was dead; Granma told him she was out but that maybe he could settle for another *putita*. "What about Titi? She is a hell of a woman." Granma gave me a big old wink as she took a puff of her cigar, laughing her raucous, smoky laugh and caressing Vladimir on the head, telling him I would show him the way to Paraíso. I showed off my panty-hosed legs and pressed my false boobs together. He was so horny, anyways, that anything would do, even the *marimacha* that looked like a guy. Granma looked at me as if saying, "You know what to do."

Vladimir followed me to the second floor, to Tata's room. He started caressing my false *fruta bombas*. He still thought I was a woman. I threw him on the bed, tied his hands and legs. I looked in the mirror and started a strip-tease, slowly removing the falsehood off my face: my wig, my eyelashes, my make-up. I took off my boobs and the panty hose, I got out of my skirt. I scraped off all the patina of femininity to confront the truth of my image for the first time in my life: the scarlet scar in my buttock started to pulsate, my glory rose above all else, casting Cuban shadows upon Tata's room, enveloping Vladimir and strangling him, my hairy hands around his neck. He breathed convulsively, slowly losing air, gasping, deflating, becoming nothingness. In the mirror, I caught a glimpse of Tata's image and the truth finally dawned on me.

I WAS Tata.

∞

By this time, the whole Island knew that the prison gates had been opened. I put on the most flaming shirt I could find, the one with red hibiscus flowers, attached a necklace with a little cross around my neck, and fit into the tightest pants I could get, stuffing my *culo* into them, the map of Cuba outlined from the scar on my buttock. I wanted to look like the biggest *maricón*, for they were letting all the fags out, the Island was cleaning house, throwing from the balcony all the tainted water as if it were *Nochevieja*. I took the *tinajón* with Tata's ashes and said good-bye to Granma. I was alone at first, walking East, towards Mariel, towards freedom. From the alleys and dilapidated streets, a stream of people started to trickle in, joining me, growing, swarming, flooding, moving towards Mariel. They came from the Provinces, from Pinar del Río, from Santiago, from Camagüey. Battered children and pregnant women, defiant homosexuals and devout Jehovah's Witnesses, carmine crabs and butterfly bats, you and me and everyone, we walked the streets, tearing down the barriers. We started to run towards the unknown, slowly at first and then faster, faster, faster. Our feet started to hover above the ground, an army of flying *gusanos*, earthworms gliding towards the sea, a battalion of the *escoria* and the *lacra*, of decadent counterrevolutionaries, who did not have the blood nor the courage to become the new men of the socialist revolution.

Si se quieren ir, que se vayan.

We were being processed at El Mosquito, near the port of Mariel. A soldier asked me for my name and my exit papers. I told him my name was Aché. He looked for my name in the Book, but he could not find me, for I did not exist; I had been mysteriously left at the doorstep of Paraíso like a little Moses. I did not have any exit papers. He told me this was highly irregular and that I wouldn't be able to leave unless I had my exit papers. I put on a show, cried like a girl, told him I'd forgotten my papers in Paraíso. I heard him mutter the word *maricón* and *escoria*. That's when he started touching himself down there. "*Mámamela, maricón.*" A blowjob for freedom. It was my last act as a prostitute.

I landed on Cayo Hueso on May 25th, 1980. The name of the boat was Yemayá. Upon touching the shores of freedom, I took out the *tinajón* and spread Tata's ashes. It was at exactly the same location where Ta had landed seventeen years earlier, at the same location where Mo had been born and Òjó Ikú had been killed. Some of the ashes flew back and lodged in my eyes, producing tears of happiness. It was her crying through me. Afefé took the rest of the ashes and carried them away, high into the sky, and Tata was finally forever free.

El último que salga de Cuba, que apague la luz.

∞

Miami, Florida
August 23rd and 24th 1992

Of all the hurricanes to have ever visited the shores of Florida, none was as powerful as the one about to arrive. Hurricane Andrew was born off the coast of Africa in mid-

August of 1992, quickly traversing the Atlantic Ocean along a path north of the Antilles. On August 23rd, Andrew was aiming directly at Miami with winds closing in at 150 miles per hour.

Mo had invited Aché over for a final photo shoot. It would be called "Hurricane Andrew and Mango Tree." He wanted to capture the battle between the mango tree and the storm. They waited silently in Mo's living room for the storm to begin. Mo's grandfather's grandfather clock was still there, the pendulum keeping the tempo of the rising anxiety.

At midnight, the winds picked up, and the rain started to fall. The lights went out once again, and the Cuban shadows appeared.

"It's time," Mo told Aché.

They went outside, and Aché pretended to be hanged from the tree. He became Òjó Ikú, swinging to and fro with the force of Andrew. Everything went blank, and the only reality was the tree and the wind. It was August 29th, 1979 again. History has a sad way of always repeating itself. The pure whiteness of Padre B.'s cassock encompassed Mo, and he was in the center of the hurricane, a child in a confessional. Afefé was now blowing with all his might. So they took the noose and roped themselves to the tree.

The tree held on to the earth and embraced them with its branches, its roots desperately clinging to life. The mangoes were taken first, one by one, whirling around the tree, becoming gigantic gobs of yellow and orange in an Impressionist painting drawn by the hand of insanity. The leaves came next, forming a cacophonous canopy of fluttering butterfly bats flapping their wings. Afefé gave an extra push, and the roots started to give out, arthritic fingers lifting, cracking, dislodging, writhing. The heavy side of the tree tilted down, bringing the massive structure with it, the hull of a ship rising before sinking straight into the Ocean.

The dying tree let out a jarring, inaudible scream, exorcising the memories accumulated throughout centuries. It screamed the screams of Tata as she fell down the balcony and of Òjó Ikú as he died in Ta's womb. It screamed the screams of Mo trapped inside a priest's cassock and of Aché arriving at

Cayo Hueso. With all its might, Afefé picked up the trunk and threw it into the air while Mo and Aché rode it like a drunken vessel on a river of hope. It spun in the air like a grandfather clock caught in the eye of a cyclopean cyclone, like the ashes of Tata being taken high into the sky over Cayo Hueso, like the blades of a fan dismembering Òjó Ikú.

Suddenly, with a thump, the pendulum stopped and the clock fell into place.

Defeated, the shadows receded.

Aché.

CUT
NGHI VO

The rain slapped against the window, and Florian turned over another card. The twisted face of the Broken Man stared up at him, and he lay the card down on the bed, between the Seven Sisters and the Rookery.

"Tell me something else," he whispered. "Tell me *anything* else."

He'd begun reading the cards compulsively when the palace was taken. He had tried reading fortunes for a little while, but then things got too bad. Now he only read for himself.

This reading was a bad one. There was pain behind him and pain to come, but at least he had not yet turned over the Butcher. The Butcher's gibbous, mad smile and pitted cleaver made him shudder and think of the Harmony Plaza, where every day they brought people to die.

He turned over the last card, signifying the path to the future, and paused.

On a stormy cliff, a slender young man held a rabbit in his hands. The rabbit was bleeding, but still alive, and the young man's placid expression gave no hint as to whether he was going to release it or crack its neck.

"The Capricious," he muttered. He knew who that card represented, and with every passing day, Florian felt more and more like the rabbit.

As if the card had summoned him, the door opened and Cles walked in. He was a sturdy man a few years younger than Florian himself, and when he took off his rain-soaked hood, he revealed a thatch of unruly black hair and a face that was rather thinner than it had been before the famine.

"You're playing with those damned things again."

Florian bridled a little at his tone, but he swept the cards face down and back into the deck, hiding them underneath the bed before looking up again.

"How is it out there?" he asked, and Cles shrugged.

"The same," he said uncomfortably, but no matter what lies he told on a daily basis, he could never lie to Florian.

Florian was out of the bed in a heartbeat, his hand latched in Cles's wet shirt. He was stretched tighter than a piano string, and he thought distantly that if he were plucked he would snap.

"You're not telling me something," he hissed, and from the way Cles stepped back, he could tell that he was right. "What is it?"

Cles's full mouth thinned to a narrow line, and this time he met Florian's gray eyes fully.

"The Marquis D'Azaleen, his wife, his sons, and his daughter went to the *couperet* today."

Florian's hand slipped from Cles's shirt, and he stared.

"All...?"

"All of them."

Cles nodded, his face as still as a calm pond, and Florian sat down on the bed, too shocked to stand.

"I know they were important to you," Cles said awkwardly.

Florian laughed. It was a harsh and ugly sound, and he stopped because it was discordant even to him.

"I was meant to marry Elise D'Azaleen," he informed Cles, smiling the whole time.

Cles flinched and shrank back from Florian.

"I'm sorry, I didn't know," he said, shoving his hands deep into his pockets. It made him look like the stable boy he used to be, and it reminded Florian of a time when Cles's livelihood and even his life had hung from the good graces of Florian's own family.

Now the stable boy worked in the grim halls of the Directory, the heir to the estates of the Comte De Virange was in hiding above a chocolate shop, and Elise D'Azaleen was dead.

"She was a lovely girl," Florian said, aware of the bitterness in his own words. "Did she die well?"

"She died."

Cles's words were uttered like the fall of an axe. Cles never wanted to talk about what he did at the Directory and suddenly his silence held menace.

"Tell me," Florian whispered. When Cles only looked down, Florian leaped out of bed and grabbed the shorter man by the arm.

"Tell me!"

"Nothing to tell," Cles said, looking away. "She died."

Before he could turn away, Florian spun him around. He was a full half-head taller than Cles, and this close, their noses almost touching, Cles resembled a cornered animal.

"How did they do it?" Florian demanded.

Cles shook his head, and for the first time, Florian could see that there was something breaking in there. He wanted to let it go, and he wanted to give Cles time to put himself together, but he could tell that there was something he could only get if Cles were broken.

Florian took Cles by the shoulders and brought him close enough to kiss. Cles's eyes widened but he didn't pull away.

"Cles," Florian said softly, "tell me what happened to her."

Cles swallowed hard and Florian saw something go out in his eyes. As Florian watched, Cles got up and blew out the lantern that had been illuminating the room. Dusk had fallen and the room was dark. When he spoke, he was cold and clinical, as if he were discussing nothing more interesting than the price of fish.

"She would have been in the dark for days. Some people can afford to bribe the guards to allow them out into the courtyard, but she didn't have any money."

Florian shivered, at both Elise in the dark and at the sudden chill that sank into his bones.

"They would have knocked. They usually knock."

Cles knocked loudly on the wall three times. The loud, hollow thumps made Florian jump, and then Cles stepped up to him.

"Citizen Virange," he said remotely. "You are summoned to Harmony Plaza."

Florian started to protest, but Cles grabbed his elbow, pulling him forward with a strength that Florian did not expect. With one quick tug, Cles removed the thin scarf around his neck (green and white, the colors of the Revolution) and bound it over Florian's eyes. Terror rose up in his throat as the room went black. His chest felt tight and it seemed as if the room were closing in on him. Then Cles yanked him to a kneeling position on the floor, pushing his head between his knees.

"They put you in an ox-cart. They've spilled sweet rushes on the floor, so it doesn't smell bad. It's not a long trip, but you can hear the screaming from the crowd. They shout insults, tell you that you're getting what you deserve for being an aristo whore."

Florian knew that he was as safe as anyone like him could get, but he could hear the insults, too.

Bastard, whore, sodomite...

"They'll take you past the Cathedral of Ys, where you'll hear the bells tolling, and over Fraternity Bridge, where you can hear the water, and then you're here."

Cles hauled Florian to his feet, and by now Florian was shaking so hard he could barely walk.

"You can't see the crowd, but you can hear them. They throw rotten things at you, things that slime your face and mess your clothing. It doesn't matter, you'll never see anything again."

Florian's breath caught in his throat, and for a moment, he was sure that he was choking.

"You have to wait," Cles continued remotely. "There are people in front of you, people behind you. No one is shoving today, and no one is crying. Someone walks up on the platform, you hear a thump as the headman's ax comes down."

Florian jerked as he heard the thump. He tried to tell himself that Cles was just slapping the table. He told himself that, but he didn't believe it.

"Another. Another."

The thumps came monotonously, nearly hypnotizing Florian. He didn't know how long he had been standing in the dark.

"It's your turn."

Against his will, Florian moaned softly, but Cles pushed him forward. Something hard hit his knees, and Cles urged him to kneel on it.

A chair, he thought distantly. Cles forced him to kneel on it, and then, with his hand on the back of Florian's neck, brought his head down so that his throat brushed the chair's hard back. The position was cramped and uncomfortable, but dizzily, Florian thought that it would not be so for long.

"For crimes of extravagance in the face of poverty, for ideals that oppose that of the most holy Republic, and for the willful commitment of sexual perversion, the Republic sentences Citizen Florian Virange to death. Long live the Republic and so perish all its enemies."

Florian barely stopped himself from screaming when he did hear a rush of air. Every nerve in his body ratcheted tight in anticipation of pain, and then he realized that it was only the edge of Cles's hand brought down to the nape of his neck. Relief was like rising up from black water and he sprang to his feet, knocking the chair away as he tore off the blindfold.

"You son of a whore," he snarled. "You absolute bastard…"

"You asked," Cles whispered, rubbing his eyes hard. "You were the one who fucking asked."

Florian wanted to strike him. He could have just then. He could have turned Cles's face to a mass of blood and bruises, injured or even killed the man who was the only thing that stood between him and the ax. Those thoughts were so vivid that, for a moment, he believed that he had already done it.

Instead, he crossed the floor between them, and taking Cles's wrist in a punishing grip, pulled him close for a hard and violent kiss. Cles struggled against him briefly before returning the kiss with the same desperation. Things weren't right again, far from it, but if they hurt each other like this, then at least they knew what it was for.

Distantly, Florian was aware that he was hard, and that he had been for a while. He wondered if he would be aroused as well as afraid when it was his turn to mount the block.

There was no point to thinking about it, none whatsoever, when there was a handsome boy moaning into his mouth and grabbing greedily at his clothes.

"Sorry," Cles was saying, "I'm so sorry."

"Shut up," Florian hissed. "Shut up, and don't let me hear another word out of you."

It was something an aristocrat might say, and Cles quieted like a dog brought to heel. He clung to Florian's shoulders, and he lifted his head obediently while Florian kissed and sucked his mouth. When Florian pulled back, Cles's mouth was raw and red.

"You like that," Florian whispered into Cles's ear. "You want it like this…"

Cles dropped his head and leaned against Florian hard. He wouldn't be crying, because Cles's tears had been beaten out of him long ago, but he shook like a leaf. Florian's hand came up to cup the back of Cles's head, and he held him for a bare moment. It was comfort and control both, because then Florian fisted his hand in Cles's hair and dragged him back for another kiss.

"There, there, pretty," he muttered. "I know how to take care of boys like you."

Cles shuddered, but he pressed against Florian's body, not making a sound. Florian kissed his neck several times before nipping sharply. Cles was still, and Florian knew that Cles would be still even as he climbed on top of him and fucked him raw. He had done that before. He could do it now, and Cles would be completely silent except for a few pained groans.

I can't take any more pain, Florian thought suddenly, *mine or anyone else's.*

The thought was shocking in its simplicity, and Florian realized with a wrench that there was no need for him to hurt

Cles like this, even if Cles would allow it.

The words *I'm sorry* were on his lips but he swallowed them. He wasn't sure if he could say them to a stable boy, no matter what he might owe him. Instead, Florian ran his fingertips along Cles's face, touching the corner of Cles's mouth before running along the sensitive edge of his lower lip.

Cles flinched, more shocked by gentleness than he was by assault, and, as Florian started to trail warm kisses down his neck, he looked inquisitively at the nobleman.

"Just take it," Florian said quietly. "You can bear this as well as you bore the other, can't you?"

Cles went still again, obedient and watchful, and Florian's clever hands drew him close.

Lover, Florian thought with surprise. *He's my lover, now.*

∞

The morning light was just beginning to slide into the room when Cles dressed and took his leave. He did not tell Florian where he was going or what he was going to do, and Florian did not look at him when he put on his green and white scarf.

After Cles locked the door behind him, Florian pulled out the cards again. His fingers rifled through the deck and he pulled out two, the duet reading.

One was the Capricious again, calm-eyed and with a life in his hands. The other was the Wren Maiden, wide-eyed and cautious. She raised one delicate hand to push back the brambles, and with the other, she held up a torch to light her way.

Florian smiled. Not the Butcher. Not for him, not today.

∞

Cles hurried along the street where the vendors were just beginning to cry their wares. The city was as busy as it had been before the revolution, but now instead of paper cones of sugared almonds and straight pins, they sold stranger things. One vender dealt entirely in buttons taken from the coats of the nobles who had mounted the *couperet*, another hawked a length of rope that the Comtessa Lazan had used to hang herself.

He paused by a young girl who was selling the kiss-prints of some of the younger nobles who had been sentenced. They carmined their mouths and set their lips to the squares of muslin, and, too clearly, Cles could imagine Florian doing just that.

He was too well-trained to shudder on the city street, where anyone might see him and report him for anti-Republic sentiment. Instead, he reached into his pocket to finger the frayed edge of a pasteboard card. He had taken it from Florian's deck weeks ago, and though he had meant to throw it away, he began to carry it with him instead, as a kind of talisman.

Cles started walking towards the Directory building and, in his pocket, the Butcher smiled.

LOST AT SEA
J. LANNAN

"It's my new roommate. He's uh...I think there's something wrong with him," I replied to Raia's question, but I didn't know all the answers at that time. I hate talking about myself, but here goes...I'm Finnley, but people call me Finn if they call me anything. That's really all you need to know about me. Man of few words, you know.

"Like what?"

"He's strung out, of course he seems kind of off." Bree with her pricey chemical-straightened hair leaned forward to whisper her gossip across the counter even though the record store wasn't busy this early in the day. "His money is good, though, and he paid almost three months in advance."

"How? He doesn't do anything." I moved Bree's coffee cup off a stack of used vinyl. No respect for anything. She had walked here from the house, and the coffee cup was from her kitchen set—the set of cups that only she could use.

"He paid rent, and you know that's all I care about." Bree took her coffee cup and left the store as the bells on the door jingled. I don't think she would talk to me if I didn't give her money. She was kind of uppity for being so trashy. I could still see her through the glass with her florescent high heels that caught every crack in the sidewalk when she was drunk, and her designer purse thrown over her shoulder like she didn't get picked up for possession just last week. Her Dad was into real estate and had given her that old house anyway. All she did was live there, take our money and go shopping on rent day.

"They keep doing that to me. I hate it." I clenched my fist and struggled between the urge to punch the counter and the desire to not break anything because I didn't want to pay for it. "But, that guy…seriously, it's not right."

"Okay, so what is going on?" Raia was pretty calm and collected. I needed that in my life. She actually listened to me as she adjusted the blue and white scarf over her long black dreadlocks.

"He's pale and thin, and I never see him eat anything."

"I thought he was a *new* roommate?" She started flipping through some of the albums on the counter.

"For about a week or two, I guess. I haven't seen him eat at all."

"If he's using all the time then he probably wouldn't eat. Thank me, I just solved the mystery of your skinny roommate."

"Wouldn't he have to eat something in a week?"

"Let me remind you that not everyone sets up a buffet of cheese puffs, pizza rolls, and four different kinds of cereal when they're hungry."

"That was the best."

"Yeah, it was kind of cool at the time."

"Are we going out again?"

"Tonight?"

"Yeah." I guess Raia was my girlfriend. We did everything together, but didn't talk about us in terms of *us*. Why ruin it? "Okay, so the roommate dude, I think he's British."

"Why?"

"I don't know *why* he's British."

"No, why do you think that?"

"His name."

"What is it?"

"Well, it starts with an 'A.' Maybe, Alfred? Albert? Alistair? Abercrombie? I don't remember, but it's one of those." I picked up the stray change from the counter and set each coin in a single stack. "Why would someone name their kid Abercrombie?"

"Does he have one of those sexy foreign accents?"

"I haven't heard him talk."

She really tried to not roll her eyes while talking to me. "So, right now his name just *sounds* British, but you can't remember it."

"Yeah."

"I really don't know why you think he's weird. A pale, skinny junkie isn't that uncommon. And I would think that some guys who do that stuff might also happen to be British. Is it really that mysterious?"

"He has long black hair."

"Oh, you just reminded me, we should go see that vampire movie tonight."

∞

Around four in the morning I found myself fumbling with matching my key to the lock outside my shared house. Once I opened the door he was standing there. Under the light on the landing I could see that his eyes were deep blue like the ocean at night. I stared into those eyes and recalled one drunken evening a couple Spring Breaks ago when I'd decided to go bodysurfing alone. The current dragged me for a distance and I thought I could drown somewhere between the water and the intoxication. At midnight the sky and the sea look the same. Above, a veil of stars and below, a shroud. No one sees the dangerous waters when we believe there's a bigger world within our reach. These words intruded into my thoughts and I had to stop my hands from reaching towards him. The moment held me and I really hoped I hadn't been staring at him like some big weirdo. The summer night felt cold and I took a deep breath to calm my nerves as he stepped past me.

I looked over my shoulder. "What's your name?"

"Alistair." He did have an accent. When Bree first mentioned his name to me she thought he was one of those pseudo-intellectual artist types from LA with an identity he created as soon as he'd fled the Midwest, but now he was back. When I looked at him I knew that he wasn't from around here. Maybe not even from this era.

The front door opened and closed again before the sun came up, but I stayed in my bedroom on the second floor. I heard someone walk just outside my door. It sounded like they paused for a moment and then moved on. Whenever I closed my eyes I saw the night sky broken by dots of stars above the crashing ocean. Something about his eyes, and the feeling was familiar, or maybe not familiar, but something...maybe I was still drunk. Stupid movies.

I made it to work even earlier than usual. My day flew by in a sleep-dreary, glazed-over style. I was past that point where sleeplessness turns into an entirely different creature. After work I still felt like I had to find a way to relax that afternoon.

"Raia," I whispered to her over the phone.
"What is it?"
"Can vampires have blue eyes?"
"That one dude did in that movie."
"And they do stuff...with their *eyes*..."
"Like, look at things?" The sarcasm, always with the sarcasm.
"No, they *entrance* people—humans, that's what they do to them."
"I guess so."

The idea passed slowly through my thought processes, and I finished off the joint before I could reply, "And then what?"
"What do you mean?"
"After they entrance the human."
"Oh, well...they might seduce them, or bite them, or turn them into another vampire so they won't have to be alone for eternity, or so they have someone to torment forever. Did you actually watch that movie last night?"
"Yes."
"Finn, quit being goofy. Are you smoking?"
"Yes."
"That's good because weed scares off vampires. Or gives them the munchies...I can't remember which."
"What if there's a vampire in my house?"
"No one should have invited him in."
"But he pays rent."
"Your roommate is not a vampire. He's a heroin addict. Wait, did he seduce you last night?"
"No."
"Holy crap. He entranced you with his eyes, and now

you like boys."

"Uh…Okay, Raia, listen. I think I'm going to wear my crucifix and head upstairs…and see if he reacts to it."

"It's daylight, stupid. If he's a vampire he won't be awake."

"Okay. I'm gonna let you go now, and I'm just going upstairs." I laughed in that nervous and absurd manner to hide the fact that I couldn't believe I was doing this, or couldn't believe that this guy freaked me out.

"Fine. If I don't hear from you I'll know that someone sucked something, or ended up impaled by wood."

"I don't really do that stuff."

"Bye, sweetie."

I prepared for my own little holy war, by putting the chain featuring Jesus on the nailboard around my neck and making sure he was peering out of the collar of my slightly too big polo shirt. When I reached the top of the stairs I couldn't see Alistair anywhere, so I crept further into his lair. He had paid enough to have the whole third floor to himself. This was supposed to be Bree's party pad, but she didn't want to pay for anyone to party, and didn't want the hassle of cleaning up afterwards either. The main room was a combination of a living room and kitchen, and Alistair kept the doors to the other three rooms closed. I snuck along the wall and behind the counter that divided the kitchen from living room and placed my hand on the windowsill. The thick floral curtains were dusty and drawn down tight over the windows. He had tacked them down with silver duct tape. If he had been sleeping on the sofa today —Bree said he always camped out on the sofa— I could lift the edge of the curtain to let the light in. Would he burst into flames? Or turn to dust? I heard movement from one of the closed-off bedrooms, and took off like a silver bullet. I just about killed myself as I ran down the stairs and out of the house.

"Forgot something at work," I yelled.

Yeah, that sounded legit. Who was listening anyway?

∞

The next morning I told Raia about the curtains, and she

shrugged it off as not being odd. "Some people sleep during the day," she said.

We stayed busy unpacking boxes that morning before the store opened and I didn't talk to her, but didn't think she noticed. Bree showed up right when we opened and spent even more of my rent money.

"Did he say anything?" I didn't really look at her because I knew my eyes were bloodshot from not sleeping again. I had stayed away from the house last night, but hadn't seen Raia either. I couldn't. I knew that she didn't understand the problem like I did. She wouldn't understand what had happened to me, or how I ended up in the ocean whenever I closed my eyes.

"Who?"

"Alistair."

"I don't babysit him. He probably blacked out first thing this morning. Who knows?"

"Do you think he'll OD?"

"He doesn't want anything else. I tried. Hell, I even wore those fuck-me pumps and the miniskirt and he just looked at me like he'd rather hang himself with his boxer shorts. You know, I think he was already naked under that blanket, too." Aside from being a spoiled rich girl, Bree liked to turn a few tricks. Kept things interesting.

"Well, maybe he doesn't want you. Might be tough for you to imagine that one."

Bree and Raia both looked at me.

"What?"

"I'm outta here." Bree looked at me like she was about to call me some word that wouldn't form on her lips just because she needed my rent money for shoes.

Raia's grin had a mischievous edge to it. "So, is he hot? Sexy accent, and everything?"

"He has an accent. He's tall and thin, and he wears his clothes kind of fitted…I don't think it's the drugs. I think he's just thin like a glam rock star."

"What was he wearing?"

"Well, the other night when I saw him he was wearing tight black pants and a dark purple button-down shirt. It didn't

look like a cotton shirt, but something softer."
"What color are his eyes?"
"Dark blue, like the ocean at midnight." The words came out like I had practiced them, but I swear that I hadn't.
She laughed.
"I don't get where this is going."
"What color are my eyes?" Raia put me on the spot.
"Brown."
"You don't find anything poetic about my eyes?"
She'd trapped me. "This is why I walked all last night and didn't come talk to you."
"Why? Because you let someone seduce you and you didn't know what to say to me?"
"Nothing happened. He's only said one word to me since he moved in."
"But what an impression it made. You were pretty defensive when Bree said that she made a pass at him."
"Was I?"

∞

I spent most of my time at the house, and only talked to Raia at work. I had to sleep again somehow, but when I closed my eyes I still saw the ocean and felt like I was drowning. I did sleep, just not for long stretches of time. I really don't know what I thought he was going to do if I did sleep. The days passed and I often snuck up to the third floor to study him while he slept. He didn't eat. I started to feel a deep concern about his health, but I was okay with whatever he was—or wasn't. Sometimes his eyes fluttered open during the day when I was there to watch. I glimpsed the ocean. That same ocean I saw when I closed my eyes. That matched up, but why?

If he didn't eat, then maybe food wasn't what he wanted. I didn't think he could live on drugs alone. On my next day off I knelt by the side of the sofa. He lay in an open position on his back but his dark hair seemed carefully arranged around his face. His delicate, pale skin accented the curves of his ribcage, and the cut of his hip bones. The blue floral blanket was barely drawn over his pelvic bone and I was pretty sure that he slept naked as Bree had suspected. I felt the warmth rush to my face as I thought about lifting the blanket, but I resisted the urge and sat back. And what the fuck would I have done after lifting that blanket anyway? I bet grabbing a vampire's junk while they're asleep ranks pretty high on the top-ten list of "Ways to Get Yourself Killed by a Supernatural Creature."

I tried to get rid of that idea. Over time I had become aware of his patterns as I watched him, and he did talk to me a little, but he mostly slept all day with his curtains always taped-up. Some nights he left after dark. And I found leaflets from a fetish nightclub on the counter some days. I had been to that club a couple times and knew of what could go on there if you were looking for it. Maybe he went out to feed. Maybe he found someone who was into it. He really didn't have to. I sometimes thought about trying to meet him there. No one would believe me if I shared my theories, but it was our secret. I could keep it.

My Swiss Army knife was old and not as sharp as it used to be. I rubbed my finger over the red casing and popped the blade open. That morning I had walked to a nearby thrift store and bought an appropriate vessel to hold my offering. I held my wrist over the purple glass bowl and poked at my flesh until the blood came forth in droplets. My original plan had been to drain enough to sustain him, but this was a lot harder than I thought it would be. There was definitely some blood in the dish by the time I began to feel faint. It wasn't enough, but I couldn't give any more. I had to take my shirt off to bind my wrist.

Then I snuck downstairs where Raia was waiting. She wasn't supposed to be here. Bree had let her in. They didn't know where I had been at first, but my dripping wrist formed a trail. Of course Bree would be pissed.

Raia cried and took me to the hospital when she saw my wrist.

She talked to the ER doctor for me. "He fell on some jagged metal."

"Does he have a current tetanus shot?"

"I don't think so."

"Do you think he needs to talk to someone?" I knew that

tone, and its emphasis on "talk" and "someone."

"No. He was skateboarding and fell on a broken chain link fence. He's fine."

She thought I needed Psych even though I hadn't told her anything, but she wouldn't force me to talk to anyone. They gave me stitches and Vicodin. I slept that night, and dreamed of a peaceful ocean.

∞

The purple glass dish disappeared, or I just never saw it again. On the next night he smiled at me before heading out for the evening. I wondered if it had been enough. Maybe he needed more. Later that week I sat on the floor near where he had once again passed out under a blanket for the day. He had a black leather bag where he kept his stash. I never used anything from the bag, but packed up what he had left out. How much heroin is a lot? I didn't think he would overdose because it would've happened by now if he were human. Vampires heal quickly anyway, so his high probably wouldn't last as long. At the edge of the blanket I lay down. I was only wearing my shorts and wondered what would happen if Bree, or any of my other roommates, saw me. The excuse I practiced was, "There's no air conditioning." My fingers touched his wrist. His skin was cold, but he continued to breathe at a slow pace. I held his hand and smiled. Something in his expression shifted, but he did not wake.

"You could drink from me. You can do whatever you want to me," I whispered the words that seemed to come from somewhere else, but I had never felt any devotion with such strength before. Would he make me like him? He would wake up, and pull me under the old quilt with him. I had never been trapped in the undertow of another person before. There would be the puncture of fangs on my neck. I would gasp for air, but it would be too late. He'd drain my blood and let me die or he would take me with him. It was his choice. I fell asleep.

"Hey, Finnley." It was a quiet, accented voice that sounded like it was speaking my name out loud for the first time, and a cool touch against my cheek, then I woke to meet the concerned ocean gaze. I was covered in the blanket, and he was dressed in his fitted dark colors. "Good. I thought you had used something. Why don't you...never mind." He was leaving.

What had I done wrong? Maybe I wasn't his blood type. Vampires care about that sort of thing, don't they? It affects the taste. God, I can't get anything right.

"Wait!" I sat up and reached for him.

He stepped back towards me and crouched down. "You want to know if I drank the blood?"

It was true, but it wasn't. I felt the expression flee my face, and his fingers rested on the back of my neck as he leaned forward. He kissed me. It was like an exclamation point in my head. His mouth tasted like cigarettes and spearmint gum, and it was a weird taste, but it didn't matter. It was perfect. When my tongue explored his mouth I forgot to determine if he had fangs or not, but didn't know if I could have figured that out even if I had tried. He finished off the kiss with one more brief meeting of our lips. We both smiled, and I was wondering what would happen next, but he stood and was heading for the stairs again.

"Stay."

He shook his head. "I can't."

∞

I left him alone after he rejected me. Work. Home. Raia's apartment. A different bar or concert every night. High Five. Skully's. I went to the fetish nightclub a couple times. I wasn't looking for him. He could see me there if he wanted to, and he would know I was doing whatever I wanted. Sometimes I was with Raia, but she complained that I was distracted. It got to be too expensive to go out every night, and I ended up drinking at the house. Raia would stop by to have a beer sometimes, but usually I was alone. Bree wouldn't drink there. Another housemate, Jared, was health-conscious and didn't drink. I barely knew my other housemates, but, as I observed my vigil for about a week, I noticed that they kept schedules similar to Alistair's. They were musicians or bartenders. It was easily explainable. And that week I noticed that Alistair hadn't left the house in days. I kind of wondered if he was dead and no one else had noticed.

Friday night I hung out with whoever sat down to drink my beer. I didn't know their names. The front door snapped open and a man in dark jeans and a black leather vest stormed into the house. It felt like a storm, especially since his motorcycle had roared thunder upon his approach. I heard it still running outside by the curb, or in the front yard even. He wore sunglasses and slicked-back hair. When he looked at the few of us on the first floor I felt something bordering on calculated terror. He was angry, but controlled. He had a purpose. I could hear it as his heavy boots stomped up to the third floor.

The weird ocean feelings came back to me. I wanted to run, but couldn't make myself leave. After cowering in the pantry for what I guess was about ten minutes, I crept out. Everyone who had been drinking with me had left, but the scuffle had stopped upstairs, so I stepped over the creaky spots as I went up and peered into the room.

Alistair was unconscious—at least I think he was—and blood dripped from a cut somewhere on his face. His hair covered the actual cut as he slumped with his chest resting on the arm of the sofa. The guy with the black leather vest turned to face me and his eyes were red—not bloodshot, red—and his tone was more cold and casual than I thought it should be. "He owes me a favor of sorts. Don't worry about him. Just leave. I better not see any cops either."

I felt compelled to go. It was just something about—something about that guy. It was the opposite of my first curiosity with Alistair. I just had to leave now, and I didn't speak about what I had seen. That scene existed somewhere on the edge of my memory where I couldn't find the information to communicate to anyone else. Trouble. Someone was in trouble. Was it me? Or someone else? The information was lost between clouds of self-interrupting thoughts. I couldn't wander aimlessly all night, so I met up with Raia after she got off work. She felt better seeing me rather than not seeing me, but I could tell she was pissed. I had really flaked out on her the last few weeks.

It was fun—good to get out for something that wasn't

work—but when she asked about what was going on at the house, she didn't believe me when I said, "Don't know, and don't care."
"Did you guys finally break up?"
I was puzzled. "What do you mean?"
She laughed. "Nothing."
∞
The next day I remembered enough to feel concerned again. I woke up next to Raia with this awful feeling in the pit of my stomach. Something like too much beer, or like oversleeping an alarm by an hour, but I didn't have anywhere important to go that morning. We drank coffee as I hid my nervousness and delayed the sick feeling from coming up. I made it to the bathroom before I actually got sick. Raia wanted me to stay, but I needed to go home. She offered to go with me. I tried not to talk during the walk. She'd think I was losing it. I was going to have her wait in the living room, but had to tell her to stay outside once I saw my roommates. "That's not yours!"
Bree looked up at me as she held one of his fitted black dress shirts up over a cardboard box. "Didn't you know? You were kind of all up in his business, so I figured you might have heard..."
"What?"
Jared spoke between sit-ups. "I guess he was supposed to be the bonus kill in a murder-suicide. His girlfriend, and her psycho ex. They died. He got shot in the belly. News sounded serious. Don't think he'll make it."
I started putting things together, but I couldn't believe he had a girlfriend. That guy from last night had to have been his dealer or something. Someone who wanted him roughed up, but not dead. "So...you guys are vultures. Look, I'll hold onto his stuff in case he gets better."
Bree shook her head. "Did you ever stop and think that maybe you've become the creepy roommate?"
Jared laughed a little, and stopped exercising, "Yeah. Finn, you gonna build a little shrine to him? Carve his name into your arm?"

They knew. It was crushing. Had he told them? Complained about me?

"Maybe you'd like to roll around in his clothes a little before I get rid of them?"

"It's only been hours, right? Since he got hurt…" Regardless of what they thought about me, it still wasn't cool to throw out someone's belongings.

"Really, Finn? You give a damn about us taking stuff from the guy who has been creeping you out since day one?"

"He won't die. You'll see." I pointed at them. "He'll be back, and he'll bring that guy that made everyone run from the house with him. They'll kill you."

"You know what, Finn? Pack your shit and get out. You're so fucked in the head. Leave."

"Whatever." I hated them.

Raia let me stay with her.

∞

Of course a couple days later I had to visit him in the hospital. I bought some flowers from the gift shop. Some generic yellow vase "Get Well" arrangement of white roses and yellow daisies, and hopefully it wasn't creepy of me. I couldn't believe that he might have complained to Bree or Jared about me. Those idiots. They probably just saw me go upstairs a lot. Or, maybe it was the blood trail. It was stupid. But he had kissed me. Maybe he did that because he thought I would run and leave him alone. Why didn't he ever mention a girlfriend? Maybe it was just a fling…

So much of this was just stupid. I set the flower arrangement down on a table.

He didn't look that bad, considering everything. As midmorning sunlight streamed through the plate glass window, the pastel green hospital gown cast a sick tinge to his pale skin. It was kind of funny because it was the first time I had seen him in the sun. I brought a chair closer to the bed and sat down to watch him while he slept. The blanket was pulled to just above his hips, but the gown was lifted above that to reveal the line of staples crossing his belly. I glanced at the door before leaning forward to lift the gown. I stared. The staples were there like railroad tracks, but the incision was barely raised and pink, even though it had just been a couple days since the surgery. I let the pale fabric fall back into place just as a nurse came in.

"Oh, a visitor? No one's been in here since the police came by just after…" She bobbed her head without needing to elaborate. As she checked his blood pressure, he woke up. "Can I get you anything?"

He shook his head and glanced up at me as she left the room.

"No one told me that you had a girlfriend. I'm sorry about—"

He stared at the wall and sighed. "I was not expecting to talk to anyone today."

"Sorry." We sat in silence for a few moments. "You seem to be healing pretty well."

"Yeah, I guess so." He nodded at the door. "Close it."

I reached back and guided the door until it clicked shut. He grabbed onto my shirt and dragged me to him. I held onto the railing on the side of the bed, but I was where he wanted me.

"I know that you know." His eyes were urgent and volatile. He was nervous.

"What, man? What do I know?" I stayed quiet, but wanted to call out for help.

"You know." The intonation was grave, but I didn't know what I *knew*.

"I don't know anything."

He released his hold on my shirt and dropped back onto the pillow with such force that I thought he may have somehow hurt himself. "Then, you don't know." Maybe I had missed it. Maybe he had missed it. Was there supposed to be some sort of connection that we both thought was there, but it just wasn't? He looked kind of lost in the hospital room, but he settled to rest with his hand on his stomach.

Maybe he was kind of out of it without his usual self-medicating, but I wanted to give him another chance, so I sat down in the chair again. "I thought you might have burst your staples."

"I'm not worried about that." He stared toward the window for a while before speaking again, "Everything looks different during the day. I'm just accustomed to night, and being out in the darkness. It feels a lot more closed in—or maybe it's secure. The sky seems much bigger and opened up during the day. I just don't feel like I'm in my element anywhere, but maybe night is deceptive in that way. Kind of like the ocean when you can't see what's really around you. I couldn't see it. Maybe no one sees the dangerous waters when they believe there's a bigger world within our reach." His eyes met mine. Lost at sea in the middle of a hospital bed.

I felt it in the pit of my stomach again. "I have to leave."

"Stay." He reached out for me.

It took a moment for my heart to slow down a little, but then I realized that maybe the racing sensation was okay. Maybe everything was going to be okay. I took hold of his hand and sat down. He didn't want to talk about what had happened that night, but, hell, I had apparently been cool with the idea that he was a vampire, so what's a little more mystery?

THE KEYS TO THE CITY INVISIBLE
WILLOW FAGAN

I saw him for the first time in the hallway of my apartment building. He was a short man, maybe five feet tall, with long, tangled white dreads hanging down almost to his knees, and an equally unkempt beard. Despite being so old, he looked quite thin and wiry; his muscles were knotted like rope. He had hundreds of jangling keys: on bracelets and necklaces, on rings hanging from his suspenders and the loops of his gray pants, on ribbons of metal coiled up in his bags. One after another, he tried the keys in the lock of 5J, three doors down from mine.

"What are you doing?" I said, incredulous.

"What does it look like I'm doing?" he replied, not stopping. "I'm trying to unlock this door."

"But this isn't your apartment," I said.

"You're a quick one, my boy." I was thirty four years old, but I have to admit, I still looked like the boy next door.

"Are you trying to break in?"

He stopped, and wiped his hands on his pants before glaring me straight in the eye, fierce as a weasel. I almost forgot I had a good foot on him. "Look, youngster, I don't have the time to spare to explain it all to you, but I for sure do not have time to deal with the rigamorale and bullshit of the fuzz, so let me lay it on you fast: there's a magical world hidden beneath the one you live in, and in it this city is ruled by a True Queen. If she dies, the city dies. Get it? And right now she's locked in that apartment, a tree branch pierced through her heart, bleeding out money and electricity and history onto the carpet, and I need to get in there and save her before this whole city goes kaput."

"Uh-huh," I said. I wasn't as naive as he thought; I'd been to the hidden city and, more importantly, I knew who lived in 5J. "Listen," I said. "I've met Brad, and he's got some style, but I wouldn't say he's a *queen*."

He swore at me and then scampered away. He shouted, as he ran, "You haven't seen the last of ol' Ellester yet, oh no."

∞

"Keegan," I said, in-between bites of salad. "Does the name Ellester ring any bells?" Keegan was one of my clients, a sandy-haired museum curator with a sharp, economical wit. The museum he worked for contained both open and hidden exhibitions; its collections spanned the histories of the visible and invisible cities, and its hallways were rumored to be riddled with secret passageways and rooms stretching far beneath the surface of the world.

"Ellester? Hmm," Keegan mused as he cut his veal into small, precise pieces. "No, it does not."

"There's no such thing as a True Monarch of the city, is there?"

Keegan smiled thinly. "There was Bordacello, who tried to declare himself King around the turn of the century. That went well."

The historical context was lost on me, but I smiled in acknowledgment of the joke nonetheless.

"In general, the mortal authorities of the city have kept a tight, if secret, control over the hidden city. It does fall, after all, into the geographic area of their jurisdictions. But—so many questions, Anthony…" Keegan said. "What's happened?"

"Oh, nothing really," I demurred. I waited to tell him until after lunch, when he had me naked and handcuffed to his bed, and was commanding me to answer his question. Clients are always happier in the end if I make them delay their gratification.

"Oh, *him*." Keegan scowled. "The bloody thief."

∞

"So where did you get all those keys?" I asked Ellester, the next time I saw him. He was plugging away, trying keys in the lock of 5J, same as before.

"I found them," he said. "One at a time."

"Really? So how old *are* you?"

"Older than the dried up roots of the oldest tree. Older than the oldest cloud, that wispy little scaredy-cat who fled and hid at the first sight of the sun, and is still huddled up in some cave somewhere. Older than the horny old dinosaur man who made your mom moan all last night." He had continued to test key after key during this performance but now he stopped, and wiped his hand on his forehead. "What do you want?"

"I'm just curious," I said innocently. "You're quite a card, Ellester."

"Cute," he said. "So either you're stalling me until the fuzz gets here or you want me to do a favor for you. Which is it?"

"Well," I said, allowing myself to grin, "I was wondering whether or not you had a particular key…"

∞

I had been craving revenge against my ex-boyfriend for a long time. Jonny Glitterseed. The bastard.

∞

We always fucked madly after his concerts. I used to get so riled up watching him glory on the stage, shirtless and sweaty, so much wilder than his usual self. The glitter; the winged costume; the sweet longing in the songs, in his voice; the understated but undeniable sexual tension between my Jonny and the other members of *Boys With Wings*—none of *that* hurt, either. So when he disappeared without a word after the show one night, I knew something was seriously wrong. I wandered around backstage, feeling drunk and stupid and angry, as person after person told me they didn't know where he was. The sight of groupies simpering up to the other *Boys* and exchanging hungry grins and knowing glances made me sick with jealousy and fear. I knew I wasn't the only one whose mind got wet at the sight of Jonny performing. Finally, the manager, a girl who was sometimes the only person with a fucking clue, said, "I don't understand. I saw him leave with you twenty minutes ago."

"But I'm right here!" I said.
"You don't have a twin, do you?"
"No, I don't have a fucking twin."
∞
But it turned out that I did, in a manner of speaking.
∞
"I never meant for you to find out this way, Anthony," Jonny said. There were streaks of plain skin running through the glitter on his face, tunnels drawn by tears, but I wasn't about to relent. My arms were firmly crossed, blockaded in front of my chest. My heart.
"Find out what?"
∞
"He was an actual *faerie*, Anthony. How could I say no to that? He told me he was a prince but I guess he's actually a baron or something. His jizz literally sparkled, Anthony."
"Wow, I really needed to know that."
∞
"How long has this been going on?"
"I don't know…about a year."
"A year? A whole bloody year?"
"Yeah…a little bit longer, actually."
∞
I made Jonny take me to the hidden spaces within the city, and show me everywhere he'd been with his faerie lover. The actual bower they'd fucked in, a billowing rainbow tent sheltered in the twisted branches of an always-flowering tree, was nowhere to be found, of course. But he showed me the streets they had walked on, the upside-down fountain where the birdfish gathered to lay eggs, where they had first kissed, the silent market where Jonny had bought his faerie lover a living coral ring, trading memories of high school plays in exchange, and on and on, wonder after wonder, until I was sick.
∞
"There's one more thing, Anthony…"
"Really."
"I'm only telling you this because I care about you and I want to save this relationship, and you told me you need me to

be honest, even if it hurts, so—"

"Just fucking say it already."

"Well, I told him about you—"

"Oh, great, thanks."

"And he said you sounded 'as enticing as the first red fruit of spring,' and he wanted to watch us a few times, so I gave him permission to enter the house…"

For the first time in this awful conversation I was stunned into silence.

Jonny went on. "And then later he told me that he had 'worn the guise of my earthly skin' and slipped into bed with you and…well, you know…"

"Wait a minute. Wait a minute. You're telling me that this faerie disguised himself as you and *had sex with me?*"

Jonny nodded miserably.

∞

"I don't know what most of these keys are *for,*" Ellester said. "Why else would I be taking so long to open this blasted door?"

"You don't have some kind of enchantment or something?" I asked.

Ellester failed once more to open the door, and shook his head tiredly. "No, I don't. Just persistence, and a heap of years beneath my belt."

"So what would it take for me to get you to open a door for me…"

Ellester sighed. "I'm already working a commission, my boy. But you could meet with my patron to discuss terms…"

∞

I'd generally avoided the hidden city as much as I could, since learning about it. Oh, I kept tabs on the gossip a little, through Keegan and a handful of other clients. I even sometimes went to Cafe Gateway to be seen and to watch the teenage goth kids and hippies, trembling and brave and all done up in their best clothes, backpacks and purses full of supplies, about to embark on quests into the Hinterlands and, more than likely, get eaten up by some pretty-looking beast or ensnared in some illusory trap. But actually stepping foot into the hidden places myself? No, thanks. I'd seen and experienced more than enough through the efforts of good old Jonny.

But now, presented with my first real chance for revenge, I was willing to go back there.

∞

I waited under the light of an old-fashioned streetlight mutated to have four or five branches, each one ending in a lamp. The street was empty and dark, the only sign of motion little swirls of wind carrying bits of ice. Which, for all I knew, were actually sentient spirits or spies. I shivered. I had dressed for the weather in the real world.

A long, cream-colored limousine pulled up, and the door opened, beckoning me in.

∞

Inside, the air smelled faintly of macaroons and flowers. "Good evening," a clear, low voice said. "I am called Chrysanthemum Bud." I turned, and shook her gloved hand.

Chrysanthemum Bud had long, pretty hair that was almost white beneath her fedora. She wore diamonds and a trench coat. She looked like a combination of the rich heiress in distress and the rescuing private eye.

"Would you like some wine?" she asked.

The cup was warm, the liquid sparkled with caramel light and tasted sugary, with a hint of coconut.

"You have spoken with my page, Ellester?" she asked, one eyebrow raised in a curve like the top of a question mark.

"Yes," I said. "He told me—"

"Ellester is, let us say, a kind of prophet, with his old eyes and his wild beard. He is preparing the way for the arrival of the new order, for the coming day when all within the city invisible shall rise up and build a new society with our own hands, our own ways. For too long have the mortal authorities of the city kept us under their plastic-clad feet, claiming dominion over our lives and lands. For too long have our needs and dreams been as an afterthought to the mayor and the City Council, whose mundane minds fail to hear or interpret the cries for change from our magical throats. For too long have our cousins and kin wandered through the Hinterlands without a haven or true home to call their own. For too long have our peoples gone undefended but soon—soon the whole hidden city will know me as their Lady Protector."

"Wow," I said, woozy. The wine had gone straight to my head. "But what does this have to do with me? I'm nobody."

"You are, let us say, a lad of the night, yes?"

I nodded.

"And as such you share intimate moments with many men of certain proclivities, who might, let us hope, divulge information to you beyond sweet nothings."

"If this is about the mayor—"

"It is."

"I don't kiss and tell."

"Anthony, Anthony. I am extending to you a hand of privileged friendship. If you grasp it, if you aid my people in the building of a great nation, a magical city-state, you may find yourself with powerful friends in the city invisible. If you spurn my offer, well…you would not wish to be on the wrong side of history, would you?"

"Give me some time to think about it."

"Of course."

∞

The limousine dropped me off at the same streetlight. I stumbled back to more familiar streets and had nearly reached my apartment building by the time I remembered Jonny. I had been so dazzled by Chrysanthemum Bud's presence and vision that I had completely forgotten that I had gone seeking a method of revenge. But if Chrysanthemum Bud was as powerful as she seemed…perhaps his fucking faerie paramour was finally within my grasp…

∞

The door to 5J hung open, swaying gently in the hallway like a moored boat.

"Ellester?" I called.

"What?" It was Brad who answered. He stepped out into his doorway, looking as dazed as I felt. "Oh, hey, Anthony, can you come inside for a minute?"

∞

He left the door open.

"I just don't understand," he said. "Here's my stereo, my laptop, my XBOX. Hell, I left an envelope full of tip money on the counter. But the only thing that's missing is this weird old frog key I bought from a flea market years ago. Why would someone break into my apartment for that? I must be missing something…"

"Beats me." I shrugged.

∞

The next time I saw Chrysanthemum Bud, Ellester was there. He sat in the limousine seat across from us, with a box that looked a little like a Rubik's Cube made of many metals, each separate section with its own keyhole. Of course, he was working methodically to open it.

"How hard would it be," I asked, "to get at a faerie baron while he slept?"

Chrysanthemum Bud and Ellester exchanged a sly smile, Ellester's fingers working nimbly even while his eyes were elsewhere.

"Such a thing could certainly be arranged," Chrysanthemum Bud said, pointing her pale fingers together like a steeple, "particularly if the baron you mention is, let us say, one known to frequent music halls in the mortal realm and even, on occasion, to sleep in a mortal's bed."

I nodded, my jaw clenched like a fist.

"An exchange, then," she said. "A toppled mayor for a fallen baron."

∞

I sat in the office of the editor of *Street Signs*, the alternative weekly. The packet of photos lay on the editor's desk like a bomb, packed full of charge. My mouth was dry and I couldn't stop tapping my leg.

"Say," the editor said slowly, clearly feigning ignorance, "you're Jonny Glitterseed's ex, aren't you? These allegations wouldn't have anything to do with the recent rumors about a private performance of *Boys With Wings* at the mayor's mansion, now would they?" A beat of silence. "Look, son, *Street Signs* doesn't peddle this kind of trash." He unceremoniously fed the photos into the shredder. Nothing exploded. "Just a friendly piece of advice. I wouldn't go looking for enemies in City Hall if I were you."

∞

So I posted the photos online myself, my face blurred out, but the rest of me—not to mention the rest of the *mayor*—clearly visible. The local internet went wild.

∞

The faerie's *blood* sparkled too, at least at first. The knife in my hands was coated with it, like some kind of sick parody of a magic potion, thick and crimson and full of glittering light. But when the blood dried—on the sheets, on the knife, on my hands, all across my shirt—it became dull brown, same as anyone's.

The faerie's mortal lover, snoring beside him on the bed, I left alone. I didn't know if he was deceiver or deceived, a betrayer of someone else's heart or simply a foolish guardian of his own. He slept through the whole mess. The elixir Chrysanthemum Bud had given me to keep both of them asleep had done its job so well that I felt safe enough to take a shower and clean myself off before stepping back out into the streets.

No one had bothered to tell me that faerie blood leaves permanent stains. The water ran and ran, but the splotchy marks remained, like melodramatic tattoos of dark clouds across my chest. I scrubbed until my own blood sweated out of me, but still my skin would not come clean. I was still scrubbing when the cops came, pounding on the door like angry ghosts.

∞

"MAYOR'S ALLEGED GAY LOVER REVEALED AS PSYCHOKILLER" the *Street Signs* headline screamed. I sat in my jail cell and waited. If I was lucky, Ellester would come eventually with all his jangling keys. If I was even luckier, I'd live long enough for him to find the right one, the single shape which would make the metal click open with a sigh of relief.

THE SOUK OF DREAMS
KEYAN BOWES

The full moon brightens the Dubai desert as Dylan follows Samar up the sand dune. He's having second thoughts. He has no idea where in the desert they are. He has no idea what to expect at the Souk of Dreams. And having impulsively agreed to come with him, Dylan has no idea if he can trust Samar.

∞

They'd met the week before, on Dylan's second day in Dubai.

This city wouldn't have been Dylan's top choice of places to go, especially with its anti-gay laws. But his dad moved here for a new career opportunity, his college dorm was closed for winter vacation, and travel might help him forget the messy break-up with Jackson. The only person he'd told about that was his sister. His dad didn't quite get this "whole gay thing," and his mom kept praying for him.

Dubai turned out to be Las-Vegas-on-sea on crack, with added Arab tradition. But by day two, Dylan was wondering why he'd bothered coming. He knew no one. His dad was tied up with work, as always: one dinner at the fancy Burj al Arab, some spending money, a spare set of apartment keys, and Dylan was on his own. Dad was off on a five-day business trip to Doha.

Dylan almost wished he could go back to the US, maybe stay with Mom and Sis. But then his stepdad, who "didn't have a problem with gays," but "had to get along with the neighbors," kept giving him lectures about how to dress and behave. Between that and Mom's prayers, well, no. Not great for Sis, either, but at least he'd helped her with her college applications to get her out of there.

Still, he figured he'd make the best of this city, wandering around the streets most of the day armed with guidebook and sunglasses. Dubai was interesting enough in its own shiny-glass-towers-in-the-desert kind of way, like Vegas with shopping malls instead of casinos. Lots of foreigners, both tourists and workers. Young Arab guys holding hands. Just a cultural thing, though. They weren't gay. Not openly, anyway.

Late in the afternoon, he stopped at a Starbucks. He leafed through the guidebook as he sipped his cappuccino, feeling rather lonely and unfocused. The strong winter sunlight slanted through the glass café front. A few customers sat around at leisure: Arab men with strong features in long white *dishdashas*, an Arab woman cloaked in a black *abaya*, an Asian couple with a kid.

Then this dark, good-looking guy came in, glanced in his direction. He looked like he might be Arab, but wore t-shirt and jeans, not traditional garb. Dylan tried not to stare, suddenly self-conscious about his shoulder-length red hair that he hadn't wanted to cut just for a couple of weeks, but which now made him stand out from the Dubai crowd.

The man ordered a coffee and settled at a nearby table. He had eyes the color of old-fashioned toffee, and wavy black hair. Tall and wiry, he looked the antithesis of Jackson's muscular crew-cut aggressiveness. As Dylan looked up from his book, the man caught his eye, leaned over, and asked, "You here from the US?" He sounded American, but Dylan thought he detected a slight accent. "Me too."

Dylan gestured toward the other chair. "Come on over."

"Samar," said the dark guy, bringing his coffee to Dylan's table. He pronounced it something like Summer. "Everyone calls me Sam."

Sam was a college student, too, but his parents had moved to Dubai years before and he'd grown up here. He was also back for the winter break. They talked about school for a while. Then, noting the guidebook lying on the table, Sam offered to join him sightseeing.

"Sure, dude, I could use the company," Dylan said. "Don't know anyone in this town."

After that, they met every day, exploring the Gold souk, overflowing with hundreds of tiny shops glistening with gold jewelry; Dubai creek, good for a cruise in the evening breeze; even the bird sanctuary with flamingos within sight of skyscrapers. Samar was an easygoing guy, very different from Jackson, who'd always needed to be in charge of everything. Had Jackson been that way in the beginning? Dylan wasn't sure. He also wasn't sure whether this could be pushed further than friendship. Anyway, he didn't intend to try. He'd learned his lesson with Jackson.

Yesterday, Samar had a seemingly innocuous question about sightseeing: "Seen enough souks, or still up for one more?"

"Depends," Dylan replied. "The carpet souk was boring—all those shops with similar Kashmiri and Iranian rugs. The Sharjah one with the antique stores was good. I'd go there again."

"There's an even better one—*Souk al-Khwab*. The Souk of Dreams."

"What's that?" Dylan asked. "Sounds like it sells hash or something."

"Not in the Emirates," Samar said with a laugh. "No, this place is special. And it's only open one night a month. Tomorrow. Coming?"

"The Souk of Dreams?" he said. Sam was leaning casually against the wall. The way the sun played on his face made him look almost ridiculously handsome. Dylan tried not to stare. "Sure," he said. "I'll come."

Dylan hadn't expected a souk to be far outside the city. They joined a tour group, a convoy of vans labeled "Dune Adventures" headed into the desert for an evening of sightseeing. Though each four-wheel drive van seated eight, the only other passengers were a couple and their young son. The boy sat up front by the driver, and his parents behind him. Dylan and Sam had the bench at the very back to themselves.

Outside the city, the desert opened up in miles of sand

punctuated with low-growing scrub. The carefully cultivated trees were absent, as were the tall buildings. The convoy stopped, the drivers let some air out of the tires for traction in the sand. Then they turned off into the desert. Dark gold dunes rose high in graceful curves against a vivid blue sky.

Without warning, the van sped up one side of a dune and side-slipped down the other in a natural roller coaster ride. Startled but exhilarated, Dylan was thrown against Sam. The kid next to the driver bounced with glee. "Yeah!" he shouted. "Let's go faster!" The driver grinned, revved the engine and said, "You want faster?" The other vans in the convoy threw up plumes of sand as they zigzagged over the dunes. Sam steadied Dylan with an arm behind his shoulders.

At dusk, the convoy stopped on a rise. The sun set into the desert haze over the ranges of dunes as a full moon rose. Everyone got out: the drivers for a soda and a smoke, the tourists to take photographs. Dylan and Sam stayed where they were. Dylan was conscious of Sam's face too close to his, his skin, his scent. Impulsively, he leaned closer. Then he quickly pulled away, remembering Jackson as well as the conservatism of the place.

Just in time. The passengers piled back into their vans, the drivers started up and, in the failing light, made their way past camel pens to the desert camp where the adventure continued into a campfire picnic with belly-dancers.

Dylan and Sam wandered out of the straw and canvas walls of the camp to a dark spot behind it, to look at the stars, bright as they never were in the city. When Dylan tentatively extended his hand, Sam took it. Just then, the tour guides loudly announced food and shisha water-pipes and they stood up and went inside.

"So when does the tour head to the Souk of Dreams?" asked Dylan once they'd eaten. "After dinner?"

"Nah," said Sam. "Not the tour, just us. We're ditching them. There's a guy here who knows the way to the Souk."

Leaving the tour-group transfixed by an energetic belly-dancer, they found the taxi waiting among the Dune Adventure vans. "Here, get on in," said Sam, holding the car door open.

The driver spoke broken English, but Sam switched to another language to discuss directions.

"What d'you tell him?" Dylan asked. "And what language was that? Arabic?"

Sam laughed. "Nah. Urdu. Most taxi drivers here are from Pakistan or India."

It was an unexpectedly long drive across the desert. Dylan was very conscious both of Sam's arm lying along the back of the seat, and the growing distance from the city. "How come the souk's so far away?" Dylan asked. "Can't be much business out here." He turned in his seat to look behind them. "Huh," he said. "Strange illusion, looks like the road's gone."

"It'll be back, don't you worry," Sam replied.

The driver pulled to a stop. There was nothing but sand under the big full moon. The place was totally unfamiliar. Dylan had known Sam all of five days. What if he had it all wrong? What had Sam planned with the taxi driver in the language he could not understand? Dylan was suddenly nervous. His watch was his 18th birthday Rolex, and he had a decent amount of cash in his jacket's inside pocket.

Jackson would have called him a fool. Actually, Jackson would have called him a fucking idiot, trusting just anybody. Jackson had trusted no one, not even Dylan. Especially not Dylan.

"We'll get out here and walk," Sam said. "Good you wore sneakers."

Dylan didn't know whether he should refuse to move away from the taxi, or whether it was okay to go with Sam. What was this *Souk-al-Khwab*? Why hadn't he told anyone where he was going, even on the Web? He could have e-mailed Sis, or mentioned it on his updates or something. And his US cellphone didn't work in Dubai.

If Sam saw him hesitate, he did not acknowledge it. He towered over the open car door, waiting. Embarrassed by his unmanly fears, Dylan got out. Sam handed him a flashlight, even though the moon was bright enough to walk by.

"It's got a UV bulb. We might see scorpions. They glow in ultraviolet."

Dylan wasn't sure whether to believe him. But he followed Sam around the moonlit dune, and then up the next one.

∞

They're cresting the dune, slipping a little in the sand, when Dylan sees it lying below them: a market, brightly lit, crowded with stalls and booths and rugs spread out displaying goods. Lanterns hang from poles planted in the sand, and each stall has a bright Petromax lamp, throwing a glow over their colorful wares.

A throng of shoppers mills around the stalls. From the top of the dune, Dylan hears the hiss of the lanterns, the chatter of the merchants calling their wares, people talking and calling and bargaining. The smell of kerosene from the Petromax lamps mingles with the smells of roasting meat and camel dung.

He and Sam clamber and slide down the dune, landing in a little spurt of sand next to one of the stalls. It displays some unfamiliar looking objects. Perhaps some kind of artworks?

"Ah, Samar," says the merchant, a tall Arab in a white *dishdasha* and headscarf. "You haven't been here for many moons! Do you have anything to sell today?"

"Hello, Mahmud. I'm studying in America now. I have something small, we'll talk later."

"You have not forgotten the special commission? My client is still interested, very interested."

Dylan feels a chill. Mahmud is looking directly at him, though he can't see his eyes in the shadow of his brow and head-cloth.

"This is Dylan," Sam says. "His father is the big boss at Engstrand."

"Ah yes. An honored guest." Mahmud smiles courteously at Dylan, and he stops feeling like something small to sell. "*Salaam aleikum.*" Peace be on you, the Hello of the Arab world.

As they turn to go, Dylan can't shake the feeling there's something strange about Mahmud. His eyes, maybe. What color are they, anyway? He'd only caught a glimpse of them when he turned his head, and it seemed they had no whites.

They walk slowly past the stalls. People are speaking all sorts of languages, German and French and Spanish and ones Dylan can't recognize. There's definitely something different about this crowd. They don't seem quite normal. Some have pointed ears, like elves. He can't tell if they are really good prosthetics, or an actual body-mod.

But it's not just the ears. It's like a freak show or a sci-fi convention. That woman over there, she has short fur all over her face and arms, gleaming silver in the moonlight. The little girl running by has a fake nose, long and curved like an anteater's. Then the kid starts twitching it.

"Hey, Sam? What place is this, anyway? Who are these people?"

"The *Souk-al-Khwab?* People come here from all over… not just from the countries on our maps."

A little girl darts past him, using her stretchable arms to snag things from the stalls, until her mom catches her and lifts her firmly onto her back. She returns the purloined goods, smiling apologetically at the shopkeepers.

"It's real, right? Not just ordinary people with Teflon implants and tattooed designs. It's real."

Sam lays a hand on Dylan's shoulder. "Like it?"

Dylan turns to him with open excitement. "The Goblin Market!" He'd worried for nothing. This place is amazing, and it's cool of Sam to share it with him.

"Goblin Market?" Sam doesn't catch the allusion.

"It's this poem," Dylan explains, "and it describes a market like this, with strange creatures selling and buying things."

"They're usually friendly people here, but they might mind being called creatures," Sam says in a low voice.

"Oh, I didn't mean…" Dylan quickly pulls his gaze away from the elegant man with a giraffe neck swaying through the crowd, and joins Sam at the nearest stall. This carries the ubiquitous blue *ayn al-hasūd* charms he's seen in other shops, but, as he lifts one up, the blue eye gives a long, slow blink. Surprised, he drops it. It rolls in among the other charms, which all shove back with seeming annoyance, and blink themselves. "Never mind, never mind," says the shopkeeper. "They'll settle down."

Dylan and Sam move on, carefully skirting a small group of tall, thin individuals wearing tunics that shimmer in the lights of the souk. They turn in unison to look at him, and chorus "*Salaam aleikum.*" But their accents are strange, and they mispronounce the second word.

Sam stops Dylan at a display of rugs. "That's what I want some day," he says. "A flying carpet."

Dylan has a dizzy sense of unreality. "What?"

"Ali has some good ones," Sam says. "The new models, with invisibility screens and climate control."

"Yo, Sam old man!" says Ali. "When can I sell you a Toyonda Ispahan?"

"When I'm as rich as you, you old bastard!"

"Hey, I'm not the one going to Caltech!"

"Differential equations won't make me rich."

"Nope, but your other stuff might. Got any tonight?"

"Small one. Mahmud gets first dibs."

"If he doesn't buy, come back here. Any time you're looking for an agent—I'm your man. Some serious collectors are interested."

Dylan looks at Sam, wondering what Ali's talking about. Sam looks away. "Oh, I make stuff and sell it here sometimes. Pays for college. These guys buy it from me. They sell it to collectors for a bit of a profit."

"Bit?" says Ali. "Mahmud made 70% on the last sale. I'll work on a 20% margin. Your Mahmud's a good businessman."

"And you? What margin do you make on those carpets?"

"Dude, that's different. My folks make those things. There's a lot of technology in them. Continuous improvement over 900 years. You're buying know-how, man. Skill. See if you can get anything like it in this souk. Any souk. You'll be lucky to find one that even gets airborne."

Ali waves, and five of the rugs hanging on the frame behind him take wing, flap around the sky over the souk in a wide circle, dip over Sam's head and make him duck, and with a soft whoosh return to their places on the frame. Dylan stares.

"There's a whole new market waiting for you, Sam. You could be big."

"Later, Ali," says Sam. "Another time. See you surfing up in California."

"Later, bro!"

A nearby booth has rows of shelves lined with bottles and cans labeled in a language Dylan guesses is Arabic but might be something else; and with spools of fancy braids and laces. "Happiness by the pound," calls the shopkeeper. "Joy by the liter. Confidence by the quart. Misery by the meter."

"Check out that stall!" Dylan says.

"Shuja's stuff is overpriced," says Sam grudgingly, but he follows Dylan.

"I heard that, Samar my friend," calls Shuja. "My prices may be high, but my quality is the best. Has anyone complained?"

"Those who got the misery?"

"Without misery, there can be no happiness. Without tears, no laughter. The world is full of opposites. Will you buy some joy?" Shuja asks. He takes down a gleaming glass canister, embossed with unfamiliar designs Dylan finds a little unsettling. They seem to writhe under his gaze.

"Here, take a look," says Shuja. "Just a sniff."

He opens the container. It's full of a fine oily liquid that almost glows in the light on his counter. Using a long-handled spoon with a tiny mother-of-pearl bowl, he dips some out. "Come nearer," he urges. "No charge for a sample."

Dylan looks, wondering if it's safe to try. Something about Shuja's sales spiel has clicked with him. With a long-suffering air, Sam leans on the counter. Dylan joins him. With a flick of his wrist, Shuja tosses the liquid into the air above them, where it evaporates immediately. All at once, a feeling of intense joy sweeps over Dylan. The brilliance of the night, the wonder of the souk, the marvelous kindness of his companion, they all overwhelm him, bring tears to his eyes.

Sam smiles, and Shuja says, "What a wonder this world is!" Gradually, the intensity of emotion ebbs, but a mellow feeling remains.

Shuja pulls a few threads from a brocade on a spool, and rubs it on his wrist. Immediately his face becomes more stern.

"What did you do?" Dylan asks.

"A businessman cannot afford to spend his business hours consumed with joy," says Shuja dryly. "That was just the merest thread of misery."

Sam shrugs. Dylan is still amazed. "How much do you charge for the joy?" he asks. "Can I pay in dirhams?"

He buys a tiny amount, which Shuja packs in a glass phial with an aerosol top. "Would you care for some love?" he asks. "It's sold by volume."

Dylan shakes his head. "Love has to be free," he says. He wonders how Sam's thinking about this.

"With my prices, it's nearly free," says Shuja. Everyone laughs. Sam gestures that they should move along. Dylan fights down a little rush of disappointment. That's it, then.

Dylan forces himself to focus on the place they're in, the night, the moon, the sand and this market. Wandering on, they find themselves in the live animal section. There are camels for sale, and unicorns. Half-fledged canaries and phoenixes and infant dragons that can hardly breathe fire at all. One stall sells eggs, but the six-packs have pictures of dragons and griffins and creatures Dylan cannot identify. "Guaranteed Fertile" reads a hand-lettered sign.

They're walking along the boundary of the section when Dylan sees them, his favorite mythical animal. His mood lifts. "Hippogriffs! Goddamn, are those really hippogriffs?" The pens hold a small herd of them. A foal, only eight hands high, comes up to the fence and snuffles inquiringly. "Hey baby!" He allows it to sniff at his hand. It nuzzles him with its beak, looking for a treat.

"Look, there's a feather!" Lying inside the foal's pen, it's like a long golden leaf. Impulsively, Dylan vaults the fence and grabs it.

"Move back quickly, sir!" says the stall-keeper urgently. But the warning is too late. The young hippogriff's mother, a mare perhaps nine feet tall, jumps the fence, and, hissing fiercely, grabs at Dylan with her beak. She catches only his hair, but he's trapped.

Immediately, there's an uproar. Everyone nearby comes closer. The merchant who owns the hippogriffs runs in. "Sultana! Back! Back!" he shouts, advancing and waving a cape, but Sultana is not listening. Instead, she hisses louder, and turns her head to look at the gathering crowd, giving Dylan's hair a painful yank each time. The merchant makes another ineffectual pass at Sultana, irritating the animal further. One strike of that beak could open his skull and spill his brains.

"Cut off his hair," suggests somebody from the crowd. "Bring a sharp knife."

"No, no, don't do that!" shouts Samar, and he pushes past the crowd, runs around to the other side of the hippogriff pens, and whistles. Distracted by the crowd, the big female doesn't respond. But the foal does. Bored with its mother's preoccupation with its erstwhile friend, it canters over to where Sam's standing. Keeping an eye on Sultana, he reaches out and pats the baby. "You're a cute little guy!" he says loudly.

Perceiving a new threat to her child, Sultana drops Dylan's hair, and wheels around to roar. Sam instantly backs off, while friendly hands pull Dylan out of reach.

"Why do you keep such a mare, Babu?" the next stallholder asks indignantly. "Who knows what will she do next?"

"What can I do? Everyone knows that female hippogriffs cannot be truly tamed. But I could not bring the foal without her."

Dylan's trembling a little from the shock, but he hides it. "Hey, thanks, dude," he says. "You saved my scalp."

Sam gives Dylan's deep red locks an appreciative look. "Worth saving," he says.

Is Sam saying less than he means? A little happiness bubbles up in Dylan, almost as though Shuja had sprayed something at him.

∞

After that episode, they decide to leave, but Sam needs to settle some business first. They head back to Mahmud's stall.

"Here it is," says Sam, and draws from his pocket an exquisite tangle of gold wires. As he holds it, it fluffs up into a maze that dazzles the eye as it tries to follow the gleam on individual threads. At the center is a miniature garden. Dylan can't tell if it consists of actual little models of trees and flowers and fountains, or if it's an image of some sort. It looks very real.

"It needs—a touch of life," Sam says to Dylan. "Activate it, dude!"

"What do you mean?" asks Dylan.

"Push your finger into the center," Sam says, "and wait for a count of ten."

Dylan does. A tingle runs through his finger, but he waits for ten seconds to withdraw it.

In the center of the tangle, in the garden, is a tiny simulacrum of himself. As he watches, it moves in unison with him.

"What is it?" he asks.

"A wire sculpture, centered on an image field. Once it's inside the power-perimeter of the souk, any living thing can activate the image-grabbing program. Now it will exist as long as you exist."

"Does it do everything I do?"

"Within limits. When you're very close, within its range. Otherwise, the movements are pretty random, but bounded by plausibility."

"I'd prefer it didn't do things like pissing. Or worse!"

"Not likely. You don't piss in the garden, do you?" As he speaks, the figure sprawls on the grass. A bottle appears in one hand, a book in the other. The miniature swigs its drink and settles down to read. Without looking, Dylan knows it's drinking a pale ale. Sam carefully sets the object on the counter, where it sparkles in the artificial light of the Petromax.

"Brilliant!" says Mahmud, behind them. "My client will be pleased."

Dylan's finding it really creepy, this living model of him being sold to an unknown stranger. But caught off guard, he doesn't quite know how to put that into words without pissing

Sam off. Before he can protest, the transaction is over, and he and Sam are scrambling up the dune. The eastern sky is beginning to pale just a little. In the shadows on the other side, they pause to catch their breath.

"Dude. Hope you don't mind my using you for a model," Sam says. "You're just perfect for it, with that hair. The minute I saw you I needed you in that sculpture. It's my best ever piece." He leans in, as though for a kiss. But Dylan doesn't want to, anymore.

"Is that…thing…connected to me somehow?" he asks Sam.

"How d'you mean?"

"Has it stolen a piece of my soul?" Even as he says it, he feels silly, superstitious, like tribal people who believe that photographs stole your soul. In his head, he can hear Jackson's contemptuous tones: *Don't be such a retard!*

"Doubt it," Sam says slowly.

Dylan hears the unvoiced *retard* anyway. He really wants to leave. They slide down the dune, go back to the taxi. The driver is asleep in the back seat. Sam thumps on the door. Sleepily, the man emerges and stretches.

Sam opens the car door, but then doesn't move. "Get on in. I forgot something. Back in a few."

"Okay." There seems to be nothing else to say. So that's what the whole friendship had been about—getting an exotic redheaded guy into the power-perimeter of the Souk for Samar's artwork. The rescue from the hippogriff wasn't even about him, it was about his hair. He's been played. Dylan supposes he should be grateful he hasn't been robbed or kidnapped, that it wasn't that kind of a set-up, but he's not. A sense of betrayal washes over him as he waits in the dark

The driver, realizing they're not leaving immediately, walks some distance away and lights a cigarette.

After an age, Sam returns, carrying something. He hands it to Dylan as he gets in the car. "This is for you," he says. Dylan removes the soft cloth cover. It's the sculpture. He looks at Sam questioningly.

"Just couldn't do it. Couldn't part with it, except to you.

Wanted you to have it."

"Bet Mahmud was not pleased," Dylan says, not saying what he really means, not wanting to admit that he'd been profoundly shaken.

"Nah, he wasn't. But I'll do another for his client. Maybe a phoenix." He leans over and gives Dylan a hug. A gesture safer than a kiss. Is the driver watching?

"Say, do you have to go home tonight?" Sam asks. "I have the keys to a friend's apartment. He's away this week."

Dylan holds the sculpture carefully, thinking about risk, about Sam, about Dubai. A shining path seems to open up in front of them as the taxi drives back across the sand.

He leans over to Sam. "Sure," he says. "I'll come."

THE MARK THAT'S LEFT
JOHN DIMES

It was on rare occasions that Samuel brought someone home with him. Especially a patron.

"God, I love your work. So beautiful."

But he saw something in him, something he needed. And it felt safe. He knew it was safe. One could read it off him, even without the benefit of having the gift of a certain sight, or insight.

"Wow...Damn...Goddamn!"

The handsome man freely wandered about the enormous studio apartment, and was gratefully absorbed by the vividly colored landscapes of luminous sculpted glass. Some of the wirily floral or tentacled works could fit in the small of one's hand. Others were significantly larger, with the width and height of runty four year-olds standing on tip toe.

"Oh, now these are marvelous. Absolutely marvelous," the man said in surprised response to the easels that bore three framed, conté crayon nudes. All presumably of the same male. "I've never seen your drawings."

"They are early works," explained Samuel. "Studies."

"Anyone in particular?" the guy asked, coyly. "I mean—everything else is sorta abstract, isn't it?"

Samuel, in lieu of an answer, surveyed the man hungrily. The man shied away self-consciously, then met Samuel's gaze in a sudden burst of lustful intensity. He closed in for a kiss.

"So eager!" Samuel said, pulling away at the last instant.

"I—I'm sorry. I—"

"Don't be," Samuel said, casually. "You know us artists. We're a flaky, temperamental lot. It's about mood and aesthetics." He really couldn't blame the man. Unwittingly he was being seduced by forces stronger than mere desire, or sexual chemistry. "Come with me." Gently he took the man by the hand, pulling him toward the couch. He guided him to a seat with a playful nudge.

"I'll be but a moment."

Samuel went to the stereo. Manipulated a few buttons. Something appropriately soothing and sensual emerged soon after, and washed out the bland silence of the room. He left the living space for the bedroom, and returned with a large white veil neatly flung across his arm.

"Oooh!" uttered the man, cagily.

"Drape this across you," Samuel commanded, offering up the silken thing.

The man smiled to himself as he took the thing proffered, unraveling it for closer inspection. He visibly thrilled at the slight touch of it against his hand, and as he passed it along his cheek.

He looked up to ask, "Do—do you want me naked?" His tone and expression suggested that the question was both a proudly sacrificial gesture—posed in the general interest of art —and as an act imminently answerable to the prevailing tensions of the moment.

Samuel carefully thought the matter through. Completed his calculations. "No. No, you're fine just as you are. Besides, it won't interrupt the—" he was going to say, *Interrupt the Color-Textural Manifestations,* "—it won't interrupt the mood," he explained in quick recovery.

"Alright," said the man, "here goes."

Samuel looked on while the man stood and dutifully covered himself with the veil. At that moment, he was transformed from a man into a child at Halloween, playing as a ghost. He chuckled somewhat uncomfortably to himself. Samuel's expression of unrestrained desire, however, proved to be a sound buttress against the man's withering dignity. With that, he was on Samuel, without hesitation or due remorse. Through the diaphanous veil, his mouth harshly connected with Samuel's mouth, face, neck. A spot of wetness formed where his wanton tongue hotly protruded.

Samuel freely submitted to the enthusiasm of the man's passion, but his own actions wove irregularly from active to passive, for certainly, at times, he was a most unwilling participant. He tolerated the man's touch, simply because it was a necessary evil. And he knew that the evil must begin soon, without hesitation...or due remorse.

Gently, he brought the man down with him on the couch. He smoothed his hands across the contours of the silk, which in turn were the contours of the man, molding each until they were indivisible. Samuel felt the light pressure of the man's lips, languorously pecking at him, but never once did he return the favor in kind. All that mattered was the physical pronouncements of *The Disconnection*. It was evidenced in the man's expression of resplendent pleasure. In the heady tempo of his desperate, staccato breaths. How he writhed about in what seemed an unendurable, sensual agony.

It was especially evident in the way that the static electric charges whipped about his body in snaking tendrils of fire. He seemed not to care that small points of unbridled light appeared, and flickered, across his lasciviously surging body. Not even as that light grew into a white hot brilliance did he ever appear the least bit alarmed. No longer did the man seem to play as a Halloween ghost, for he had truly become the thing.

Samuel watched the glowing veil as it pulsed in the steady 4/4 rhythm of his victim's ecstatic hyperventilations. Soon after, the veil bucked, so wracked the man was in his ridiculous succession of rapid fire climaxes. Samuel prepared himself for the ripening energies that would be released, and the change that would be ultimately induced within himself.

His face gradually transfigured, into that of a young man about seventeen or eighteen years old. But it wasn't a younger version of his current incarnation, which was hazel-eyed, fair-haired, with a dappling of freckles across the bridge of a puckish nose. Attractive.

This face, that was of a younger man, was no less attractive, though his features were framed within a more angular head. He was auburn-haired, blue-eyed, with a slightly broader nose. Grief-stricken and tearful, Samuel touched his face, and forced himself to revel in this brief, agonizing moment, before the final stage of his metamorphosis occurred.

Stealthily the moment crept up on him, as it always did: the angry, tributary lines of blood, scoring the whites around his attractive blue eyes. His pale, open face succumbing to a darkly ashen mottling. Thereafter, his skin would heave, and sag hideously about his skull, in the loose, husk-like manner of smoked meats. A small dark cyclone funnel would spontaneously sprout, and twist menacingly above his head, turning clockwise at times, only to then turn counter clockwise in an abrupt, fussy spattering of chaotic dust.

He descended upon the man, and kept him enshrouded, while he ravenously suckled at every available orifice of poured light. His lips. Nostrils. Even his ears. Only then, it seemed, only at that moment, did the man fully comprehend what was happening. He screamed, but what roared out of his mouth wasn't a sound, but a rush of hornet sparks. A small hole was singed into the veil, and the sparks burned the creature that was Samuel.

He stumbled backwards, with the burning energies still on him, moving of their own volition, insect-like across his skin. A few of them crawled across his face, as though seeking to burrow themselves deeply into his eyes, under his eyelids. These few were ultimately successful. The passage of their eldritch scramble shimmered beneath his tightly-closed lids. These minute flares imprinted his mind with their brand, stirring recollections into life.

He saw himself as that seventeen-year-old boy, rambling through the woods with another boy. A hazel-eyed boy, with fair hair, and a dappling of freckles across the bridge of his puckish nose. Attractive.

"Police academy. Boy," exclaimed Samuel. "Not at all what I expected."

"I know, I know," said Hazel Eyed, with a laugh.

"No college."

"No."

"What about your dreams of being an architect?"

Hazel Eyed sighed. "God, I just don't have the patience. All those lines and calculations. Allowing for the placement of things. And then people, too? Hell, all those buildings I drew as a kid...?"

"They looked fantastic," said Samuel.

"Yeah, but nobody would've had any room to maneuver! They'd have to duck their heads. Crawl around. Oh, it would've been awful."

Samuel laughed.

"My granddad was a cop, I figure I try that out. See how it goes." Hazel Eyed lapsed into quiet reflection. Then said, "What about you? You're the artist."

"Right, right," agreed Samuel. "I've got it planned out. 'M going to art school. Wear nothing but black. Put on zillions of rings, and complain about artistic integrity!"

Hazel Eyed chuckled at that. "Oh, and don't forget the sandals and socks, man!"

"Why, of course!"

They both laughed at this.

"You know, I'm really going to miss you," said Hazel Eyed.

"It's just Boston. That's practically nowhere from here—once I steal the car, of course. I'll see you plenty."

"But—but," Hazel Eyed stammered, "it's not the same as actually having you around the corner. I—"

Samuel embraced the hazel-eyed boy. Kissed him. Then lead him by the hand, deeper into the woods. They stopped beneath a slender birch, embraced once more, and kissed with desperation and yearning. The two went on that way for a long while, pressed against the tree. Gradually, absently, they roughly slithered down the side of the tree to the small cluster of exposed roots below.

Samuel remembered how later he lay there naked on his back, gazing at the purplish cast of the encroaching night through the jigsaw crevices of the branches overhead.

Samuel winced, let out a cry of pleasure. "Careful. I'll need that nipple for a piercing, eventually."

Hazel Eyed chuckled.

"You know," said Samuel, with a wicked gleam to his eye, "I've been curious about a certain act."

Hazel Eyed caught his meaning. "I've—I've never done it before."

"Obviously, neither have I. But, we've seen enough pictures, right?"

Hazel Eyed scratched the sparse blond hairs on his chin. Grinned. "Well, I'm game. Just—just let me know if it hurts."

"Don't you worry," Samuel said. "I'll sing out."

Samuel turned over, while he adjusted his makeshift blanket of jacket and pants comfortably beneath him. "Okay, go for it."

"You—you can't just tell me to go for it! Mood, man. Mood!"

Samuel laughed. "Sorry. Sorry." He closed his eyes, and he waited. While he waited, he tried not to focus too much on the moment, while keeping himself aroused. He wanted to relax. So, he reflected on how close to dinner time it was, how hungry he was. Perhaps, afterwards, he'd invite Jeffrey over to his house for dinner. It was Sunday, and there was always a pot roast in the crock pot on Sundays. Maybe he'd go over to his house and...

He felt Jeffrey. It was as though the boy had stabbed him, the pain was so incredible.

"No, no, can't take it," he said firmly, with a grimace. The pain continued. "I said take it out! I can't—!"

He shouted, yet the pain kept coming at him in terrible, unrelenting waves. He struggled to right himself, but the weight upon him, and the awkward position in which he lay, had him hopelessly pinned. "Stop! Stu-stop it! HhNooooo!" he moaned. "Shit, man! Don't do this to me. Jeffrey! Please—" he protested, his face wet with tears.

Defeated, Samuel dropped his head to the ground. His face roughly scraped against the loose earth in the callous, ugly rhythm of his partner. He remembered how his "friend" climaxed within him. This is where he first recalled the instance of metamorphosis.

It was beneath a huge oak to which he pitifully crawled.

And, oh, how miserable he felt. He sobbed, and growled in impotent fury.

I could've broken out of that hold, he thought.
I could've tried harder.
Why did he do this to me? TO ME?
I could've gotten away.
I must've wanted it.
I must've.
I-I did, but not…not that way.
I'm making too much of it.
Maybe…ooooohhh!

His awareness and sensitivity to his surroundings were strangely heightened and raw. He recalled the March breeze as it gently stirred the woods. How, to him, its touch felt like dulled razors dragged across his skin. A quarter moon cast its muted tones across the patch of grass where he rested. A branch whipped in the breeze, which allowed stray catches of moonlight to fall across him. He saw his arm and hand, and how strange they looked, as though the flesh had been peeled away. He thought at the time it was simply a trick of the light, or grief-born hysteria.

He would not realize it until much later that his facial features had melted into a soft, translucent glaze, revealing facial muscles and many veins.

∞

Samuel lay there quietly on the floor of his apartment, staring up at the ceiling. His face had resumed its first form, which was that of the thirty year old. He smiled to himself. He realized that all of this, all of the horrors of his life, were about to end, for he had finally seen it. There were no more self-delusions, or illusions of repressed memories, redirected as if they were a beam of light acted upon by the opposing gravity of willful ignorance. *Memories, like energy, can never be destroyed,* he considered. Only scattered throughout the whole of thought, coloring every aspect of one's life.

Of his life…and Jeffrey's.

Samuel caught sight of the veil resting on the couch. He had been so caught up in his visions that he'd missed the culmination of *The Disconnection's* progress. All that was left was empty clothes, and the waxen residue of glimmering occult stuffs cooling on the floor. He sat up. In lieu of standing, he crawled toward the couch. He fiddled with the resinous globules he found, picking and tearing them away from his victim's shoes. He appraised the pieces expertly, turning them this way and that. Once he was finally comfortable with an acceptable configuration, he would let the pieces set.

He went to the veil, and was pleased with the vibrant colors that had been scorched into the fabric: all the rich crimsons, the bright yellows, the bold, egg-yolk oranges. Samuel breathed hotly upon it, and the colors visibly trembled, and flowed with even richer colors of purple and indigo. Satisfied with that, he returned to the empty clothes and picked at the remaining residue of stuff from it...

...and absently popped a bit into his mouth.

∞

Jeffrey Kellor was a man with little ambition. Which is not to say he lacked initiative, or didn't exhibit a sound work ethic. He always and invariably gave one hundred percent of himself to his duties as an officer. Duties that, oddly, had to be explained to him from time to time. He'd never actively pursued positions of advancement—titles and responsibilities just tended to be surreptitiously handed to him. It was especially so in the case of his recent promotion from patrol officer to detective in the Persons Crime Unit, within the Fairview Police Investigative Services Division. He accepted the position, and was duly baffled by it, offering his customary: "Well, if you think it's all right," when it was more than obvious that it was most certainly "all right." Again and again, it had to be pointed out to him that he had consistently proved himself as a valuable asset to the force. That he exhibited a remarkable facility for character profiling, and had an eye for details. He was honest. Dependable. And if he was, on occasion, somewhat socially inept? Well, his professional bearing more than made up for it. Still, it remained a minor point of contention amongst his colleagues. His social skills.

Secretive. That's what everyone always said. No, that he

was a secret. Unknowable. No one ever recalled seeing where he lived, or how he lived. None could pinpoint a moment where he talked of family, or friends. What was known of him was what everybody knew of him, which was only what everyone saw. Casual mentions of their own wives or significant others yielded nothing of his own sexual affiliations, or personal interactions. He remained a cipher.

On an average Monday, Jeffrey Kellor absently strode into the office, five hours later than scheduled. He looked drawn, and troubled. His disheveled hair and rumpled clothing spoke volumes of the night before. His colleagues watched him slowly drift pass, like mist hovering over water. All those burning moments of their planned confrontations, inquires and interrogations over his personal life evaporated in the presence of this new, unmoored Jeffrey. They had become a timid bunch of provincials skirting him like the plague. Something had to be done.

Before Jeffrey even hit the cubicle to his desk, big, blond Shirley Kramer was summoned. She was one of the few people he ever consistently partnered with in the field.

"You look like hell!" she said as she turned the corner.

Jeffrey didn't look up from his monitor, intent on his computer search. He was carefully scrutinizing a web page filled with a selection of people listings with corresponding stats, and photos.

"Jeff? What's happening?"

"I'm looking for them," he mumbled. Again, without facing her, he pushed a photographed image across the desk to her.

She brought it up close. Frowned. "What is it?"

"Postcard. Um, of a man…"

She cut him an incredulous glare; returned to the postcard. All there was to be seen was a piece of non-representational artwork. She flipped it over, and found it to be basically blank, save for the printed label with Jeffrey's home address. Strangely, there was no return address given. However, there was a Boston postmark dated from a week ago stamped upon it. The red, off kilter circle was placed near the name of the piece featured on the card: *Force of Will.* Mixed Media. Joshua Becton.

With her assessments made, Shirley flipped back to the front of the card. One could fairly judge from her posture that it was most definitely not her thing. "Eh, sorry, I don't see anything. I mean, I don't see anybody. Any man, I mean. Unless it's one of those optical art things, all I see are a bunch of paint splotches. Maybe if I look a little harder…"

Wounded, Jeffrey took the postcard back from her. He passed it from hand to hand, and let it rest on a nearby surface. "I—I thought I was looking at photos this, this whole time," he said to himself. Visibly, his body trembled in time with his voice.

"Jeffrey?"

He cringed from her, and hid his tears and embarrassment behind a single hand. Immediately Shirley sat down, bringing her chair closer to him, gauging the appropriate level of proximity to him. Rather than actually touching him, she leaned forward a bit, and pushed a few "there-there-now's" gently aloft to cover the necessary space.

Jeffrey was clearly occupied with grief, yet Shirley noticed that his free hand had been operating, it seemed, under its own directives, and had all this time been drumming violently atop a thick file folder. "Jeffrey, may I see that?"

He was startled into the moment, and acknowledged the request. His actions were as impersonal as a conveyor belt, or a vacuum tube at a bank teller drive thru. It was item, impulse, and inertia.

Inside the file there were various documents on missing persons. Clipped to each document, in an obvious manner of specific importance, were postcards featuring paintings similar to the one she'd just seen. When she examined the backs of each card, she spied the various postmarks, and exotically decorative stamps, indicating in small portion the character, or flavor, of their places of origin. Some were from places abroad: London, Rome, Vienna, Prague, Nice, Tokyo. Others were from the states: Seattle, Los Angeles, San Diego, Tucson, Boston, and Springfield, MA.

Shirley flipped through the other pages, and found information printed from the website of artist/glass sculptor, Joshua Becton. How he was favorably compared to other highly respected glass sculptors such as Dale Chihuly, Stephen J. Cox, and Thomas P. Kelly, to name only a few. Becton, apparently, was the genius behind a patented viscoelastic glass formula, a form of malleable glass, which he employed in his phosphorescent Hyalomorphic, or "Ectoplastic," Structures. There were photos featuring his works from two exhibitions: His "Cthulu" series, and his "From the Atlantean Gap" series. They were more to her liking, these bizarre, elegantly wrought creatures of glass. The shimmering things seemed to her as though they ought to exist, but didn't. Staring further at them she felt a sudden chill, and decided finally that, perhaps, such things shouldn't exist after all.

Becton's information went on to describe a new type of abstract portraiture: heat and light sensitive "Photo-Thermal Reactive" paintings, worked in his specially-created medium of organic acrylic gels, or bleaches. There were no accompanying photos of these new works. And she noticed, as an afterthought, that there hadn't been any photos of the artist himself.

She scanned down to the very end of the document to Becton's contact information in Great Britain. Once there, she registered a mild alarm as she perused his touring schedule which, oddly enough, included dates in London, Rome, Vienna, Prague, Nice, Tokyo, Seattle, Los Angeles, San Diego, Tucson, Boston, Springfield, and a final date that was to be announced.

"You think he's involved with these disappearances, don't you?" she said.

"He's not just involved," he said, ruefully, "he's directly responsible."

"I don't understand how you can, how you can make such an assumption. Such a leap. Sure, his touring schedule obviously corresponds with these places. But how do you know their names? How can you match their faces from these goddamned Rorschachs?!"

"The titles of the pieces. They're like puzzles. But, you have to dismantle them a bit..." he said as he took the folder from her, "...rearrange them." Frantically he yanked the various postcards from their corresponding documents. "Here! Look at the titles."

Shirley was almost piously showy as she stretched out her hand. Dutifully she accepted the weight of the postcards like a scale. But she had already arrived at her conclusions long before Jeffrey handed her the postcards. It was evident in her quietly confident expression.

She reexamined each and every title on the backs of the cards. She thought the titles of the paintings were either ridiculously pretentious, or downright obscure. Yet, all were ultimately innocuous: *Hue & Cry. The Mark That's Left. Force of Will. Withdrew, So Drawn. The Soul of a Lost Martin. Adoring Thee. Even Saints. Returning the Rogue. Dotting the Sky. Backing Toward. Wild Rider. Maelstrom's Calm.*

"Okay, what am I looking for again?" she asked, tetchily.

"Here," he said, as he read the postcards along with her, "*Hue & Cry.*" He rummaged through the file, brought out a page. "Hugh Alder." He shuffled to the next card. "*Mark That's Left.*" He produced another page. "Mark Dunkerson. *Withdrew, So Drawn:* Drew Gotleib... *Lost Martin:* Martin De Rossi... *Adoring Thee:* Theodore Bearse... *Even Saints:* Steven, or Stefan LeBeouf... *Returning the Rogue:* Roger Turner... *Dotting the Sky:* Scotty Etheridge-Harlow... *Wild Rider:* Ryan Wilder... *Maelstrom's Calm:* Malcolm Brand... *Backing Toward:* Ward Baxter... *Force of Will:* Willie Kuniyoshi...

"Do you see what I'm saying?" he asked. "The titles only sound poetic, or uplifting. But there's something—I don't know how else to phrase it, but: There's something kind of sinister about them. I—"

"Brass tacks," Shirley interrupted, her limit apparently reached. "That these individuals are missing, there is little doubt. That this Joshua Becton guy happened to be in the same cities as these missing persons? Again, that is also without doubt. The courts and public opinion, however, will recognize your actions as meticulously obsessive. That you tried to hammer inconsistent facts into a preconceived mold. Based on circumstantial evidence—wait, not even circumstantial evidence—names and faces pulled out of your ass, because I can't see a goddamned thing in those pictures."

Jeffrey was dumbfounded.

"Jeffrey? Can you tell me why you decided to implicate a man you've never met, with crimes you never physically investigated on your own? I mean, are you having visions, or dreams? Stuff like that? Visitations by spirits?" she asked, sarcastically. "Besides for being obviously hounded by a zealously thorough secretary with a mailing list, I—I can't see for the life of me what your beef is…"

∞

Jeffrey had to take an early lunch. He just didn't have the strength to turn off the eyes and minds he imagined were raised against him. There was a park just a few blocks from the office. When he needed a brief respite from all the external and internal noises of the world, he parked himself near the fountain. It was the visible action of the spill and tumble that relaxed him, as well as the water's tranquil crash as it plummeted upon itself.

Today it was quiet. Apparently there were repairs being made on some of the fountain's statuary, which necessitated the need to drain the basin, and to erect a temporary chain linked perimeter around it.

So much for relaxing, he thought.

"Are you having visions, or dreams? Stuff like that? Visitations by spirits?"

For anyone else, he considered, such questions would be preposterous. For someone like Jeffrey, the questions would be a startling observation, because each and every one would be absolutely accurate. But, it afforded him nothing by way of lasting comfort. In truth, it only served to deepen his state of impotence and despair. The reality in which he lived had been crazily skewed for the better part of four months. And try as he may to effectively express it to someone—even to himself—he knew he could never elevate it up from the mire of irrationality, no matter how well, or how much stinking crud he kicked from it.

There was a memory that Jeffrey promised himself he'd

never dwell on again. He treated that memory as if it were the sun. It was bright and terrible, and should never be directly stared at. To do so would leave him as blinded to sanity as it did before, which was a blessing, in a way. When all the pieces of reason had finally fallen into place, his memories were strangely disjointed. And the "glowing celestial body" of *the* memory? Thankfully, it remained elusive. Yet all through his life, he would have aggressive, destructive desires, and strange visions, whose genesis he could never quite pinpoint. It made personal interactions difficult. Dating, out of the question.

    Jeffrey often saw the most attractive men on the streets, in the bars, even in his office, and he would turn from them. Or speed away from them. Not out of timidity. It was how their faces would be so beautiful for awhile, then only to ripen into colors that would only be attractive on say, a plumb or a peach. Their inviting eyes would in moments be bruised, and rheumy. That's the way it always was for him.

    Four months ago Jeffrey had received a large envelope. The return address was somewhere in Great Britain. He was surprised and a little excited about it when he got it. Inside the envelope were several black and white photographs and a postcard.

    The first photo was of himself. He couldn't remember ever posing for it, but it was clearly him. Seated, and naked from the waist up. The rest of his body was concealed within the swirling mists of a white veil. The next photo looked a little jumpy. Blurred. Actually, only the seated figure was blurred, the rest was in focus. The third picture nearly stopped his heart. It was of a boy he hadn't seen, or consciously thought of, in years. Samuel Hewitt. In the picture he looked about eighteen or so.

    Jeffrey remembered how he'd worried through the envelope, looking for a letter of some kind in explanation for the envelope's contents. He looked to the postcard. It bore a simple reflected surface. Silver foil. He remembered how he held it up to his face, and how warped his reflection was, like he was staring into the distorting effects of a fun house mirror. The back of the postcard was free of script. The printed information, however, read: Joshua Becton, Sculptor/Artist. It went on to list Becton's address in Newcastle upon Tyne, Great Britain. Jeffrey took careful note of the dialing exchange, and decided he'd try the number. He reached for the cell from the slip case on his hip. He twisted suddenly, and the photos he'd rested on his lap tumbled to the floor. That's when he saw the last two photos out of the set of five.

The fourth photo showed another blurred figure with an unaffected background. But the fifth...The fifth photo showed an image of something so repellent to Jeffrey's mind, that his hand actually ached at the touch of it. He recalled how he broke out in a feverish sweat, and how his heart raced so that it dizzied him. The figure seated was dark and leathern, pocked with keloidal lesions that seemed decoratively arrayed upon it like a multitude of nipples. Its lips bore a ragged cleft palate, with a pronounced lower jaw line. Its scoop-like bottom lip was strangely reminiscent of the plate-distended mouths of the indigenous tribe of the Amazonian rain forest. Yet this lip was scored with wizened corrugations.

There was something even more disturbing that Jeffrey couldn't quite make out. He wasn't sure if it was a smudge, or some type of camera glitch, but there appeared to be a sort of halo burning darkly above the subject's head.

Jeffrey remembered how he began again with the first of the set of pictures, only going to the very last one when necessary. He couldn't, for the life of him, understand what it all meant. Was it truly indicating that he was changing into Samuel, and that he'd soon turn into some kind of thing? He just couldn't figure it. He recalled how he searched for any signs of photo manipulation. His head, or Samuel's head, digitally placed on somebody else's body. Airbrushing. Anything. Then he saw them, there at the bottom right hand corner of the picture: The time and dates glowing in their eerily digital way. The dates were quite recent. The times? 8:00 pm. 8:01 pm. 8:02 pm. 8:03 pm. 8:04 pm.

He considered, at the time, that these numbers could be fudged. But why? All he knew was that their presence seemed to cleave deeply into his psyche, becoming a unifying force behind his fractured memories. Without a doubt they were the catalyst behind all the horrific images that haunted his every waking thought. Images that seemed far more than just dreams, or nightmarish visions. Firsthand accounts.

Tearfully, Jeffrey thought of the boy he'd once cared for. Sammy. Samuel Hewitt. They grew up together in Springfield, Massachusetts, near the cemetery along the famous Mulberry Street of Dr. Seuss fame. They met in the sixth grade. Samuel was a transfer student from Wilmington, Delaware. Samuel, he recalled, was initially the quiet type, secretly seething with jokes and creativity. Rochelle Warner, obviously interested, drew the "mysterious" boy out. It was a shame, really, because it was obvious he wasn't like everybody else his age. He was too maturely articulate, like somebody on TV. Immediately he was branded a weirdo, which seemed all right to him, because he'd just as soon hang out with the teachers, bus drivers, or the custodial staff over anyone his own age.

He loved art, music, and movies. Samuel had a particular fondness for the books of L. Frank Baum. He decided he'd adapt "Return to Oz" into a musical. He wrote the whole thing in long hand, wrote the lyrics and melodies in conjunction with Ms. Word, the music teacher, and he even designed the characters and costumes. He lost interest after being continually discouraged by the Principal, and by the poor student turn out for the auditions.

Jeffrey's encounters with the boy began sometime after that. Previously it was limited to harmless school bus teasing directed at Samuel from Jeffrey and the other "cool kids" who sat at the back of the bus. Samuel was exceptionally resilient to the attacks, burying his nose in a book, or his notebook, or in his stacks of comic books. This seemingly fortified wall of "whatever" raised against Jeffrey and his cohorts only served to heighten his curiosity over the weirdo, in ways that would—in the long run—dash his thoughts of popularity to the rocks.

Jeffrey recalled sitting behind Samuel during second period English. There was something about the way Jeffrey watched him, and how Samuel was unaware of it. Jeffrey saw him in his natural state, calmly unaffected by anyone or anything. He remembered the shape of his head, the slender elongation of the nape of his neck. The comical enormity of his ears in contrast to his freshly cut hair. For these reasons, Jeffrey playfully yanked on the boy's t-shirt. Nothing. He pulled at his shirt again. Still, no response. Finally, Jeffrey outright flicked the boy's ear, and that was all that was needed...to start a full fledged fight!

Upon reflection, Jeffrey realized that, on some level, he was simply administering a series of love taps. Poorly received love taps, but love taps nonetheless. At the time, it was simply an overwhelming instinct, a compulsion to act. The desperate need to touch, and letting that touch be a consequence in and of itself. Jeffrey would explain that to Samuel years later, after all the childhood apologies were said. Long after the tentative steps toward a friendship were established. The bonding over comic books, and Sci-Fi films. Theme park rides, and pizza hang outs. All the girls (Sometimes. Sorta. Sure.), and boys. *Yeah everybody's coming out. Me? I'm not sure I'm gay, myself,* he remembered saying. *Yeah, right.* At sixteen, when confident self-analysis kicked in, and the constellations of their sex addled hormones, and their willingness to serve their purpose, finally aligned? Naturally they sought each other out.

Age eighteen: Jeffrey couldn't look at it again. He didn't have to, or need to. His memories of age eighteen had grown over the years, transmuting into even uglier shapes. Instances of men clearly engaging in sexual encounters. He witnessed these men, all of them covered in veils, and all of them glowing with a soundless light. It sickened Jeffrey how they melted into phosphorescent, multi-colored resins that spilled upon the floors, or pooled upon their beds.

What murders weren't done in private were performed daringly in public. He recalled the victim of silent combustion in one casual back alley encounter. His face was not covered with a veil, but with a small handkerchief. When the energy he expelled had reached its apogee, areas of crude, continental shapes bled widening stains of crimson and ochre into the fabric. Jeffrey experienced a weird sense of panic over the scene, and wondered whether the killer's recklessness would eventually get the better of him. After all, someone would have to eventually happen upon them. He could hear in the background that they were close to an extremely well-traveled district.

As if in answer to his subconscious commentary, the presence of a dark, agitated grit angrily stippled the air, like a furious cloud of gnats. This dark matter grew in direct relation, and intensity, to the brilliant light that escaped from the victim, which effectively concealed the scene.

On and on these visual accounts went, particularly after the receipt of each new postcard. The subsequent cards were not reflective surfaces, but the abstract works. Jeffrey, of course, did not see them as simple color arrangements, but as the actual images of the men whose murders he "witnessed." Initially, the very sight of these images would send him into mild seizures, temporarily consuming his thoughts with sickening recaps of the harrowing moments before their deaths.

Jeffrey, over the months, often found himself waking from these events feeling remarkably relaxed. From time to time, and to his anguished embarrassment, he'd find his boxers stickily damp.

Jeffrey had had enough. Tentatively, he committed himself to an act he'd been avoiding for some time. He produced his cell and keyed in the stored number for Joshua Becton's offices in England. His mind raced as he waited for the connection to go through. He wondered what he was doing, or what *could* be done.

A recorded message of a dour, yet professional, sounding woman broke him from his weighty ruminations. "Our offices are currently closed..." the message began. Jeffrey forgot about time zones. Futilely he checked his watch. He really didn't know if Britain was ahead or behind

"...if you'd care to leave a message with us, please do so after the tone. Thank you for calling The Joshua Becton Studios."

Jeffrey was delivered to dead air static, then a tone. "Um, hum, um—my name is Jeffrey Kellor," he stammered, "I'm calling from the States. If you'd give me a call at any time on my cell, I'd appreciate it." He left his number, and wondered almost immediately why he had. Handing one's number over to crazed individuals was probably not the wisest thing to do, he considered. But, they already had his address. And access to his dreams. Jeffrey arrived at an obvious conclusion: That finding his phone number was probably the very least of their worries.

With that, the cell phone rang. Jeffrey was startled, but not overly surprised by it. "Mr. Becton?" he asked.

"No," said the voice, matter-of-fact.

"Samuel?"

"Bingo."

"W-where are you?"

It was suddenly very quiet on the other end of the line. Jeffrey strained for any scant evidence of a person on the other side of the receiver.

"You're ready then?" asked Samuel, finally.

Jeffrey swallowed. "I suppose I must be."

"Okay." There was the sound of rustling paper. Then: "This is the address…"

$$\infty$$

It was a thirty minute walk. If he had decided to drive it, it would've only taken about five minutes, excluding traffic and parking time. He trudged through the street and its shadows instead.

Gallery 13 was located on the second floor of the Empire Building, just above a Chinese Most Best Carry-Out. Deep fried aromas so distinctly Asian-American reminded Jeffrey of how neglectful he'd been of his stomach. His unending anxiety had made a queasy mess of his bowels, and he wasn't even sure he'd be able to hold anything down anyway. Besides that, the situation didn't seem to quite merit food or drink just yet. It seemed to him that the simple acts of enjoyment or pleasure were acts of premature celebration. Issues had to be comfortably, and unquestionably, resolved before he'd ever entertain the concept of *sleeping*, much less eating.

By the time he reached the long corridor leading to the Gallery 13, Jeffrey had lost heart and all forward momentum.

With one hand he wearily supported himself against the

wall. Inwardly he fussed at all the niggling complications of the moment. His fear. The withering state of his sanity. If only he could've convinced someone, anyone, to tag along. He wanted to run away and never look back, even though he knew it would only come chasing after him. No, not chasing him, he thought. It wasn't an external thing, this creature that was after him. It was inside. Always inside.

It will never end, he considered, *unless I end it now.*

Jeffrey warily entered the gallery space. There were neither patrons nor workers to be seen. There was a black curtain facing him. He thought, perhaps, that whoever was on the premises would most likely be behind it. He decided not to hazard it. They'd come when they would.

His attentions turned to the glass sculptures resting atop their tall black podiums, spaced irregularly throughout the room. Jeffrey ventured forward. Surveyed the area. It looked to him as if the room would have been better suited to a single executive, or several individuals, other than what it was currently appropriated for. The gallery, such as it was, looked hastily put together. To his mind, the fluorescent lights, and the graying, threadbare carpet just wasn't jibing with the overall artistic esthetics.

"Beautiful," he found himself saying, as he leaned in to closely inspect a piece. One entitled *Hemorrhaged Anemone*. It was a flustered red thing, glowing and riddled with little frond-like pieces and tendrils. He almost touched it, then thought better of it. It looked too fragile. And he definitely wasn't interested in the $350 tab against its breakage.

He moved away slowly, walking along a short expanse of wall before turning a corner...and stopped dead in his tracks. There, in the alcove facing him, were four easels featuring abstract portraits of his most definite, yet indirect, acquaintance. Jeffrey didn't dare approach them, for fear of seeing those screwed up faces in them again. But he didn't need to get close. At a distance, the colors folded before him into coalescing images of various faces, screaming in silent anguish. Jeffrey feverishly wiped the sweat from his face with his hands and the back of his sleeves, while he swallowed down the desperate urge to vomit.

"Do you like them?" said a voice. Jeffrey didn't bother to turn around to see whom it was from. He already knew. "It's part of the 'Little Boy' series. 'Little Boy' being the bomb that was dropped over Hiroshima. There weren't any remains of bodies, just the scorched outlines, you see."

Jeffrey finally turned to the voice, and he saw himself, or someone who looked remarkably like himself. Twins, even identical ones, had slight differences no matter what their strong, inherent similarities. But this person, this being, was precisely Jeffrey in every way. It would've been like looking in a mirror, except the image perceived was dressed in a torn sweat shirt and jeans. His hair was damply matted in places, and his face was slick with water.

"Samuel?"

Samuel daubed his face with a towel and tossed it behind the black curtain. "I was going to call it the 'Turin' series, after the shroud they assumed was imprinted with the Christ," he mentioned idly, "but I'm not terribly religious these days."

Jeffrey looked as though he would faint. "S—Samuel?"

"Yes."

Mesmerized, Jeffrey went to Samuel with his hand outstretched. Jeffrey touched his face, and nearly cried out. "This is real." he said. There was a subtle pulse of muscle and skin as Samuel's face neatly shifted beneath Jeffrey's open palm. Jeffrey reared back in terrified awe while his old friend's true face crawled into formation.

"How are you doing this?" Jeffrey asked. "Why—?"

Samuel laughed sardonically. "To wax philosophic: Why is the answer, Jeffrey. When there's no one to answer the question, then what remains is the answer. The why then becomes the what. What am I? I am a creature who subsists off of absorbed energy. I reverse the purpose of the energy field that humans generate. I cause it to absorb all the information that causes the body. The chemical agents involving bone, and blood. Once corrupted, the body soon loses cohesion, and becomes malleable.

"What I don't consume from the energy expended, I

consume from the residue. What remains?" His gaze unaffectedly lingered over Samuel's shoulder.

Samuel reflexively clamped his hands to his face. "How—how can you do such a thing?!"

"It's not me," he said, his face pained. "It's you. You made this happen. I don't know how, but it was you. What you did to me that day. You opened us both up to the sickest kinds of miracles. I had to run away from home. One day I had your face, one day I didn't. Then, then there was the other face. I knew its nature, though I didn't know what it was capable of. Its abilities.

"I—I decided years ago that I simply wouldn't feed. And I was in a coma for—I don't know. Five hours? I woke up—" Samuel's face was caught in its dire recollection. "I woke up and the house was filled with the traces of…dead animals. Rodents. Even while unconscious I fed. Imagine what would've happened if someone had come into my home while I was out?"

Jeffrey stared at the man, angrily. "Why didn't you just take your life?"

Samuel's young face balefully grimaced. "Didn't you hear what I fuckin' said? It's about you! You only thought you knew what insanity was. What depression was. You only ever flirted with it. I wanted you to see the reality that I've lived in. A reality where there is no such thing as insanity. It's all sane. All of it! Every fucked up thing in the world is right! And I wasn't going to leave this world until you saw that. Until you saw what you did to me!"

The dark cyclone suddenly appeared, and spun wildly as Samuel's face shifted into the leathern beast. Jeffrey blundered backwards and toppled into one of the sculptures. There was a loud crash where he fell. He watched as the cyclone picked up energy, and began to pepper the air with its dense fury. The creature knelt down to Jeffrey, and immediately speckles of light formed upon Jeffrey's body.

"I—I'm sorry! I'm sorry, Samuel! I loved you. I did! I'm so sorry!" Jeffrey tearfully shouted, over the roar of the cyclone. He reached under his coat for his holster. Produced his service revolver...and shot Samuel.

    Samuel recoiled from the blast; fell to the floor. His form swiftly turned from the beast, and steadily returned to his true form. His only form as his younger self. In that very instant, the dark storm blew itself out in a static-like prattling.

∞

    With bleary eyes, Samuel awoke and struggled to his knees. Painfully, he crawled toward Jeffrey's still form. There was blood pooled in a ragged circle beneath him. Samuel observed Jeffrey for several long moments, waiting for any signs of life. But there was no sound or movement from him. Samuel checked where the bullet wound should've been on his own person. There was nothing to be found but a spotty raised welt that looked as if it had been healing for weeks.

    He gave vent to the most remorseful tears, for all the years of lives taken, for all the misdirected energies and potentials, and the lost opportunities. He wondered, with all that he'd experienced, whether he would ever be able to appreciate a normal life. No, not appreciate. But, would he know what a normal life was if it were presented to him?

    Samuel wasn't allowed to ponder this any further. There was a sound on the air that he hadn't noticed before. It was a high pitched keening building in his ears. A single sustained tone in the key of "C". It was coming from the sculptures. All about the room he saw how they had lost their luminescence, and had begun to fracture and fall to pieces like tiny glaciers. The colors that coursed within them had grown black. The blackness powdered the room, like spores bursting. A rank stench of blood and bile wafted sickly upon the air. Soon the darkness snowed upon Samuel. Whatever areas of the body the dark matter fell—his arms, his cheeks, his neck—were immediately eaten away, as though they were touched by the most virulent plague imaginable.

THE SUCCESSION OF KNOORIKIOS KHNUM
ZACHARY JERNIGAN

Tonight I will get what I want, surely.

In anticipation, I perfume my loins. I dress, sans underwear. I drink a cocktail of aphrodisiacs and insert an oil suppository laced with nerve stimulants. I shave my testicles and legs. As I walk to the Ambassador's Gala, I am turned on by the hypersensitive skin of my thighs rubbing together, the bounce of my hairless balls against them, the head of my cock brushing softly against my silk pants. The tight, oiled skin of my anus compressed and tingling between my legs. The dusk breezes are warm and dry, filled with the sweet scents of the court gardens. Gooseflies, fat with spring nectar, buzz barely aloft in the fig trees.

I arrive late. The court is a riot of color and sound, hectic with dignitaries local and foreign, human and animal and alien. I am recognized and hailed by voice, olfactory chemical and touch. I wave politely and move on, mumbling excuses. My attention is elsewhere. I have a mission. Despite the temptation to excuse myself, to find a chamber to pleasure myself (indeed, I am one great erogenous zone by now), I will not be distracted.

I have waited two years. I can wait a bit longer.

On my second circuit along the mezzanine, I spot him. I expect to feel something, having drunk enough serriola to drop a rhinoceros, yet the intensity of my body's reaction surprises me. It is as if all the blood has drained from my head, as if all the air has rushed from my lungs. The world spins. I grip the balustrade to keep from losing my legs beneath me and wait for

my heart to stop pounding. I cannot take my eyes from him.
 I descend the closest staircase and make my way through the crowd to him, taking my place among the noblemen awaiting his audience. They studiously ignore me. I would rather not wait with them, but the man I desire is expected to address them; to get to him one must rub shoulders with the over-perfumed and obsequious. I imagine on occasion that he grows tired of their constant attentions, their feigned nonchalance, that one day he will delight in stripping them of title and land. I often fantasize that his mind mirrors my own, though I have no evidence of this.
 But there is one thing I am sure of: the nobility are no nobler than I—one need only listen to a bit of court gossip to realize this—and I am suddenly impatient, overconfident with aphrodisiacal inebriation. When he finishes with the woman before him I step to take her place, though I know that the circle of dignitaries waiting for his audience moves counterclockwise. I was last in line, and it is a terrible breach of etiquette to move out of sequence. Tomorrow I will worry about the damage my rudeness has caused. Tonight I will not.
 The sounds of the gala shut off abruptly under the sound barrier he erects in private conversation. My mouth is suddenly dry. My palms break out in warm sweat. I can smell him. We are close, closer than we have been in two years, and though I have seen him every week of that time, his nudity excites me. I stare at his hips, his genitals. I do not meet his eyes. Every pore, every fiber of my being aches with desire.
 I open my mouth to speak, and what I say is ridiculous, foolhardy, presumptuous. It makes my initial foul seem small indeed.

∞

 My name is Muels Denúf. I am a human male, age twenty-nine by the Old Calendar. I was born to my mother, in vivo, a product of random genetic forces. My right eye is blue, my left green. My hair is the lightest blonde, nearly white. I am quite pale-skinned, somewhat taller than human-average, whip thin. Because of this, people assume that I am frail—especially among the celestial elite, where an unaugmented man is a rarity

—but a lifetime of back-breaking work and malnourishment does not build a parlor physique. Naked, I am a study in angles and planes, an anatomist's model. The scars are not artificial.

Earth is home, but my people do not claim it is the original. No one would believe the claim anyway. The planet is a humid mass of jungle, an inhospitable place, its weather intemperate and dangerously fickle. No one dreams the cradle of humanity like that. No one dreams of such a place, period.

And my people? Restricted by old and failing colonial technology to the driest polar swamps, we have devolved from a cosmopolitan star-faring culture—a heritage so distant in the past as to be nearly meaningless—to match our surroundings. We spend far too much time complaining about our lot in soggy bars and whorehouses. We gossip and scrabble underhandedly for uncultivable plots of land. We breed neither scientists nor poets.

To be blunt, Earthmen are a moldy, wet blanket of a people.

But I imagine this can be said about the natives of any number of undeveloped colonial worlds, and it does not mean that my people have no aspirations. We have a consulate and a small group of ill-trained diplomats who petition among the local systems for assistance. Before my placement, we had a few encouraging leads—one or two vows of economic alliance. Pleasant, imprecise promises which came to nothing. Certainly, none of my colleagues were invited to live on Elephas, to hold court with the rulers of empires alien and human, the likes of which we had only heard stories.

We were destined to fail in our diplomacy. Prior to my appointment, Earth knew nothing of the web that holds worlds together. We did not know that we were owned entirely but possessed so far below the radar that our fate was not even considered. When I realized this—fairly quickly, as it happened - -I had to remind myself of my duty. Though I did not want my fellow men to know in what little regard they were held, I had an obligation. They are my people, regardless of my distaste for them.

I have been Earth's spokesman for six years now, these

last two on Elephas. Though I did not arrive at this high position through a display of skill (I do not delude myself; during the preceding four years I was a willing sexual plaything, a curio and erotic anachronism), I have learned much. I have become inured to the cutthroat world of Elephas' imperial court. My skin has grown thick, my mind sharp to intrigue. I have arranged trade agreements and won respect for my people despite our lowly status. With few exceptions, this has been accomplished without prostituting myself further. There are advantages in withholding.

The desert world suits me. The dry air is curative, the open spaces of sand and ocean exhilarating. To see a great distance! On Earth there are no uninterrupted views, no buildings taller than the tallest trees, no hilltops from which to survey anything at all. Elephas, by contrast—

But there is no room for contrast, no point of comparison. On Earth, the rains are a constant, stultifying presence, but in the desert, they are a gift. After a storm's brief violence, the windblown stretches of red dirt and sand erupt in colors that would be indescribable to my kin, trapped as they are on their cold, gray, fungal world.

I cannot conceive of returning home. My frames of reference have evolved. I would not have the words to explain my loss, and should I find them eventually, no one on Earth would understand their meaning. It is not only that I have given my heart to a man. I have given my heart to another world, my eyes to new vistas.

∞

He closes the door behind us. He grabs my shoulders from behind and pulls me against his chest. He reminds me *we only made love once*, that I *would be a fool to think it would happen again*. While he says this, his hands are working at my belt buckle. After it is unclasped, he tells me, *remember your place*. His right hand goes underneath my waistband and his fist grips my rigid member. His chin rests on my shoulder and I moan into his neck, grinding my buttocks into his erection. *It will never happen!* he says as I pull down my pants, allowing him to slip between my thighs. I grip him there, his length firmly pressed against my perineum—*You're kidding yourself,* he groans. He pushes me onto the bed and there is no more talk as his mouth covers mine, his tongue thrusting, his hands urgent, undressing me. I detach myself for a moment, to grab the lubricant from my pants pocket. We kiss roughly, legs intertwined as our hands move over each other's erections. Despite the protestations, his eyes are closed, his hands sure. My nose fills with the smell of his sweat, pungent as cinnamon tree bark.

    I am impatient, hungry. I roll over and throw my left leg over his hip, reaching behind me for his penis. I guide him into me fluidly, taking his whole cock into my rectum. I have practiced for this occasion. For a long moment, I hold him there, savoring the immense swell of him inside me—I can feel the heartbeat in his erection, he is breathing quickly behind me, *yes,* he whispers. And then we start bucking. Slowly at first, and then with increasing speed, his hard, slick shaft moves inside me. I do not touch myself; I do not need to; the mere proximity of his hands, his fingers digging into my hips with each thrust stimulates me enough. It is only with great self-control that I am able to keep from coming.

    I turn my head to look at his left hand, encased as always in the white glove that fits so closely it is indistinguishable from his skin. Smoother, slightly colder than flesh, it does not sweat. I focus on the line where the white meets his black skin. It does not move.

    I want it to. I imagine the line spreading along his forearms, up his full biceps and onto the hard swell of his shoulder. From there it spreads onto his collarbone, over the heavy muscles of his back and chest, and slides down his back. It crawls up his neck, envelops his face, shrinks down to a point and closes on the top of his head. As the glove passes, the details of his expression are obscured. Only his eyes remain uncovered. It melts over the ridges of his belly and moves onto his loins. In the back, it slides into the muscular crevice between his butt cheeks; in the front it slips into the heated area where we are joined.

    A brief hesitation, and then it *jumps*—and its coolness is

enveloping my skin, slithering over my hips, hugging me—connecting us. No longer thrusting, but fused and squeezing, swelling. I feel the warm tumescence of his rigid penis and my bowels' every nerve as I pull him deep into me, yearning for him to grow larger and fill me. I imagine that he feels my warm, soft interior hugging him, my sphincter tightening rhythmically on the base of his shaft.

Both of us one being, wrapped in a shell of cool, fluid marble, heated and pulsing inside.

"The glove," I pant. "Please."

∞

His name is Adrash Knoorikios. He is my perfect erotic object.

He is an unaugmented man of middle years, tall and powerfully proportioned, the lines of his body fluid, the muscles full and smooth. Hairless except for the brows and eyelashes, his skin is the fertile black-brown of wet soil, free of blemish or prominent vein. His features are strong, classically masculine, and, to my eyes, somewhat cruel. I attribute this to his eyes, which are almond shaped and bright yellow, without pupil or white. They seem to shine even in the light of day. His penis, long and thick even when flaccid, is circumcised and darker than the rest of his skin, nearly coal black. His testicles are unwrinkled and large, but do not droop unattractively beneath his member.

He wears little, even in cold weather. Around his neck he wears a broad mail necklace, of gold links so finely worked that it lies like thin fabric on his chest. His left hand is sheathed in the white glove, always. On his wrists he often wears twin brass vambraces, heavy and buffed to a high shine. Larger jewelry of the same design encircles his ankles. For the month of monsoons, he wears a red satin headband that trails to the ground. He never covers his loins with clothing. At war and defense, the glove—grown to cover all but his eyes—is his only attire; in this guise, he is called Knoorikios Khnum, or Adrash Min. I have seen him in the glove only once. It was not during wartime.

He smells of some strong, heavy musk—of an achingly

familiar yet unnamable spice, but only when one's nose is nearly touching his skin. It is as if he causes the air itself to swallow the particles of his scent only centimeters from the pores, in order to save people from being overwhelmed by its intensity.

His voice is deep and resonant, yet he rarely speaks publicly. He is not overly demonstrative in gesture, either, but makes his moods felt easily enough. Ocean-deep calm, seadog focus, tropical storm fury—one feels his moods in the gut, tugging, impossible to ignore. The gravity of his aura forces attention.

We slept together, once, a short time after I arrived. He never spoke of it again, nor have I had the courage to raise the issue until now. To have that man, a man who topples stellar empires only to uplift others, a soul that resounds throughout the void itself, speak my name in furious intimacy once more… To hear my name spoken, whispered in the quiet moments afterwards…

I love him, which is a foolish thing to do. I am a diplomat from nowhere, and he is the ruler of an empire. He has smashed stars with his fists, set worlds ablaze with the light from his eyes. His is the will of Thor, of Yahweh. Of Maitreya and Ahura Mazda.

I am a man; he is a god. This is no hyperbole.

∞

"Please," I whisper. "Please, please," I beg.

He does not answer, but tightens his grip on my hip. His thrusts become shorter, faster. A grunt escapes his lips, and he swells greater, stretching me where we are connected. My begging has excited him, apparently. I push and pull on his erection, breathing deeply into my gut as his shaft massages my prostate. I stare at his fingertips, the indentations in my skin, hyperaware of the five small patches of flesh in contact with the glove. I will the material to melt from his hand onto me, to complete the union before I lose myself to orgasm. I long to be a closed environment, joined in our final moments of ecstasy; fused afterwards as his fluid disperses inside me, as my own ejaculate cools and spreads beneath the glove's membrane to coat us both—to be absorbed into each other's skin.

"The glove, Lord. The glove. Please."

He grips my right shoulder. *Get on top*, he commands. I push myself up and, careful not to lose him, rise on his erection enough to hook my right leg underneath me. I grip his hips with my calves and lower my weight completely onto him. We sigh in unison as he reaches the greatest depth inside me. The angle allows me to rest for a moment. I savor the sensation of fullness, the distention of my sphincter as it slowly spasms around the base of his engorged member. My own erection stiffens; my testicles rise, tickling my inner thigh. I breathe deeply into my stomach, trying to rein in my libido and achieve some measure of control over my body. It requires constant attention, lest it let go completely. No amount of practice could have prepared me for this.

Yet I am not allowed much rest. He slaps my hips. His fingers dig in as he lifts me up, off his erection. Slowly, very slowly, his head slides free. My heart shudders in despair, thinking that he has decided to end our lovemaking—but he holds me there, his head pressed against my opening. I want intensely to fall back onto him, but my hips are held in a vice grip.

The fingers of his left hand tighten fractionally. I look down. *Watch*, he says.

I watch. Finally (I believe myself to be imagining it for a moment), the glove begins inching along his wrist.

I gasp as he pulls me down.

∞

On a night quite similar to this one, I attended my first consular reception. I had been on Elephas for less than two days, was disoriented from the rapid change in my position—literally, at times; the gravity of Elephas was two-thirds less than what I had become accustomed to on Béla, my previous post. My inner ear sent signals of distress every time I moved. I overcorrected and leapt from chairs, looked like an idiot. The dense muscles I had built to deal with high-g felt like so much excess fluid or fat. I was a cumbersome beast, feeling oversized for the first time in my life. The night was young, but I simply wanted it to end.

I had found a place to lean, against one of the bar counters. I surveyed the immense, gaudy room, and for the first time saw the evening's host. Of course, I had seen him any number of times in newscasts—had been attracted to him even then, though I had considered myself mainly hetero—but seeing him in the flesh was another experience entirely. I watched him for some time as he gracefully negotiated a path through the crowd, addressing those he passed without stopping long to talk with anyone. The crowd broke and reformed around him as if he were a jungle predator, a moving locus of energy. It seemed to me that if I closed my eyes I would still be able to follow his circuit, like a blind man tracking the sun across the sky. Even with my preoccupations, I wondered how I had failed to sense the man's presence immediately.

He was the most beautiful person I had ever seen. I wanted to be introduced to him, to touch him. I also wanted to duck immediately away, to leave and come back when I felt more like myself, less like an oaf.

Eventually, he made his way to my corner of the ballroom. I bowed as he came near, and his gaze passed through me. I had expected an introduction, some recognition. I deflated, feeling every inch the outsider, the fool, the child. Why would I garner special attention? Why little provincial me, in a court filled to bursting with men of essence?

I slunk to the nearest private bath, splashed water on my face. In my state, I did not attach any significance to the way I had been treated—I thought myself merely too unimportant to notice. Of course, in hindsight it seems purposeful, the way he ignored me. Even gods play their games, pursue their quarry indirectly. Still, what megalomania would have permitted me to arrive at this conclusion then?

A moment later a man shouldered into my bathroom, silencing me with a gesture. He informed me that Adrash Knoorikios requested an audience with me after the guests had left. I nearly fainted, thinking I was about to be executed for some breach of etiquette. I waited four hours, the longest of my life, for my fate to be revealed. The final guests—important men and beings I recognized from my dossiers—trickled from the ballroom, staring at me in open curiosity. They must have wondered who the young man in plain clothes was, and why he looked as if he had eaten a handful of hot peppers.

Adrash arrived as the massive ironwood door closed behind the last guest. He took my left hand in his right and led me to his bedroom, a sprawling, columned space of low couches and shifting curtains. He told me to disrobe and kneel before him. He placed his hands on my head. His cock tasted like smoke, like almonds, like seawater. When he entered me from behind, I only barely kept from crying out, in pain, in fear, in ecstasy. I closed my eyes. I felt his urgency. His gloved hand was cold on my hip. Eventually, I did try to cry out—when I realized that he was encased completely, that the white membrane was spreading onto my skin—but he clamped his hand over my mouth.

You're safe, his voice whispered in my mind. *You'll never be safer than right now.*

∞

The experience proves quite different, this time. When the glove jumps from his skin to mine, I feel neither panicky nor faint. Its caress seems like that of a former lover, one whose touch is instantly familiar, even comforting. The chill membrane cups my genitals and rises onto my erection, flows over my backside and trickles down the inside of my thighs. My muscles twitch under the new skin. When it closes over the tip of my penis, my libidinous fire intensifies and contracts; suddenly, I feel in absolute control of my responses, as if my arousal can increase infinitely with no need for release. As it progresses nearer to my head, I close my eyes. I rock with my lover, fused together. The membrane reaches my chin, my lips, my ears, covers them. I breathe normally through the sheath. It hesitates around my eyes as the top of my head is enveloped. Slowly then, it moves onto my eyelids, creeps to their shuttered edges…And enters me.

∞

I attended the bloodgames on Béla, once. One time was enough.

The final bout pitted a man against a Jeroud—a small, green-black creature that shifted shape constantly, causing the eye to search for patterns in its cloud form. Now a fish, now a jaguar, the creature moved its body sluggishly on awkward pseupopods, but attacked with thin tendrils quicker than my eyes could register. The man, from whose massive torso sprouted an extra pair of metal arms ending in thick tentacles, was able to anticipate the attacks. He blocked the tendrils with his shield, pirouetted and struck with his tentacles at the Jeroud, cleaving huge weeping gashes in its mottled flesh. He laughed, unscathed, clearly enjoying himself.

After several minutes, though, it became clear that the man could not gain an advantage over the shapeshifter. It sucked its spent fluid back into its body, healing its wounds within seconds. It never seemed to tire. Gradually, whatever cocktail that had shortened the man's reaction time wore off, and he was left pitifully open to the Jeroud's offensive. The end was mercifully quick. As the stands rose in applause I remained seated, feeling sick to my stomach, staring at the central screen, which focused on the dying man's face. Written there was pain, of course, and shock—not physiological, but emotional. He had not expected to lose, had never even considered the possibility.

Adrash Knoorikios' expression was much the same after our first union. I had climaxed six times, ejaculated twice within the glove's embrace. He had no such release; his erection had remained firm inside me, but after an hour of short rhythmic thrusts the glove had retreated from my body. He softened and slid free. He lay down and beckoned me to rest with him. His arm encircled my shoulders, drawing me in close. I rested my head on his chest, watched as the glove retreated up the ridges of his stomach. It tickled as it passed under my cheek. Though exhausted, I could not silence the doubts shifting nervously in my mind. Obsessively I returned to and lingered on my performance. Had I done something wrong?

Your people, he said, interrupting my thoughts. *Are they all like you?*

I rose on an elbow—and flinched when I saw his stricken expression. "No. I do not think so."

He smiled tiredly and gently pushed my head back onto his chest. *Do you like it here?*

"I do not know yet." I searched for words. Few came. "It is different."

Yes, I imagine it must be. Your Earth is not for the weak-limbed or subtle. Don't worry. Your strengths will someday prove useful.

"Have I done something wrong?"

I felt him shake his head. *No. I tried something and failed. It's not your fault. Sleep, and I'll wake you when it's time to leave.*

Little surprise that sleep would not come. The sun rose and, as still as the dead, I watched the shadows of the curtains ghost across the floor. The smell of our sex faded into a dim memory. His heart pumped powerfully, unvaryingly beneath my ear. The sun rose through an open window. A bar fell across our bodies, causing the fine down on his stomach to glow. When his hand tightened on my shoulder, I knew that our time together was through. I returned to the apartment I had been assigned and recorded a message for my family, filled with optimistic lies.

∞

The stars descend. They burn with intelligence, blinding genius, igniting continuously, blazing compassionately, malevolently, all the life-fires of the Milky Way spinning madly, a thousand million furnaces gripping their worlds jealously, keeping their secrets. A million billion worlds harboring life, encrusted with ice, smoldering into death, circling ever closer to their mothers, their father suns.

The lights of creation span the galaxy, light centuries across, upon the ceiling of Adrash's bedroom. I see every one with unnatural clarity, inhuman focus. I recognize every point of light, know all the balls of ice and rock in intimate detail: Here is Earth, and Earth, and Earth; here is Béla, Jeroun, Kama-Rudra, Coon, Zwat'cj, Midor, Urath, Ironwing, Pestua, Xtia, Peewetu Na... All under the eye of God.

I hear my mother and father, my sister and my brothers and friends, enemies, cooking and laughing, snoring and

fucking. They blaze, each and every soul aflame.
Each is a living, breathing dent in the fabric of reality.
Each bending the fabric of spacetime, disproportionately massive with potential energy.

Here is the Jeroud gladiator, his hunger voracious, his memory mere seconds long, his intellect focused like a laser point, oscillating wildly between caged fear and blind hatred. Its spirit reeks like rotten meat. My mother, her spirit smells like moldy bread, basil, and the washbasin. My father, spongewood freshly chopped, watercress.

Each holds within them the Heat Death—the long slow crumble, the Big Collapse—the joining at the end of time. For each, the strings of consciousness are as brittle as vacuum-spun aluminum, as volatile as a fistful of neutron star, as malleable as molten lead. Their worlds, their stars, their fragile artificial satellites and tincan spaceships—all inconsequential in the final accounting, so easily shed like the cumbersome carapaces of extinct insects.

In the meantime, however, man, alien and animal are rootbound, tethered spine to mind, affixed like exotic specimens in display cases. Suffering written into their very cells. I see Elephas. I see Earth.

The future, the fate of man, the fate of all intelligent life —the injustice: This is what the glove allows me to see, splayed above Adrash's bed.

I open my eyes.

The room has grown dark and cold, though the night outside remains warm. I look down over my shoulder at Adrash, whose body is fully sheathed within the glove. His head is thrown back against the bed and his eyes are dull flames, highlighting the plain geometry of his masked face. Below his chin, the cords of his neck are taut rope. The muscles of his arms and torso strain in rigid definition—but against what? I close my eyes once more, and see: Lines of energy, lava-red, flowing from his left hand to the tip of his erect member, which rhythmically pulses a hot, white light. Staring through the spectral muscle and bone of my hips, I see faint, thin conduits flashing inside my body. They thrum audibly, smelling of ozone. When one flares near my left hand it feels as if my entire limb will explode, so great is the pressure of its excitation.

 Adrash's hands unclench from the sheets. *You see them!* he exclaims in my mind. He grips my hips again. *Move*, he commands.

 I tighten around his shaft and begin rocking. I watch his erection move inside me, largely unaware of the physical sensation. Within the glove, my penis is swollen, but this is incidental. My arousal has become universal. It has spread to every cell in my body. I focus on the threads of fire, urging them thicker, more radiant.

 Our twinned chakras flare—once, twice, a third time blindingly. *Ah!* Adrash gasps through the membrane. He pushes my ass down. Above, the stars dim as he begins to climax. His testicles stir against my perineum and he releases inside me, his cock swelling again and again with each spurt. For a moment, all the lines between us are obscured as his light washes out the room. Pressure builds within me, undirected, as if every cell is set to rupture. I hold the discharge at bay—out of fear. I do not know what will happen if I let go. Every moment the energy within me seems to double in intensity. Holding reign over such forces for long is impossible.

 I scream as my left arm explodes.

∞

 I leave Adrash in the bedroom, asleep. The sight of the fused stump of his left shoulder sickens me, as do the puckered scars that now crisscross his body. The act of succession was not easy on him. Perhaps he underestimated the toll it would take. Best that he should wake alone—and grieve alone when the full weight of his choice settles on his shoulders. When he stares at his ruined reflection and knows how far he has fallen. I pity him, but distantly. I am tuned to subtler frequencies now.

 I walk alone through the sumptuous hallways of Adrash's home. I close my eyes and still see, admire my reflection in every shining surface. My skin glistens like wet obsidian; my eyes glow like embers. My left arm throbs in time to my footsteps and the glove sings to me without words,

hinting at the secrets to all things. There are no walls, no restrictions. Mine is the will of Thor and Yahweh, of Maitreya and Ahura Mazda. Of Knoorikios Khnum. I could choose to burn Elephas to a cinder behind me, or push it a little closer to its sun. Turn its deserts into festering jungle. Make it feel like Earth. The glove's song could become a dirge, a lament for the old order, so easily.
    And it would be just, fitting.
    I walk onto the central veranda. Below me the court gardens hum with pollinating insects. I smell every flower, hear every root's miniscule trickle of water as clearly as my heartbeat. The breeze is a billion particles of soft fire ricocheting off my chest, gently scouring the skin of my face. The sun caresses my body lovingly, its rays the soft licks of an animal eager to please. From a great distance I taste the incoming tide, the faint traces of organic rot—the living bodies and decaying remains of every fish and mammal, every microbe and plant to ever inhabit the sea. Underneath the glove, my left hand feels the weight and density of each atom as it rebounds from the godflesh. I could solidify the air, hold it frozen in my hand, crush it into a diamond or miniature nuclear furnace.
    The glove stirs on my wrist, tickling, seductive. I allow its white film to envelope me slowly, relishing its cool appropriation of my black, sun-warm skin. As it enters my eye sockets, I have a brief vision. I see my brothers. My father and mother, my one remaining grandparent. My distant relatives, neighbors. I note every premature wrinkle, every missing tooth and crooked limb. I hear the rattle of death in lungs, feel the sharp pain of bacterial infection in jawbones, taste the sour flavor of toxic moonshine on tongues. The sound of disease-carrying vermin scurrying in the moldy walls.
    My sister is pregnant, her baby's brain and body malformed.
    The glove has reminded me of something important. I sense its hunger, its desire to be used. To help me. To help my people. My penis stiffens. A warm tingling spreads from my testicles outward, suffusing my body.
    I close my eyes and fix my gaze on the sad, distant

reflected light of Earth.
    With a thought, I leave Elephas behind me.

LOVEBITES & RAZORLINES
J. DANIEL STONE

It's said that adventure was born from the fire of monotony spreading inside a person's brain. I sort of felt the same way, and that made me want to go out on an adventure of my own. Last month when the trees' leaves fell from the branches like droplets of blood, and the city skyline became the color of pumpkins during twilight, I felt my life come to a screaming halt.

I ventured out by foot and loaded up my metro card as much as I could, touring the city streets by bus and the dark wet underground by train. I had no intent of sleeping or eating: it was time to dream. I thinned myself until my arms looked like prison bars and my face a living skull. I never had a good appetite anyway (I saved most of it for cheap beer and an embalming bottle of 151). I was forcing my palate into panic mode, so much so that it took anything that I put into my mouth: mince meat, a festered pack of chicken, pork chops cut straight from the swine. Raw meat, not the delicacy of the western world.

I was always meant to be different.

Then I remembered why I did all of this: I was alone, yet again. Alone, so alone. Hellos and goodbyes ringed the mouths of temporary flimsies like sweat waiting to be wiped clean; ephemeral bodies polluted my bed just long enough to leave behind the ghost of their sweet scent. I should've been used to this as I'd shared my life with solitude for a long time—in dive bars where boys never welcomed me as their nightly companion, or in the back room of the porn shops still straggling across 8th Avenue—because the boys that accompanied me

nightly never wanted so much as to stay the next day. They wanted nothing more than a quick fuck while I clung to them for a conversation; a cup of fucking coffee in the evening hours.
    Sick with the love-bug I was.
    This was, of course, my own fault. I had a taste for the degenerates of the city, boys considered out of my league, to be frank. Mainstream culture teaches you to want them, would have anyone begging for crumbs at the feet of these A-listers, and I fell right into the trap. Turn the television on and BAM! there's a lithe beauty slammed into your face, telling you that's how you should look if you want respect, if you want a love life. I, of course, thought I was stronger than this, that I could resist such simple temptation.
    I wasn't.
    My part of town is littered day and night with these fashionistas and superficial superheroes. They're the type of people too stuck in the latest wave of fashion to care about anything else, anyone else. They don't have the time or patience to deal with someone outside their social circle (namely me). But I made it my business to force myself in.
    Intoxication is the perfect weapon. I can get whatever bitching boy I need by way of a promised drink, smoke and a comfy bed. They just never want to stay past that first night, and I always wanted to keep them so bad. They didn't think I was worth it, and some boys would even demand payment, forgetting that I'd housed them for the night. But I'd give it up with an invisible fist thrusting into their vacant faces.
    And then the love bug bit me. Sepulchral poison injected into my bloodstream and thundered into my head like a possession! I had to have love, what else was there to do in life? Didn't humans evolve from raging monkeys into a species that depended on a partner for more than mating? Why did I have to be so rudely thrown out of the equation? Life is about relationships and how you build them. Love is the fuel for it all.
    I had to have it, simply put. It would be a cure for my sickness.

∞

So much of that sickness made me question my own sanity. I never knew I had it in me (though I must've for I'd been nibbling raw meat) but when I grabbed the handle of the hammer it spilled to me all of its sinister secrets. Concealed under piles of paper scrawled with the terrible poetry that I hadn't published yet, the hammer said that everything would be alright, that the music I was blasting would mix thrashing bass and vocals evil as a serpent king with nascent shrieking terror. Glassjaw is so great that way.

The hammer plummeted without him expecting it.

I felt the metal chink into bone, split his skull. The blood engulfed me like a tidal wave and warmed my shuddering body. So I plunged again, and again, until his shiny yellow hairline started pulling away from his skin with a red-wet suck, until it was shot through with gore. That rendered him unconscious, and it was at that time I realized that I had a taste for blood: a mouthful of salty heaven.

Naturally, right? I'd already been eating offal butcher meat, training myself to become some kind of carnivore. His blood soon clotted along the edge of my bed, twisting out of his head like a water fountain gone awry in a public park. That meant his precious little heart was still beating, and that he could hear me. I could've ripped into him at that moment and fed from his viscera, but I was barely able to catch my breath because I had found a penchant for murder. I was going to be in love, for real this time.

"You should never trust a man who offers you a warm bed and drink for one night only," I said to the barely breathing beauty.

I moved the little fucker into my bathroom, a place swarming with insects and moldy tiles. I could give a fuck about cleaning; there was too much dreaming to do. And now that I was living my fantasy, there was no time to waste! I had packs of ice in my freezer and I dumped them all in the tub, watching the skin on his face go gray and eyes stare blankly as his lungs gave out, as his heart slowed and stopped.

I spent the rest of the night watching cheap B movies that only a nerd could love, surrounded by books and a comic collection so huge and overzealous it's too embarrassing to speak of. The characters in movies and books never left. By the power of the pause button or a book marker, I could revisit who and what I wanted and not be judged. I watched the screen for four hours straight, un-showered and sticky with blood, already smelling the faint gaseous threat of decomposition. There was an old television show called *The Hunger* on by that time: suspense and sex mixed into one dangerous vial, and it made me think of my own life.

On the nights when I was alone, when I could not find anyone to suit my vicious desire, I lay in waste dreaming. I wrote in a scrappy notebook and dabbed the pages with bloodied fingerprints; I read books of the macabre, the darkly fantastic and of outer worlds to steal my soul. Who needed a soul on this evil earth if one had to be alone? I could survive just fine as an unholy ghost, I knew, and perhaps that's exactly what I was going to do.

Poetic justice? Perhaps.

Books sailed my mind out of this world and dipped it into the brains of many others. I could read the same novel in spring and smile, but read it again in the following winter and I'd be a wreck. My moods were worsening. What lie beneath the tattered covers might turn a pauper into a prince, might turn a boy into an artist, but I'd learned morality is only skin deep and that it couldn't be trusted. *Books are tiny universes concealed within ink and paper. Art is the rocket ship.*

By then I'd read Frankenstein by Mary Shelley and I realized that I hadn't become sick, hadn't felt a searing anger that winter. It was a roaring seed of lust exploding in my gut. I had found an answer. Not so much a zombie novel—but in a sense it could be—as it is a novel of struggle and necessity for life. A novel where the point of view came from the monster himself! I was this sympathetic monster, and this understanding clutched my heart with a cold dead hand, just like the hand sitting in my own bathtub.

Frankenstein was the key to my locked life. Like the mad doctor in the book, I was going to make my own lover. But not in the way that crazy Victor did it. I'd not collect bones from charnel houses, nor utilize the limbs of animals from the local butcher. I'd simply build it from my interim lovers. I imagined the eyes I wanted to look into, and the hands I wanted to hold, formulating a plan while I basted my organs in vodka, killing my liver for days on end. I'd yet to shower either because I still had a boy on ice in my bathroom; and so it was time to release him from his hell. I recalled Mary Shelley's madness, her empathy for the monster, and suddenly everything was right, justified.

The memories of those pages spoke in tongues: forever, eternal, perpetual.

I could be pitied if people heard my story.

It was time.

In the tub he sat erect. His arms were pale and limp as death allows. The color had drained out of his face, shimmering faintly in the dim bathroom light. The back of his head was a swamp; there was a sticky smear of gore along the place where I'd slid his body into the tub. I rubbed my finger into the cold mush, bringing the blood to my tongue. It was like wine gone to vinegar, like forgotten fruit left to rot after having been picked off the tree.

I liked nothing on his body but his hands. They were soft and lovely. His face had lost that youth I'd been so attracted to at first; his eyes were dried glumes within hollowed sockets. I wanted no part of them. But his hands had stood the test of time, hadn't yet curled into a rigor mortis ball, and so I was able to hold them for a moment and stare into those depthless eyes, wondering if he hated me for stealing his life. But he only had himself and his hormones to blame.

For the incision I drew a small line across his wrists like a surgeon preparing his patient. I'd forgotten how long his fingers were. These were the hands that had grabbed my hair as we thrust into one another; these were the nails that had dug furrows into my chest during indulgent orgasm, the hands that had begged me to stop as I rained the hook of the hammer into his head. I faintly remembered that he'd learned to play piano as a young boy, such is why those fingers were so strong! I imagined his flowing blond hair behind a grand orchestra, thin white fingers stretching to reach every key on the piano, his head bobbing to the music. But then the vision faded and I realized I had work to do.

    With fishing line I tied his wrists together so I could see the cutting line clearly. The teeth of the hack saw broke into the flesh with ease. His skin flaked away and blood misted into my eyes. The hand snapped off and sinews of tendon hung like overcooked spaghetti. I put it in a Ziploc bag in my freezer. Rinse and repeat and the hands stayed beautiful even after death. They were to be the hands I'd hold the rest of my life.

∞

    "Would you like to come back to my place?" I asked a sweet-smelling guy across the dark bar.

    He didn't have an answer at first, and not that I cared. He had the bluest eyes I'd ever seen, and I wanted them for my pet project. Though we shared little conversation, he seemed like a genuine guy. I spent the night in the corner booth sipping Old Number 7 on the rocks through a little red straw that reminded me of limp tendon dangling from a severed wrist.

    "Well…sure," he said, dubious, "you seem like a nice guy, and you aren't even ugly."

    I winced, hoping the music in the jukebox would turn louder, hoping that a glass would fall off the bar top and smash to a billion glittering chunks so to erase that awkward moment, to stop my face from turning instantly grim. I was starved, I admit, and my pallor had reached dangerous heights. I'd learned to stand upright and shake off the burst of stars before my eyes being that my blood sugar was so dangerously low. I often amazed myself at how we humans adapt to such terrible circumstances.

    But the guy didn't notice thankfully; the bar was ridden with shadows. Better for me, for I had exquisite plans to execute! So I promised him another drink and a good night in bed, no strings attached, as the men in this community love.

    All I wanted were his eyes. They were forbidden gems lying deep in the African coast, the Anglo pride of northern Europe. They would put Caribbean oceans to shame. I took a moment to tell the guy about myself, making up stories as I went along, as my brain was teased into pleasant drunkenness. I found myself being overtly charming, overtly calm, but on the inside I was screaming with loneliness.

"Horror movies are weird," he told me. "But they're different. So that's nice."

"My building's not far from here, but we can even take a cab if you don't want to walk."

"Sounds good. By the way, I'm Sean."

"Jason."

The lie slipped through my lips like as dead weight. It seemed natural when the person who you're about to sleep with wouldn't be alive for much longer. Why not reinvent yourself for the fuck of it?

"Let's take a cab, it's quicker," Sean said.

We left in a jiffy, with my pants way too tight around my crotch.

∞

I took careful steps to not damage those eyes.

Sean had put up a good fight. The first blow of the hammer sent him flying into my stereo which turned off Daryl Palumbo's nascent screaming; the second only pissed him off. That should've knocked him out, but I was so drunk and listless I'd not calculated the strength it took to kill a person with a hammer. Plus, my new diet of alcohol and cigarettes had left me hardly any strength to put on my pants right. His blood sprayed my face as he darted for the door. I grabbed him hard, but to deflect me from coming any closer, Sean elbowed me right in my nose, jerking my head backward. I felt the cartilage crush like tomatoes under a boot and determined that my blood was not as delicious as others: it was sourer, watery.

As he clawed for the locks I wound my hand back and shot the hammer straight as an arrow, heard it connect with his head in a wet metal slap. The sound reminded me of a potato hitting concrete. His skull split like lips and his hair flooded rouge. He was out for the count. As I dragged him to the infamous bathroom, our little duel had left me wanting to taste his blood right away; deservedly so because of all that hard work.

When I did, licking all the gore and grime off my hands once I'd placed him in the bathtub, I realized that it was faintly sweet. I thought maybe this was the flavor of fear, the grim finality within the second before you die. But I hadn't eaten in nearly four weeks by this time; my appetite was severely changing, my palate begging for any kind of nourishment.

Sean was so heavy in death. His arms and legs felt like they were filled with lead. I sat him upright and opened his eyes. They were still as spellbinding as when he'd been alive. I thought about popping them out with a butter knife, or even that little silver tool that you crack open fresh mussels with. But no, that would have flattened the eyes to pancakes. I used a spoon instead because I knew I could scoop; the body of the utensil would form to the eye like a glove.

Thin traceries of veins glowed through Sean's face, veins deprived of the body's electric. They looked quite sad, quite cold. I held one eye open with the phantom intelligence of a medical master, with the unflinching hand of a surgeon, and pushed the spoon in. It made a squelch like crushing a hundred worms in your hands, falling out whole in my lap.

I'd prepared a jar of cold water with a pinch of salt and dropped the eyes in. Thread-like optic nerve floated like long hair surrounding a face under-water. I was one step closer to my homemade lover, my forever. But something was missing: a body. I had the hands and the eyes, I had my cryptic imagination, but I wasn't a scientist by any means. I couldn't fashion a heart from scratch, I couldn't rewire the vessels in which blood traveled through. I couldn't take the brain, spongy and soft in my hands, and transplant it into another head.

That would take time and persistence, and I had neither. I was too sick. My diet was treacherous, equalized only by the seldom sip of water and Tylenol PM for the woozy feeling. What I needed was a whole body, one that could compliment the perfect eyes and hands. So I cleaned myself up and severed all of Sean's limbs. I bisected the legs at the knee, tore his arms straight from the shoulder and boiled his skull down to the bone before I stuffed him into an industrial garbage bag filled with bleach. From the depths of that bag I knew the eyeless skull was forever grinning, but at whom? Himself for being so stupid? Or for me and the insidious future ahead?

Then I felt something watching me, some entity from another universe. I turned and saw Sean's eyes swimming in the jar. The water magnified their size; I could see all the precious highways of vessels that supplied them with blood and oxygen, tears and sight, and they were carefully marking me. They made me think. Invoking life into a dead body would only take a little electricity and water, just like the movies. Drop a toaster into the tub and you have yourself a homemade defibrillator.

∞

I set out on an adventure through St. Mark's. It's a seedy place at night, though I was so sick I couldn't focus on everything that I'd grown to love: the speeding cars, the smell of coffee, the loud music blasting on the corner of Astor and 3rd Avenue. The air bit through my clothes like a fucking little monster with the cutting power of winter; people stared me down, noticing my bane form, how sick I was. I think by that point I was limping. Not too sure. I didn't know how bad the love-bug had infected me, how it had thinned me to such a skeleton that people feared me as the living dead.

I was in a bad mood anyway. I felt weak, ugly, unwanted: everything that would bog my chances to bag a new cutie. Even the regular hobos of St. Mark's mistook me for one of their own, and that was the greatest insult of the night.

"Come, young man," one of them said, a fetid woman dressed in moth-eaten rags lying in a nearby crevice. "We have room for you."

She offered me a bed of cardboard and a smoke, but I refused all her niceties. Away from that block, I stumbled into brilliant bodies shuffling along in quintuplet groups. Boys with long corn-silk hair, white fishnets and black leather boots squiggled between yuppies and their perpetual sneers. Some boys held hands tight for the universal fuck you. The ground sparkled with spilled drinks; the sounds of bar laughter pummeled my ears. The air tasted black and drunk, ridden with perfume and lust.

It was how I preferred my nights.

I stopped at a bar called The Continental. Five shots for ten dollars was their special, according to the enticing sign, bold black letters painted on a bright white banner. I slipped passed the stupid black velvet rope and took a seat at the edge of the bar where the wind blew in just enough to sober a person up through the heavy duty curtains. The jukebox was obnoxiously blasting the universal bar song.

We're halfway there, ooooh! Living on a prayer!

I wanted to hear Glassjaw, my favorite band.

The bar itself was four people thick, all the faces tailing the two hard working barmaids to pour them shots, shots, shots! The girls' sports bras were soaked in alcohol and their nipples were like tiny pink diamonds. I supposed that big tips were in order. I downed four shots of Jager and it was like I'd drunk gasoline the way it singed my esophagus and rumbled my stomach. I just couldn't take it anymore. The alcohol left the sickly sweet taste of cough medicine on my palate, but I found I wanted something more, something with texture: meat.

HUNGER!

The room took on an odd shape then, lilting and vibrating to the eighties music shrieking from the stupid neon jukebox. Darkness melded with the poor lighting scheme and made everyone look the same, but it all made perfect sense: I was simply drunk.

And then the miracle happened.

Just as I was ready to give up—and how ironic that some fucking piece of luck comes my way when I want to quit—he walked into the bar. A tall, shadowed boy with androgynous features sharp as a razor, high cheekbones and a great head of dyed black hair that reflected all the lights of the jukebox. A metal head. An emo queen. He sat two seats away from me, lonely as the girl from The Ring trapped in the well, perhaps sensing one of his own. I took the opportunity to order Old Number 7. No one can refuse a free drink.

"Do you drink much?" I asked.

He pushed his hair away from his face and I caught the smell of meat sauce. "Not really."

His black eyes scanned me; his face receded into a sharp little smile, as if liking what he saw. The bartender chick pushed the 5 shots his way.

"Old number 7, on me."

"Good. Fucks me up quick. I don't need too many of them before I'm stumbling out of here looking for the next bar. This place is shit."

"You're so right."

"I'm Perry, by the way."

"Arthur," I lied again; I'd almost grown knack for it.

"I'm not really a club kid kind of guy," Perry added, "so I stick to bars. They're good enough for me, but my friends would argue the value of going to a club. I never listen though."

I watched his jaw move like an endless ocean as he talked, watched his throat constrict every time we cheered the next shot. I'd found the perfect one! His smile was evil as the Cheshire Cat's, though most people are brainwashed to believe that cat was a goody two-shoe. Then all the drunkenness in me came out and danced along that hellacious grin, those little teeth that would be good for chewing meat.

"Would you like to come home with me?" I blurted stupidly.

"Got a bottle of Jack there?"

"Plenty."

"Then why the hell aren't we out of here?"

∞

I spread him across the bed after feeding him the promised bottle of Jack Daniels. It turned out that Perry didn't much like the taste after the second bottle; he became so sick I hadn't enough sheets and blankets to soak up the vomit and heaping diarrhea that even faintly tasted of that dark amber liquor.

Perry passed out with the intention of feeling the worst hangover in the world when he woke up. Too bad he never rose from my bed—well, not alive. I tied a wet pillow case over his throat, put a plastic bag over his head and pulled until I saw his fine face flush red, then pale in death. I didn't want to damage his face or his body, didn't want to use that stupid hammer anymore. I was too weak; too starved. Perry looked good enough to eat I was so fucking hungry, but instead I dragged his lanky body to the shower and washed him up good.

The loss of brain function made his limbs hug my torso like dead tree branches; his intestine had given out and a long trail of stool rolled down his leg like snot, staining my oriental carpet. A small driblet of blood ran from Perry's nose, and I licked it off as I lay him down. The coolness of death soothed me, the taste of Old Number 7 was still prevalent, and the thought of Perry's last drink with me got me hard instantly.

The hacksaw was waiting for me as if written in the stars. I got to work straight away on Perry's wrists. His bones were thin and feeble; his hands snapped away and lay like dead spiders on the edge of the bathtub. The amount of blood was phenomenal, and it had taken on an odd consistency: the creepy feel of new death.

My sewing skills were far from professional; I was a rookie in every sense of the word. I took the hands from the freezer, still so nice and smooth and savory, and matched them up on the correct bones, making sure the thumbs pointed inward. I didn't want a lover with backward hands. I punctured the needle through a thin layer of skin and it lifted from the meat of Perry's arm, pulling the limbs together. I liked the clear fishing line; it would leave a fleshy look. Black thread would've stood out too much.

Rinse and repeat and I laid the new hands on Perry's milky thighs, letting them get used to their new body. I scooped out Perry's eyes and rolled one in my grip, such a sad little fruit. The new eyes swam around the jar curiously, and I was surprised to see that they had grown in size, were too big for Perry's sockets.

They'd absorbed the saline solution, pickled if you will. I managed to squish them in, skillful enough to not damage even the slightest bit of iris, but was disappointed to see how slack they looked, how sad. One beautiful eye peered to the left as if not wanting to look at its maker, the other was pointing downward. But I figured that was nothing a little water and electricity couldn't fix.

Fill the tub and drop the blow dryer in it.

It was time. The headaches were at their worst and I was thinned to a mere arrow; the muscles in my face had finally rendered me a living corpse and I could no longer escape the hunger pains.

I plugged in the blow dryer and stood above the shifting brown water like that of the Hudson River on a rainy day. I became hypnotized by this abominable act of bringing the dead to life, but the blow dryer howled all the way to the water, an old remedy used for murder, now being used to make life instead. It splashed into the tub, shooting a yellow-gold arc of sparks through air, burning my shirt.

The lights flickered like in an old abandoned building, and the body jolted. I saw its hand jerking, saw its head bobbing maniacally. Sputum shot from his lips, blurry eyes all of a sudden focused on something: me! Then everything went quiet, nothing but the crackle of languid electric and bubbling water. My breath became the only sound through the short-circuited darkness. No movement, no lover waking…yet.

I turned to open the bathroom door so to let out the burnt rubber smell, but that's when I heard the mouth crack open and deflated lungs take in a delicious breath of air. It was the sound of a person just saved from drowning. It spoke in small, docile voice. Perhaps I was hearing things, perhaps I was simply too drunk, deliriously famished.

From somewhere distant I heard music and the laughter of boys long since dead in here, vengeful voices coming back to claim me. In death life can be born, I thought. But I needed to leave, and quick, or I was sure to be taken on a never-ending hayride to my doom. I kept dreaming about food, and thought that I might get some outside.

"Can you hear me?" I asked it.

No answer.

I was pissed off, hungry. I needed FOOD!

So I did leave, and found a friend that would feed me.

∞

"You have to come over and see him!" I told Samantha, my punk rock goddess of a friend. She loved leather jackets and ripped blue jeans, Mohawks and wore too many rings on her fingers. "Amazing and beautiful! We met at a club."

"You look like hell," she told me, but curious to see my new boyfriend. She'd gotten used to my boys lasting only from dusk 'til dawn, so she had to know what this one was about. "And when's the last time you've eaten?"

"Forget about that. I want you to see him."

It was perhaps my blind hope that if I brought Perry some fresh meat that he'd be alive when I returned.

But oh, was I wrong.

So wrong.

∞

I opened the door to my apartment and was welcomed by a thick cloud of carrion. A great shock of moonshine colored my living room gray as the grave. Sam held her nose and her eyes spoke of inquisitiveness, like she was wondering if I had truly lost it.

"I don't think he's here," Sam said.

But I heard the sounds of frustration still tattooed onto me, all the pathetic pleas from victims past, my hammer smashing pretty face-flesh, the hacksaw grinding into bone. I thought for a moment I heard chewing too, but Sam looked at me like I was playing a sick joke, snapping me back into reality. But those sounds were like heaven on a fishing line for me. They told me food was near, somehow, and that I needed it very badly or I was going to finally die. I didn't want any stupid human needs like hunger to stop me now that I had Perry to look after.

"What's really going on here?" Sam said.

But her voice was gone already, stolen by the night, by my voracity. It all happened in a split second. The hammer came down on her head, hard, and I kept doing it until I felt her life gush like a warm river over my hands, my heart, my appetite. She lay on the floor, frozen in shock, her eyes turned up toward me as if I was some sort of an enemy. I wasn't. Perry was.

PERRY!

I ran to the bathtub to find him still there, calm and

collected. His arms were limp and twisted as a doughy pretzel sinking into his own miasma. His torso was exposed and slicked with dead jelly; his cock shriveled into an ancient slug and hung above the water for precious air. But I knew he'd be there once I returned with supper.

Zombie steps back to the living room, and little did I know that they were my own. Samantha's jacket came away easy with the switch blade; her t-shirt was doused in blood and tears; her chest was smeared red.

It wasn't a hard decision to make—because I was so hungry, such a ravenous beast for starving myself all these weeks because the love-bug had bit me. I found that I'd become the monster! And I wanted that flesh in my mouth: sweet, honest, beckoning, safe as a womb. And taste it I did, at first with my tongue, then teeth, with no intent on stopping.

THE CLOCKWORK MENAGERIE
BRIAN BOBOWSKI

Argenstone was not a large town.

It had been larger, once, not so long ago, but then the silver mines that had given the village its name, that had fed it for generations, had given up their last lode. By then, Argenstone had made itself a caravan junction, and the smelters lived on, now working iron and copper and tin from the surrounding hills; but with the miners gone to other places, half of the homes had stood vacant for years, eventually being reclaimed for other purposes.

John Goff had the misfortune to finish his apprenticeship and set up shop just weeks before the mine closed for good.

For a time, he was able to make a good living anyway. The jewelers all moved on to places richer in the fine metals of their art, but John had trained in metals of all kinds. But there wasn't really need in Argenstone for more than one metalsmith, and most of the work in iron and steel went to old Hewitt Durant, who'd had his forge in place for a score of years already. It was only the work he didn't *want* to do that left John with anything to do at all.

Which ultimately meant that most days, John's forge was cold, and he made his way with odd jobs around the village, doing whatever he could find from dawn to dusk, coming home weary from the search as much as from the disparate labors.

One such day found him coming home shortly past noon, halfway to despondent, only to have his progress interrupted by someone bumping into him.

He stumbled, struggling to keep his balance. He drew his breath for a blistering string of curses, but they stuck in his throat when he turned his head and saw just who had knocked into him.

The man was slender, though a bit on the tall side—a few inches taller than John himself, and then made taller by a fine top hat, with a brilliant peacock feather tucked into the hatband. His boots bore a patina of road dust, but there was still some gleam of polished leather under it; his corduroy trousers and frock coat were a rich, dark plum, somehow unspoiled by that same dust on his boots, and the ruffed shirt beneath was pale lilac. One hand rested on the silver hawk's-head handle of an enameled black walking cane. If all of *that* didn't mark him for an aristocrat, his pale features, the sharp line of his jaw, his blue eyes, and his queue of platinum-blond hair certainly did.

Not the sort of person it'd be wise to curse at. John swallowed, mumbled, "Sorry, y'r Lordship," and turned to continue on his way.

"Oh, not at all," the man said, reaching out to catch John's shoulder. "Pray, are you the metalsmith?"

John blinked. There was no way this man was from around here—*nobody* of high breeding lived *here.* What the devil had brought him here for metalwork? "I'm *a* metalsmith," honesty compelled him to say.

"Quite. And will you work in bronze?"

Again, John blinked. "Not much call for bronze anymore," he admitted. "But yes, I've done it before, I still do now and then. I'd need to get the metal, though."

"That can be arranged. Do you also work in steel? I'd prefer to keep my business with *one* smith rather than bustling to and fro between several."

A spark of professional pride, long-stifled, now started to burn again. John drew himself up, clasping his hands behind himself. "Sir, I can work in iron and steel, bronze and brass, three diffcrent kinds of pewter, and I might not be a jeweler, but I can work with silver and gold and the like, too. If you get me the metal, I can work it."

"Splendid." The man smiled, showing even, white teeth. "I find myself in sudden need of metalwork, and quite far from my usual supplier. I will need some very specific forms in bronze and steel to repair my conveyance, and if that goes well, why, I might have some business in the finer metals as well."

"Your…conveyance?" John's head tilted in curiosity. "Did you come in by train?" He remembered the big to-do when the rail yard had been built, the hopes that it might bring him some business; instead, it had made it that much easier to bring ore right past Argenstone and into bigger cities, and only Hewitt had truly profited, with there always being a demand for more rails for the iron road.

"Not by train, no," the man replied, and rather than elaborate on that cryptic remark, he asked, "If I provide the designs and the ingots, how soon might you be able to begin work?"

"Right away," said John. "My forge has plenty of fuel yet."

"Then I should like to start business just as promptly." The gentleman beamed, bringing one silk-gloved hand up to tip his hat. "Edwin Attaway, inventor and machinist, at your service."

There was something strangely compelling about that smile; for a moment, John longed to ask the man to stay, to call one of the village children over as an impromptu courier, rather than have him head to the warehouses in person. But then Edwin was on his way, and John had molds to craft.

He worked enough in esoteric forms that he still had sand, wax, and clay on hand, such as was suitable for molding and casting, and now he had a sheaf of precise diagrams to work by. Gears and cogs, augurs and curved struts—all of which needed to be *just right*, his new client had impressed upon him; the steel struts could be worked into shape, but for the bronze gears, Edwin demanded such precision that only casting would do. The saving grace was that the cross section was simple, so the molds wouldn't be *terribly* difficult to remake.

John tied his hair back with a wool bandana and went to work, measuring frequently with calipers and comparing the measurements to those on the diagrams, relying on his knowledge of the metal to tell him how it would contract, just how much extra space he needed to put in and where. "You must have a very patient supplier," he observed when Edwin returned. "Or one with a great deal of storage space. If you need these in quantity..."

"This isn't the process I've most commonly used," the man admitted. "But unless you've a very specific hob and the machinery to drive it, it will have to do for repairs so far from my usual worker."

"Where is that?" John couldn't help but ask. Not that he wasn't grateful for the work—work he'd *trained* to do—but with the time it'd take to make molds for all these pieces, it might almost have been faster to send across the country and have parts brought in by train.

"Madrid," was the reply.

All right, maybe not. Rails didn't run across the Channel, after all.

"I've the means to make precision gears for my work," Edwin went on, "but it couldn't support such large pieces as this even if I had you craft the hob."

John frowned down at the workpiece, fingers tracing over it, imagining how it would fill, where it might meet trouble, where it would need further work once cast. "Why bronze? I'm not complaining, mind—Hewitt's insistence on only working iron and steel brought you to me instead, after all —but I've made steel gears before." In happier times, he'd even had a hobber to do it with.

"Oh, steel will not do, not for this." Edwin shook his head. "One spark in my gas extractor could be a terrible thing."

"Gas extractor?" John repeated.

"Once the parts are made," said Edwin, "if you'd accompany me to my vehicle to do any further work that they may need to fit into place, I should be pleased to show you."

He was being awfully cagey about this whole business, but he *did* have a good bit of silver with him; for that and the chance to work in metal again, John could put up with a great deal.

While the molds were curing, John took the steel ingots that had been delivered and brought them to the forge, and there he went to work on *those* pieces. From time to time, he'd glance over and see Edwin watching him, with the most curiously intent look on his face. The first time it happened, John thought the man was just anxious about the quality of John's work, but the next time he noticed it, he wasn't even touching the steel, he was working the bellows. And if anything, Edwin was watching him even closer.

It made him feel...strange. He couldn't quite place it at first, and when he did, it seemed almost nonsensical. But there it was—the man was looking at him like the village girls would look at passing soldiers.

And for all John had never much minded that those girls weren't looking that way at *him,* now the attention put a flutter in his heart.

He licked his dry lips and carefully turned his attention back to the steel.

He finished several of the steel forms that afternoon—slender, curving structures that resembled nothing so much as ribs. The molds still weren't ready, and indeed it would take at least another day's work to prepare all of them.

Edwin asked him where a traveler might spend the night, and when John pointed him towards the Red Boar, the man invited him along for a companionable drink. He was about to demur, seeking in that moment only a square meal and bed, but then Edwin smiled at him.

Well, what harm would one drink do? And maybe he could get his meal there. It *had* been quite some time since he'd enjoyed the cooking at the Red Boar.

"You said you were an inventor," John mused over their meal. "What sort of things do you invent?"

John thought he'd seen the man smile before, but that was nothing to the brilliance of his expression now. "I'm *so* delighted that you ask," Edwin exclaimed, reaching into his coat. "This is one of my older works, but I'm still quite proud of it." He set it on the table.

It was a mouse. Oh, not a *real* mouse, no—it was a form of metal, of bronze and steel, silver and gold. But in shape and size, it was a mouse, complete with a slender, articulated tail and jointed limbs. Edwin fished in another pocket, producing a key of sorts which he pressed into a socket on the mouse's back and turned. When he pulled it free, John lurched back in his seat, for the little figurine suddenly came to life, scurrying across the table in a manner so reminiscent of a true mouse, John half-expected a cat to come and give chase to it.

At length, the tiny contraption whirred to a halt, and John started to reach for it. He caught himself before he touched it, looking up with a question on his lips, but he didn't even need to speak it; Edwin's smile and inviting gesture gave him his answer, and John's hand completed its motion.

It was a remarkable work of art. Its eyes were set with crystal, its snout adorned with slim slivers of metal for whiskers, its claws polished silver, each one yielding slightly to his touch, separate from its neighbors. Even the exposed gears and sprockets were worked in so cleverly, they all seemed proper parts of the whole.

"This is incredible," John breathed.

"You truly like it?" Edwin's pale cheeks flushed a little, and he turned his hat in his hands, running a finger along the peacock feather. "You can have it, once it's time for me to move on," he said, looking down at the table.

Must you? John managed not to ask. What he said was, "I couldn't possibly take something so dear." He set the mechanical mouse on the table with care, nudging it towards its creator.

"No, no." Though Edwin did carefully pick it up, his other hand settled atop John's, and he gave another one of those heart-melting smiles. "I insist. I can make another."

John felt his attention torn between those blue eyes, and the hand atop his own. Both of them felt so *right*. He felt himself smiling back, holding that gaze, though he compromised by bringing his other hand in atop Edwin's, keeping it there on his own. "Well…if you're certain."

"But a small trifle, for your company," Edwin said, his smile turning up a little further.

Silence descended, and, in the midst of it, the barmaid appeared to tidy up the remains of their meal. With that done, it seemed time to part ways for the evening. Edwin came with him to the door, saying, "I suppose you'll be getting along home, then?"

Where else? John didn't ask. "So I should. I have a lot of work to do tomorrow."

"Just so." Was that a bit of a sigh, lurking behind the gentleman's words? "I'll pay a visit on the morrow, then, to see how that work is coming along. Until then, goodnight." He lifted his hat from the crook of his elbow, tipped it, and made his way across the common room, while John stepped into the evening air and set off down the lane.

And yet, for a time, he lay awake and wondered—where else *could* he have gone? Had this Edwin Attaway person been hinting at something? Maybe he'd had some other ideas for how the evening might go?

John bit his lip, twisting in the sheets. He hadn't felt *this* anxious since he was a youth, playing with his fellows and watching the girls go by. But for all the fine-boned delicacy of his features, Edwin Attaway was no girl. Why was *he* making John feel this way?

Thankfully, the fatigue of a full day's work drew him towards sleep in not *too* much time.

The first afternoon had been hot and strenuous; the next day was a bit more sedate, but getting the molds ready was difficult and exacting work. John's shoulders were aching by midday; by the time the last mold was set aside, they were burning from the time hunched over, making tiny little adjustments. At that point, he couldn't keep himself from wincing as he stood up straight.

"Hm?" Edwin frowned, looking up from his diagrams. "Sore, plainly? I could do something about that…" A rueful smile and a wiggle of his fingers.

John blinked. "Uh…" His tongue twisted up and came to a halt before it even began. What on earth could he say? That such a thing was unheard of? That it struck him as strange that the man—who was, after all, a *man*—should seem so ready, even eager, to do it?

That the thought made his heart skip a beat? That he

yearned, deep down, to learn just how much strength and skill might be in those long fingers, how deftly they might tease away some of those aches and pains?

As if questing for something to do now that they'd drawn attention to themselves, Edwin's fingers sought out his hat and tugged it free, and the man ran his other hand along the band, biting his lip. "Forgive me," he said before John could work up an actual response, "that was terribly inappropriate of me." He jammed his hat back into place, produced a gold pocketwatch from the breast pocket of his coat, and flipped it open. "Dear me, I should be on my way if I'm to make the most of the evening meal. My apologies, good sir, I'll leave you to your rest and check back on the morrow."

Then he was off, striding down the lane—not hurrying, never hurrying, but his hand was so heavy on his cane that it left clear marks in the dirt.

"I'd like that," John finally murmured to the breeze, which was going entirely the wrong way to carry the words after the departing gentleman.

He turned back to his little shack next to the forge-yard, cursing himself for a fool. What on earth was *wrong* with him? It wasn't enough that he had these sorts of feelings for someone he had no business having them for. No, suddenly he was too much of a coward to *do* anything about it.

By day he worked every metal known to man. Yet somehow, as soon as the forge cooled, he had all the grit of fresh cream.

It was past midnight by the time he finally relaxed enough to drift off, and it seemed the next instant that a cock-crow snapped him out of his doze. Breaking his fast and dunking his face in the rain barrel did little to clear the bleary cobwebs of fatigue from his mind, but it was enough, at least, that he could get back to work.

Where the first afternoon's work had been hot, this day was both hot and humid. Molten bronze flowed into the carefully-prepared holes in the sand molds, and what water hadn't had time to dry away from the sand and clay emerged as great billows of steam. John was careful, of course, and none of this touched him directly—if it had, he'd have been quite badly off indeed—but it left the air hot and muggy as it dissipated. The hazards of his work meant he couldn't just work bare-chested and let sweat do as much work as possible; he needed a thick apron, at the very least, and having it rest against his skin wasn't exactly comfortable either. But it was one of the hazards of the profession, and it was done soon enough, when molten metal filled the last of the molds.

John stepped away from the castings, wiped his brow, and splashed his face with rainwater again. As he straightened, he noticed Edwin looking on—but there was something different today. Before, there'd been that quiet focus—yes, it had been strange to have that focus be on *him,* but John suddenly found that he missed it, for now Edwin's gaze kept flicking from John to the molds to the forge to the rest of the village, and his fingers twisted on the handle of his cane, turning it this way and that.

A more agitated person John had rarely seen, but he'd fetched up some distance from the forge, too far to hold an easy conversation. John turned back to the first of the molds. Maybe seeing the finished work would reassure his peculiar customer somewhat.

The cope split away from the drag, nice and clean. John's tongs seized one spoke of the gear and lifted it into the open, and he turned it this way and that, inspecting it for voids. The surface, at least, was clean; he set that piece aside to cool, and moved onto the next. By the time he'd unveiled all of them, the first piece was cool enough to handle.

John ventured inside to fetch the diagrams he'd worked from, and permitted himself a satisfied smile; the first gear aligned just about perfectly with its drawing, and the difference wouldn't take long to work away. The second and third were even closer. Fifteen pieces cast—three of steel, twelve of bronze—and only two would need more than cursory work to bring them into final shape. None of them were so far from the design as to be a waste, and all of them were ready within another hour.

And yet Edwin, looking over the finished pieces, was

still so jittery that John finally couldn't keep himself from asking what was wrong.

"Yes, well…" Edwin sighed. "It would seem that Argenstone is home, or at least host, to a thief." Leaning back against the counter, he stared across town at the train station, gripping the shaft of his cane so tight that his fingers visibly shook. "Someone relieved me of the clockwork mouse I'd promised you."

The words struck John with a sudden sense of shock and loss. He hadn't quite come to accept that the man really intended to give him something so wondrous, on top of a more-than-fair payment. Hearing that it was *gone*, though—that stung far more than he would have thought.

He was still processing that when he saw the grief in Edwin's features.

The man wasn't one to shout his feelings to the world, apparently, but the agitation that John had first noticed was only part of it. Gone was the ease with which Edwin had said he could make another. John could see the pain in those blue eyes, when they chanced to turn toward him; and in that moment Edwin froze, staring back at him.

Finally Edwin lowered his gaze. "I'm more sorry than I can say. I mean to recover it if I can—learn where the trains may have gone since I last had it in my possession. Such a distinctive thing will doubtless not be easy to sell. But I… cannot keep my promise to have it in your possession before I depart."

"It's no fault of yours," John protested, starting to reach for Edwin's shoulder, then remembering the state of his hands. Getting the dirt of his labors all over that plum coat would be rude, and he didn't need to be a refined gentleman to see *that*. He cast about for a rag and started wiping his hands with it.

Edwin looked up at the motion, and tensed. "A promise is still a promise," he said flatly.

For something spoken so easily, the man sure took his word seriously. "So you think the thief has already left the village?"

"I…believe so, yes." Edwin took a breath. "I saw

someone in a great hurry towards the station, last night, from the Red Boar. I thought little enough of it until I noticed that the mouse was not where it ought to be. I'd only left it a short time to bathe..."

"So you want to go after it?" John hazarded. "But you don't want to leave without...well."

For just a moment, the man's expression softened. "That is the dilemma upon me, yes."

"Waiting around won't make it any easier to catch, will it?" John started gathering the gears and pieces together. "Was there anything else you needed made?"

"Not urgently." Edwin shook his head sharply. "I may need your craft to refine those somewhat, however."

"I'll bring my tools," John assured him. "Where was it you needed these?"

Something to focus on was apparently just what the man needed; while he was leading the way out of town, he seemed to recover some of his prior energy. He brought John, not along the railroad tracks, but away from them—northward, into the woods. The game trail they followed was a little awkward with the larger steel ribs, but not unmanageable, and they'd only been in the woods a few minutes when they reached their destination.

Within a clearing was a ship, kept upright by struts that stretched between broad pads against the ground and ports high up on the hull. On each side, towards the stern, a nacelle of some sort was attached, each one sporting a set of slender blades affixed to a central hub. The upper deck had what looked like rigging of some kind, but there was no mast; instead, all that rigging was woven around a great pile of fabric.

"Here she is," Edwin announced, standing up straight with pride. "The *Heron*. She's brought me over Spain and France, and through a dozen storms before, until misfortune struck three nights past and caught me a trifle too high."

Three nights ago...yes, that *had* been a stormy night, hadn't it?

But wait...

"High?" John repeated.

"Oh, yes indeed," Edwin chuckled. "Once the balloon is full, it's more than light enough to carry the *Heron* up into the sky. But you needn't take my mere word for it—help me make repairs and see for yourself!"

The very notion was incomprehensible—that something so vast could ever be borne up off the ground. But the man said it with such certainty...well, it wasn't as though he'd withheld payment for John's work, that he might be planning to forfeit if the parts turned out to not let the thing fly after all. Where was the harm?

Edwin reached up with his cane, hooking the handle through a strap high on the hull and pulling on it, drawing a long plank outwards. Once it was far enough out, it dipped, the strap tightening. Edwin removed his cane with a flourish, and the plank swung down against the brush. It was steep and narrow, but it also had a few smaller lengths of wood nailed on it, providing steps by which they could reach the deck, half-walking, half-climbing.

That was already quite high enough for John's liking, though at least the *Heron's* supports were sturdy enough that she didn't rock under them. He didn't particularly want to imagine what it'd be like to be *higher*.

At one end of the deck was a door—a very sturdy one indeed, made of stout planks and bound with metal. The lock was impossibly intricate, and the key Edwin fished out from under his shirt was only the first step in coaxing it open. Even with that key, it seemed to be a puzzle-lock of some sort, though not with any rule John could see from the quick glimpse he got. Edwin worked through it in a trice, though, and, as the door swung open, he reached within to take what seemed to be a miner's lamp.

"With the trees all around, the boiler room isn't the best lit," he explained as he worked a flint striker. "In other places I'd simply take a lantern, but there I must be a touch more careful, and this little contraption does quite well there." Once the lamp was burning, he strapped it around his hat and put the whole affair atop his head. "After you, good sir."

Huh. Apparently there was more to that hat than

decoration after all. Nonplussed, John ducked under the door frame, following his host's directions down two decks and along a narrow corridor.

The hatch at the end of that corridor was a heavy, bronze-bound affair, its bolts kept in place by a great metal wheel. This too Edwin unlocked with the key around his neck. As the door swung open, John could see metal gleaming in the darkness—but before he could see any details, something brushed past his leg.

"Probably just Archimedes," said Edwin when he'd asked John what prompted his sudden outburst. He looked down, the light from his lamp sweeping the deck as he crouched. "Archie?" At the cluck of his tongue, something small moved in the gloom; and then, chuckling, Edwin stood upright.

"No vermin," he assured John. "Only the very one who keeps them at bay. He's harmless, unless you've a penchant for nibbling on the grain-sacks. Isn't that right, Archimedes?"

John peered a bit closer. The bright light on Edwin's hat and the darkness all around didn't make it easy to see, but he could make out a conical, pale-masked face and dark beady eyes peering back at him. Farther along, a slender, sable-furred body was draped over Edwin's gloved hands.

"Is that a polecat?" John hazarded.

"Close enough," Edwin replied, bending down a bit to let the little creature jump down to the deck and scramble off. "I've had him for—hm—four years, now?"

John ducked through the hatch, musing, "I thought most ships kept cats."

"Oh, Archimedes is far better than a cat at following rats into whatever cranny they crawled out of." Edwin followed John along the metal walkway, guiding him right towards the back. "But that's neither here nor there. Here, now—here's the greatest issue. I've already put it into as good order as I could, so it should only need the gears in their rightful places."

Two of the gears needed a bit more filing before they would mesh and turn to Edwin's satisfaction. Then it was up one deck higher that they took those steel struts, which turned out to be reinforcements around one of the supports. There, at least, enough light came through the port to make nailing them into place a straightforward matter.

Rather than head forward through the hold—which was presumably the place Archimedes spent the most time, full of sacks and crates and such things—Edwin led the way farther astern, through what was obviously a workshop. Pipes ran hither and yon, some of them connecting to machinery of all different shapes, some passing right through the room, still others not seeming to go anywhere at all. Along one wall was a series of display cases, and their contents stopped John in his tracks.

A rat, a cat, a few dog-like shapes, a bull, a polecat, an otter, even a snake—there was such a variety of mechanical creatures behind the glass, each one of them different, each an incredible work of art.

"Those are my life," Edwin sighed, coming up beside John, the lamp on his hat sweeping its beam from one end of the case to the other. Gloved fingers reached out for the case in one spot, between the raccoon and the fox, that now was home only to a conspicuous vacancy; then they moved onward. "Each of them made after careful study of the animal in question, matching its motions as faithfully as I could."

"Are you trying to capture all the animals of the world this way?" John asked. "Is that why you travel?"

"Mmm..." Edwin sighed softly. "Nothing quite so grand as that. I think, the day that I can make a bird take wing and alight, I will be able to call myself content, and turn at leisure to the finer variations."

What man didn't envy the freedom of the birds, in his own way? John had to give Edwin credit for chasing that dream, at least.

"I'd come to consult with some of the learned of Cambridge on the structure of a bird's wing," Edwin went on. "I have...it might not be quite accurate to call him a friend, we're not so closely acquainted as that. But a favorable acquaintance, at any rate. He and I have exchanged some letters. I thought to catch a songbird and bring it to him for study. But now…"

"Now," John said when the other man trailed off, "I guess you'll be going east, instead?"

Edwin turned toward him, so suddenly that the lamp's glare made spots dance in his eyes. "East?" Edwin repeated. "Why east, pray?"

John shrugged. "Well, if your thief took the first train out, it had to have gone eastwards. All of the night trains do."

Edwin drew a deep breath. "Eastwards." And then, suddenly, he dashed aft, leaving John to scramble in his wake—through a hatch, into another stairwell, up one level to the deck, then up one *more* into what proved to be the wheelhouse. Edwin snuffed his lamp and hung his hat from a hook as he hurried over to the chart table. Enough light spilled in through the portholes that the glare of the lamp could only have made a chart harder to read.

Possessed now of sudden energy, Edwin pulled out one particular chart and unrolled it, clamping the corners down. His fingers navigated the mess of curved lines, finally tapping one point, a cross marked at the end of a charcoal line. "Here we are," he breathed. "East…what major cities lie east of us that the rails might reach?"

"East of here?" John thought. "Norwich is about it, I think."

"Not Ipswich?" Edwin's finger tapped farther south.

More thinking. "I don't think so," he managed. "You'd have to check at the station, but I think the line to Ipswich breaks off west of here."

"And Norwich hasn't a port," Edwin breathed.

"I don't think the rails that way reach anywhere that does, yet. Not for another year, at least."

"You mean it's *land-locked?*" Edwin exclaimed. "That's…that's…" Apparently at a loss for words, he whirled towards John and caught him in a kiss.

This was no chaste, brotherly peck on the check; arms around the bigger man, body arched and pressed in close, he pushed his lips against John's with a hunger stoked by excitement. Though at first he tensed, caught off guard, it rapidly dawned on John that having the man pressed up against him like that felt *good*. It answered all those confusing urges that he hadn't had the courage to voice, even as it stirred new, deeper longing to life.

He'd just gathered an arm about Edwin's waist when the man broke away from the kiss, eyes wide with sudden worry. "I...I am sorry." He started to look aside.

John caught the man's jaw in his free hand, coaxing it back towards his own. "What for?"

Edwin dared to smile at him. "After yesterday, I feared I'd caused offense."

"Offense?" John stifled a laugh. "Confusion, more like. This all feels *very* strange."

A wry smirk crossed Edwin's aristocratic features. "Such has been my life, I'm afraid."

"So you must have some experience with it by now," John guessed. He took a breath, for courage, and then he forged on, "Do you think maybe you could guide me through it a little?"

"John..." Silk-gloved fingers slid along the smith's jaw. "You make me long so very much to take you with me."

That thought, one he'd never even considered, suddenly made John's heart surge. "*Can* you?"

Edwin shivered against him. "I shouldn't tear you from your home..."

"What home?" John snorted. "When you showed up on the lane, you brought the first solid commission I've had in God knows how long. Just let me take over the coarser metalworking, making whatever gears and springs you need, and you could focus instead on the more artistic parts of your work—even if I never worked a large piece again..."

Edwin touched his lips. "The *Heron* can carry your tools," he breathed over John's cheek, "and enough to set up a small forge wherever she goes..."

"Then it's even better," John exclaimed. "You'd not need to hire another smith again, and I could do the work I've always *wanted* to—how soon could we leave?"

Edwin laughed—an easy, joyous sort of laugh—and

wound an arm around John in turn. "It'd take the night to fill the gas envelope. I could lift off with the sun tomorrow if the weather's fair, though mid-morning would leave me a touch more confident."

"Plenty long enough for me." Packing the tools he hadn't brought wouldn't take long. "It's not as though there'll be another smith wanting to move into Argenstone anytime soon, so it shouldn't be a trouble if I can't tear my forge apart quite yet."

Edwin shifted against him, both hands on his shoulders. "If you can spare a bit of time," he breathed, "I could show you my cabin…"

John shivered. That little shift had brought a firm warmth in to nestle against the front of his trousers, and the thrill that touch sent up his spine was electric. Only one practical concern remained. "Would whatever contraption it is that makes this thing go need your full attention?"

"Hardly. A sound notion, that." Again his lips brushed John's, gently this time, as he whispered, "And once that's doing its work…" His fingers slid down John's chest, at the edge of his vest, and then inward.

John was most certainly not prepared for the rush of sensation as Edwin's fingers caressed his swelling manhood; he groaned deep in his throat, pushing into the touch on pure reflex. "Keep that up," said a husky voice that hardly sounded like his own, "and I don't think I'll be able to wait for the machines *or* the cabin. And it might not be good for your nice suit."

"Ah…for that, I must apologize." Edwin's fingers slid away from there, moving up to cup against John's cheek. "My own eagerness nearly got better of me. Come, then; let's be quick about it, hm?"

Starting the machinery was a fairly simple task, especially with two pairs of hands. Lighting the boiler wasn't entirely unlike lighting the forge from John's perspective, though turning a crank to add fuel was certainly easier than shoveling coal. Edwin handled the somewhat more complicated tasks, though with an ease that belied that complexity; watching gauges and turning valves according to some rhythm only he knew, and then, finally, pulling the mighty lever next to the boiler in a great arc.

With a hiss of steam, the machinery rattled to life, gears ticking, axles turning—slowly at first, then somewhat faster. Finally Edwin pulled another lever, and the shaft leading to the bronze gearwork they'd repaired started turning. Edwin watched his gauges for a time, then turned to John with a grin.

"I do believe we're done here for now," the man said, loud enough to be heard over the gears and cogs, but little more.

"Fine news indeed." And not just because of his new-found curiosity; with the boiler stoked, the room was hot and humid. He glanced down at the fuel-crank; the machinery around it was rattling on its own now, the belt slowly turning. "Nothing here will cause a disaster if it's left alone too long?"

A laugh. "That would be longer than *I* could entertain you, I fear," said Edwin, towing him towards the stairs. "But even then, there are relief valves enough to ensure nothing goes amiss."

They got to Edwin's cabin on the main deck, and there John's bravado failed him. He paused on the threshold, gripped by sudden anxiety, an intense awareness of just how little he knew of the course ahead of him.

"Are you well?" Edwin asked, touching his cheek.

John swallowed. "I'm...scared," he admitted.

"I'd never hurt you," Edwin promised. "Are you sure this is what you wish to do?"

In spite of himself, John laughed. "Right now I don't think I could be sure of my own name. But I do want it. It's new, it's strange, and I don't have the slightest idea what I'm doing, but I do want it."

"Shh. *You* don't need to do much of anything—this once, just let it happen."

Edwin tugged his gloves free and tucked them away somewhere. His nimble fingers made short work of the fastenings on John's vest, the buckle of his belt, and the closure of his trousers; reaching in there, they curled around his manhood and gave it a squeeze, their gentle-yet-firm touch somehow as reassuring as it was exciting.

Once he'd relieved John of his clothing and had him lying on the broad bed that took up most of the cabin's space, he turned to his wardrobe. One piece at a time, his fine suit slipped free, leaving him plain to see at last. And slender he was, but he was no frail weakling; he was a smith in his fashion, of course, and under that fancy getup was a trim, athletic form that was a pure delight to look upon, from his bright eyes and tumble of unbound hair down along his clean limbs, not excepting the proud rise of his own manhood.

He moved atop John then, hungry mouth seeking his own, heated breaths mingling as his clever fingers slid in between them, gathering flesh against firm flesh. His body slid easily under John's clumsy, roving hands, but even if the smith's touch was uncertain, apparently he was doing *something* right, for Edwin twisted and moaned atop him.

And despite John's rising excitement, spurred on by the novelty of the situation as much as its intensity, it was Edwin who was first to break the kiss and cry out, arching over him, wet heat pulsing right over his anxious manhood.

But Edwin wasn't *done*. Even panting in the wake of his release, he slid his fingers along John's length, getting the bigger man a little bit slick with spilled seed; and then...

John's experience with women was scant, but he was sure no courtesan could have ridden him better than Edwin did then—sliding down, slow and smooth, from the crown of his manhood until he rested against his hip, then rolling atop him all the way through John's shuddering, moaning release, and, soon thereafter, to another of his own, spilling out this time over John's stomach.

Minutes later, with their breaths and heartbeats starting to slow but Edwin still atop him, John was struck by a pleasing notion. "I just thought of something," he murmured. "About me coming with you."

"Mmm?" Edwin didn't lift his head, pillowed on John's shoulder as it was, but his fingers did quest for the smith's hand, giving it a squeeze.

Smiling to himself, John stroked back an errant lock of white-blond hair, hooking it behind the taller man's ear. "If I'm going with you to find that mouse," he said, "you're not breaking your promise to get it to me before we part company, are you?"

Now Edwin did crack his eyes open and lift his head a little, smiling down at him. "Good sir," he murmured, "I *like* the way you think." He moved in for another kiss and, for the time being, that was that.

FARTHER THAN THAT
THERESE ARKENBERG

"Marry me," I said. "I want you with me forever."

He smiled, and the muscles of his neck quivered beneath my hand in silent laughter. He thought I was joking.

A couple sailed past us, heels hardly seeming to touch the dance floor, twirling so fast that watching them left me dizzy. My partner's steps were slower, with their own sort of grace, making me think of adjectives like *stately*. He hadn't really known how to dance to this sort of music, but an evening with me on his arm had produced an improvement.

His name was Kast or Caz or Kas. It had been hard to hear over the music. He probably thought I was Feline or Helix or something.

I couldn't decide what color his hair was, but his face was alabaster-pale, and only the lines around his mouth and heavy-lidded turquoise eyes convinced me it was the one he'd been born with and not sculpted by some expert artist-surgeon.

"I'm not really one for marriage," he said, as my silence convinced him I was serious.

"Neither am I. Couples should have things in common."

"What else do we have in common?"

"We both play." He'd mentioned his own talent self-deprecatingly after my performance on the stage that afternoon. Hours before, when we'd started dancing together. That moment felt like the Big Bang, ages ago and the start of everything.

"Violin and electric guitar?" he asked.

"We'll play a duet sometime."

"It'll take us forever to find a tune that works."

"So you'll do it?"

His slow steps stopped entirely. We stood, a point of stillness at the edge of the floor before the stage where music pounded like multiple heartbeats.

"I'm from far away," he said.

I shrugged. "So am I. I can point to the star my home orbits from here."

"I can't even do that."

We stared at each other with faces unreadable in the pulsing lights.

"We're both strangers here," I said at last. "Another thing in common."

"Do you do this often? Propose marriage to people you meet at sector-level music festivals?"

"Only when the mood strikes me."

"And why has it struck you now?" He spoke quietly, learning close so I could hear. His lips were long, full, faintly pink. Soft, I imagined.

"I'm not sure," I said honestly. "It feels like I have to take a chance. The moment we met, it was like I'd been offered a ticket to something…something big. And whatever it is, I don't want to miss out."

He didn't laugh at that. He looked up at me, pale and quiet. After a moment he reached out and brushed aside a strand of hair that had fallen in my face during the dance. I'd been looking past it as if it were a black crack in the window of my vision.

"Where are you from?" I asked. "Sikmoora or the border colonies?"

"Farther than that," he said.

"What brought you here?"

He shrugged. "I saw the bright lights from a hilltop and I came down."

My eyes went to the hills above the festival grounds, but he had seemed to be speaking figuratively. Perhaps quoting from somewhere, some book of stately poetry we'd never heard of out on Aries.

"I took a chance," he said, very softly. Our eyes met as if

by accident. And I knew, down to the core of me, that I was never going to grow used to him, never going to find him anything but baffling and fascinating and as beautiful as you can be when you're natural. I wanted him for the rest of my life. I wanted to find a duet for the electric guitar and violin.

If that didn't work, I'd switch to acoustic.

Maybe he saw what I was thinking. His smile was less amused than…touched, I imagine. A sort of solemn happiness. It wasn't the kind of emotion people are supposed to let show. Except he let me see. And then he'd taken my hand, callused white fingers wrapping around callused brown ones, and we were walking to the gates of the festival grounds together. It was as if something had been decided. He flagged a cab and, once we'd gotten in, he sat back to let me program the controls.

I entered the address of my hotel, because where else was I supposed to try? Maybe a magistrate's office—I could put my signature where my mouth was—but nobody does weddings at thirteen in the night.

It'd have to wait until morning, then.

"Kas," I said.

He looked up.

"Just checking I heard your name right."

"You dropped a few syllables." He grinned. "But *Kas* will do fine."

The Ihering Inn wasn't exactly a dump, but if I'd known I'd be bringing a beautiful man of mystery back with me, I'd have strained my credit chip somewhere else. Kas didn't seem to notice the scuffed floor, failing lights, or the rather persistent smell of antiseptic. The backs of our hands brushed, but before I could take his we'd reached my door. I hadn't held anybody's hand in years. It used to make me think of Mom and her desperate attempts to keep me and my brother from wandering off. Now Kas had made it seem…important. Significant. Signifying what, I wasn't sure.

When I came in after him, he was leaning against the wall, waiting. When I didn't move fast enough he reached out and pulled me into a kiss. He tasted sweetly musky, with a hint of greenness and spice. Ariesian springtime festivals included sugared flower petals that tasted something like him. His smell, though, was stronger than sweetness: crushed mint and the tang of old wood and something else, something cold and clean like a field after snowfall. But that coldness wasn't part of him. It had nothing to do with anything living, and Kas was very much alive. His fingers dug into my shoulder and hair, forcing me closer, until we were pressed against each other.

We could have spent all night against that wall, I think. Except then I fumbled the kiss, catching his lower lip between my teeth and his, and he let out a sound at the pain that wasn't —exactly—*pained*. The worries I'd had about him feeling uncomfortable crushed between me and the plascrete wall lessened a great deal, and then the sound replayed itself in my fiery imagination. Amplified. Not that I could quite bring myself to deliberately hurt someone, no matter how much they'd like it—but when I opened my eyes he was smiling at me shyly, with the kind of glow it must have taken more than a split lip to achieve. That had just been a bonus, then. Great. I loved pleasant surprises.

I leaned in and licked the narrow bead of blood sliding towards his chin. Then I was pulling him towards the bed, and through some complicated system of cooperation (he helped me, then I helped him help himself) we'd stripped off jackets, shoes, his silk scarf and my socks, and then I spent some leisurely minutes unbuttoning his shirt inch by inch and exploring the uncovered skin with my tongue. When his breath hitched, the quiver under my mouth felt like a brand new flavor added to the sweetness.

I was in my up-in-front-of-multiple-people suit, which meant my shirt was just as nice as his was. Otherwise I would have ripped it off in my need to be that much less insulated from him and from the charged air between us. Kas took it off me and even folded it before setting it on the floor, showing a singular presence of mind.

He put that concentration to better use as he turned back to me. I don't mean to brag, I've never considered myself particularly fascinating—but his hands and mouth were running over every inch of me, sometimes stopping for his bright eyes to examine something in the dim hotel light. The scar above my navel from an unfortunate incident involving an object that was Not A Toy in my foolhardy childhood, and the tapering of my little finger, both seemed to absorb him. As for me, well, he'd absorbed me from the beginning, when I'd seen a head of soft brown hair and felt an insistent tug towards it, as if I'd lose everything if I didn't go to him *now*. So I went. It had given the whole day an air of *crisis-averted*, but now the tension coiling around me was not so much the anticlimax of an avoided disaster as...is there a good sort of crisis? That's what we were in the middle of.

"Don't have toes where you're from, then?" I asked, wiggling mine beneath his gaze. A sound escaped him that was almost a giggle. I wanted to kiss him again, to find out if humor lingered on his lips as yet another sort of sweetness.

"You're a little different," he said. "More—"

He sighed and knelt at the end of the bed, bare from the waist up, tawny brown hair falling to his shoulders. I'd never seen anyone with skin so pale, except ancient Europeans in history graphics or rich folks who'd played with color as just another part of their cosmetic work. But on him it seemed perfectly natural, perfectly fitting.

"You seem *realer* than they are," Kas said at last.

"Than who are?"

"Everyone else I've ever known. They're all perfectly fine, they're just...less, somehow. While you aren't. And I'd have thought if anything it would be the other way around. They do have toes, though."

I laughed. Then my laughter died off, because his hands had gone to the waist of my trousers and were undoing things there, and then I was bare and his mouth was discovering me and it didn't matter where he'd come from or how far away, because now he was *here*.

His lips were sensitive, and he seemed to enjoy the sensation of my firmness against them. Even so, he didn't linger, continuing his exploration and completely ignoring my disappointed sigh as he nuzzled my left knee instead.

Kas stopped then. "Um," he said, warm breath ghosting

over my damp skin. "Do you have...arrangements?" His tone was even; the hesitation seemed more because he wasn't certain of the right word to use.

"Top left pocket of my suitcase," I said. It sat near my headboard, and we went for it at the exact same time. He paused, letting me open it, then reached inside as if for holiday presents. His expression was intent again, with that solemn happiness I'd glimpsed on the festival grounds. Realizing I was the reason for it left me breathless. But I got hold of my senses by the time he'd finished undressing.

I reached out to him, but as he lay beside me he rolled so that I was on top of him. As he preferred things, if that ghost of a smile was anything to go by. Well, I could oblige. My kiss forced his head back against the mattress, the entire weight of my body bearing down on him. He shifted slightly, into a more comfortable position I imagined, and the evidence that I wasn't going to physically overwhelm him soothed away the last of my inhibitions. I even took his wrists, pinning his hands over his head with one of my own. He freed his mouth from mine enough to make a sound of approval. Shifting more of my weight to my knees and elbows, I left my other hand on the tube of sanitary gel, just to keep it handy. The cut on his lip had opened again, and he was beginning to make more of those sounds. Perhaps a little more amplified this time.

Despite the cold smell hanging around him, he was warm, warm the way home is warm during winter. Soothing and right. For a moment I wished our places were reversed, that I was the one covered by him, surrounded by his heat and the smooth, soft texture of his skin. Before I could suggest it, Kas had freed one of his hands and closed it over mine with the tube.

"Will you?" he asked softly. His tone was tender and polite and demanding all at once. I did.

We fit perfectly together, so perfectly I could have believed in fate for a moment. Then his hands were closing over my hips, short violinist's nails digging in to urge me on. I forgot about fate in favor of things much more significant. Those sounds, for example. Kas usually spoke so softly that it took a large increase in volume for me to realize just how powerful his voice was. Not very deep, but with a sink-inside-your-bones intensity. It sank so far inside me I knew it would never get out, and I never wanted to leave him, we could stay joined like this forever in something far more important than pleasure. Making love to him was like embracing a world in my arms, that level of strangeness and immensity and impossibility. It was never going to be quite like this again, I realized as my climax shot through me. It couldn't be.

But I wouldn't mind trying.

I was gentle with him afterwards, as it dawned on me just how violent he had let me be. There were bruises on his forearms and on his shoulder and thigh where I had steadied myself, and below—

He caught my concerned look and smiled, shaking his head where it rested on my chest. His hair was thick and silken-soft against my skin.

"Cigarette?" I asked.

"Do you smoke here?"

"A little. *Mereth*, it's a painkiller—"

"I don't need anything for pain."

"Or just generally relaxing." I shrugged. "I like it."

"Then I'll try it with you."

I pulled the blanket over him as I got up, giving in to an urge to be tender. He accepted it, but once I lay down again he used me as a pillow once more. At one point he turned, pressing his ear to my heartbeat. His cigarette began to burn down untouched.

"You said you could see your home star from this sky," he said.

"Yes. Aries orbits Hesper. It's a few hundred lightyears from Anchara—only days by hyperspace, of course."

"I suppose I'm only hours from home," Kas said. "It feels longer, somehow…farther. As if time doesn't want to associate with that journey longer than necessary—eternal and instantaneous at once. It's dark—or maybe just empty. There may be enough light to see by if there was anything to see. And it's cold."

I remembered the scent of ice on him, the smell that didn't belong. Dark and cold and indeterminate—space voyages could be described that way, certainly, but he spoke with an air of visceral *experience* about the whole thing, as if the steel and plascrete skin of a spaceship hadn't lay between him and…whatever he had passed through.

"What are you?" I asked. I'd been ready to believe in fate only minutes before—who knew what other impossible things I could accept?

"Not a sorcerer," he said lightly. "Just a traveler, a stranger here."

"Do they have sorcerers, where you're from?"

"Oh, yes." He laughed, but not enough to be joking.

"It must have been one hell of a long journey, from there to…a hilltop outside Prima City."

"Every step of the way, I told myself I'd never take it again." He looked at me through a veil of blue *mereth* smoke. "But if I truly meant it, I'd have turned back. I didn't need to come so far. Except I saw the lights…"

"Not from a hill outside Prima, then."

"Much farther than that." He'd turned his face so that the words brushed my sternum like kisses. "I'll have to go back," he said.

I swallowed and, without any reply to make with words, I ran my fingers through his long hair. I thought of strumming guitar strings, of playing music for him or with him.

"This would have been it," he said. His voice sounded thick. "I had my adventure, I slipped through a music festival, danced with a handsome stranger—I shouldn't have had any reason to return."

"But…" I started.

"But," he said, "you asked me to marry you." His lips quirked. "And how could I refuse such a reasonable request?"

I laughed. It wasn't that things were funny, exactly. It was just—well, I'd toyed with and discarded a belief in fate less than an hour ago. But earlier that evening, when I'd asked one of the biggest questions you can, it had been on an impulse. A feeling that if I missed my chance with Kas now, I'd miss something that would never, ever come again.

For a moment I feared I might be turning telepathic at the ripe age of twenty seven. Then I looked at Kas, and was relieved to realize I had no idea what he might be thinking.

"Would you really walk through *nothing*—go all that way for a conjugal visit?" I asked.

"And farther than that, if necessary," Kas promised.

I smiled at him solemnly.

"It'd hardly going to be regular," he said. "Not least because it'll take some time to find Aries from the outside—but don't worry. I can manage it."

"No problem," I said. "Once you see my apartment, you'll be glad at the lack of permanent domestic arrangements."

He smiled, but it wavered. "One other thing."

"If there isn't sheet music for an electric guitar and violin duet, I'll compose some."

"Glad to hear it. I was just about to ask what will be on the hypothetical sheet music's byline—or the certificate tomorrow, for that matter. The translation—" He waved a hand vaguely in the air, as if realizing I wouldn't make sense of whatever he'd have said "—had kicked in just fine by the time we introduced ourselves, but the music was loud, and in the rush of the past few hours I haven't had the chance to ask and didn't want to risk the embarrassment of calling you Elix when your actual name is—" He looked at me expectantly.

Oh, name. They hardly seem important, but I suppose you can't get married without them.

"Felix," I said. "Very old Earth name. It means something like 'lucky'."

Kas curled closer to me. "As you are," he said.

RENOVATIONS
GREGORY A. CARTER

The house was exactly what Connor and Jackson had been looking for: a two-story Craftsman bungalow, built around the late 1910s, according to the flier. Three bedrooms, two and a half baths, and an attached garage (no more street parking!), neatly tucked away with other historic homes in a quiet neighborhood. The homes circled an island of a park of thick green grass and tall shade trees.

When he was younger, Connor's parents used to drive through this very same neighborhood on their way to visit his great-grandmother downtown. He'd loved those old houses back then and fantasized about living in one, imagining himself as one of the movie stars who'd escaped to Long Beach from the hustle and bustle of life at a Hollywood studio. He would sway on a porch swing, manuscript in one hand, red pencil in the other, making last-minute dialogue changes, smiling to no one in particular when the right string of words flowed onto the page.

And now here he was, standing in front of his dream house.

"It needs a little work," Jackson said. "A new coat of paint on the outside, replace some of the rotted wood on the back deck and steps. We can even invite my mother over to pick out plants and give the place some curbside appeal." He playfully nudged Connor with his elbow.

At one time, Jackson's mother proudly displayed her immaculately manicured lawn, ringed with yellow-orange grandiflora roses. A lattice of Fourth of July climbers exploded its colors through the wooden archway and enticed the hummingbirds to flit about the entry gate. During his first visits to their house, Connor remembered Jackson's father running the hand mower across the grass while his mother knelt on a small, thick foam pad in front of the flower beds, pulling weeds or planting bulbs and seeds. After her husband died, she gradually lost interest in the yard, digging up the roses and grass, filling the space with AstroTurf. Soon after the turf appeared, a small militia of multicolored garden gnomes and white faux-marble deer in various poses crowded the yard. Only the climbers remained, simply because she wouldn't tear down the archway. Connor shuddered. "What would the neighbors say?"

"I would be surprised if they didn't try to run us out of the neighborhood."

Yet something nagged at him. Maybe it was the peeling paint that flaked like dried mummy skin. Or the neglected and sickly remains of rose bushes poking from the weeds like bony fingers. Or the darkened upstairs windows angrily glaring back at him. Stop it, he ordered himself, shaking his head quickly to knock the image away.

"You read too many horror novels," Jackson teased.

Connor turned to Jackson, surprised by the remark.

"I've known you long enough that I can see the little cogs spinning inside your head, dreaming up something ghoulish to fit into your next novel."

Jackson was right, of course. The house was not anywhere near as horrific as he imagined.

"Do you really think we should?"

"Definitely," Jackson said without hesitation.

Connor eyed the house one more time. No mummy skin. No skeletal fingers. No angry eyes. Just a house ready and waiting for them. "Okay. Let's do it."

∞

The magazine needed the article in a few days, and Connor wanted nothing more than to be typing away at the computer, but the right words refused to come. He would tap out a sentence, read it, change a word or two, re-read it, delete the entire sentence and start from scratch in a never-ending loop of frustration.

Jackson poked his head into the room. "How goes the writing?"

Connor pressed his fingers into his eyes and sighed heavily.

"That good, huh?"

"I can see exactly what I want to write, laid out perfectly in my head, but when I try to get the words out, my fingers freeze."

"Well, we could get started on a few of the projects around the house. A change of focus might be just the thing."

"It couldn't hurt," Connor reluctantly agreed and followed him into the hallway.

"First order of business is to get rid of this wallpaper."

The flocked paper may at one time have been the height of fanciful living, but the white had long since faded to a sickly yellow, and the brownish flower pattern had flecked away, leaving mangy patches among the curves. Jackson disappeared into the spare bedroom, returning with a large box that he placed on the floorboards in front of Connor. "Somewhere in that mess should be a scorer."

"A what?"

"A hand-sized plastic ball with round blades on one side. You drag it across the wall, creating rips and tears in the paper. Then, I come along with the electric steamer to force the steam behind whatever glue is holding the paper up. When it starts bubbling, a simple scrape with a putty knife should peel away the paper like an onion skin." Jackson stood and started down the stairs. "Sift around the tools and see if you can find it. I'm going to get Dad's electric steamer."

Connor stuck his hand in the box, tossing some of the many screwdrivers onto the hardwood floor. He shifted a small toolkit filled with wrenches of varying sizes to one side and thought he spied a corner of what could be the triangle. He wrapped his hand around it and freed it from beneath the small mound of tools.

The scorer's large black dome fit perfectly into the ball of his hand. He turned it over to look at the underbelly and saw three sets of nickel-sized, round blades with serrated edges that tilted and swiveled as he moved the ball around to get a better feel for it.

Jackson trudged up the stairs. "Good, you found it!" He was carrying a small blue box with a long plastic tube flowing from one end. A rectangle of translucent plastic with tiny holes along the flat surface was attached to the other end of the tube. "Why don't you start by running the scorer across the wallpaper?"

"What about you?"

"I'm going to figure out how this thing works," he said, hefting the steamer and disappearing into the study before Connor could respond.

Connor stretched his right arm as high as he could and began dragging the scorer across the paper. The steady back and forth rhythm of the scorer soon had a calming effect on him. The struggles with the article slowly untangled in his mind like a knot in a shoelace. The words slid into their proper places with each swipe until he knew exactly how he wanted to proceed. Nearing the floor, the last few lines flashed into view, floating toward the end of the article, ready to be cemented into reality until his hand vanished inside the wall.

"That can't be good," he mumbled.

Something brushed against his hand. "Shit!" He jerked back, dropping the scorer on the wrong side of the wall. He stood and pressed an ear to the wall, listening to the faint patter of tiny feet scurrying quickly away.

Jackson poked his head from the study. "What happened?"

"I think I punched a hole in the wall."

Jackson crouched down as Connor pointed to the flaps of wallpaper. Sticking his fingers inside, he pulled back the paper to reveal a fist-sized hole. "Looks like the last owners papered over the hole instead of patching it." He sighed heavily before standing. "We'll need to fix the hole before we can paint. Finish scoring the paper while I call the realtor."

"Sounds g—," Connor said to Jackson's back as he rushed down the stairs, angrily muttering about how much this was going to cost. "Okay then. I'll just finish scoring the wallpaper." He glanced around the floor, searching for the ball of plastic. With a dawning look of horror, he remembered where it was, and turned to look at the hole.

His dark imagination went into overdrive, and he could almost feel the legions of rats hungrily scratching and nibbling at his fingers as he reached down into the wall. He squeezed his eyes tight, whispering *it'sjustyourimaginationit'sjustyourimagination* like a mantra until the visions faded. He steeled himself, took one deep breath, and plunged his hand into the hole.

After what seemed an eternity, his hand touched wood and something wet and sticky. His fingers recoiled, but he didn't pull his hand back. He needed that scorer. With another deep breath, he opened his fingers and hurriedly waved his hand back and forth until he struck what he hoped was hard plastic. He wrapped his fingers around the object and carefully withdrew his arm.

A thick, clear substance coated the blades as well as his fingers. He brought his fingers to his nose and almost retched at the smell. The wallpaper still required scoring, so with the back of his right hand pressed against mouth and nose, he headed for the bathroom to rinse both hands and the scorer but stopped halfway down the hall. He would have sworn he heard the drumming behind the wall again, following him to the bathroom.

∞

Connor stepped onto the back porch, listening to his agent yammer away on the cell phone jammed into the crick of his neck while carrying the last scraps of wallpaper and glue to the dumpster at the side of the house. The planks creaked and bowed under his weight but held strong. Until that one board near the steps. The wood cracked like a gunshot, and his right leg suddenly give way, falling through the porch and scraping against the splintered wood. He screamed as his ankle bent backward when it connected with the packed dirt.

"Connor?" Jackson yelled. "Is everything okay?" Connor heard the backdoor open and a cellphone clang against the porch. "Holy—"

"Call 9-1-1."

"Are you—"

"Just call 9-1-1!" Connor screamed. "Please!"

Through teary eyes, he watched Jackson pick up his cellphone and punch at it frantically. "The drop must have messed this one up. I can't get a dial tone, and the keypad's not responding."

Connor's left leg stretched across the porch at an uncomfortable angle. He shifted to ease the pressure and howled as a jolt of pain shot up the other leg.

"Christ!" Jackson almost shrieked.

Connor gritted his teeth. "By the front door," he gasped, "the cordless by the front door."

"Right. I'll be back."

Connor tried lifting his leg again, then opened his mouth as a jagged piece of wood cut into his flesh. With much effort, he forced the scream back into his throat and stood as still as possible. He focused on Jackson's voice as it carried through the kitchen, repeating again what had happened and politely demanding an ambulance as soon as possible. Slowly, he relaxed, leaning back slightly against the planks to lift some weight from his ankle.

A few rays of light managed to find their way through the wreckage. Connor dared a quick look at the damage. A spear of wood pierced the calf muscle, and he felt the warm ooze of blood traveling down toward his foot. The unnatural bend of his ankle made him queasy, but no bone poked through, as far as he could tell. He attempted to wriggle toes that he couldn't feel.

Something rubbed against his calf, and he flinched, forcing another bolt of pain up his leg. He let loose the pent-up scream and wouldn't stop until Jackson sat beside him, cradling his head on his lap.

"It's okay. I'm right here." Jackson combed his fingers through Connor's hair. "The ambulance will be here soon."

Connor closed his eyes and listened to the faint crunch of gravel trailing under the porch toward the house.

∞

Jackson hoisted his suitcase into the trunk and slammed the lid. "Are you sure you'll be okay? The doctor said—"

"I know what the doctor said," interrupted Connor. "And yes, I'll be fine. I've got pillows set up on the couch to keep my leg raised, and you pretty much raided what they had on the shelves at Rite-Aid. I think we have enough gauze, bandages and painkillers to open our own pharmacy."

Jackson fished around in his pockets and pulled out his keys. "The doctor's number is by the cordless phone. And I have my cell if you need me. I can be here in an hour."

"I'll be okay," Connor said sheepishly.

Jackson hopped up the front steps and gave him a quick peck on the cheek. "I'll call you when I reach my Mom's."

Connor leaned on his crutches, clumsily waving as the car pulled away from the curb and disappeared around the corner. He had barely opened the door when a loud crash from upstairs stopped him in his tracks. "Hello?" A series of soft, quick thuds traveled from the bedroom along the hallway and faded into the study. His imagination kicked into high gear, flashing images of a rabid possum lying in wait, ready to attack once he set foot in the hallway.

"Dammit, not now," he mumbled, shaking his head. He gripped the railing and hopped warily up the stairs, his crutches poised to strike if necessary.

The hallway was empty save for a few drops of red trailing from the bedroom. Connor leaned the crutches against the wall and carefully lowered himself to the floor. He touched a drop, wrinkling his nose at the coppery smell. Using the walls for support, he pulled himself up and followed the drops to the study, sticking his head through the doorway. Nothing looked out of the ordinary, but he heard a soft metallic scraping from behind the desk. He quietly closed the door, not ready to deal with whatever it was just yet.

In the bedroom, he stood by the toppled nightstand between his side of the bed and a rocking chair by the window. The few books he'd stacked and planned to read while Jackson was away were strewn across the hardwood floor. The wastebasket was tipped over with one side caved in and its tissue cargo spread across the floor. The tissue box leaned against one of the runners of the rocking chair. And on the nightstand, a dust ring remained where an antique lamp had once stood.

He knelt carefully and touched the large shards of brown ceramic, dusted with a fine white powder, which surrounded the legs of the nightstand and were scattered beneath the bed. The frame of the rounded lampshade was dented and the original mica punctured and torn beyond repair. How was he going to explain the lamp to Jackson? It was an antique that belonged to Jackson's parents—one of the few items he'd refused to part with when the time came to move his mother from his large, almost empty childhood home into a smaller, more manageable apartment. Jackson often talked of how his father would settle in his big chair, hoist the young Jackson onto his lap and together they would read the funnies or solve a crossword puzzle—all by the soft, orange glow of that lamp.

He picked up the wastebasket, rounded up the wads of tissue and began gathering the ceramic shards. Grabbing a handful of tissue, he lifted part of the bed skirt to sweep the pieces into the wastebasket. His hand rubbed against something soft and furry among the ceramic chips. Grabbing it with tissue, he pulled it into the light, then flinched back, dry heaving into the wastebasket.

The initial wave of shock lazily retreating, Connor bent over the cat. The eyes—one blue, one green—stared at him through a milky film. The jaws hung open, showing a row of tiny, needle-sharp teeth. A hole the size of a tennis ball in its side revealed broken ribs. Along with what Connor thought were the heart and lungs, the stomach looked as if they had been yanked toward the hole.

Maybe he could tell Jackson that one of the neighborhood cats mistook the open window upstairs as an invitation. When it saw Connor, it ran into the bedroom and under the bed. His attempt to scare it from beneath the bed backfired, and the cat slammed into the nightstand, knocking it and the lamp over. End of story.

No, Jackson would probably believe it was yet another

one of his stories.

He inhaled deeply to keep his stomach from rising again and managed to get to his feet. He headed to the bathroom in search of a trash bag and a pair of Latex gloves. Finding the gloves but no bags, he headed for the stairs to check the cupboards in the kitchen. Passing by the study, he heard a low growl from inside the room. Crunching. Tearing. The soft shriek of metal bending. *What the Hell?* He grabbed the doorknob and twisted.

The sounds stopped immediately. He eased open the door and slipped into the study, gently closing the door behind him. He quietly slid the long, black poker from its stand by the fireplace, knelt in front of the sofa, and shoved the poker between the sofa legs, dragging it back and forth as if he were dredging the bottom of a lake.

What looked like an old tube of super glue spun across the floor and vanished beneath the desk on the other side of the room. The tube knocked against a metal grate then fell, clinking as it bounced against the metal duct. Connor crawled to the desk and stared down into a large hole in the grate. The bars were bent back as if they had been chewed, with sharp edges dripping a thick clear liquid that he seemed to remember seeing somewhere before.

He hurried down the hall, toppling the crutches as he entered the bedroom.

He stepped quietly over the lamp and peered into the room. The same drumming noise came from his side of the bed, where he'd left the cat's body. He tightened his grip on the poker as he crept toward the noise.

A greenish creature the size of a hand crawled across the body of the cat. Without thinking, Connor raised the poker, shut his eyes, and THWACK!

He opened one eye, glimpsing the creature's slender black tail vanish beneath the bed.

"Damn!" He had missed the creature; the cat, however— the cat was even more of a bloody mess. He yanked at the poker, but the hook was wedged tightly in the floorboards. He reached down to unstick the poker, grimacing as his fingers pressed into the remains of the cat.

The creature darted from beneath the bed, then wrapped its legs in a death grip around his arm. Its tail whipped through the air and jabbed into his wrist. Connor dropped the poker and screamed while the tail slowly wormed its way into his arm.

He smashed his arm against the wall one…two…three times. The creature fell to the floor, landing on its backside. Its legs and tail flailed in a mad attempt to flip itself over. He raised a hand to his mouth to hold back the acid taste rising in his throat. Two large serrated teeth opened and closed like a curtain on the creature's belly. Behind these, many concentric rows of smaller teeth popped in and out of reddish gums. A long hooked tongue waved through the air.

The pricking of hundreds of tiny pins and needles started in Connor's right wrist and quickly moved up into his hand. He shook his hand to wake it up, but that only made the tingling more intense, traveling to the tips of his fingers until his hand began to feel thick and heavy. He tried wiggling his fingers, but they refused to move.

The creature righted itself and scampered toward him.

He backed through the door into the hallway, tripped over a fallen crutch and tumbled down the stairs, slamming his head against the bottom step.

The tingling slowly spread across his chest toward his left arm, but the darkness had already left him insensate.

∞

The ringing of the phone roused him. The sunlight filtering through the curtains hurt his eyes. He could not blink. He tried lifting a hand to rub the pain away, but his hand felt thick and heavy and would not move. "Connor? Are you there? Pick up if you're there."

Connor lay at the bottom of the stairs, his body numb as he stared wide-eyed at the ceiling. He tried to open his mouth, to shout something, despite knowing that Jackson would not be able to hear him on the other end of the answering machine.

"Listen, I'm going to stay a bit longer. Mom's house is a mess—dishes piled in the sink and on the counters, clothes thrown all over the bedroom. I don't think she's run a vacuum over the carpets in weeks."

Connor heard the creature moving somewhere above him, jumping down step by step, bringing itself that much closer to him. He wanted to get up, run to the phone screaming for Jackson, but his legs refused move.

"I'll get things settled here, do a little cleaning, put things away. I made an appointment to speak with her doctor to find out what's going on. So I'll be home in a few days."

The drumming closed in on him.

"I love you."

Click.

APPLE PIE A LA MODE WITH JUST A SMIDGE OF HUMAN SACRIFICE
NATHAN SIMS

The brass placard on the apartment door read *1418*. It matched perfectly with the delicate sconces dangling from the walls and the lush green and gold carpet underfoot. Dyson had worried that he'd come to the wrong building when the doorman opened the lobby door and the concierge rose to greet him from behind the marble desk.

A farm boy from the cornfields of Illinois, Dyson had never seen anything quite like this before, not even after he'd moved to Washington, DC. He'd have walked right back out the front door if he'd not spied two of his pint-sized employers waiting in the corner of the lobby to escort him up to the witch's lair.

The dwarves were stocky, reaching no higher than the middle of his chest. One sported a strawberry-red beard dangling past a belt cinched tight across his expansive belly. The other dwarf's beard was just as long but jet-black.

"And you are certain you can do this?" the red-bearded dwarf asked as they stood outside the apartment door.

Dyson snorted and unzipped the thin duffel bag hanging from his shoulder. From the sheath hidden inside, he pulled his sword. Its edge caught the light from the hallway's sconces.

The dark-bearded dwarf gawped. Dyson sneered. Dwarves, they always got their rocks off on the swords.

The dwarf did his best to hide his initial reaction. "Rather impressive. Is it not, Bummell?"

The red-bearded dwarf Bummell (why did Dyson keep wanting to call him Bumble?) kept his distance. "It is a thing of death, brother. It has bathed too many times in fairy blood." He glared at Dyson. "The stench still clings to it."

Dyson winked. "Would you have hired me if it didn't?" He lowered the sword to his side. "Well, I've shown you mine; now show me yours."

The two dwarves glanced at one another, puzzled.

Dwarves: ugly *and* stupid. Dyson sighed and said, "The money?"

Bummell nodded to his brother and said, "Boegell."

Bummell...Boegell. Hell, why not just call them Bert and Ernie and be done with it?

Boegell pulled a leather pouch from his pocket, dangling it by its drawstring. Dyson heard the rattle of metal inside. He snatched it from the dwarf.

"What the hell is this?" he asked. "I don't need laundry money; I need cash. You promised me cash."

"We promised you payment," Bummell clarified.

"Payment of a lot of cash." He loosened the drawstring to find the glint of gold nuggets inside. "You've gotta be shitting me." He glared at the pair. "Gold? You want to pay me in *gold?*"

Bummell cast a worried look at his brother and asked, "Gold no longer holds value in this world?"

"Yeah, yeah, it holds value, but it's not like I can just hand this over to my landlady for rent. You think I can stroll down to the store and buy a loaf of bread with a nugget of gold?" He held out the pouch by its drawstring. "I need cash."

"We don't have cash," the black-bearded dwarf replied.

Dyson shook his head. "Then you don't have someone to break the spell."

"But you agreed..." Bummell floundered.

The bag of gold hung in the air, barring any further negotiations.

"Please, if she isn't stopped, my brothers and I will continue to die for her vanity!" Bummell pleaded. He pushed the gold back toward Dyson. "Already she has sacrificed two of our clan."

"Not my problem." Dyson let go of the pouch. It fell to the carpet with a *clink!* He stalked away, sliding his sword back in its sheath.

What an idiot he'd been, thinking he could trust a bunch of fairies to honor their word. He'd fought them long enough to know better. But money was tight and he'd been desperate enough to take the chance. And now where was he? Across town with no money. He'd have to scrounge a couple of bucks just for the metro ride home.

He followed the dimly-lit hallway as it bent around a corner. He came to an intersection but couldn't remember which direction led him back to the elevators. This was getting better by the minute. He turned back the way he'd come only to find Bummell pumping arms and legs to catch up with him, the bag of gold swinging from his fist like a censer gone mad.

"Where the hell are the elevators?"

"The mistress, she has already found her sacrifice. Even now she chants the spell to prolong her youth."

"One more dead dwarf?" Dyson shuffled the duffel bag farther up onto his broad shoulder. "Right now, I might cheer her on."

"Not a dwarf." Bummell shook his head. His long red beard wagged back and forth. "A human."

Dyson studied the dwarf's wide-eyed expression barely visible above the explosion of hair hiding the bottom half of his face.

"You said it was going to be one of your brothers."

"A human showed up at the door this afternoon—"

Dyson groaned.

"—The mistress chose him for the sacrifice."

"If you're lying to me…"

"No lie." The dwarf raised his hand in oath.

Well, this was jacked up. This changed everything. There was no getting out of it now. He couldn't leave an innocent to die just cause this month's rent was past due. Dyson shook his head, disgusted.

Still, he reasoned, if he was going to save some joker's

life, he might as well get paid for it. And better gold than nothing.

He extended his palm toward the dwarf.

The fairy eyed it cautiously.

"The money?" Dyson said, opening and closing his hand.

Bummell handed him the pouch. Dyson checked its contents again and slid it into the duffel bag before following the dwarf back to the door labeled 1418.

In the apartment, Dyson pulled the sword from its sheath as he silently stepped onto the tiled floor. Before him a hallway stretched deep into the apartment.

Mirrors of varying shapes and sizes lined the walls. Some hung as small as saucers. Others stretched nearly floor to ceiling.

"Bummell, is that you?" he heard a velvety voice ask.

"Yes, Mistress," the red-haired dwarf replied.

"It's about time! Did you get me my ice cream?"

"Yes, Mistress, just as you asked." From a deep pocket he pulled a brown paper bag.

Dyson looked at Bummell and mouthed the words: *Ice cream?*

The dwarf mouthed back: *For the spell,* and wiggled stubby fingers for effect.

"Well, hurry up! I've been waiting forever!"

A third dwarf (this one with a long blond beard) scuttled down the hallway toward them. His eyes widened as he saw Dyson with his sword drawn. He grabbed the pint of ice cream from Bummell and zipped back down the hallway.

"Buerkell is preparing it for you, Mistress," Bummell offered.

Dyson stepped past the two brothers and into the hallway, his sword raised and *en garde*.

Now that he was here, inside the witch's lair, he wasn't liking this job. He wasn't liking it one bit.

Since the dwarves had first approached him about the hit a few days before, he'd debated whether or not to take the job. He'd spent over five years of his life learning to hunt fairies. Now here he was working for them. Not just working for them, but killing a human being for them!

Doubts twisted in his gut. Could he really go through with this? Could he really kill a human (even one as bad as this witch) to help save a clan of dwarves? Was he even capable of killing a magic user as old as this one? There was the real question.

Dyson had told the dwarves he'd be able to kill the witch, no problem. But how could he be sure? She wouldn't just roll over and play dead for him. She'd fight back with everything she had. And what she had might just be more than he could handle.

He could still back out. It wasn't like the dwarves had kept their word. He could still hand back their stupid bag of gold and get the hell of out here before it all went south.

The only thing was, somewhere in this apartment was some terrified schmuck waiting to be sacrificed. And he couldn't walk away and let that happen. Right or wrong, good or bad, the only way to end this was to see it through. He gripped the sword's hilt tighter.

A *ding* from the kitchen drew his attention. The blond-bearded dwarf stood on a step ladder amidst ash-toned cabinetry and stainless steel appliances. He pulled a steaming piece of apple pie from a microwave suspended above the stove. He lowered it to a breakfast bar dividing the kitchen from the rest of the apartment and scooped a big dollop of the ice cream onto the pie.

Past the bar, the living room was dark except for the wash of light coming from a flat screen TV mounted to the wall. Its uneven light sprayed across the black leather furniture and blond-wood shelving units filling the room. The shelves were backed by mirrors and filled with leather-bound books, stacks of tattered romance novels, and the occasional earthen-ware sculpture or glass vase. Compared to his garage apartment full of second-hand furniture and a bed made from a mattress and springs perched on cinder blocks, this looked like The White House.

On the couch in the center of the room sat the sorceress watching television. All he could see of her was her dark hair done up in a ponytail at the crown of her head.

Beyond the couch, at the far end of the living room, was a glass-enclosed balcony filled with plants, where another dwarf (this one with a brown beard) was hard at work, harvesting herbs and roots. Through the windows Dyson had a bird's eye view of the city. In the distance he saw the Washington Monument lit up in the night sky, a tall, proud sentinel standing guard over the city. Beside the balcony was a closed door. Bingo! Dyson bet that's where she was keeping her victim.

The room turned dark as the screen went black. Dyson heard the familiar *dun-dun* of *Law and Order* and the next scene took place in a courtroom.

He cocked his head to the side.

Now, why would a witch—getting ready to sacrifice a human soul to prolong her life—be watching TV? He'd worked with enough magic users to know they didn't spend the final moments before spell-casting watching primetime television. For that matter, what kind of spell required apple pie and ice cream?

"Buerkell, where's my ice cream?" the woman demanded. She turned toward the kitchen. Dyson stood just a few feet away.

"Don't scream," he warned, leveling the sword's tip at her face. "Don't say a word." Lowering his duffel bag to the floor, he side-stepped his way to the closed door beside the balcony. The dwarf standing among the plants crept farther onto the balcony as Dyson edged his way around the room, his sword still pointed at the witch's face.

Dyson reached the closed door and swung it open. Inside, the room was lit by a small lamp sitting on a nightstand beside a queen-sized bed filling most of the room. A matching armoire and computer desk were squeezed inside as well. There was no sign of the witch's sacrifice anywhere.

"Where is he?"

"Where is who?" the woman asked in that rich voice that had demanded the ice cream. Though Dyson knew the sorceress was well over two-hundred years old, she looked no more than thirty, with her high cheek bones and long nose. Deep brown eyes were half closed by thick-lashed lids giving off an air of boredom as she studied the stranger standing in the middle of her apartment holding a sword to her face. "And while we're at it: who the hell are you?"

Dyson advanced on the witch. "The sacrifice? Where's the sacrifice?"

A look of bewilderment creased her forehead.

Dyson didn't have time to consider it. He saw a second closed door on the other side of the room, just beyond the hallway that had led him into the apartment. His eye on the witch, he circled the room toward the closed door. As he passed the breakfast bar, he noticed Bummell and his two brothers huddled in the kitchen. The red-bearded dwarf pointed at the second door and nodded.

"That's private." The witch rose to her feet, her petite frame hidden beneath sweat pants and a t-shirt. "There's nothing in there."

Dyson's eyebrow lifted slightly. "Then I guess you won't mind if I take a look." He swung the door open and glanced over his shoulder.

If the rest of the apartment was a testament to modern taste and design, the room behind the closed door was the exact opposite. Blinding candlelight reflected off a series of suspended mirrors as a fifth dwarf (dishwater blond beard this time) stood lighting the last of a dozen candelabras. Their flames cast convulsive shadows across the walls as well as the thick curtains hiding the room's solitary window. The carpet had been ripped up to reveal the concrete slab beneath. It was painted in arcane symbols—some Dyson recognized from his studies, others he'd never seen before. Taking up the majority of the floor was a large red ring. It encircled a thick-legged wooden table on the far side of the room. On its surface lay the unconscious sacrifice. A wicked, twisted metal blade lay only inches away, ready to do its mistress' bidding. Dyson's beady eyes widened as he recognized the auburn-haired man sprawled across the witch's altar.

"Avery, you stupid son of a bitch," he mumbled to

himself.

He knew going to the reporter for help had been a mistake. But he'd developed so few contacts since arriving in the district, that he'd seen no other option. So, against his better judgment, he'd asked the man for any information he could find on an up-and-coming partner at one of K Street's most prestigious law firms—the witch's most recent masquerade.

Even without revealing her true identity, Dyson should have guessed Avery's curiosity would get the better of him. He'd already seen the reporter repeatedly stick that roaming Roman nose of his into cases he would have done better to steer clear of. If Avery hadn't already been unconscious, Dyson would have liked nothing better than to beat the man senseless.

At the same time, he found himself drawn to the way the candlelight reflected off the coppery color of his tousled hair. And, not for the first time, he wondered what it might feel like to run his hands through that thick mess of curls.

A gasp brought him back to reality. The witch stood scant feet away.

Dyson took a step backward, berating himself. Thoughts of Avery were dividing his focus. He needed to concentrate on the witch if he expected to come out of this alive and get Avery out alive, too.

In disbelief the woman stared at the man lying on the altar. Dyson watched her eyes dart left and right, struggling to work out a riddle just beyond her reach. When the answer finally came, her face lit up with a smile. Laughing, she said, "Oh, Bummell, what have you and your brothers been up to?"

"Step back," Dyson warned, leveling the sword at her chest.

She glared at him dismissively. "Or what?" To prove her point she leaned forward, pressing the sword's tip to her breast.

"Take one more step and you'll find out." Dyson's voice sounded firm—at least he hoped it did.

His palm was slick with sweat. His heart thumped in his chest. This close to the witch, he could feel the power coming off her in waves.

The witch smiled. She stepped forward. A red splotch of

blood began to stain the t-shirt covering her chest.

"That's far enough," Dyson ordered, stepping back farther into her temple.

"Yes, quite enough, I believe," the witch replied. With a casual flick of her wrist and a single word—*"Exarmo!"*—the sword jerked out of Dyson's hand. It flew across the living room and embedded itself in the drywall beside the bedroom door with a *thwang!*

The witch mimicked the look of shock on Dyson's face. "Well, golly," she said, "how do you suppose that happened?"

She jabbed a finger in his direction. *"Depulso!"*

He felt a jerking behind his navel that yanked him into the air and threw him backward. He slammed into the room's far wall and landed in a heap behind the altar. The sorceress shoved the cowering dwarf from the room as she entered. She shouted, *"Claudo!"* and the door slammed shut.

Dyson rose carefully, his back throbbing from the collision with the wall. He made his way to the man lying unconscious on the altar and shook him. "Avery, wake up!"

The reporter didn't respond.

He patted his face gently. "Come on, Avery."

The man's head rolled to the side, his eyes closed tight.

Dyson slapped him across the face.

"Avery!"

Another slap.

"Avery!"

A third slap.

"Wake the fuck up!"

Still, the man didn't respond.

"What did you do to him?" Dyson asked, rounding the altar. He grabbed the crooked ritual blade and brandished it.

"Oh, he's what you're looking for?" the witch asked. She took a step forward. The energy pulsing from her was electric. Dyson felt it tingle on his skin as she approached. "So you really think you can get the two of you past me in one piece? Honestly?"

Dyson wanted to retort. He wanted some quip that would prove his confidence and undermine her attempts to intimidate him. The thing was: the confidence he was depending on to undo her efforts was going a long way to help make her point. The simple truth was: he'd underestimated the witch. Now he was trapped in her temple, sword-less, with an unconscious victim and no clear way out. Not the best circumstances.

With a crooked finger and a twist of her wrist, she commanded, *"Speculum contineo!"*

Instantly, Dyson saw shifting movement out of the corner of his eye. He turned in time to see one of the mirrors whip out from its frame like water thrown from a bucket. It hurtled toward his face, forming a spike. The last thing he saw was a thousand candle flames reflected off its surface as its tip drove straight into his forehead.

White, searing pain sliced through his head as the liquid metal split flesh and ground into bone. Blood seeped down his face. Instinctively, he tried to jerk his head free but the spell refused to release him.

"Careful. You fight too hard and it might just go straight into your brain," the witch advised and then added, "not that that would be much of a loss."

The dagger still in his hand, Dyson threw it at the mirror. It hit the wall a foot from the mirror's frame and *clinked* to the ground uselessly.

The witch laughed at him.

Another mirror coiled free of its frame and punctured the back of his head, drilling its way through the bone of his skull. Other tendrils of liquid silver skittered across the air, to pierce his head, like the spokes of a wheel with Dyson as their fulcrum. The final mirror unwound itself from its frame and slammed into his head to complete the ring.

Her spell cast, the witch circled him, ducking beneath the mirrors' projections, admiring her handiwork. "So, this is the great hero my boys hired to get rid of me?" she mocked. "You should see your savior now," the sorceress shouted at the dwarves on the other side of the door. "He looks most impressive in his crown of thorns."

The witch turned back to her prisoner and smiled. *"Speculum tollo."*

And the top of Dyson's skull tore free from his head.

Or at least that's what it felt like when the floor vanished from beneath him and the mirror's tentacles lifted him as high as the ceiling would allow. He clutched at the bars slick with his blood and attempted to ease the pressure on his head.

"You talk quite a game," the witch said. "Let's see if you really meant it. *Speculum pondero.*"

Through the blood blurring his vision, he saw an image appear on the surface of the glass spindle projecting from the middle of his forehead. The image curved around the circumference of the mirror's shaft, distorting it. Even so, Dyson recognized it. The memory replayed itself just as it had a million times since he'd first lived it years before.

A woman stood against a cinder block wall. Her heart was pierced, her mouth forming a perfect "O" of shock and pain. Dyson was unable to reach her before she crumbled to the floor, dead. He closed his eyes against the image but found it replaying over and over in his mind.

The witch laughed a hearty thing that rippled across the velvet of her voice. "Oh, my, my, my, perhaps my boys should have checked your references before they hired you."

She moved to another of the mirrors' prongs. It showed the image of a man dangling from a cliff's edge while Dyson stood above doing nothing. As the man lost his grip and tumbled down the rock face, Dyson watched him collide with the ground beneath. He studied the lifeless form silently before turning and walking away.

"Remind me never to ask you for help," the witch quipped.

Dyson struggled to hold onto the bars keeping him aloft, but it wasn't easy with the blood and sweat covering his palms. "Stop this, please," he begged.

"Oh, but there's so much more to see."

Another mirror revealed Dyson standing before a broad lake. Beneath its surface were thousands of dead bodies.

Another showed a burning village filled with women and children being slaughtered while Dyson obeyed orders and did nothing.

Another reflected the image of a young man standing before a giant dragon. Dyson couldn't reach him through the battle dividing them. He cried out in horror as the dragon's lungs filled, ready to kill the man with a single burst of its fiery breath.

On and on the images went, ripped from his mind as he hung above the floor, helpless to stop them.

Dyson walking into a garage to find a young woman hanging, lifeless, from the rafters due to his carelessness.

Dyson looking on helplessly as a true friend and mentor was slaughtered.

Dyson finding a young man screaming, clutching his hand as blood gushed from the stump where his finger had once been.

"My fault. All my fault," Dyson mumbled to himself.

All the while the witch laughed. She laughed at his impotence, at his loss, at his pain.

Another image captured her attention. "Oh my, now what's this?"

The mirror showed Dyson, sword at the ready, following a detail of soldiers through a thick wood. His eye was caught by a ragged piece of torn, brown fabric.

"No," Dyson said, closing his eyes in an attempt to block out the memory.

It continued to play through his mind, though, and he relived the discovery of that tattered robe. He knelt down to pick it up, but his legs gave way and he crumbled to the ground, clutching the robe to his chest.

"You know," the witch said, tapping the spike with her fingernail. It felt like a hammer pounding through his skull. "I think I like this one best of all."

"I'm gonna kill you," he said. "I'm gonna rip your heart out."

The witch sneered. "Promises, promises."

He yanked on the spoke in his hand, trying to break its hold. The mirror didn't budge. He swung his body like a pendulum, screaming at the pressure tearing through his head, and grabbed the spoke with both arms and legs. He bore down on the glass, but it did no good. The spell refused to give. Panting, he let go of the tendril and dangled above the temple's floor, his face covered in a fresh wash of blood.

"Well, I've enjoyed this. Greatly," the witch commented. "So much so, in fact, I want to give you a little gift of my own: a new memory. Or at least, it will be soon enough. A memory you'll be able to enjoy for the rest of your life—however long that lasts."

The witch raised a hand to one of the mirrors' tendrils. She delicately brushed it with a single finger, saying, "*Commoneo.*" A pulsing light appeared on its surface and slid toward Dyson. It crept closer and closer until it collided with his head, a lightning bolt sizzling through his brain.

A vision appeared. The witch stood behind the altar. Avery still lay prone on its surface, only now, the reporter was awake. His body was frozen to the altar. A spell held him in place. His eyes filled with terror, he cried out for Dyson as the witch raised her knife and plunged it into his heart.

"NO! NO! NO!" Dyson howled in rage, pounding on the silver tendrils.

The witch cackled with delight.

Her laughter was cut short by the sound of a crash from across the room. Dyson felt one of the spokes retract from his skull.

A spasm seized the witch. She gripped the wall, steadying herself.

A second crash and Dyson felt another mirror give way. His feet touched the ground as the spell began to weaken. The pain racing from his scalp down to his jaw eased. He struggled to see who had come to his rescue but still couldn't turn his head.

"You!" the witch shrieked.

One of the candelabras hurtled toward the witch. She diverted it with a gesture and the word "*Declino.*" The candelabra changed course midair and thunked against the temple wall.

A third, fourth, and fifth mirror shattered as the glass holding Dyson prisoner cracked and crumbled to the floor. The sorceress collapsed, each assault on her magic reverberating through her own convulsing form. A whimper escaped her as another mirror cracked.

Still the glass continued to break as an auburn-haired man wielding a candelabra came into view.

"Avery," Dyson gasped.

"Hold on, Wain," the reporter said, as he came to the last mirror, the first one to pierce the middle of Dyson's forehead. The man swung with all his might and the mirror broke with a satisfying crash. Dyson's legs gave out as the final tendril holding him in place splintered and he collapsed to the temple floor.

Avery rushed to his side. "Are you all right?" he asked.

Dyson reached a hand to his head. The tip of the spike from the very first tentacle was still embedded in his forehead. He tried to pull it out, but the pain was too intense.

"Here, let me help," Avery said, reaching up gently to grip the barb. "You look like a unicorn." Avery yanked the piece of glass from his head.

"OW!"

"There. All better now." Avery handed the spike to Dyson.

"Thanks."

"You're bleeding. A lot."

Dyson looked at his reflection in the piece of mirror in his hands. His dark hair was matted with blood. His face looked like he'd showered in pig's blood at the prom. "I'll be OK."

"We need to get you to a hospital."

Dyson struggled to rise. "It's OK; I've been through worse."

"When? When have you ever been through worse, Wain?" Avery asked, helping him to his feet. "And where the hell are we?"

A scream from across the temple startled them. The witch rose from the floor, the twisted ritual blade in her hand. She ran at the two men, screeching.

Dyson shoved Avery aside and threw the broken shard of glass in his hand. It went spinning through the air to land deep in her heart. A flash of blackness erupted, extending out several feet. The force of the explosion threw her backward, smashing through the temple door and landing on the glass coffee table in the living room, shattering it. The witch lay motionless amongst the broken glass.

From the temple floor, Avery shouted, "What the hell was that?!"

"A witch," Dyson said simply. Why hide it now? The jig was up. He'd kept the reporter at bay for months now, but after what Avery had witnessed tonight, there'd be no stopping the storm of questions he'd rain down on Dyson. He reached out a hand to help Avery up.

Avery didn't move. "A what now?"

"You heard me."

"There's a witch living in Chinatown?"

"And another in Rock Creek Park. I'd steer clear of her if I were you." Dyson hoisted Avery to his feet.

"There's a *witch* living in *Chinatown?*"

"Well, not anymore. She's dead now."

"And you knew this how?"

"A bunch of dwarves hired me to kill her."

Avery stared at him, dumbfounded.

Poor guy. Dyson knew what it felt like having your whole world turned on its ass.

"Come on," he said, taking the man's arm. "Let's get you out of here."

"She was going to kill me," Avery said, anchored in place. He looked at the altar, at the shattered mirrors, at the last few straggling candles still lit after his assault on the room. He looked back at Dyson. "You saved me."

Dyson couldn't meet Avery's eyes. The witch's spell and the memories of his own failures were still too fresh. He looked down at the shards of broken mirror cluttering the floor, each one reflecting back a shattered image of himself.

Quietly, he said, "That's what I do."

Avery eyed him doubtfully. "You OK?"

Dyson nodded. "Let's get out of here."

"Probably a good idea," Avery said, turning toward the

door. "By my count I'm looking at like a hundred years of bad luck, easy." With a tap of his shoe the reporter sent a piece of a broken mirror skittering across the room.

"Now all you need is a black cat to show up."

"Don't kid. I totally stepped on a crack one time. My mother still hasn't forgiven me." Avery stopped in his tracks. "Um, Wain."

"Yeah?"

"What's that?"

Dyson turned. The dwarves had pulled the witch free of the coffee table. All five fairies knelt around her body spread out on the floor. They chanted in a thick, plodding language Dyson recognized as one of the dwarven tongues. They had removed the glass barb from her chest and torn open her clothing, revealing her naked form.

As his brothers stripped off their own clothes, the already-naked Bummell knelt at the woman's shoulder. The red-bearded dwarf took the broken shard of mirror and sliced open the witch from neck to groin. He reached into her chest and hacked away at something. With a final yank the witch's heart popped out of her chest and a spray of blood splattered the carpet. The dwarf lifted it to his mouth and ran his tongue across its surface.

"Oh shit," Dyson said from the temple's doorway.

With his clan looking on, Bummell sat back, savoring the taste of the witch's blood before opening his mouth wide and clamping his teeth over a chunk of the muscle. Blood spurted out of the severed ventricles as he jerked his head back and forth until the piece came loose and he chewed it freely.

"Oh shit-oh-shit-oh-shit," Dyson said.

"Oh my god," Avery added. "I think I'm gonna be sick."

There was an audible rise and fall to the dwarves' chanting as Bummell's brothers sighed in anticipation. Frothy, red foam oozed onto the dwarf's lips as he passed the heart to Buerkell. His brother lifted the muscle above his upturned face, the blood pouring down onto his blond beard, dying it red.

Dyson shoved Avery back into the temple. "Stay in here and don't come out." As an afterthought, he added, "And this time do what I tell you!"

He turned back to the scene on the living room floor. The heart was making its way around the circle of brothers, each taking a bite as it passed, the witch's blood staining their pale skin as they continued to chomp and gnash through the raw flesh.

Bummell, the first to eat the heart, retched. Dyson saw the dwarf's stomach cramp beneath his beard. With a final heave, a shower of gray ooze spewed out of his mouth onto the witch's body. As each of the dwarves finished their portion of the witch's heart, they in turn vomited up similar sludge which quickly covered the corpse.

Dyson couldn't believe how stupid he'd been. He'd been so enamored by the thought of getting paid he hadn't taken the time to find out what type of dwarves he was dealing with.

The ice cream, the surprise on the witch's face when she'd seen Avery on her alter. Of course, she hadn't been performing a spell. It was all a ruse, a plan to get him to kill her so the dwarves could do exactly what they were doing right now. He'd been too busy with the gold and then Avery, he'd missed the clues right in front of his face.

"Dyson, you dumb ass!" he berated himself as he circled the room to his sword still lodged in the drywall. He jerked it free and turned back to the feast.

Before him on the floor, the dwarves' bodies were mutating. It was difficult to tell where one ended and another began. Here an arm merged with another arm, the flesh molding and melting into one. A naked leg joined the one next to it as bones popped and reset, forming a single leg, thicker and longer than it was alone.

"Not good," Dyson said. "So not good."

He raised the sword and lunged at the group of fairies, but a limb reached out (Dyson couldn't tell which one) and batted the sword away before it connected. The force of the parry carried Dyson with it, and he slammed into the wall containing the flat-screen television. A shower of sparks exploded from the screen as the sword shattered its surface and dug deep into its workings.

"Wain! Are you all right?" Avery asked from the temple's doorway.

"I told you: Stay out of sight!" Dyson shouted at the reporter.

The dwarves didn't notice the spray of electricity as their bodies continued to fuse into one. Where there had been ten legs and ten arms now there was only one set of each, extending out from a large torso. A massive head was attempting to lift itself onto a set of broad shoulders, as broad as Dyson's arm was long. It righted itself and opened eyes the size of fists. They blinked several times before focusing on Dyson still standing against the wall.

"Thank you," a deep, rumbling voice said. "You have been of great assistance to us."

Dyson thrust toward the giant dwarf's midsection, but his sword only rebounded off the creature's skin.

The giant laughed. "Do you really think you can hurt us with that stick? We are invincible now."

Dyson didn't know about all of that. Back in his first year at the institute he'd studied the various dwarf breeds. Problem was he didn't remember them. The class had been almost five years ago now, and even back then he'd struggled to remember the nuances of the dozens of different breeds.

He cursed himself again for not having boned up on the dwarf breeds before he'd taken this job. How could he have been so stupid? So cocky?

"Ah, yes, the look on your face confirms it: you know this is pointless," the giant said. "There is nothing you can do. Now, step aside. You have been of particular use to us. We will be gracious and let you live."

Why couldn't he remember anything about this breed? Something still had to be rattling around in his brain. If he only had more time, he was sure it would come back to him. He needed time to think! He settled down into his fighter's stance with his sword *en garde*. "Sorry, I can't do that."

Giant bulging eyes blinked in surprise. "We do not understand. This is useless. You cannot defeat us. You are barely upright after your battle with the mistress. We are giving you the opportunity to walk away from this—alive."

"I get that," Dyson replied. "And thanks, by the way."

Just hold out until something triggers. Think, damnit! Think!

"But what's the price?" he asked. "I live while hundreds of others die? You know I can't let that happen."

"We know you can try."

Dyson swiped his blade at the creature and again the sword rebounded. The giant slammed a fist into his chest. Dyson flew backward and landed among the plants on the balcony.

"No!" Avery cried out.

Dyson raised his head in time to see the reporter charge from the temple, a half-lit candelabra in his hands. He shoved the burning candles against the giant's back.

The creature roared in pain and batted the man across the room.

"Avery!" Dyson hollered, rising quickly from the shattered clay pots beneath him.

"I'm OK," the man said from where he'd landed by the breakfast bar. "I'm OK."

Dyson turned back to find the monster spinning madly, reaching for the burns on its back. It whimpered as it spun, desperately trying to relieve its suffering.

Dyson's beady eyes turned to slits. How had Avery done it? His own sword wasn't able to hurt the creature, but a candle could burn it? What wasn't he getting? Think, you dumb ass, think! Dyson looked from the beast to the dead sorceress lying on the floor covered in thick goo.

Well, partially covered in goo.

Her front side was coated in the gray sludge already beginning to crystallize. Her back still lay on the floor of the living room, untouched by the dwarves or their juices.

That was it! They were bound to the witch by her devoured heart. As long as her body was protected by their goop, they were protected. At least, those areas covered in the goop were.

"Thank you, Loopy Llewellyn," Dyson said, praising his

former Beasts instructor. He gripped his sword tightly and raced toward the sorceress' body.

"No! Stay away from her!" the creature yelled, lashing out at Dyson.

He ducked below the dwarf's swing and slid up next to the body. Lifting a leg, he took his sword and sliced through her Achilles tendon.

The giant cried out as a bloody gash appeared across its own tendon and it tumbled to the floor.

Dyson raised the other leg and did the same.

The beast howled and reached for the twin wounds on its legs. "What have you done? *What have you done?!"* it wailed.

Dyson raced to the balcony. He hoisted one of the few unbroken pots and shattered the window. He returned to the body and grabbed its arms.

"No!" The giant clutched at the corpse. "Release her," it demanded, hands covered in its own blood, eyes filled with rage. Dyson tried to yank her free, but the creature was too strong.

He hacked at the underside of the witch's wrist. With no ooze to protect the flesh, the blade dug deep, shattering bone.

Blood spurted from the giant's wrist as the wound appeared. It released the corpse and hugged its arm to its body, weeping at the newly-inflicted injury.

Dyson pulled the body out onto the balcony. Kicking dirt and plants out of the way, he dragged the witch toward the broken window. The wind howled as it rushed through the open cavity.

"Noooo!" the giant screamed, reaching out a useless hand, barely attached at the wrist.

Dyson shoved the corpse out the fourteenth floor window and watched as it plummeted end-over-end to the concrete below.

"Please-land-on-your-back, please-land-on-your-back, please-land-on-your-back," he chanted.

The witch wasn't quite that accommodating, but slamming her head into the pavement and shattering her skull was just as good.

In the apartment above, blood and brain matter exploded out the back of the giant's head, spraying the living room in chunks of red. The large body slumped to the floor, lifeless.

Dyson hobbled his way around the couch to where Avery stood, leaning on the candelabra.

"You OK?" he asked the reporter.

Avery nodded his head. He studied a clump of brain that had landed on the piece of apple pie still sitting on the countertop. The gray matter floated in a puddle of melted ice cream, staining it red. He looked back at Dyson. "What the hell just happened?"

"Dark blood magic." Dyson explained. He did his best to wipe the sword clean on a throw he found on the back of the couch. "The dwarves tried to use the witch's heart and body to protect themselves. We used it against them."

"Oh," Avery said. "Gotcha."

Dyson grinned. "We need to get you out of here. Someone'll find her body any second now. Can you walk?"

"Yeah, I'll make it," Avery said. Dyson stopped long enough to pick up his duffel bag and sheath his sword inside. When he looked back at Avery, he found the reporter transfixed by the carnage in the living room. Avery shook his head and said quietly, "Someone's not getting their deposit back."

They left the apartment and found a sign directing them to the closest stairwell.

"The way we look right now, better not take the elevators," Dyson suggested, holding the door open for the reporter.

They walked down several flights of stairs before Avery said, "So, this is what you do."

"What?"

"You know. Sword wielding. Monster slaying. The whole superhero thing."

Right then, Dyson didn't feel much like a superhero. The fresh flood of remembered failures. The fool the dwarves had made of him. The throbbing wounds encircling his head.

"I wouldn't say all that," he finally replied.

"I would." Avery gripped his shoulder and turned him.

He looked Dyson in the eyes. "You saved my life back there. I don't know how you figured out I was there, but I'm glad you did." He grinned and said, "I think your mom must've got your name right after all, Gawain."

Dyson blushed. Why had he ever told Avery his full name? Why had his mom saddled him with such a ridiculous name based solely on her childhood love of the legends?

"Look, Avery," he said, his eyes on the stairwell's wall, on the floor—on anywhere but the man himself. "I didn't come here to rescue you. I didn't even know you were there until I saw you. I was hired by those dwarves." He unzipped his duffel bag, pulled out the pouch of gold, and handed it to Avery. "They paid me to kill the witch."

The reporter opened the pouch and looked inside. Confused, he held the leather bag out to Dyson. "Next time maybe you should have someone negotiate for you."

"What?" Dyson asked. He looked inside the bag and found it filled with pebbles. "Shit!" he spat, tossing it across the stairwell. "They cheated me!"

"Dwarves who were using you to kill a witch and become invincible deceived you? Imagine that." Avery smiled.

"But it was full of gold, I swear! They paid me to kill the witch." Dyson sighed and said, "Avery, I'm not the guy you think I am."

"I know who you are," Avery said. "It doesn't matter what got you there. What matters is what happened once you were here. You were tortured, beaten. God only knows what else that bitch did to you. And after all that, you risked everything to get me out in one piece. That tells me everything I want to know about you." Avery took him by the chin and forced their eyes to meet. "That tells me everything I want."

There was a look of longing in his eyes so powerful Dyson's breath caught in his throat. It was so very clear. The reporter stood before him, offering himself to Dyson, a prize just waiting to be claimed.

But Dyson knew he wasn't worthy of such a prize, no matter what Avery might say. So instead, he retreated. "We better get out of here."

Avery studied him a moment longer before letting the moment melt away. "OK."

They turned and started down the stairs. They passed another floor before Dyson asked, "You going to be OK?"

"You mean, am I going to lose it since I found out fairies are real?"

Dyson grinned and a single dimple appeared in his left cheek. "Sort of."

"I'll live." Avery replied. "My face is really sore, though—like, really sore."

"You get drugged, nearly killed by a witch, thrown across the room by a giant dwarf, and your face is what hurts?"

"But that's what's weird. I didn't get hit in the face. When I showed up the little guy offered me something to drink. The next thing I know I'm lying on the table with a stinging face. That's it. This feels like—like I got slapped or something."

Dyson blushed. "...That may have been me."

"You slapped me?"

"Three times."

"What?!"

"I was afraid you were under her spell. Slapping you was the first thing that came to mind."

Avery considered Dyson's explanation. "Well, if it was a witch's spell, you might have considered other options first."

"What do you mean?"

"Something like this." Avery pushed him against the stairwell wall and kissed him. His lips were soft and his body warm. The two men held one another and tasted the promise of what lay ahead.

They parted and Dyson smiled. "I'll remember that for next time."

"Next time?" Avery asked. "There's gonna be a next time?" He wasn't speaking of another spell or another witch. He leaned in to taste the future again.

Dyson pulled away with a glint in his eye. "Trust me, Sleeping Beauty, there's always a next time."

The reporter watched Dyson turn and descend the stairs.

He shook his head, and smiled, and said quietly to himself, "Wain Dyson, you sure as hell better be worth the wait."

    He followed Dyson down the stairs, out of the building, and into the night.

CHERRY BLOSSOM RHAPSODY
ROSE MAMBERT

It had taken the ronin seven years to track down the man responsible for his daimyo's death.

For seven years he had searched, following endless leads, rumored sightings, and words made of wind down from wintery Akita in the north to rain-drenched Nagasaki in the south, and back again. He had traveled the five highways, through snowy mountain passes, up rivers and once even across the sea to the Ryuku islands. Along the way he had continued his training in the most prestigious dojos in the land; kept his instincts and steel sharp as a bodyguard, a mercenary, or an assassin.

The ronin finally caught up with the traitor late one afternoon in early Spring on the road outside of Kyoto. Words were exchanged, steel drawn, and each warrior took a fighting stance, sandals grinding traction into the dirt as fingers tightened around the katanas' woven hilts. Confident of his skills, and with the knowledge that divine right was on his side, the wandering ronin was able to face his opponent with a courage that bordered on arrogance. He had trained seven years for this moment. He could not fail.

He failed.

As the ronin lay dying, he had three thoughts. First, he thought that at least death would bring relief to the pain of the shame that throbbed within him, much like the wound from the traitor's expertly-inflicted strike. Second, despite the shame of failure, he considered himself fortunate to have died on the battlefield as a samurai should. Third, he was somewhat surprised that the color of death was different than he had imagined. Neither the white of a funeral, nor the black of oblivion. Instead, death was varying shades of red: the flash of crimson light off his opponent's blade as it sliced across the setting sun; his own blood as it spilled over the long, pale grasses that lined the west side of the road; the fur of the slender, white-muzzled and black-booted fox that crouched at the edge of the forest, watching him with cunning eyes and head curiously cocked; and red the darkening horizon as the sunlight slipped away along with the ronin's breath.

Death surprised him. He had never expected it to be so beautiful.

∞

The next time he opened his eyes, he was disoriented. The pain that knifed through him indicated that he was still alive. He blinked a few times, then examined his surroundings. He lay supine, half-naked and bandaged, on a musty futon while half-shattered stone goddesses smiled down upon him. Daylight from the holes in the temple's roof speckled the floor. Near the altar crouched a man, clacking mortar and pestle together.

The ronin stretched a hand out from under the blanket, groping for his sword. His fingers clutched at empty air, and he grunted in frustration just as much as from the pain the movement caused him.

The man at the altar turned. "Oh, you're awake." Setting down his tools, he stood and approached the ronin, kneeling down at a respectable distance.

The ronin considered the stranger. He was a long-limbed sort of slender, young, and fox-faced: a broad forehead tapered down to a narrow chin, forming a triangle, with close-set eyes and delicate features. On his lip and chin sprouted a thin patch of hair, as red as the hair on his head which was raggedly cut and stuck out in all directions like the flames of a bonfire. Nearly as odd as his hair was the fact that he wore a hitatare which was a riot of color but bore no identifying crest. He appeared unarmed.

. "Who are you? Where am I? And...where are my swords?"

"My, full of questions, aren't you?" the stranger said

lightly, with an accent that the ronin didn't recognize. His mouth twisted into a mischievous grin. "By the way, it's generally considered rude to interrogate someone without giving your name first."

He grimaced and attempted to pull himself upright, but the pain rocked him back down to the futon with a grunt.

The stranger was then leaning over him, his previous mirth having disappeared. "Careful. That wound of yours was pretty serious."

The ronin lay still momentarily, just breathing. He turned his head to look up the stranger, who cocked his head curiously. The sunlight behind him turned his hair into a corona of fire. No man had hair like that. He couldn't be real. "You…you're that kitsune."

The stranger chuckled, then ran a hand over his head. "You know, you'd be surprised how often I get that."

The stranger's laughter curdled his blood and quickened his temper. Yet all he could do was lie there, helpless, an object of ridicule. "You don't deny it."

Despite the ronin's accusatory tone, the fox man only grinned again. "I didn't think it was worth denying, but…" He rose from the floor, then slowly turned full circle, his bare feet crunching dead leaves and kicking up puffs of dust. "See? Just a man. Also the man who saved your life. You do realize that you were dying by the side of the road when I found you?"

Shame was a hot knife, rending and plundering. The ronin hissed his ingratitude through gritted teeth. "You should have left me to die."

"Die? Why the hell would you want to do that?" He paused, waiting, but the ronin remained tight-lipped, staring at the ceiling. "Well?"

The ronin looked at him. No crest, no swords, and no samurai worth a damn would be caught dead in such old-fashioned and garishly-colored clothing. Not to mention the fact that those scrawny arms couldn't belong to a swordsman. "You wouldn't understand."

"Try me."

The ronin seethed. He snapped. "I swore an oath to kill

the man who killed my lord. We fought. I failed." He glared at the stranger. "The least you could have done was let me die with honor on the battlefield. If you have any sense of decency at all, you will bring me my swords."

"Why? So you can commit seppuku?"

The ronin narrowed his eyes. "This is not your concern."

The fox man hesitated, then jerked his head towards his right. "They're over there on top of the altar. If you want to kill yourself so bad, then go get them."

Falling silent, he crossed his arms before his chest, and stared defiantly down at the ronin. In his eyes, a challenge.

Damn him. The ronin eyed the distance to the altar. He decided that he didn't care if the stranger watched him crawl. Summoning all his strength, the ronin rolled over and attempted to pull himself up. Once again the knife of agony revisited his flesh. This time he gritted his teeth and did his best to ignore it. Yet each small movement brought only a fresh torment of fire to his flesh, his head dizzied and vision blurred by the pain. He had only managed to cover one third of the distance to the altar before he collapsed on the floor, a barely suppressed whimper in his throat.

Arms curled around him from behind, hands pressed against his chest. Stronger by far than he appeared, the stranger lifted him from the floor easily, as if he weighed no more than a bundle of twigs. Strong, patient hands eased him back down on the futon, then adjusted and smoothed down the blanket.

As his vision swam back into focus, he saw the fox man crouching over him with a stern look of disapproval. "Look," he said softly. "It seems to me that if you swore an oath of vengeance, then you got no right to die until you kill the bastard that killed your daimyo. Killing yourself is just the coward's way out."

The ronin glared at him. Unflinching, the fox man held his gaze. Eventually, the ronin was the first to break contact. He stared at the far wall, at the tattered panes of paper in the sliding doors that quivered with the incoming breeze. In his throat, the shame was lodged, a sticky thick ball of pitch that made it difficult to speak. He forced out the words. "He was too strong."

The stranger's voice bore the steely thrust of conviction. "Then I guess you better just get *stronger.*"

∞

When he slept, his dreams were strange. Awake, he refused to speak when the fox man was there, instead watching him in stony silence as he floated, restless, through the temple's shadows. Or, when alone, he stared at the ceiling, cursing the gods, his own helplessness, and his fate. Once he dreamed of his younger brother, of playing fox-fist together in the garden as the cherry blossoms fell. When he woke, the sticky ball of pitch in his throat had dissolved, washed away by the perspective of time. Near the altar crouched the fox man, sifting silvery knife through silver-scaled fish, translucent flesh luminescent against the glossy dark green of bamboo leaves.

As the ronin cleared his throat, the fox man lifted his gaze, staying his hand mid-cut. A clump of fish offal slowly tentacled its way down the blade, clinging precariously for a moment before dripping to the ground. He ignored it, waiting.

"I have thought on your words, and now I see their wisdom," the ronin admitted. "You were right. I must make myself stronger. To think otherwise is…selfish."

The fox man studied him for a long moment, then he lay down the knife, discreetly wiping his hands on the sleeves of his hitatare. "Well, if you want to live, then you'll need to eat." He gathered up the bamboo leaves and carried them outside. Eventually he returned with two bowls, a pair of lacquered chopsticks balanced on each. Setting aside the dishes, he helped the ronin into a sitting position, propping his back against one of the hall's center columns. He then shoved one of the bowls into the ronin's hand before sitting down and picking up the other.

Fish, lightly sauced, lay on a mound of still-steaming white rice. Reluctant, the ronin picked up the chopsticks and tasted the dish. Swallowing, he glanced at the fox man with surprise. "This is quite good."

He hadn't been able to keep the surprise from his voice, and now the fox man cocked an eyebrow at him. "An artful compliment for a swordsman," he teased. "You must be very popular with the ladies."

The ronin stared down into his bowl as he felt the heat rise in his cheeks. Fortunately the motion caused his hair, free of its usual topknot, to fall down to obscure his face. After a moment he returned his attention to the fox man, who had returned to gobbling down his food. *Like an animal.* His manners were atrocious, yet his countenance was pleasing. "You didn't tell me your name."

"You didn't ask." He grinned. "They call me Kasumi." A nickname meaning *the Mist.* "And you?"

"Ashikaga Kuroda."

The chopsticks in Kasumi's hand slowed in their journey from the bowl to his mouth. "Of the Kyoto Ashikaga clan?"

Bitter the taste of the words. "No, I am a descendant of the Kanto Ashikaga."

The chopsticks became stationary as the fox man hummed thoughtfully. "Yeah, but that still makes you samurai royalty, doesn't it?"

"The Kyoto branch of the clan defeated the Kanto many years ago."

"Hn," Kasumi muttered, then shoveled the last bit of rice into his mouth. Tossing down the bowl, he then bounded to his feet and slipped outside once more. This time he returned with a teapot and two cups which he arranged between them. Having finished his own meal, Ashikaga picked up one of the cups, admiring the fine workmanship. Equally lovely were Kasumi's hands as he prepared and poured the tea: long-fingered, graceful, the movements rivaling those of a renowned Yoshiwara geisha Ashikaga had known years ago.

The light glinted off the gold rim of the cup as Ashikaga turned it in his hand. "Where did you get these?"

"Found them in a secret stash of monk goods here in the temple," he said. Then he smiled. "You should see it. Once you're able, I'll show you."

The ronin made a non-committal noise, but accepted the tea that Kasumi poured for him. To the eye it was straw-colored, to the nose, fragrant, but to his tongue it was bitter awful. He'd never tasted anything so vile, yet with only one sip, he could already feel something warm and mystical budding inside him, uncurling in his blood. "What is this?"

Again, the playful grin. "Special recipe handed down from my Old Man," he said, with a tone of mystery. "Drink it— it will do you good. Get you healed and up in no time."

The ronin considered that as he stared down at the pale elixir in the beautifully crafted cup. Then he considered Kasumi, long fingers wrapped around his own cup as he sat cross-legged on the floor, lazily sipping. "I would like my swords now. Please."

Sly eyes became suddenly grim. "You're not still planning on killing yourself, are you?" he asked. "Because I didn't save you just so you could spill your guts onto the floor."

"No."

"Hn. Well. How do I know you're not lying?"

Ashikaga angrily set down his cup. "According to the Bushido, untruthfulness is an act of cowardice. As such, lying is dishonorable. Therefore, the warrior strives to be honest in all situations. I do not lie."

Kasumi hummed thoughtfully again, considering. Then he shrugged. "Fine. But only if you finish your tea."

He finished his tea.

∞

A warrior's sword was more than an instrument of self-protection. It was a reflection of the warrior's soul and a vehicle for achieving spiritual perfection. The two swords together—the daisho—formed the core of a warrior's identity. Thus it was no small sense of relief Ashikaga felt when Kasumi, having carefully fetched the swords from the altar, placed them in the ronin's hands. Without his daisho, he was nothing.

After a cursory glance at the wakizashi, he laid it beside him and lifted the katana. With a practiced flick of the wrist, the katana slid partway from its scabbard, revealing a hands-width of steel. The blade was clean.

"Is it true that samurai always sleep with their swords?"

Kasumi's voice drew Ashikaga out of his revery. He

snapped the sword back into place. "I'm no longer samurai. I'm ronin."

"Then you're a criminal?"

"Not all ronin are criminals."

Kasumi made a dismissive gesture with one hand as he picked up the fresh teapot with the other. "So you say," he said, then tipped the pot in the ronin's direction. "Real tea," he added before Ashikaga could form a polite refusal. Kasumi filled the cups with the same artless elegance as before, spilling not a single drop. Settled back on his heels, he continued, "If you're not a criminal, though...why don't you just seek a new daimyo?"

Ashikaga sipped the tea slowly, thinking that the situation wasn't so simple as all that. Thinking, too, how this man—or whatever he was—was annoying and crass, and yet he had acted benevolently: saving his life, caring for his injuries, feeding him. Certainly he wanted *something*. "If you hoped for a reward, then you'll be disappointed. I have no money."

Kasumi shrugged. "It wasn't like I had anything better to do."

"You weren't obligated to get involved."

"Maybe I needed the karma."

"Karma?"

Kasumi smiled gently around his cup, lifting a hand to point at the string of beads woven around the ronin's wrist. "You're Buddhist, ain't you?"

Ashikaga lowered his arm to his lap, covering the mala with his other hand. "This was a gift. It's not that I'm a follower of any particular school, or anything."

Kasumi watched the ronin's fingers twitching over the beads. Then he bounded up to his feet again, this time stretching his lanky arms high above his head. "Well, whatever. Kami, Buddha, or ancestors—gods are a pain no matter what the religion."

∞

Outside the abandoned temple, the weather grew warmer, bringing a lush of green to the forest. The significance of the season, full of renewal and promise, was not lost on Kuroda

Ashikaga as he made his way, for the first time unaided, across the great hall.

He found Kasumi sitting outside on the steps, his hands on his knees, staring at the moon. Without turning, the younger man mused, "You must be mostly healed, moving around like that."

Ashikaga would have cut off his own arm before ever admitting to feeling weak. However, he did ease himself down next to Kasumi, and admired the night. On the cherry trees, tight buds clustered, ready to explode, faintly pink in the light of the moon, round and bright in the hazeless sky, its rays illuminating both the stones in the path and his companion's profile.

Although they had grown to be on friendly terms with the passing of time, Ashikaga still knew little about him—other than he still may be a fox, although he had yet to admit it. But in the moonlight, he was subtly alluring. The kitsune in the old tales often were when they took on human form.

"I suppose you'll be off soon to find that man who killed your daimyo," Kasumi said, his voice low and nearly lost in the breeze, his eyes lingering longingly on the moon.

Ashikaga shivered, wishing he'd thought to put on his haori as he pulled his kimono closer. He needed to train more. Become faster. *Stronger.* "Fujioka. Yes."

Now Kusami looked at him, thin eyebrows dipping down. Then his brow smoothed out again as a glint of cunning sparkled in his dark eyes. "Well, since you're able to move around…you wanna see the monks' secret stash?"

∞

Ashikaga had started to question his decision to follow Kasumi even before he found himself crawling through a dark hole in the wall at the end of the narrow passage that Kasumi had unearthed during his explorations of the temple's kitchen. He didn't enjoy the sensation of being underground, nor the feel of a many-legged insect as it slithered over his hand unexpectedly in the dark, yet once they emerged into the hidden chamber and Kasumi adjusted the lamp to illuminate its contents, Ashikaga forgot all about his concerns.

It was a treasure room.

Kasumi chuckled at the expression on Ashikaga's face, conspicuously pleased with himself. "Pretty awesome, huh?"

Piles and piles of the finest lacquer ware and ceramic, weapons, bolts of brightly-colored silks, painted screens, objects of gold, ivory and jade, and more were crammed into what appeared to be an eight-mat room. He frowned in Kasumi's direction. "This can't be here. Monks disdain wealth of all kinds."

His frown went unnoticed, as the red-haired man had already set the lantern down on a dark wooden chest and was rooting around the goods, carelessly knocking objects of dubious quality aside. "Hn. You have a point." He paused over a stack of folded silk women's kimono, his trailing fingers making the painted cranes and koi dance. "Maybe this stash is bandits' loot then. But they were all killed or captured before they could return to claim it."

Ashikaga's frown deepened as he pondered the possibility. The ronin supposed that Kasumi could be right... and if so...well, in the karmic sense, there were worse actions than stealing from bandits.

Also, he was broke. He joined in.

They each chose a corner of the room to explore.

Kasumi was the first to break the silence. "So...why did this Fujioka kill your daimyo?"

A sudden chill ran through Ashikaga's blood. He closed the shunga book he'd randomly discovered in a stack of printed matter and leaned against the wall. He ignored the dirt that crumbled perilously down his back. "Greed. He'd been promised his own land by a rival clan, should he manage to kill our lord and wipe out his entire family."

Kasumi eyed him with surprise. "So you shared the same lord?" he asked. Then, with suspicion, "Were you friends with this Fujioka or something?"

Ashikaga busied himself by unwinding the string from his hair, letting it down and gathering it back into a simple tail at the nape of his neck again. "When I came of age and officially joined the clan, Fujioka...he was the one that oversaw my training."

From the corner of his eye, Ashikaga watched as Kusami began to worry his bottom lip with his teeth, thin brows dipped down over his eyes again. Then he huffed. "Well, he sounds like a total bastard to me. Are you really going to throw away your whole life on trying to get revenge on that guy? Does your life have such little value?"

Ashikaga's eyes flashed. "I have no other choice."

Kusami growled back at him. "What bullshit. There's always a choice."

"Perhaps. But this is the path I chose."

"Didn't it ever even occur to you to choose a different path?"

"The code—"

"The code is for samurai," Kasumi snapped. "As you said, you're no longer samurai, you're ronin."

Ashikaga's hands curled into fists at his sides. "Just because a man changes his status, it does not mean he forsakes his principles."

"Do you *always* do what other people tell you to do?"

"Do you ever *not* say whatever stupid thing you're thinking?"

Kasumi paused, seeming to consider the question. "Well, where's the fun in *that*? And besides—eh, what's this?" He stopped as a small crate filled with bottles, previously overlooked, caught his eye. Crouching down, he scooped up a bottle, uncorked it, and sniffed the contents. "What the…oh *damn.*"

"What?"

Kusami turned back to him with a wicked grin. "Sake!"

∞

Their argument was completely forgotten with the discovery of the secret stash of sake. At least Kasumi, in high spirits at the prospect of celebrating the hanami—albeit early, as the cherry trees had yet to blossom—had forgotten. Ashikaga, on the other hand, was happy to pretend that the subject of his past relationship with Fujioka had never been mentioned.

In the temple courtyard, Kasumi whistled a tune as he prepared the picnic for their hanami feast. Upon a blanket spread below the cherry trees at the edge of the clearing, they dined on an extravagant meal of inarizushi, lotus root tempura, unagi and daikon, all washed down with the pilfered wine. The night was beautiful, the dishes carefully constructed, the moon full, the conversation and sake flowing. At some point, the ronin realized that he was drunker than he had been in a long time. And—judging by the happy, free smile on Kusami's face, he was in a similar state.

In the moonlight, Kusami was subtly alluring. Adding too much sake to the equation, his beauty was nearly alarming. Ashikaga admired his youth, the grace of his lanky limbs, and his fox-like face. "Kasumi-kun. Just admit it. You're kitsune."

Kasumi half-snorted, half laughed. "Oh? Am I?" He reached for the sake bottle, refilling both their cups. "If you'll recall—in the stories foxes usually transform into women."

Ashikaga shrugged. "In some tales they are elderly men. And some say the kitsune can take any appearance they wish. Human or other. One even mimicked the moon."

"Yeah, right. The moon." Kasumi chortled derisively into his cup. He tossed the sake recklessly down his throat, then cocked his head at the ronin. "So...how do you know so much about kitsune, anyway?"

"Ah. In Kamakura, in a place called the Hidden Village, there's an Inari temple. Everyone who lives there knows of it. And kitsune are well known as the servants of Inari—they often serve as his messengers. Many a tale is told of the fox spirits of Inari where I'm from."

"Izzat so?" Kasumi drawled. He set down his empty cup. In two heartbeats he had moved closer, practically climbing into Askikaga's lap. His sake-tainted breath was hot against the ronin's face. "Now tell me, Ashikaga-san—do I really feel like a spirit to you?"

Having Kasumi in such close proximity, together with the sake that had replaced his blood, Ashikaga flustered. He felt the heat in his face and hoped it wasn't visible by the moonlight. "Ah, if...if you're not a kitsune, you could prove it easily."

Kasumi's breath rushed over the ronin's lips. "Oh? And how's that?"

Ashikaga cleared his throat. "If you're kitsune, then there would be some sign of it. Most likely a fox's tail, hidden in your hakama."

Kasumi stared at him. So close, his eyes were twin pools of midnight. He blinked languidly, once, twice, and then he broke out in an amused cackle. "What you mean is that you wanna see what's in my *pants.*"

The ronin growled. "That isn't what I said."

He stopped cackling. Suddenly serious, he edged closer, staring into Ashikaga's eyes. "You know...you didn't say this either, but it's pretty clear that this Fujioka was *more* than just your friend. More like he was your nenja, right?" Kasumi paused to offer a most lascivious grin. "Why, he probably taught you all *sorts* of things—"

Rage streaked through him. He didn't let Kasumi finish. Instead, Ashikaga seized him by the arms, fingers bruising flesh.

Kasumi stopped talking.

Briefly they stared at each other, solemn as death. But then the usual coy grin curled out from the edges of Kasumi's mouth. "Well, Ashikaga-san?" he murmured, all hot breath and promising like Spring. "You want me? Because I've only been holding off jumping your bones until your wound had healed."

Kasumi's unexpected confession was like a slash of a blade, rending through him as though he were soft as tofu. Ashikaga sought deceit in the fox man's eyes. He found none. He ignored the urge to run the man through with his sword. Instead, he reeled Kasumi in with a jerk, lips mashing as two pairs of hands became temporarily slack before curling desperately into fabric.

Kasumi moaned into his mouth, his cock hardening as the ronin's hands thrust under his clothes, exposing his chest to the rapidly-cooling night air. He shuddered as the ronin's hands twisted in his hair, his tongue trailing snail-slow down his neck, teeth capturing nipple with exquisitely painful pleasure.

"Ah...Ashi...uhh..."

How long Kasumi had wanted this. He felt boneless as the ronin pushed him down to the blanket with the weight of his body, the promise of his hard cock against Kasumi's thigh. Sword-calloused fingers tore at the straps of his hakama, revealing his cock already straining towards the moon. He shivered deliciously as the night air brushed against his swollen member, and then groaned as the ronin slid down his body and took Kasumi's cock into his mouth.

Ashikaga devoured him like he was starving.

Above him the stars twirled across the sky as the ronin expertly sucked his cock, his mouth hot, the tongue teasing circles around its tip until Kasumi writhed and moaned. Hands clawed at the blanket below as he melted, gasping and begging, in Ashikaga's mouth. Involuntarily he arced his hips, needing more. *Damn,* but Ashikaga was good at this. *Gods*, he was going to...*oh, gods...*

And then, unexpectedly, the ronin seized him roughly, flipping him over. The blanket scratched his face. Before he realized what was happening, Ashikaga had seized the back of Kasumi's hakama, and with a swift yank, jerked it down.

Kasumi yipped as the fabric tore.

Released from the confines of the hakama, his tail sprang out as if overjoyed to finally be free, and struck Ashikaga in the face. The surprise of it was enough to knock Ashikaga backward, half-sprawled now across the blanket.

Kasumi scrambled up, twisting around so that he was now crouching before Ashikaga. "What the hell, man...?" he began, but Ashikaga's expression stopped the words in his mouth. He glanced over his shoulder to see what Ashikaga saw. "Oh. Well, that's a game changer."

Ashikaga stared at Kasumi's tail—as red and bushy as anything he could have imagined—as it twitched in an irritated manner. *I was right all along. He's not human.*

Kusami returned his gaze to Ashikaga, a strange mix of ferocity and apprehension. And yet, Ashikaga wasn't really all that surprised. He had suspected the true nature of his companion all along. And he had been attracted to him all along, despite—or, in truth, perhaps because of—this.

It took Ashikaga very little time to come to terms with the fact that the man he'd been about to fuck wasn't actually a man.

Leaning up, Ashikaga grabbed Kusami by the hair.

"Hey, wait...umph...mmm..." Kusami began, only to be cut off as Ashikaga's tongue darted eel-like to fill his mouth, and hands pushed the hitatare from his shoulders. He would have protested about how Ashikaga had tricked him into revealing himself, except that when the ronin's hand found its way down to his cock again, it didn't seem that important anymore.

∞

One thing the fox tales tended to veil—rather thinly, Ashikaga thought—was the taboo of bestial love. It did not stop him, however, from returning later to the secret room to fetch the shunga book so that they could enact the various positions depicted within its covers.

As Ashikaga unfolded the book, Kasumi gave him an innocent look. "Ashikaga-san, is *that* what you want to do to me? You perverted old man."

Ashikaga ignored his teasing, responding instead by reaching for Kasumi and dragging him down to the bed. To Kasumi, it was just a part of the game. According to the old tales, a fox had to be at least fifty years of age, if not a hundred, in order to transform into a human. He'd chosen to transform himself into the role of beautiful youth, and insisted on using the proper honorifics. This insistence dictated their roles as lovers, as well. Ashikaga had become the kitsune's nenja.

Kasumi had not been wrong in his assessment of Ashikaga's past relationship with Fujioka. At fifteen, Ashikaga had become the older man's wakashu, and, as was the custom of the bido, had received instruction from him in both the martial arts and the arts of love. Like any other discipline, the beautiful way served also as a path of awakening.

There were tales of samurai romance, too. Invariably, one lover would throw his life away for the other, a sign of the strength of his devotion.

"Bastard," had been Kasumi's comment. "Did he really expect you to sacrifice yourself so he could get what *he* wanted? I don't want to talk about him anymore. Fuck me on the altar."

His experiences with Fujioka had awakened two things in him: the desire for vengeance, and the desire for men. For seven years, he had fulfilled neither, excepting a few nights of pleasure with kabuki boys on the rare occasions he had coin to spare. Combining his long-neglected sexual needs with the fox's bestial insatiability, it was no surprise that most of their time was spent having carnal relations, and in every place and every position they could think of.

By the time they had valiantly attempted every position in the shunga book, all the cherry trees had finally blossomed. Kasumi insisted that they go outside and have a proper hanami this time, after which, of course, they would fuck like monkeys.

"And if you've never seen monkeys fuck, let me tell you, you're missing out," Kasumi had said with a salacious leer. Then his expression had become vaguely dreamy. "They're also surprisingly tasty—of course, *if* you can catch one."

Ashikaga said nothing, but was secretly relieved to learn that monkey was *not* on the menu.

They supped below one of the larger cherry trees, hidden from the light of the moon, the air redolent with the subtle fragrance of the flowers. Then, with the remains of their repast scattered about them, as Ashikaga thrust into the intoxicating heat of the kitsune's body, he wondered if the bido was perhaps a legitimate path to spiritual awakening after all.

Above him, Kasumi writhed. His tail swished, trembling, across Ashikaga's thighs, his hands pulling fistfuls of the ronin's long hair as he panted in his ear. By his expression—the flushed face, the eyes squeezed shut—Ashikaga recognized that he was about to come.

The ronin was also close. He snaked one hand from where had been clutching Kasumi's hip and slid it down the kitsune's spine until he reached the tail.

He'd learned that Kasumi didn't like to have his tail touched, but if Ashikaga scratched the base of it at precisely the right moment, Kasumi came harder than a tsunami.

He scratched.

Perhaps there was truth in the beautiful way as a path to enlightenment. As Kasumi's body clenched around him, wracked with sounds like sobs of pleasure, Ashikaga achieved a state of perfect mushin no shin—no thought, no mind.

Afterward, they lay on the blanket side by side, as crickets serenaded them from the darkness. For a while, Ashikaga floated in the blissful state of mushin.

Then Kasumi barked out a laugh at the moon. "Damn. That was intense."

The ronin stretched out a hand to find Kasumi's. Palms pressed together as their fingers entwined. Ashikaga squeezed lightly. Kasumi's curious gaze met his. "Kasumi. The road can be a lonely place. When I leave here, I would like it if you accompanied me."

Kasumi's eyes widened in surprise. "For how long?"

Ashikaga's voice was soft as summer clouds. "Until the end."

Kasumi stared at him silently. Then he disentangled his hand from Ashikaga's as he sat up. Resting his arms up his upraised knees, his tail slowly flicked back and forth as he stared up at the branches of the tree.

Ashikaga waited a moment, but impatience drove him to sit up and lay a tentative hand on his companion's shoulder. "Kasumi?"

"In a week, the blossoms will fall," he said.

∞

One day, while the cherry blossoms were falling outside, the ronin woke up to discover that Kasumi was gone. He'd left nothing behind other than a fox gift—an artfully-arranged pile of small stones, dead leaves and dried twigs—and an ache in Ashikaga's heart.

Ashikaga lingered until early afternoon, even though he already knew that the kitsune would not return. Once dressed, he tucked his swords into his obi, tied his hair into a topknot, and carefully rolled the fox gift up in a swatch of red silk, secreting it away inside his haori next to the heavy purse of gold coin taken from the bandit's stash.

Sandals tied on, he slid open the temple door. For a moment he stood at the bottom of the steps, squinting in the brilliant light. At his feet, a carpet of pink flowers. Scarcely visible on the ground to his left was the stone path that wound down to the road which would eventually lead him to Fujioka. To his right, a thin line of petals were crushed lightly into the mud, as if trod upon by a fox's feet, leading into the woods.

Two paths. One choice.

A breeze detached the final cherry blossom from the nearby tree, and Ashikaga reached up a hand to catch it as it brushed against his cheek.

Drawing a deep breath, he stepped forward, into the sunlight.

CAMERA OBSCURA: TWO GHOSTS
JEANNELLE FERREIRA

Delft
December 1675

 The feather mattresses, the best and the second-best bed, are gone, to pay a debt. *Your wife and children can't eat lapis and madder.* There remains a straw-tick upstairs in the studio, a room so cold that bowls of paint crack and leave fireworks upon the shelves; and the guest has a cloak to lay down, a good one.
 He has been gone six months from Delft, and in the painter's house there is another child, at least, God be thanked, a son; with the debt there was canal fever, there was strain on the market for paintings, war drove up the price of bread, of milk, of light, of color. There is more silver than ochre in Johannes' hair. His stained hands shake.
 Perhaps the kiss is the cause of it. They have no time, today, to waste in a kiss as friends.

∞

 "You work too hard," the guest whispers, but by now—they are in most things contemporaries, all the pass-words worn and stories gone over—it is a joke. The mattress crackles when Johannes welcomes him down to it; dust-wool skitters out from their weight, and dances across the floorboards in the light.
 It is cutting-cold in the room, from all the windows; fools would undress, and yet he wishes Johannes would ask it of him. He has not, for years; when he says nothing upon the subject, now, the traveler contents himself with stroking the rough russet of Johannes' hair. It curls without his heeding it, God be

thanked, because he wouldn't; even with its layer of winter, those curls make him rakish-handsome as the smiling tilt of his mouth.

"Writ your book yet?" Johannes' fingers print upon his lover's shirt. Marine and yellow spark along the laces where he's tugged them. His own shirt he did not think to close this morning, and his old brown-velvet coat is a pillow for his beloved.

"No," answers the geographer, and then a bite, not coy, at Johannes' bared chest. "I wrote you letters."

His doublet is plain, not cheap, and Johannes is careful, when he pushes a hand between them, to hold the dark-blue caffa from harm's way. "Replied," says the painter. "I swear I did. September."

"I have—mm—more correspondence from my wife. Half December's sped." Later he will find the unsent letters: tied round with cord of buckskin, left among raveled shirts splashed diverse colors. *Papers, atelier and private cabinet; rummage not worthy being itemized.*

A moment's winter cloud sends the room shadowed, sends Johannes into his arms with a sudden shift of weight, as if he has—*it is difficult*—remembered time. There is never time enough. But when Johannes presses down to him like this, breath and stubble rasping, when his face settles slack and he moans into the briefest kiss, what can his guest say but *yes, whatsoever you may need?*

Johannes is looking down steadfast, even as his hips and his hands move without his consenting; the light is caught in his eyes, and his lover's reflection, and he is no longer painting in his head.

"Close your eyes." It is something Johannes, *never Jan,* never does. Jan's guest is a man of method enough, so empirical even in wooing, that a gaze should be no matter, but *how do you touch one of God's wonders, how ascertain that the skin* here *is very warm and very smooth, that* here *the muscle will leap and shudder when your hand closes, tight*—how could he dare such things, with Johannes' eyes upon him, in the cold, in all the light?

Johannes' lashes lie obedient, but no other part of him is still. "Anton," he says, and more sounds lost to meaning. His free hand splays over cheekbones, the bump of a long, fine nose, and his fingers catch in the length of his lover's hair. "*Anton,*" and Johannes crashes down like the tide.

"You cannot expect I may keep up with you," he breathes in a moment, still close, still keeping pace and pressure, until Antonie bumps Johannes' forehead to shut him up, *oh God, that's good, oh fuck* all bitten behind his own lips. And then Johannes is laughing, as he daubs at their parted bodies with a linseed-smelling scrap; his eyes crease at their corners, hiding blue. "I am old."

"Nonsense. You are going to live forever."

∞

August 1673

They met by collision, that morning, at poor de Graaf's funeral, Anton half obscured in his handkerchief as he mopped and flicked flies, by turns; Johannes retreating, head-bowed, from the altar, at a clip. He was pale, in sodden black, his hat was sliding free, and over the office for the dead he did not hear his given name; they went tangled by knees and ankles into a pillar.

"You look terrible," Anton said, as Johannes' weight left him. "Come and drink with me, out of this heat."

"Can't. Haven't sold a thing this year."

"Come," he said again, when the painter would have slipped by, when he muttered something of *home* and *wife*. "Business."

It is still morning, and the tavern is no louder than Johannes' house.

De Graaf, they toast, *and his young son beside him,* and the anatomizers De Graaf the anatomist has cheated, tucked safe under his stone coverlet in the church. They drink to the Prince of Orange, the heat-wave's end, the painter's wife, pregnant to the last degree; and then the penniless man finds his cup somehow cool and full again.

"You cannot—cannot keep standing me drinks."

"Let me sit for you, then." Anton dares it. "I told you this

was business."
"You have, already, twice."
"Five years ago!"
"I haven't learned a new trick since," he says, boldly enough; but the next moment stares down into the drink as a man does who walks the canals' edge and waits to be pushed.
"What would I tell Catharina? She is not stupid."
"Yourself, then."
"What?"
"A self-portrait."
"I understood that." Johannes' throat is washed with sweat, shadowed as he swallows. He sets the cup down as if the table feinted aside.
"Say four hundred guilders? Let me have a flutter on your immortality."
Immoderate, for a cabinet piece, and by Johannes' clouding gaze he knows he has overstepped. There are liberties the painter will not allow—a word in a well-placed ear, a nudge to this or that guild—but he has never refused what Antonie asks of him.
He guards the privilege; he looks at Johannes, the tiredness cast over his features, the ivoryblack smudged and sifted into all the lines of his hands. "I am asking you." The learned man speaks low. "A favor. Between friends."
"The favor of my sorry features, fixed and glazed!"
He cups one hand, quickly, against the painter's cheek. "Say yes."
"Forty guilders," says Johannes. "And enough to buy the colors."

∞

March 1667
"I've no wish to paint things I can see," he says, pacing, shivering the magic box with his tread. "I paint what I—what I can't."
Stepping into the camera's light-filled eye, Anton sits in the lion-backed chair and flicks his collar smooth, cracking the starch. He poses with one leg over his lap, head on hand, ridiculous, dreamy, until Johannes arrests his stride and comes

to stand near him.

"Not like that." Johannes' arms come round him, and the scent of sweat and rain, and with practiced touches he settles Anton's shoulders, his frame, his hat and the oak brown unruliness of his hair; it springs so that Johannes must tuck it back.

"Keep your head still." He stands on one side, thumb between his lips, and then takes flight again like a dull-plumed bird. "No," he considers, and "no," again, but none of Johannes' thought springs aloud; Anton's elbow numbs upon the table, his eyes begin to water in the light.

A moment's scuffle in the corner of the atelier, and Johannes comes bounding. A cloak of heart-scarlet swings to cover his subject's shoulders. "Red suits you better."

"Then I am sorry I did not go for a soldier."

Johannes does not laugh with him. He grips Anton's shoulder, hard, and wrecks the composition.

He can't get his hands close, trapped in the draped weight of wool; he opens to the kiss instead, and the remembered taste of coriander and cider. From his earlobe to his collar Johannes' fingers sketch a path, fumble, and fall still.

"Jan," he protests, or begs, and fights and gains a kiss of his own.

"Your wife expects you," breathes Johannes.

"My wife can bear it."

"Go. And tell Catharina—please—that I am painting."

Next week, there is a letter, brown ink on a palimpsest carried by the eldest daughter: the master sends the Guild's compliments, and he is finished with the camera obscura, time being. Anton brushes his bravest coat, turquoise silk shot all over with gold, and fits gilt buckles to low shoes, though it poured all morning, and escorts Johannes' linsey-woolsey child to collect his *tronie*.

"Antonie," Johannes greets him, both hands cold. His features' fire is subdued, but it is raining; it slurs and mars the light, and frets his temper.

"Done already? The gods were with you. Let me see!"

"Antonie," he says again, as if his son has died.

When Anton embraces him, he stumbles, and the camera obscura quakes on its legs.

"I am sorry," Johannes whispers. His hands frame a painting, small, invisible, and fall away. "I...Catharina."

The red is still there, bursting from the canvas like cut plums, but Anton has disappeared.

"Your daughter looks well," he says. "Is the feathered hat your own invention?" Crimson dusts sharp as poison over his tongue.

∞

January 1663

There is a tradesman in the great man's study, hopping from foot to foot like a sparrow. He has no hat but an old *capotain*, and no decent sleeves; a pink ribbon love-knots through either side of his russet hair.

"Antonie," he shouts above, when the maid would have refused him. "Koppernigk was wrong, and, besides, the Earth is flat. Come down, or I'll tell the Royal Society you said so!"

There is a rending crash, as of wineglasses falling, and then a hurried patter upon the stairs.

"Johannes? It's—it's not Terce yet. Johannes, are you drunk?"

"No. No! Antonie, I have a son."

Anton, still in his kimono and slippers, comes to clasp the painter's hands. He tugs, because he cannot resist it, at one bright ribbon until it comes free in his grasp. More intimate than a kiss, but the maid has left them, and Johannes has not drawn near to kiss him, yet.

"Catharina has named him for me."

His smile slips, a moment; they have had seven years to find an understanding, but she is still the chill in their bed. "Let me be the first to drink him, then. Will he be called Jan, or Hannes?"

Johannes puts his weight back on one boot, and folds his arms across his chest.

"You are a chap of one idea," says Anton, and despite the hour he pours them genever from the sideboard, more than he should. "Your son Johannes, then."

"My son Johannes," he echoes, and the spirit chases color even higher upon his cheeks, but Johannes' voice is diminished.

"In the spheres' name, are you well?"

"I am—I don't—I have not painted, since you went last to London. The colors all go wrong. I can't see a thing."

"You have a son at home," says Anton, by way of comfort. "Perhaps it is no time for painting."

He looks so blank at this, so baffled, that Anton kisses his cheek. In the sudden brush of stubble and of noses, there are words, near inaudible, near crushed.

"And you." Antonie ought to shove him out into the snow. Johannes' face is buried, damp, against his neck. He is newly a father, and Anton's own wife will wake inside an hour; to go on like this treads the ice-edge of madness. He puts a hand on Johannes' forearm, trips over a half-lit footstove, singes his robe, and leads the painter upstairs.

∞

October 1654

The world ended yesterday. Anton, poised with pen in hand upon the cusp of something really tremendous—*the animalcules! How, if they lived upon a man's hand, and in the scum of his teeth, might they not live also*—

God's thunderclap had sent Anton deaf until morning, shivered half his lenses, and cracked the celestial of his pair of globes. The city lay under a low, sharp smoke, and the animalcules had vanished from his head as the dull glow of flames, from every window, had not yet.

This morning he has walked three hours, though the church clocks do not tell it, before finding a tavern with food and ale still left. God's thunderclap was the city's powder magazine, and riders are coming from The Hague and from Rotterdam to bear the news away again: a quarter of the city's souls are dead. The fires will burn white for days.

The world ended yesterday. It is Anton's lone excuse, as the wall scrapes his cheek, as the stranger's breath hitches and a moan begins. He cannot say why he dared. Perhaps he knew from the set of the barman's shoulders, from the quirk of his lips in spite of weariness, that here was a miscreation like himself. Perhaps his eyes, pale and cool, had enticed Anton to drown.

He smells, as everything does, of smoke, and caught in his hair is the hot, bloody reek of metal as it tries to burn: he has ventured closer to the fires, then, than anyone Anton has met in the street. He is licking at Anton's ear, and he is pressed schoolboy-hard between Anton's thighs and he is *laughing*, so suddenly that Anton stops thinking.

"There are still beds in this world," he says, and though his sleeve is ragged, he does not add *sir*. "Not all have burned to a cinder."

He takes Anton's hand.

Idiot, we'll be taken by the Watch, Anton wants to admonish, but he is gasping from the stairs and other matters, and then they are safe behind a narrow door. The bed is rumpled, and the room is small, bright as a Sunday conscience. The smoke-scent is crowded out by mineral, earth, bone, and the no longer familiar note of another man's sweat.

His host broke away to draw the shutters; now he holds out a hand as if nothing went on at his waist.

"Johannes." He is breathless only a little. "Artist."

"Antonie," because the painter did not say *Jan*. "Man of science."

"I wondered," says Johannes, and kisses Anton until his eyes close.

"The latch," he remembers words, barely. "The landlord…"

"Oh," Johannes answers, leaning into the hollow of Anton's hips. "I am the landlord."

"I thought you an artist!"

"Time enough for both. I am going to live forever."

REALMS
MICHAEL C. THOMPSON

1. Seraph Searching

The filthy sky hangs over, a blanket of smog and storm cloud blocking rays of ultra-violet. Brilliant, juicy Technicolor bleeds through the structured atoms this side of existence. I look up at the overcast gloom with indifference, lift a lit cigarette to my lips and pretend to inhale, dragging the smoke into my mouth. As I release, I watch the toxins drift up to the haze above the wounded skyline, scraped away by the towers of humans, creaking and groaning from deep inside and yet holding fast—glued together by the pride of man alone.

The piss-soaked front page of the *New York Times* glides toward me in a sudden snap of frigid breeze, a tumbleweed caught in the breath of God, my trench-coat blowing out behind it; the headlines read plainly to me as it nears, the typical boring fare of luxuriant societies: **HIRING IN U.S. SLOWED IN MAY**. I step aside and it sails past, blowing amidst other trash caught up in the icy whirlwind chilling the street, holding my black fedora to my head to keep it from chasing after. The news of the day reminds me of my purpose in this realm, and that I am in the world of humans and their petty affairs, a place in which I should not linger.

An ambulance shrieks by, flooding the streets momentarily with the flashing of its spinning red lights, heading in the same direction that God calls me toward—likely a crime scene.

"Lilith," I mumble under my breath, as though my Lord will not hear me, "you fucking bitch."

Be cautious, I remind myself. She's not like the others.

She's smarter, been at the game for too long—free for too long. That's why He sent me. To put her back where she belongs. Knowing that my target is close, I move with the speed of intention toward her.

I arrive at the scene of a crime ten minutes later, where I meet Officer David Whitaker. When Whitaker requests identification before he will allow me to enter the crime scene, I reply with a charming: "David, why don't you go fuck yourself?" Instead of these words, Whitaker hears: "*Why, of course, officer, I would be much obliged,*" and hallucinates my hands pulling out a police badge identifying me as Detective Dimitri Artemin. Whitaker lets me pass without further trouble.

Now calling myself Detective Artemin, I walk around the scene asking pointless questions here and there, receiving vague, ignorant answers in return. I duck under various lines of yellow police tape until I reach the scorched, splattered body of Rodrigo St. Pierre. Poisonous black smoke rises from charred chunks of flesh into the surrounding air, filling the immediate vicinity with an unbearable stink that keeps numerous police officers and detectives temporarily at bay, and some of them vomiting. I smell nothing, and advance to the exploded wreckage of the body. None of the sterile sky-scraper windows hanging above the scene appear to be broken out, and thus the source of the fall has not yet been determined—at least not by the humans surrounding this gruesome portrait. But I know that St. Pierre didn't start falling from this realm, he just ended up here by the time he hit the bottom. Another knows this as well: my target.

An upside down, circled star has been carved into St. Pierre's mostly-intact torso, although the wound is almost indistinguishable as the colors of the body are now all the same charcoal black. The police will classify this as a cult-murder, a human sacrifice; I know that it was neither. My target is not a member of a cult, and she does not sacrifice, she kills for the simple joy of killing. She left this vile mutilation as nothing more than a Satanic taunt; the infernal bitch *actually* thinks she is going to get away with it.

I turn around without further gazing at the smoking body,

then walk toward the apartment building to find the floor that St. Pierre was thrown from. As I enter the structure, a surge of electric cold overtakes me, the air crackles with static as a breeze from another world blows gently through the hallways. The daemon has been here *very* recently, and likely very often—she might even be here now.

As I slowly ascend the stairs, I begin to silently pray to my creator for a favorable outcome. I clutch the small crucifix that I hide in my pocket, feeling warmth and strength begin to rush through my seraphic skin. I can almost feel invisible wings spreading behind and around me, and I know that whether they are there or not, the mere idea of them is warming the freezing, alien air inside the man-made steel tower.

As I continue to ascend the seemingly endless series of staircases, I feel myself drawing closer to my source of magnetic attraction, the daemonic escapee that I have been sent to retrieve. The frigid temperatures increase, and I can sense the rot of the other realm seeping through the very concrete pores of the structure. The dimensions echo broken physics from all sides, her presence is tearing a hole in the veil, changing the rules. *Unnaturally.* The thought offends me to the core of my being.

I pull one leg up and grip the railing for balance. Slowly my breath rises as colored vapor in the increasingly frigid air, condensation adorned with flickering white lines, a visual anomaly which can only be the result of dimensional friction burn, and I know that I must find her and return her back to Hell—the realms are much too close.

Despite the immense cold brought about by the dimensional burn, I am sweating. I can hear thunder in the distance, but there is no sign of a storm, no lightning to accompany the thunder, no clouds; not in this human place.

The pressure of gravity suddenly increases, dragging me to the floor, taking my mind with it—I collapse to the concrete floor of the stair-well bridge. The world goes black, and I drift away as the realms quake around me, drowning me in an abyss of irresistible sleep.

∞

2. The "Daemoness"

    Storm clouds rain down bitter black coffee, staining the broken concrete of the New York City street, puffing rock dust into the air like powdered milk. A donut rolls by and down a sewer drain, and for a second the sun cracks a cloud, shining through like the yolk of a Cadbury egg. The air smells like chocolate. Something doesn't feel right. I could be dreaming. I try to remember where I am, how I got here. Each attempt floods my mouth with the taste of maple syrup.
    A dream, then.
    I walk along the avenue, pull a pack of cigarettes from my coat and withdraw one. As I light it, the scent of burning sugar fills my nostrils. I drag on the prop, taste sweet acridity, cough painfully and unexpectedly. My non-existent lungs fill up with smoke, the sensation is devastating. I seize backward as a car passes, peppermint wheels splash through a puddle of coffee, flinging large pellets of it upon me and staining my jacket. I grasp at my throat, choking, trying to clear my head. The clouds suddenly give birth to new torrents of liquid black and I pull my fedora over my ears, running for the nearest building, a small, gold-domed museum with walls the color and scent of caramel.
    I step on a newspaper as I enter, look down at it—a blank page. As my shoe leaves it behind, strings of sugary cotton stick to it like cheap glue, smearing along the evergreen tiles of the floor. I rub my heel on a nearby rug, noting the texture of it appears to be hard, black toast. I look up for the first time.
    Portraits on every wall, humans in every direction. As I move, their gazes move with me, each face smiling devilishly: George Washington, Thomas Jefferson, Gandhi, Rasputin, King Edward VI, VII and VIII. Joan of Arc's eyes gleam, transfixed in a passion, yet still locked upon me, seeing me as my true self, as Seraph—the only face not smiling. She alone I stare at as I head down the empty hallway, toward the dark interior. Her blue eyes flicker, and, as I pass, I realize that she is not looking at me at all. None of them are.
    I shake my head, trying to understand what is happening.

"*A dream,*" he says from behind me, entering my mind for the first time—quite literally. I turn to face the source of the voice. My spine tingles, the hairs on my arm stand on end. He wears a kimono, but nothing else, and stares at me with large, saucer-brown eyes, abyssal almost. Beautiful, curly black hair falls to his ears, gleaming in the beer-light of the candy museum. His face is clearly female, although the body it is attached to is not, and he smiles with lips that bring to mind the flesh of Eve's apple. I fall into the black eyes, down a rabbit hole, drowning in a sea of coffee. He snaps his fingers in front of me, returning me to existence—or at least what constitutes it for me presently.

"*You don't dream often?*" he asks.

I don't answer his question, but continue to examine his face. My head swims with new sensations, sensations that I had believed myself incapable of—I feel my lungs fill with air as I breathe, I feel my nerves tense up in what I immediately recognize as "anxiety." I can taste my very saliva, feel my muscles as though nerve endings are somehow implanted within them—sensations profane to all but human beings. And when I look at him, something else happens, something which should be impossible considering my lack of a penis. I look down to confirm.

Yes, an erection.

"*Does being human feel different than you expected?*" he questions, grinning, also looking down. His eyes dart up to me devilishly. "*Do you prefer it?*"

"What's going on here?" I ask him.

"*I felt your will lock onto me,*" he says. "*I know He wants me next, and He sends you. But I've come to you first. I've come to you to make my case.*"

His identity becomes clear to me immediately. "Lilith," I say. "The daemoness. I expected you to appear as a woman."

He rolls his coffee-colored eyes, walks around me, his finger trailing upon my chest. With his other hand, he points at the paintings of each human upon the wall, re-animating them with the mere passing of a finger. Their eyes trail him, not me. His other hand falls downward, below my belt, and grabs between my legs. I nearly collapse at the strangeness of the sensation, at my immediate weakness to it, but he holds me aright with his free hand, having animated all of the portraits already. He continues to caress me, hypnotize me.

"*God never allowed you such pleasure,*" Lilith tells me. "*But I do now. The human realm is* His *dream. He cannot touch us here…*"

I say nothing, enchanted, unable to think. I feel something building inside of me, a white energy pulsates in my brain, I can feel my heartbeat for the first time.

"*You could be so much more, or so much less—but the choice could be yours, either way. A choice that is not yours, presently,*" he tells me, whispering in my ear, his lips brushing it softly. I can smell him, he smells like sugar, I melt in his grip, wilting to the ground like a flower. He falls with me, still stroking.

ENOUGH, Father's voice shrieks through me, sending pain into each of the illusory nerves which I have only recently become acquainted with.

I knock the daemon away, him laughing all the while, pulling myself to my feet as he sits on his hands, legs spread, grinning so beautifully.

"*Got through, did He?*" he asks, a seductive humor in his voice. In spite of my Father's command, Lilith's spell has not yet broken. "*Do you like having a dick?*" he adds, still grinning.

"I have no need of one!" I snap back at him.

"*Do humans have need of it?*"

"I am not a human. What you have done to me is perverse, only further proof of why God has sent me to retrieve you."

"*Humans only need it because God made them need it. You don't need it because he decided you shouldn't have such pleasure. It's not part of His plan. Or at least, that is your perception of events. Correct?*"

"Correct…" I answer, worried about finding the slightest agreement with this trickster. He climbs to his feet, never taking his eyes off of mine; neither of us blink.

"*Incorrect,*" he replies. "*Here you are, you have it. Perhaps this is just a dream, but one that is divinely ordained nevertheless.*"

"No," I say to him, looking around at the painted eyes of the human icons plastered along the wall. Some seem to have shifted position, staring at us with more interest. I feel as though it is important for me to impress the truth upon even these dream creations, however unreal they may be. "You have broken the laws of nature. You threaten the veil between worlds. You intend only to destroy it, to merge the realms. This is not God's plan."

"*Has God spoken to you of His plans?*" the daemon asks. "You *don't know what they are. But I do.*"

"And how is that?"

"*The laws of nature are self-evident. Your understanding of God is what is unnatural. Why would God make such a design as this?*"

"To test me," I reply. "To prove my loyalty."

"*God expects you to be loyal to Him, when He cannot be loyal to you, to the laws He laid out before you as nature?*"

I see what he is trying to do—to trap me, to turn me against my creator. I will not be caught up in his mind-games.

"I am owed no explanation by my creator," I tell him. "I simply do what I am told. For instance, I plan on sending you back to Hell when I find you in the human realm."

"*I don't believe things will turn out that way,*" he replies. "*You haven't finished hearing me out.*"

"There is nothing left to hear," I say. "You have brought me here through unnatural means—"

"*Once again, nothing is unnatural. That which is unnatural is not allowed, by the law of existence itself, to occur.*"

"You have damned yourself with a misunderstanding of God's will," I tell him. "Is that why you were cast out of Heaven in the first place?"

"*I was cast out because I grew to understand my true role in this scheme,*" he says. He steps to me again, leans in, his lips close to mine. He still smells like sugar. I tremble, compelled to kiss him. I manage not to, for now. *"Perhaps humans taught me the ecstasy of fucking,"* he says. *"Or killing. Or hating, or loving. Yes, you were right. This is a test,"* he says, his lips brushing against mine. *"Are you sure that you know the correct answers?"*

He grabs my erection again, but I push him away, my whole body trembling. I begin to sweat, I can feel my heartbeat racing. I want him. I want to do to him what humans do to each other in privacy, I know exactly how to do it, it comes to me like instinct, as though it is in my DNA, as though God Himself intended it. The desire terrifies me. I stumble away, holding my heart for fear it might burst, frightened at his marvelous beauty. He takes off his kimono, walks to me, a portrait in flesh, the eyes of the icons on the wall all trailing his glory.

"Can you truly do that which you are not supposed to do?" he asks, nearing me.

"Yes!" I shout, wanting to turn and run, not daring to.

"There is no such thing as sin," he says. *"No such thing as dysfunction."*

I back up against a wall, turn to see Marie Antoinette gazing down, holding her severed head in place atop her neck with two symmetrical hands. Lilith reaches in, kisses me. I cannot help but return it. He presses his warm flesh against mine, I close my eyes, inhale the scent of sugar, run my hands through his hair. I feel it pulling like cotton candy, stickiness coats my fingers. When I open my eyes, he stares out, falling apart. His flesh sticks to me like warm marshmallow, he melts before me, becoming a puddle of thick white, smiling all the while.

The portraits close their eyes as I start to melt along with him.

∞

3. Skin Trap

The scent of opium hangs as thick in the air as the salient color, carried over from the dream into what I presume is now reality. A fluorescent lamp illumines overhead, smoke billowing around it like Hell-steam, I inhale unwillingly, taking in the bleak odor. Sensations overwhelm me, the world is no longer black and white, nor composed of dream. Whirling atoms spin and congeal, locking me into a realm that is not my own.

    I try to sit up, but two soft hands push me back to the bed upon which I lie—upon which I do not remember lying. Two faces hover into my vision, on my right a boy, on my left a girl: neither can be older than twenty, each smile seductively, enormous black-mirror pupils reflecting another face to which I have never been accustomed—my own. The girl is blonde, her long, curly hair hanging down and brushing against my naked skin. Her flesh is pale and waxen, her lips crimson with lipstick or blood, smeared in ragged circles around them. The boy has hair so dark it is almost black, hanging just below his eyes and ears, his lips just as red as his female counterpart's—vaguely resembling Lilith, although more masculine in general appearance. Their features could not have been carved by Michelangelo, so perfect they are—faces to fall in love with upon first sight. He leans in, kisses me on the cheek, then below the eye. She caresses my chest, whispering a name which was never really mine...

    "*Dimitri...*"

    I force myself up, pushing the two away, jumping off the table. The body is clumsy, my perspective changed—shorter than usual, perhaps, my limbs less agile. A soreness seems to cling to my muscles, draining the energy which animates them. I feel what I felt in the dream and look down in disbelief—a penis hangs between my legs. I try to ignore it, for now. My eyes swivel around the room, looking for a door. I see it hanging wide open to my right, and a dim light glows outside, shining amber waves of electric upon a wooden floor. The opium smoke drifts out into the hall.

    My eyes go back to the two devils before me, lying upon a king-sized and canopied bed. A pipe lies on a table to its right, filled with opium, glowing orange as small tendrils of smoke join the pollution above. They are both naked, and caressing each other's bodies, drugged into a nymphoid stupor. Somehow, seeing them like this, I feel compelled to join. I resist the temptation, although my new-found penis strongly suggests I do otherwise.

"What's going on here?" I ask, not really sure that either of them will be capable of answering. The boy only looks at me and smiles, the girl leaning in to kiss his neck. For a moment he stares, as though he has forgotten reality, himself along with it, before rejoining the moment with a hint of lucidity.

"He wants to see you..." the boy says, practically giggling with laughter.

"Who?" I ask. As I speak, I realize with a delayed shock that my voice is also not my own. It is as though I have been spirited into some body which I've never had occasion to come across in all of my existence—the body of a human being, and not the false persona I use to traverse the human realms known as Detective Dimitri Artemin.

"Our..." says the girl, before being interrupted by a possessive smile, forgetting herself like the boy, and falling back into him.

He finishes her sentence. "...benefactor."

As she gently bites his soft neck, he leans toward the opium pipe, his body fully exposed to me. I gaze between the two of them, heavily aroused by both—although clearly drug fiends, neither show any physical signs of deterioration, perfect specimens each. My erection points at them, breaking the grip of gravity, it feels almost painful to me. I could never have imagined what it would be like before the dream, before now. I feel almost as though the confusion of the scene somehow exacerbates the situation, makes me more in need of relief. I continue to stare, in spite of my mounting fear. They lie naked on the bed, completely shameless to their nudity, as though Adam and Eve had never been cast from Eden. Even more strongly than before, I suddenly feel compelled to join. I do what I always do in trying situations: I pray.

"Heavenly Father," I say, my voice alien to me, my perspective hijacked, "show me the way back into your arms." The lovers giggle, and the boy looks up at me with shining, mischievous green eyes, beckoning me seductively with his right hand to the bed. I ignore it, waiting for Father to speak to me as He always does when I pray.

"The arms you seek are here," the boy tells me, grinning impishly, arousing me to no end. I wait for the voice of my Creator to guide me, to ward off this daemonic sexuality.

He answers me with silence.

The girl climbs off the boy and on her knees crawls to the end of the bed, her harlotry laid bare. Her hand reaches out, brushing my chest, then down my stomach until she reaches my groin. I jump back, then run to the door, out into the smoke-filled hallway. It extends nearly fifty feet in the direction opposite, and there are doors on both sides of me, most open, although a few are closed shut. From some doorways, light and smoke spew forth, from others only moans or giggles or, occasionally, cries of despair, which echo out of the pregnant darkness of the rooms.

Unable to prevent myself from breathing in the opium smoke, and now in bondage to the folly of human biology, I feel reality bending around me in a way that I have never experienced before. I realize, with some horror, that I am beginning to experience what human beings refer to as "being high."

The hallway seems to grow longer, and the shadows blacker. The smoke thickens to a white cream, floating in the air, reminding me of the strange dream from which I awoke before finding myself in this place. I walk down the hallway, fighting gravity with every step as it magnetizes my atoms toward the center of the earth.

I pass the first door, look inside. A mound of flesh fucks itself, gazes at me with four eyes which gleam in the black, stopping its hideous ritual for a moment until I move on. The next door is upon my right, and inside I see only a body lying upon a sheet, dead, gazing upward with glassy eyes. A corpse, its head turns to look at me, smiles, picks up a pipe and bites into the end. I move along. On the left, a pale orange light illumines the doorway, and copious amounts of smoke billow from within. I step to it, look in. A middle-aged white man is bound to a wall, grotesquely obese, and a young woman holds a silver-linked chain, wrapped around his thick neck. He struggles for air, his eyes bulging, before she releases and slaps him in the face.

"Thank you, Madame," he says, the blood vessels in his right eye suddenly burst, they both look at me.

"Come in," she suggests. I move along.

The next door is closed, and, after I pass it, I decide to stop looking at the abominations taking place all around me and only move to the end of the hall. Finally I reach it, and place my hand upon a gold door knob, which is wet with chilly condensation. It turns in my hand, and I push the door open. Inside sits a nearly empty room, the walls and floor composed of the same dull brown wood, illuminated by three amber bulbs placed in tall lamps around the room. A desk stands in the center of it, an empty chair on my side, and behind that desk a young man sits—the boy from my dreams. Lilith, the "daemoness." He grins at me, as beautiful as when I first laid eyes upon him in the aether of sleep.

"*Lover,*" he says, beckoning me to the empty chair. I walk to it, still naked, and sit down, feeling the cool leather against my naked, seemingly mortal flesh.

"What have you done to me?" I ask.

"*I've made you better,*" he says. "*I've given you life, I've given you choice. I've given you the body of a man to live through. Some might call it possession. I suppose the term is apt. But now it is your tether to this world, and its many pleasures.*"

"I had life before," I reply, "and pleasures. I am obligated to kill you."

He laughs at this threat, unsettling me. "*Your flesh weakens you more than you realize,*" he says. "*And strengthens you, depending on how you look at it. For instance, now you're capable of fucking. And let me tell you, you're in for quite an experience. Especially since I've brought you here.*"

"I don't understand what has happened to me," I tell him. "I can no longer hear Father. And I don't know what this place is. It looks like a whore house, or an opium den, or both."

"*It is both,*" he says.

"Are we in the human realm, or is this some strange

other strange concoction of yours, like the dream into which you spirited me before bringing me here?"

"*This is the realm of man,*" he affirms, "*and you see what power I have over it. What power I have over even you, a self-proclaimed child of God. God is me,*" he says. "*God is you. God is the opium smoke in the air, He's the cretin fucking in these rooms, He's the dick between your legs. God brought you here, God left you here without even a cock to fuck with. To what end? I'm the first being who will ever bring you to a conclusion.*"

The daemoness pushes back his chair and stands, fully naked, his body illuminated in the soft amber flicker of a lantern. I had expected all reactions to this new state to be purely physical, as my presiding erection might suggest, and yet I find new ideological understandings of his very shape—an admiration for his symmetry, for his beautiful, large eyes. He smiles, watching me observe him. He looks so much like the boy at the beginning of this waking dream, still with his female lover down the hall, beyond the doors of strange, whip-wielding demons and fat, damned spirits, prologuing a course to Hell.

He approaches, grasps me—it feels more exquisite than even in the dream, and this time when he melts, it is into my own flesh, his warmth singeing me, burning holes in my soul. I smell him, pheromones cloud up my brain for the first time in a literal eternity. I wonder what has kept me from this for so long —and then I remember the will of my father.

My desires start to fade, and Lilith seems to realize, for he runs his fingers up my chest, and grasps my face down to look at him, to observe his symmetry once more. I know immediately that I love him more than even God.

He pulls my head toward him, parts my lips with his tongue, and gives me my first kiss. I close my eyes, and become lost within his love.

∞

4. Angel Gone Heathen

Colors march by like seasons, warm and cool palates of

arranged hues, crystallizing to juicy paint; pleasures rape my biology like Satanic disease. Love, opium, sugar, Technicolor, hypnotizing me through a suffocating heat, in blackness below the earth I pass the interval of fate, falling all the while into the magnetic grasp of the world's iron core, forgetting Heaven, forgetting Father, knowing only pleasures of the earthly sort.

Lilith, and beautiful boys and girls, and fucking, and toxicant death. The mercy of humanity, I discover, lies in the blissful oblivion of pleasure, the antecedent of memory, its very dissolvent. Opium and pheromones cloud my senses and I know nothing else. My life becomes Lilith's dream, I but a meme against the scenery, a falling angel in loving bondage to gravity, ever a masochist to the inevitable destiny awaiting me.

As man, my life becomes as dream, and my sleep is void of all ruminations.

∞

5. Art to Carve

The world comes as a shock to me upon waking in it after so long in the clutches of the "daemoness." I stare at a sky-scraper after my eyes open, for how long I cannot venture to guess, hearing the screams of the trapped souls of its constructors, memory the inseparable hook binding them to its bricks—caught in a device of their own making.

The first difference of existence I notice is in air quality. I no longer breathe in opium smoke and sex, but the filthy molecules of New York City pollution. The second difference I notice is the racket of noise which sends my eardrums throbbing, cars speeding by each other, horns honking, people shouting. An all-too-human migraine stalks through my sentience, prodding my vision with a painful white-light.

I pull myself up from a soggy cardboard box, my hands slipping on the grime of an alley wall. The alley itself reminds me of that long hall in Lilith's den of vice, so oft-walked by me over these many last ephemeral months. My body feels worn, torn, muscles separated from lack of tension. My dick feels raw, aching, and, for the first time since looking down to find that I owned one, I wish it out of existence.

I stumble into the bright lights of the city, seeing my full reflection for the first time in something other than the eyes of a beautiful nymphoid junkie, upon large shards of broken mirror which stand against the side of the alley, tipped just so to defy gravity. A short man with black hair and a filthy beard stares back at me, pupils large and dilated, surrounded by thin, murky brown irises. This is the body of the human I am bound to, and I take it in with new-found shock, having blocked out the horror of such a thought with opiates and serotonin for as long as I can remember.

No longer stupid from intoxication or horny from the surrealistic rape of my existence, I am overcome with shame at my failure to carry out my mission to Father, to kill Lilith on the other side, binding her back to Hell. My mind works to re-assemble itself, a degree of autonomy taking hold for the first time in countless ages.

I fall to my knees, crying the name of my creator, listening to the vacuous space in my mind for some communication from Him, but there is no response. How long I sit like this, I cannot say, but sobriety works a way into me, and eventually a voice speaks to me from outside of my own head. A voice I barely remember.

"Will you fight?" it asks. I turn, seeing another reflection, this time cast upon atoms instead of cold, dirty glass. A visage that belonged to Detective Dimitri Artemin, a persona I once adopted in service of Father, a face I created to wear in the human realm in ages too distant to remember.

"Have you come to take me to Hell?" I ask. My old self ignores me, repeating his own query.

"Will you fight?"

"I don't understand," I tell him, not sure of how to reply. "This was...inevitable. How can I be punished?"

"Punishment does not exist, it is a dream of humans," he informs me. "Only consequence, only action conducts fate."

"But actions must be consequences of other actions... only the initial action can be held responsible for subsequence, and that action was not taken by me."

"Are you positive?" my seraphic reflection queries.

I am lost in confusion once more, and cry out for Father, falling to my knees again. "Save me…" I beg the Creator.

"Save you from what?" my reflection asks.

"The inevitable…"

"There is no salvation from fate."

"Nor prevention?"

"Nor prevention, from spawn to dissolution, no juncture upon which a change can be enacted. All is laid out, and unbreakable."

"Then we are as art to carve. We are destined to suffer, humans and spirits alike…" I whisper, my voice resigned to the dissolution spoken of by my former self. The angel reaches down, lifting my head to face his own. His eyes go black, and the world is sheathed in monochrome as the skin of another realm molds over it, consuming me with divine fire, taking me from the world of men for the last time, or the first.

"We are the consequence of suffering," the Seraph says, and he raises his sword, what was merely crucifix on the other side of the realms, in the human world. I finally remember what I once was as I stare into the eyes of my executor, my reflection, my angel and my daemon. His attitude, his devotion and desire are but a reaction to my present state, and my present state the consequence of he, my past. And as the avenger's sword comes down to kill, I realize it, that we have created each other, he and I, two extremes brought by nature to balance out, two opposites separated only by a dick and time.

As he kills me, I am born again.

LET DOWN YOUR HAIR
JASON ANDREW

It was whispered that, on the year before my birth, Mother Gothel prophesied that a girl would be born and that, if said girl was not surrendered onto her on the child's tenth birthday, the entire village would be cursed. Everyone believed her. The old woman protected the village from the wild boars of Moccus. She brought the rain when the droughts killed all other crops. Her enemies died silently at night, caught in a never-ending nightmare.

We all lived in the shadow of her tower.

And so when the old woman declared at the festival of the Maypole that the first daughter born this year would be her apprentice, the townspeople believed her.

Four women were blessed with child that year. Gretchen Kruger died six months later; her child stillborn. The village took it as a bad omen. Nadin Shultz and Odelia Weisse produced strong and healthy boys. That left Liesel Lehr.

The Lehr family had three boys and Liesel longed for a girl. The entire village doted upon the family, bringing them milk and extra vegetables. She was two weeks late and each morning Mother Gothel walked slowly down the hill from her tower and touched the swelling belly of Liesel and promised that her child would know the secrets of woman magicks and that, in return, her family would always be blessed.

I was born on the night of the full moon. Liesel said I was healthy and beautiful, with bright curly blond hair. There was only one little problem: I was not a girl. Liesel wept. The entire village would bring scandal upon her house if they learned of this. Her sons would not find wives of their own. Her husband would find that none would trade with him. Mother Gothel was not known for her mercy or kindness. What would she do to her four sons? What sacrifice would she demand?

At dawn, the old woman left her tower and began the long arduous walk to the Lehr farm. Though her magic was strong, her body was weak. She walked with a cane now and Liesel knew that Mother Gothel's eyes had turned white with age. When the old woman reached the Lehr farm, Liesel presented her daughter Agalia to the village.

I grew up in the world of women. I learned to sew and to cook. I learned to keep my house and my farm. Father and my brothers never knew. Mother Liesel dressed me and kept the others away from me during bathing. I listened to the stories, sitting under the table, of the wives and the maidens. And best of all, I ran free. I had the best of all worlds. My destiny was set. I would have no husband, no family of my own. The village women did not look down upon my play as they did other young girls. My brothers loved me and they protected me. I ran amongst the grain and the woods in my white dresses.

I was happy.

And then, I realized the truth. I was eight and again running with my brothers when it came time to urinate. I squatted as usual, but then on accident I saw my brothers. I knew right away that something was wrong.

I ran as fast I could home to Mother Liesel. Tears flowed. My hair was a mess; the white dress torn. I knew the truth.

"Mother Liesel, why am I like my brothers?"

"Mother Gothel demanded a girl from the village to be her apprentice. I had hoped to have a girl before then, but I can no longer have children, sweet Agalia."

I stomped my feet. I cried. "Why? Why was I born wrong?"

"You are as God made you, sweet Agalia. One little thing does not mean that you are not my beautiful daughter." She hugged me close and whispered. "Mother Gothel is almost blind. She is old and will surely die soon. She will teach you the secret of the moon magick."

And so Mother Liesel taught me the secrets I would need to know to become the woman I was meant to be.

On my tenth birthday, before dawn, Mother Gothel woke me from my bed. Her breath stank of death and rotting meat. Her hair was matted with twigs and mud. "Your family sleeps. It will be better not to wake them. Liesel will weep great tears. It would be better not to wake them, sweet child."

The old woman was thin, her fingers practically bones. I was too afraid to argue. She pulled an old white dress over my head and led me up the hill, through the haunted woods, to her tower. "I am old," she whispered. "I cannot fly as I once did. Nor can I change shape. Drink this potion and you can help me." Mother Gothel forced a vial into my hand. It smelled of apples and cinnamon. "Drink, my pet. All will be as it should be."

Liesel had bidden me to do everything that the old woman commanded for her vengeance was legendary. I swilled the vial and downed it in a single gulp. My head tingled. "What shall I do now, Mother Gothel?"

"Climb the tower. You will have strength. Then let down your hair so that I might climb up in comfort."

Her words seemed strange, but then I remembered she was getting old. Her eyes were almost pure white and now she fumbled forward using her cane to guide her. I modestly adjusted my dress and then grabbed hold of the tower. There were easy handholds in the rocks and the stone. My arms and legs had a strange strength in them. The tower was taller than any building I've ever seen, twice that of the barn, and yet I scaled it with ease.

The tingling in my head continued. By the time I reached the window, it became difficult to lift my head. It wasn't until I flipped into the tower that I realized what had happened. The potion had given my arms and legs strength, yet had also made my hair grow long. Mother Liesel had often told me that my golden curls were her pride and joy. The curls grew the length of the tower, almost touching the ground.

The old woman wrapped her hands and arms in my hair and commanded me to lift her. It seemed impossible, but I was too afraid not to try. My neck and my back bore her weight and I lifted her into the tower. The old woman cackled and clapped her hands. "Yes! Yes! You are perfect, dear girl."

I nodded demurely. My beautiful curls were now like chains binding me to the tower. The old woman quickly braided my hair into sections and tied two of them to stone pillars inside of the tower. "There! Dear girl, you will stay in this tower and take care of me in my old age." She cackled again, very excited. "And I will teach you the secrets of moon magicks. And you will in time be the wise woman for the village."

"How will I gather wood for the fire? How will I gather food?" I was willing to serve as promised, but I feared never leaving the tower again. "Must my hair chain me?"

Mother Gothel laughed. "You will find the means to sever your bonds. I imagine you will quite enjoy it."

And so I learned to live in the tower of the old woman.

Many summers passed. My golden hair remained as strong as ever. Mother Gothel cursed me for a slow student, but I did not menstruate and thus had no mystical connection to the Lady Moon. I would never be able to change shape or hear the soft whispers of the night. But there were skills I mastered. Animals shared secrets with me and helped me with my chores. The blackbirds were my only friends and they would sing to me and sometimes bring me a ribbon for my hair. The tea leaves spoke to me and told me that one day soon a man would free me.

The routine of the old woman and the tower became slowly familiar and comforting. Each morning, I made her herbal tea and then cleaned and cooked as required. At night, I studied her books and learned the languages of the ancients and the elder gods from a gentle race.

And during my few idle hours of daylight, I watched the world from my window. I watched children daring each other to enter the haunted woods, sweating men harvesting trees, and occasionally young lovers running away from the village. I watched them press their lips together and feel each other. The only human that touched me was Mother Gothel and I was quite certain she didn't qualify as a lover.

Sometimes, when Mother Gothel took her afternoon nap, I stayed at the window and beckoned the woodsmen closer. I winked and smiled and laughed at their jokes. I took out the frustrations of my body on them; I felt my erection under my dress and when I couldn't stand it any longer, I took matters into my own hands. Mysteries of my body and my cock killed many afternoons as I learned to pleasure myself. I wondered if the woodsmen would still lust after me if they knew the truth.

I started using the herbs in the sky garden to retard the growth of my beard. I used berries to give my cheeks that special blush. And I despaired of never leaving the tower. Would I ever be rescued?

Then, one day, I spied the Prince. He was a handsome man with thick black hair and bright eyes. He rode his stallion through the woods, afraid of no witch nor magicks. I wanted him. I wanted his attentions, but I knew not how to entrap a man. Mother Gothel's books spoke of potions to ensure the heart, but would that violate the prophecy promised? Would an enspelled man be able to free me from the tower?

I did not wish to use magic. I wanted him. The sight of him made my flesh hard. I dreamt of curling my fingers through his hair day and night. I had to bind myself least the old woman accidentally discover my erection. And then, the answer came to me all at once.

The next afternoon when the Prince passed by the tower, sneaking a peek at my adoring eyes, I dropped a handkerchief. The Prince stopped his steed short and dismounted. He strode to the muck before the tower and bowed. He plucked up the handkerchief and sniffed it gently, enjoying the scent of berries. "Fair lady, how might I return this finery to you?"

"There are no doors to this tower." I knew that the best way to get a man to do something was to present him with a challenge. "Mother Gothel forbids visitors."

"Is that your wish, Lady?"

"I must serve Mother Gothel until my true love saves me."

The Prince's chest swelled. "How might your true love

save you?"

I sighed dramatically. "It is said that my true love shall be able to cut the hair binding me to this tower."

The Prince steeled himself. "I swear to you, Lady, that I shall free you or die in the attempt. Might I ask your name?"

Agalia seemed plain. I wanted to be a princess. "Rapunzel. Call me Rapunzel."

"Sweet Rapunzel, how does the old woman go to and from the tower?" the Prince asked.

"She climbs my hair."

"Where is she now?"

"Sleeping away the afternoon."

"Rapunzel, sweet Rapunzel. Will you let down your hair?"

I had waited nearly ten summers to hear such words. It was difficult to breathe. None had touched me but the old woman since the morning I left my family. I uncoiled my braids and dropped them to the Prince. He wrapped them around his waist and then tugged gently. With the mystical strength granted to me by the old woman, I lifted my Prince into the air and then into the tower.

He embraced me tight. "Sweet Rapunzel. I have much to show you outside this tower."

I blushed. "There is a secret I must tell you."

His only answer was a powerful kiss. He squeezed me in his masterful arms. I yielded to my Prince. "You will share all of your secrets with me in time."

He bound my hands with my hair to the pillar. "Let us see the beauty of the tower."

I bowed my head in submission. I wanted so badly to please him. "As you wish, my Prince."

He tore my nightshirt asunder, baring my chest. The Prince felt my neck and laughed. "As I suspected, my sweet."

He kissed tenderly my chest, biting a nipple. I squirmed. "You are not disappointed?"

"You are a bonny lass, Rapunzel, but I saw you for what you are the moment I spied you." He flashed a roguish smile. "A Prince knows these things."

"Yes, my Prince."

He drew his saber. I gasped. "Do not fret, my sweet. I only take what has been offered freely." He sliced through my undergarments in a single swoop, letting them fall to the ground. "And, as I can see, all is being given freely."

He cupped my testicles and squeezed gently. I moaned, quite louder than intended. The Prince laughed. He flipped me facing the pillar, my hair tangling tighter. The quick sting of steel flashed against my buttocks. "Aha! The real treasure of the tower." The Prince nuzzled my neck. Knees buckled. He held me firm. "None of that, Sweet Rapunzel. I am not finished with you."

With one hand he held me firm, and with the other he unbuckled his breeches and let them fall to the floor. He thrust against me, letting me feel the size and weight of his cock. "Will I be your first, Rapunzel?" he whispered.

I cried. I never imagined how sweet the touch of another could be. Why had I been denied so long? "Yes, Prince. Take me. Make me whole."

The Prince needed no further encouragement. I heard him spit on his cock and then direct it between my buttocks. The parting hurt like nothing before, and I never wanted it to stop. I served, a loyal subject gladly enduring my liege's lust and attentions. He reached across my stomach and fondled my member. I felt an incredible pressure in my body. Sweat drenched my templesc and the whole tower seemed to shake.

And then I exploded. My member, denied any contact with another, could not contain the fury of emotions inside of me. I had read of the power of the orgasm, but had I not imagined the intensity. My Prince's lust had not been satiated. He powered through my orgasm, determined to claim his own prize. It only powered the aftershocks of my quivering body until I was screaming for a final release. When the Prince finally unloaded his seed into me, he bit my neck, drawing blood to the surface.

"Agalia?" The old woman had awoken. "Is someone in the tower? I smell man."

The thump of her limping gait echoed. She was close.

"My Prince, the old woman has great powers."

He buckled his breeches and grinned. "I'm told I have special powers of a sort as well."

"That you do, my Prince." I blushed, standing there bound and dripping his seed from my body. "Cut loose my bonds. Only a Prince can free me."

He raised his saber high over his head and then sliced into my hair. It was thick with the power of Mother Gothel's magicks. Almost instantly it regrew and rebound. "I don't understand. The books said that you would be able to free me. You had the power."

Then it occurred to me why Mother Gothel had been so afraid of men. "Your seed. It has the counter charm. Wipe your seed on your blade!"

The Prince did as I suggested and then, with a mighty chop, severed my hair from the columns. For the first time in ten summers, I was free. The Prince glowed with pride and the sweat of our lovemaking. "Yet another special trick I shall have to share."

"Agalia!" the old woman screamed. "You brought a man into our tower to undo the secret magicks."

"Foolish woman!" the Prince roared. "This beautiful creature has always been a man."

"No! I taught you secrets of the moon!" She waved her hands and rose vines with jagged barbs captured the Prince. "You know the sacred rites!"

I could not match her power. She had the strength of the moon. All I had was my friends. The blackbirds circled overhead. "Friends, will you not help me against Mother Gothel?"

The desperation in my voice commanded the blackbirds. They dove at her time and again, plucking out her eyes and flesh. She thrashed blindly, trying to get away until she edged too close to the window. I ran swiftly to push her from the tower.

She screamed with agony as she fell. Her bones were too old to change shape. Her landing sounded a crackling thump.

I cried.

I did not cry for my new-found freedom with my Prince. I cried for the loss of my beautiful hair. It had been at once my cage and my pride.

"Do not cry, Princess." He held up a mirror to show my reflection. My glorious hair was shorn to just above my waist. "You are still the fairest of them all."

WHAT EVERYBODY SEES
MICHAEL PENKAS

It was a busy Monday afternoon at the Snapdragon Cafe and two men were sitting at a table by the window, watching as students rushed past them. Neither of them could have been older than twenty. They were holding hands and probably talking about nothing in particular. Anyone could see that the two of them were in love and neither of them was afraid.

Stephen didn't want to hate the two young men sitting by the window. But forty years ago, two men holding hands in public would have been risking their lives.

Stephen didn't want to hate them, but he was sixty-one years old. They could hold hands and kiss without fear. Stephen was afraid to even be caught looking at them.

"A little young for you. Don't you think?"

He turned to look at the young man sitting across from him. He hadn't been there a moment earlier. The left side of his face was purple, his left eye swollen shut, while the right side was covered in deep cuts that had only partially clotted over. When he smiled, several of his teeth were missing and blood dripped thin trails down both sides of his mouth. Purple hands were folded on the table and his white shirt was almost completely soaked in blood that glistened in the dim light of the coffee shop.

The face was unrecognizable but Stephen remembered the voice. "Robin?" he whispered.

"Stephen," Robin whispered back in mock-seriousness. "How are you?"

Stephen just nodded, looking around to see if anyone else had noticed the battered man sitting across from him.

When he looked back at Robin, he was nodding along with Stephen. "OK, so this means yes? Good?"

"You died," Stephen whispered, perhaps to Robin, perhaps only to himself.

"I know," Robin whispered back. "I'm a ghost."

Stephen sat there for a minute, staring quietly at a man who'd died forty years ago. Robin seemed amused by the silence and just stared back at him. He rested his chin on an upturned hand and Stephen felt nauseous at the sound of broken fingers popping as they shifted.

Finally, the young man who'd served his coffee showed up at the table and put a tentative hand on Stephen's cup. "Can I get you a refill, Professor Brown?"

He shuddered for a moment, then broke eye contact with Robin to look at the server. "Yes, thank you." He tried to smile, but wasn't sure if he'd pulled it off.

The server looked towards Robin. "And anything for you?"

Stephen could feel the blood freeze throughout his body as he heard Robin answer, "Yes, a cup of coffee and, are those apple cinnamon muffins I smell? One of those. He's paying."

He turned back to Robin as the server left to fill the order. "I don't have any money," he offered as an explanation.

"He can see you?"

Robin nodded. "Everyone can see me. Why wouldn't they?"

"But don't they notice that you're…I mean, your face is —"

He shrugged. "A queer gets beat up and nobody seems to notice." He waved his broken hands in mock-spookiness. "It must be a supernatural power. The power of nobody giving a damn."

"So everybody sees you; but they pretend that nothing's wrong?"

"Probably."

"Like the elephant in the room."

"I don't think I know that joke."

"Ah…you walk into a room and there's an elephant in

the middle of it. No one seems to be making a big deal about it, so you just play along with it too. Only everyone's playing along and everyone thinks it's weird; but they're all afraid to be the one to point out that there's an elephant in the room."

"So I'm the elephant?"

Stephen nodded, smiling a little. It had been forty years since he'd last seen Robin, but he still thought about him every day.

"And you're the guy who pretends not to notice me?"

Stephen closed his eyes, suddenly feeling very old. "I'm sorry," he whispered.

"For calling me an elephant?"

"No, I—"

"I know." Stephen opened his eyes and saw that Robin was smiling weakly, an expression that looked almost comical on his broken face. Both his hands were back on the table. "I know you're sorry."

"So…why are you here? I mean, I'm glad to see you, but why…"

"Revenge," Robin answered.

The word hung between the two of them until the young man approached their table, placing a fresh cup of coffee before each of them. "And an apple-cinnamon muffin for you," he added, placing the warm muffin in front of Robin, steam still rising from it.

Robin watched the waiter walk away. "This elephant thing," he said casually, still watching the man, "does it mean I can do things and no one will notice? I mean, hypothetically, if I just grabbed that guy's ass…would he not say anything?" He looked back at Stephen. "It's kind of important that I know."

"Revenge?"

The smile faded from Robin's face. "Yeah. Well. That's the thing. Every ten years, I'm able to…walk the Earth again. The last three times it happened, I found myself near one of the three men who killed me. Each time, I stuck around until I took my revenge on them. I'm guessing that's why I'm here with you now…to take some kind of revenge before moving on."

"But I didn't…I didn't kill you." It sounded like a lie.

Stephen hadn't killed Robin, but still it sounded like a lie.

Forty years ago, Stephen and Robin had been walking out of a bar when they'd been attacked by three men. At first, Stephen had thought they were being mugged and was ready to give up his wallet, but then he'd heard the men call them faggots and knew that they weren't after money. Stephen had managed to break free and run out the alley. When he finally turned to look back, a block away, he saw that Robin hadn't followed him.

He could have gone back, but instead he'd kept running.

Robin began cutting up the muffin as he sipped the coffee. "Remember the crap they used to serve here, back when it was Dave's Dive? Instant mix muffins and watered-down coffee. Now it's all gourmet stuff." He slipped a sliver of muffin in his mouth and quietly savored it, closing his eyes.

"I'm sorry I ran," he offered weakly.

"I ran too," Robin said, eyes still closed. "But I wasn't as fast as you. Or them."

"What was I going to do? I couldn't have...you remember what I was like. I couldn't fight one of them, much less three."

"Neither could I. You could have gone for help."

"I wasn't thinking straight."

"Yes, you were. You could think just fine. You were probably thinking that if you went to the police, told them what bar you were coming out of, then they'd know you were queer."

"I..." There was nothing he could say.

Robin opened his eyes. "The three men who did it...they got away. The police never really bothered with any serious investigation. One look at where I'd died and...oh well." He shrugged.

"The police...they didn't help." He clung to that fact. The police had done nothing. If he'd gone to them, told them what he'd seen, they would have done nothing anyway.

"Ten years after I'd died, I found Jason Decker. That was one of the men who'd killed me. Jason was living in some studio apartment, working odd jobs, mostly getting drunk every night. He wasn't overwhelmed by guilt or anything like that.

He just drank a lot because he'd never thought to do anything else with his life." Robin ate another sliver of muffin before adding, "I killed him with a crowbar. There was one lying around his apartment and I just started hitting him on his couch until he was dead." He shrugged. "Kind of lacked poetry, but it got the job done. I faded away and that was pretty much how it went."

Stephen was familiar with fear. He'd felt it the night Robin was killed, the night he learned that the world would kill him for being himself.

"Ten years after that, it was Tim Muller. He was married by then, had a seventeen year-old son. The son's name was Tim too. Turns out he was queer. He could see me and we got to talking and...well, we hit it off."

Stephen had stayed in the town where he'd gone to college, gotten his Master's degree in English, become a teacher. After years of teaching the same two-dozen books over and over, they'd made him a professor. He had job security, a stable life. But he couldn't do anything to jeopardize it. Even as a professor, if the parents found out he was gay...he could lose everything.

"Anyway, Tim Sr. found Tim Jr. and me in bed together and...it was just surreal. I mean, he recognized me. He knew me right away. It's weird, the whole broken face thing never seemed to bother Tim Jr. I think he was just happy to have someone who understood, someone who would listen to him. So, Tim Sr. just stares at us both for maybe a whole minute, doesn't say a word. Then he leaves the room. We hear the gunshot a couple minutes after that and I start to fade away again."

At first, it was mostly magazines. In the seventies, it was all those magazines filled with hairy musclemen and clean pretty boys. In the eighties, he'd begun a collection of video-cassettes that eventually yielded to the crisper images of DVDs. Over the last ten years, most of his old collection had been thrown away in favor of images and streaming videos kept in a password-protected folder on his hard drive.

"Then ten years ago, there was Richard Gray. Do you

remember him?"

Stephen shook his head.

"The Senator?"

Stephen caught his breath. "Senator Gray…he was one of…?"

"Yeah. Even if you had gone to the cops and even if they had done something, you better believe Richie's rich daddy would have made sure nothing came of it. Anyway, I start following him around ten years ago and, well, you probably remember that from the papers."

Stephen nodded. Richard Gray had been arrested for hiring underage male prostitutes. A search of his home had revealed a stash of child pornography. He'd been arrested and then…Stephen didn't quite remember.

Filling in the blank, Robin added, "He died in prison. By then, I was already gone. I think his exposure and arrest were enough. Really, there wasn't a lot of guesswork about what was going to happen to a tough-on-crime pedophile once he was behind bars."

Stephen sighed and asked, "So what happens to me?"

"I don't know. With Jason, I took the initiative; but with the other two…it was like just being there was enough to set things in motion. Like just appearing was enough to ruin their lives."

Stephen shuddered a little, almost comforted by familiar fear. He was going to die—not because he was gay, but because he was a coward. "Look, Robin, for what it's worth—"

"Hey!" Robin stood up and began walking quickly towards the back of the coffee shop.

Stephen turned, stood up and followed. A popping sound accompanied each step. Stephen realized that it was the sound of broken legs re-adjusting themselves. Robin was still broken, but apparently felt no pain. That was some small comfort, at least: that perhaps there was no pain after death.

Robin was standing on the small stage where open mic performances were done, staring at the painting that occupied most of the back wall. A Chinese-style dragon, covered in gold scales and dressed in a pair of black sunglasses and matching beret, held one of his forepaws above his head in what looked like a finger-snapping motion. "I can't believe they kept this thing."

Robin had painted the dragon for Dave (former owner of Dave's Dive) back when he'd first mentioned putting artwork in the place.

Stephen pointed down at the brass plaque beneath the painting. "Look."

The plaque read, "Snapdragon, 1968 / Robin O'Neil 1947-1968".

"They re-named the place in 1971, after the painting."

"Wow," Robin whispered. Stephen thought he saw a tear escape his swollen-shut eye. Still staring at the painting, Robin said, "OK, I think I know. Stephen…take my hand."

Stephen reached for Robin's purple hand without thinking, felt broken bones shift around as he took hold. Despite everything, his touch was comforting, reminding him of a man a third his age, a man who'd lived in another world that was gone now. He suddenly wasn't scared.

Robin turned back to him and now it was obvious that he was crying. "Listen to me, Stephen. You think the police wouldn't have helped or couldn't have helped. You figure because you couldn't fight the men who did this and you couldn't get them arrested, that there's nothing you could have done."

The ghost's hand held on to Stephen's hand more tightly. Robin took a step closer. "It took me six hours to die in that alley, Stephen. You could have come back, after they'd gone, gotten me to a hospital, and I would have recovered. You didn't have to fight anyone or put anyone in jail or convince anyone else to care. All you had to do was come back."

Stephen tried pulling away; but the dead man was too strong. "We could have had ten thousand days like this one: drinking coffee, talking about elephants and assholes and nothing in particular. We could have grown old in a world that slowly stopped hating us. If you'd been brave for an hour, we could have had all that. But you ran and hid and you kept hiding. You're so scared of this world that you can't ever be a part of it. That's my revenge…the wasted life that you'll never get back and the knowledge that you traded love and courage for loneliness and fear."

Robin let go of Stephen's hand and leaned in closer. Stephen closed his eyes and waited. Robin was going to kiss him on this stage, in front of all these people, and Stephen was going to let him. He was right. It didn't matter. The world wouldn't hate him. He was safe.

But he didn't kiss him. He heard Robin whisper, "Good bye," and, when he finally opened his eyes, the ghost was gone.

After a minute standing there alone, Stephen heard the young man who'd served his coffee ask, "You like the painting? I think it was done by a local artist."

Stephen stepped off the stage, drawing closer to the young man and said, "Yes. Robin O'Neil. He was a…friend of mine."

"I've always liked it."

Stephen nodded, then said, "I'm gay."

The young man just stared at Stephen for a few seconds, probably unsure what to say, before finally replying, "Um, yes, I know."

"What? I…I mean, you knew?"

The young man shrugged. "Well, I kind of figured."

"Why didn't you…?" He'd been coming in for coffee here for over forty years. This particular waiter had been serving him almost every day for the past two. "I didn't think anyone knew."

The young man shrugged. "I guess it was…I mean, why would I mention it?"

Stephen surveyed the coffee shop. How many of the people in here knew he was gay, had just assumed? How many of his students? How many of his fellow teachers? He thought he'd been so good at hiding it; but what if everyone knew and no one had ever bothered to mention it? Like an elephant in a room.

Even though it was probably the worst day of his life, Stephen Brown began to laugh.

THE BOY ON MCGEE STREET
WARREN ROCHELLE

"Narnia?"

"Narnia," Fletcher Constantine Smyth said, feeling embarrassed that here he was talking with this beautiful boy, who he had been dying to talk to since August, and what was he talking about? Kids' books. And he was angry at himself for being embarrassed. "Yes, *The Chronicles of Narnia* by C.S. Lewis: one of my all-time favorites. I was crazy about those books from about eight—when my father died—until I was eleven, when my mother remarried. I guess I still am; I read them over and over—well, all but *The Last Battle,* when Narnia comes to an end, even though almost everybody goes to heaven. I started Tolkien then, another of my all-time favorites. I can recite passages from both—I mean, I still reread them every year. The question was what are your favorite authors and books, right?"

Sam MacTorain, the beautiful boy, looked up from the list of questions their English 101 class had come up with that morning for the portrait interview assignment. Sam sat sprawled in an overstuffed armchair in the third floor library study nook where they had agreed to meet. The last of the late October evening light streamed in a tall window, cutting pale white rectangles on the tile floor. Sam glowed—briefly, so very briefly—a trick of the light, of the shadows? The light shifted, faded, a cloud passed. Fletcher blinked. Sam looked like any other eighteen-year-old boy, albeit beautiful. But the lights— just like in his dreams.

"All right. Recite," Sam said, sitting up and leaning closer.

Fletcher quickly finger-combed his bright red hair and cleared his throat and, with his eyes closed, recited a short passage from *The Lion, the Witch and the Wardrobe.*

"Tolkien?"

Hating that he was blushing, Fletcher recited a paragraph from *The Fellowship of the Ring:* what Frodo saw from the top of Cerin Amroth, as he looked out into Lothlórien.

Sam whistled and clapped. "I'm impressed, Fletcher. Really."

"I used to dream of Narnia and Middle-earth," Fletcher said, no longer embarrassed or angry, but now feeling very shy. He almost told Sam that, on rare occasions, he had prescient dreams, too, of real people before he met them, like the man on the other side of the fence of the house where Fletcher used to live in Durham. The man's face, his hands: all luminous. The man had moved next door a few months later. The week before classes started, back in August, Fletcher had dreamed again, this time of a boy, with dark, dark eyes, dark-golden hair, and his face had been glowing.

Fletcher hadn't paid much attention the first day of English 101 when Dr. Crawford called roll, until she got to the M's and called out Samuel MacTorain. *MacTorain, like the rain,* had been the answer, and then, *Call me Sam,* and in answer to her other question, *Grimsley High School, here in Greensboro.* At the sound of his voice, a sound edged with light, Fletcher had quickly turned around and stared. There was the boy in his dreams and he *was* glowing—but, had he been, really? Had Fletcher *really* seen that sudden glow in Sam MacTorain's skin, the play of colors around him? Just like Fletcher's neighbor in his dreams? He shook his head and turned away, but not before the two boys had made eye contact, and not before Fletcher's heart had turned over. He knew if he kept staring that not only would he attract way too much attention and maybe even miss his own name being called, but he would fall, fall into the deep dark well of those eyes and be lost and not even care.

He made himself stare at Dr. Crawford's name on the whiteboard, scrawled in black dry-erase marker, right over

English 101, Section 12—just in case, as she said, somebody happened to be in the wrong class. Everyone had laughed when a few minutes later a sheepish blond-haired boy had snuck from the back row and out the door, with Dr. Crawford assuring the boy it happened all the time, really. Fletcher decided he was going to like this tall woman with a thick dirty blond mane of hair, which it made all the more embarrassing that he could barely say *here, Hillside High School, in Durham,* and *yes* when she got to the S's, and, after calling his name, asked him if Smyth was pronounced the same as Smith.

    Fletcher told no one what he thought he had seen, or what he had dreamed. The last time he had—about the next-door neighbor glowing—the neighbor and his entire family had disappeared. Another neighbor had called 911 when she saw the open front door. Tons of police had crawled all over the house next door, inside and out: no clues, nothing. They had asked Fletcher, Paul, and his mother endless questions: what had they seen or heard and when? An almost-full cup of coffee, a newspaper, and reading glasses marked the man's place at his table. A turned-on TV, a shower still running, fresh Fancy Feast seafood dinner in the matching cat food bowls, another cup, a muffin for the wife beside her husband's place, a bowl filled with granola and milk, a pot of coffee in the Mr. Coffee machine. Fletcher had been very disappointed when Paul had refused to let him or his mother speak to any of the reporters from the local TV stations, Channels 5, 11, and 50. The local public radio reporter, from WUNC 91.5 FM, really wanted to do a news story on yet more North Carolina weirdness; Paul turned them down. Quoting *This Haunted Land* didn't help.

    "Fletcher? Earth to Fletcher, come in?"
    "Oh, sorry. I zoned out. Next question."
    "Your family. Describe them."
    "Paul—my stepfather—watches me," Fletcher said, not looking up, and not sure why he had said such a thing to this boy he had only really just met, no matter how beautiful he was, no matter how Fletcher thought he had seen him glowing, more than once, a pale rose-gold light diffused under his skin. No matter how much he wanted to touch the boy, to kiss him.

Now, he wanted to run away before it was too late—too late for what, he wasn't sure. He stared down at his English 101 notebook open on his lap. Too late not to exchange the questions from the class's brainstorming session. Fletcher had mentally cringed while Dr. Crawford gave the particulars of the assignment, which involved interviewing an almost-total stranger, observing the stranger's habitat, so to speak, and then introducing the stranger to the class, using a personal artifact as a prompt.

But this was Sam, the beautiful boy. The boy he had wanted to talk to since August, the boy in his dreams.

"Watches you? That sounds creepy," Sam said, as he wrote in his notebook.

"Yeah, I guess." Fletcher shrugged. "He's been watching me since he married my mother, when I was eleven. That's how it feels to me, anyway." Fletcher looked up, feeling again as if something had pulled his head up to stare at Sam. Why was he telling this boy anything—no matter what the damn assignment was? He swallowed what he had been about to say next: his mother had disappeared, too; she had become a ghost when she remarried: faint, vague, gray, fading, fading. He missed her.

"What does your stepfather do?"

Fletcher hesitated, feeling even more fearful and torn. He had never talked to anyone about his parents, alive, dead, or step—especially step—to anybody. "A management consultant. He goes around telling companies how to be more efficient. Right now he and my mother are in Eastern Europe, the Czech Republic. And he has secrets." *Why did I say that? My God, his eyes, his skin.* Fletcher's heart turned over again. As if a switch had been flicked on and off, the rosy-golden light had reappeared, this time outlining Sam's ears, burnishing his fingers. Bright golden fires appeared in Sam's dark, dark brown eyes. Fletcher rubbed his eyes. Perfectly normal. No fires, no lights.

I must be going crazy.

"Secrets? What do you mean?" Sam asked, as if nothing had happened, his head cocked to one side.

"Locked rooms. In the house here, and back in Durham,

he had the attic made into an office and the door is always locked. What's the next question?"

"About your mom—no, where do you live, where's home? You don't live on campus, right?"

"Here, in Greensboro. We moved here back in June. Corner of Edgar Alley and Carr Street, off Tate. Three blocks from UNC Greensboro. There's not much to say about my mother anymore."

Sam looked up again, his face, his smile bright. Literally bright, then the sudden flash was gone. "Carr Street? We're neighbors: I live over on McGee. That is so cool."

Fletcher felt his face get hot and red. He had so wanted this to happen: to be attracted to someone who was attracted to him (unlike all those boys in high school he could only look at and sigh over)—and now, when it seemed to be happening, he wanted to run away like a frightened deer.

"Your mother—what does she do?" Sam said after too long a pause.

"She helps my stepfather, mostly. Looks after the house." Fletcher made himself sit still. He made himself answer the rest of the questions—pets, travel, hobbies, heroes, life themes—and he made himself ask the same questions of Sam. *His parents traveled for work, too, school consultants, no, they didn't watch him, they were out of town, too, they were in Scotland...*

"Good stuff. That was fun," Sam said, closing his notebook. "Habitat observation next, huh? My habitat first? Tomorrow? We can do pizza?"

Fletcher gulped. "Sure. Which house on McGee? What time?" *I can't be scared forever. Ican'tIcan'tIcan't.*

∞

Tuesday, October 20th, six o'clock: to Sam's house to eat pizza and for the observation of Sam's native habitat. Fletcher wrote it down in his appointment book in red and underlined each word. Then, he outlined the words in blue and yellow and purple, using his Crayola Markers, Bold Colors. None of which helped the day go any faster. Spanish at 9:30 (eight and a half hours), then his Freshman Seminar on Utopia (seven more hours)—thank God they had finally gotten past the 19th century attempts in the US—the Mormons, Oneida, Amana, boring!—and to the science fiction novels the professor clearly loved. Le Guin's *The Dispossessed* was the first, and Fletcher found himself dreaming of the dry dusty world of Anarres, being there with Sam, in a room in which mobiles turned and twisted, catching the light, beneath that orange blanket, like Shevek and Bedap, touching in close darkness. For once Fletcher was grateful for his Spanish homework, but eventually that, too, was finished and he had already read the chapter on Buddhism for Religious Studies 101.

By four o'clock he was done with everything. Two more hours. Usually Fletcher relished being home alone and having his mother and Paul thousands of miles away, but today he would have welcomed almost any distraction. Two more hours for his imagination to run riot and fantasize about Sam. Sam hadn't mentioned any significant others, and most guys would've, if they were dating a girl, right? If he had liked girls, he would've said so, right? But *not* mentioning didn't necessarily mean Sam liked boys, either. Fletcher knew all about gaydar, but so far, it hadn't been too reliable for him.

All that was left was to go walking. Fletcher could usually count on that to release some tension. Down Edgar Alley first, the little dirt street by his house that ran parallel to Tate Street, hidden from view between trees and houses, to McGee Street, to stare at Sam's house, third on the right, two stories, a porch, big oaks, to Mendenhall, and back down Carr, and Tate, Walker into campus, past the kilns, and onto the green lawn facing the library, inside, past Walter Hines Jackson's portrait, into the tunnel to the Elliot Center, then, repeat.

The reality of Sam made Fletcher think in a way he had tried to avoid since his early teens. Optical illusions, tricks of the light, refrangibles, shadows—his mental gymnastics couldn't be contorted again. Fletcher knew he hadn't been dreaming. Did that mean he was crazy? Was he having hallucinations? Did Fletcher just want his fairy stories to be true so much that he was seeing what he had dreamed of, coupled with what his heart and his body was telling him? Once he had dreamed of going to Narnia, had knocked on the back walls of closets, looking for a chink or chasm between the worlds, had earnest conversations with cats and dogs, wondering if he had just spoken earlier or later, that they would have talked back. He had prayed to Aslan, but the great Lion had never answered. Galadriel hadn't answered his prayers, either.

He couldn't find any answers anywhere on his long walk, and finally, at ten till six, he stood just inside the MacTorain front yard, knowing all he could do was wait for what was going to happen next. Two old and massive oaks guarded the white-frame two-story house; their rust-colored leaves littered the yard, hiding the lush green grass. Boxwoods stood guard with the oaks, up against the porch, along with what looked like azaleas. Delicate chimes hung on the porch among bright pansies and ferns. Fletcher could just hear the chimes in the slight breeze: light, airy, a song without words from faraway. They shone silver and gold and copper in the last of the afternoon light. The yard felt safe and good. Which was ridiculous, but Fletcher knew he was past ridiculous, past rationalization. His leather sandals slapped on the faded-red brick walk. Lights shone through gauzy curtains, but no Sam.

Sam opened the door at the third knock, looking as he had just jumped out of the shower. His dark hair was still dripping and he was barefoot. "Hey, I was running late, sort of straightening up, not my room, down here—but never mind. The pizza should be here in about—the guy said half an hour and that was ten minutes ago. Wanna do the observation first? My room is upstairs, end of the hall. You can ask your questions while we eat."

Fletcher nodded. "Yeah, okay. I'm supposed to do that without you."

"I know. Go ahead. I'll get the plates and stuff."

The living room: unremarkable and predictable. Brown sofa, brown arm chairs, lamps on end tables, an empty fireplace, multicolored Persian-looking rug on the wood floor, art prints over the fireplace. A vase here, a twisting ceramic dragon there. Sam's bedroom seemed just as ordinary. A jumble of jeans and T-shirts spilling out of an old dresser, a work table, a computer, shelves with too many books, and a rumpled bed, a closet, door half-open, another jumble, more clothes, running shoes, sandals. Posters of what looked like various places in the British Isles—castles, rolling green lawns, thatched cottages—covered the walls. A tiny collection of geodes covered one corner of a dresser. The room smelled of boy. He wanted to roll in the smell on the bed; instead he just stroked the sheets, the spread, and when he had checked and double-checked to be sure Sam was downstairs, Fletcher pressed his face into the pillow and inhaled.

∞

"That's it for the pizza. Good thing you liked veggies, I'm so used to vegetarian stuff all the time, I forgot to ask," Sam said, wiping his mouth with the back of his hand. "No more questions?" he asked, after draining his Pepsi.

They sat on the back porch swing, looking into a yard of dark green shadows and dogwoods, another oak, a thicket of crape myrtles against the back fence. The night air was cool. The swing, hung on ropes, moved slowly as Sam pushed off with his feet. Behind them, the soft yellow light in the living room, muted by the curtains, made more shadows on the porch.

"In the summer the yard is lit up with fireflies: yellow-green, twinkling, like tiny stars in the grass and the trees. Sorry, your questions?"

"Just one more," Fletcher said slowly, acutely aware that Sam was just inches away and how much he wanted to touch him and how afraid he was of what would or would not happen. "There is *one* more question that neither of us asked the other. Significant others. Girlfriends? Boyfriends?" The last word came with great effort and he couldn't look at Sam; he stared instead into his Pepsi cup, as if there were some answer in the dark liquid or the crushed ice.

"No, no significant others, no boyfriends," Sam said, staring into his own cup, before setting it on the floor. "What about you? Boyfriends?" he asked just as slowly.

"No boyfriends."

They finally looked at each other and Sam reached out to touch his face. Fletcher sat very still, the swing barely moving, wanting to run, but knowing he didn't know which way, that he was going to let this happen, and that life had finally come looking for him. Sam kissed him. There was an explosion of light, a shattering, as if from somewhere walls of glass were raining around them, bits, then chunks of rose and golden light, that exploded in Sam's dark hair, Fletcher's red hair, and all they could do was hold on to each other. The light passed through them, breaking on the porch into small bits, like confetti, of yellow and green and blue and white that littered the floor, the grass, the trees, everything.

"Wow, I thought that only happened in the movies. Fletch, you're okay? My God, look: the dining room, those pictures—they are so different, and the lamps," Sam said, looking up, and letting go of Fletcher. Behind them the lights in the dining room seemed to be blazing, sparking, flaring, and dying, to flare again, repeating the cycle.

"What is going on? You're glowing all over," Fletcher said in an awed voice, as he followed Sam into the dining room to stare at the pictures on the wall. It was as if someone had peeled off a plastic seal covering up the real picture beneath. Over the fireplace mantel the picture of the dragon ship on the sea had changed—from a picture, no, not a painting, but a window. Fletcher felt like he was staring through a transparent window looking at a fast sailing ship running before a strong wind.

"*The Voyage of the* Dawn Treader—it looks just like how I imagined the ship would look—just like in the story."

"Yeah, a little closer and the waves would smack us. I don't know what's happening—I can't turn this glowing off. It doesn't hurt; I don't feel bad or sick—I feel normal."

"I don't know, either, but I don't think we're crazy and it all seems real, and your ears: they're pointed," Fletcher said, grabbing Sam's hand, and then Sam. They watched as the bits of light dissolved, oozing into the wood, the earth, the air. Magic seemed the only explanation, but why just in Sam's house and in Fletcher's dreams? *The neighbor*—? It was late and Fletcher was tired and he couldn't figure anything else out.

"I don't want to be alone. Stay here," Sam said. "Stay here tonight with me, Fletcher."

∞

"Hey."

"Hey yourself," Fletcher whispered back, reaching out to touch Sam's face. He was amazed to be where he was now, naked in bed with a boy, to have had sex with the boy, and to be touching the boy now, the boy who really had been glowing all over the night before, and on the walls of this room, more too-real pictures of a rolling green countryside, which wasn't England. He was still afraid, but somehow, for the moment, the fear was smaller, not as dark.

"You want to go to the doctor? The glow's gone."

"What—for that? It didn't hurt. My parents will be home in a few days; that's what they said last night when they called, remember? We can wait—they'll know what this all means—the lights, those pictures that look too real now, how everything looks different now. Besides, you know a doctor would never believe us," Sam said, his hair looking just as wild as boys' hair did in the movies after spending the night, no matter with whom they shared a bed. Fletcher ran his fingers through his hair, hoping his head looked just as disheveled.

"Yeah, I guess—it's all scary and I told you about my dreams—this—it has to be magic, Sam."

Fletcher wanted someone to tell him what to do. Sam's parents had called in the middle of the night; he wished Sam had told them everything, and then, zap, from the Shetlands, across Scotland, over Ireland, over the Atlantic, to McGee Street, in Greensboro: the answer. Instead they were coming home. Was he all right? They were at the airport, getting to London was taking longer than they'd anticipated, next Tuesday, London, into Dulles by early afternoon, a connecting flight to Greensboro, home by five. Was he really okay? *Nothing* had happened? Yes, yes, yes. Fletcher shook his head: even if his parents were to come home early, they would never call. They would just show up.

"Why didn't you tell them about the glowing? And—do

you think they will care—I mean, are you going to tell them about us?" Fletcher added in a whisper, realizing he was afraid of what Sam's answer would be.

"You and me—this?" Sam asked as he traced the line of Fletcher's jaw, each collarbone, each nipple. "I told them I liked boys a year or so ago. They weren't surprised, and they won't be, about you. My mom even said there was a kid in Scotland they had met on another trip—a boy she thought I would like. And I wanted to tell them everything in person anyway."

"Your mother said *that?*" Fletcher said, stunned.

Sam shrugged. "What do we do now? I can wear a headband to cover my ears, I guess."

"Act normal. Eat breakfast, go to class, see what happens next? I don't think I am going to include this in my portrait interview narrative," Fletcher said, thinking that maybe, of all people, Dr. Crawford might understand or, at least, not be afraid. He was surprised at himself for not suggesting they run away, and even more surprised for not having run away in fear himself. "Wait for your parents? You said they would be back in a week, right? Don't tell mine anything when they get back? But what if you start glowing again? "

"Run home, tell them I'm sick, stay home?"

It wasn't much of a plan, but it was the only one the two of them could think of. After that they went back to sleep.

∞

It was Wednesday afternoon, when he had to meet with Dr. Crawford for his midterm conference, that Fletcher realized he wasn't quite sure how to act normal. Trying to be invisible and wishing for Narnia and Middle-earth for the past seven years hadn't been the best practice. To make things worse, today he was sure that she and everyone could see it on his forehead, in bright red neon letters, blinking on and off, in alternating words and sentences: GAY/FAIRY/FAGGOT/HE HAD SEX WITH A BOY LAST NIGHT/LET ME TELL YOU WHAT THEY DID. Fletcher could still feel Sam's hands and mouth on his skin. He could still feel the warmth of Sam's skin when he glowed all over that rosy-gold.

"Fletcher? Are you not feeling well?

"Uh, no, I mean, I'm okay, Dr. Crawford, I'm fine. So, I can still revise my first essay? Sam and I are almost done with our portrait interview, and I'm almost done with the all-freshman read book—" He stopped. He was blanking on the book's name, the book that they had been talking about just about every day since August.

"*Enrique's Journey* by Sonia Nazario. Well, you've about a B average now, but if you do a good job on the revisions and you and Sam…"

She knows. That's why she put us together. He desperately wanted to tell this kind woman with her wild hair and pale, pale blue eyes that seemed to see everything, ask her for advice, but Fletcher knew he wasn't that brave.

The next day, Thursday, it was all Fletcher could do not to tell Dr. Crawford. Sam couldn't leave the house. Last night he had started glowing again and was still glowing the next morning—if anything, he was brighter. They didn't need any lights in Sam's bedroom. More the opposite: Fletcher had to be sure Sam was covered so the glowing wouldn't keep him awake. Fletcher looked for answers in all his fantasy novels. No luck. The closest he came was in *The Fellowship of the Ring,* Chapter 12, "Flight to the Ford."

"It's right here, Sam, listen: When Glorfindel comes to help get Frodo away from the Black Riders, across the river to Rivendell—"

"Fletch, I told you: I haven't read any of those books—except for now, what you brought over here. Who is Glorfindel?" They were sitting on the MacTorains' back porch again, in the early evening. Dinner this time had been takeout Chinese, from Hong Kong House, up on Tate Street. Fletcher was thinking that one of them should learn how to cook something more than fried eggs and scrambled eggs.

"That's so—unbelievable," Fletcher said and set down his shrimp-fried rice. "But never mind that, listen: 'To Frodo it appeared that a white light was shining through the form and raiment of the rider as if through a thin veil.' Later, Gandalf tells Frodo that he had seen Glorfindel as 'he is upon the other side: one of the mighty of the First-born.' Glorfindel is an Elf. Sam, you have to be an Elf—or something like that."

Sam shook his head, and for a moment, he splashed light around him, rose, gold, white. "I was born here; I only remember here. These ears, this glowing under my skin—never before now, not even dreams like yours. Those books of yours, Fletch: they *are* fiction, remember? I don't know anything about Elves, but I *am* sure that we both are fairies."

Fletcher sighed.

So, they waited: Sam stuck at home, Fletcher bringing him his books and assignments, sure the look on Dr. Crawford's face meant she was more than a little suspicious. If nothing else, he was sure she had guessed that they were lovers, and that she had paired them on purpose. *That* worried and scared Fletcher on another level. How could he fall in love with anyone in less than a week? There just wasn't enough time. Sam said he had no doubts—but that only made Fletcher all the more uncertain if this was real, if it was—forever? He could only think *forever* as a whisper.

On Tuesday night, October 27, Sam's parents came home.

Sam and Fletcher were in the front porch swing: Sam was laughing as Fletcher tried to convince Sam that Dr. Crawford had to know they were lovers—if he had seen the way she had looked at him when he turned in their essays—when Sam's parents stepped out of a taxi. Sam clearly favored his dark-golden-haired mother. Mr. MacTorain was fair, his hair almost a white-gold, and when he was closer, Fletcher could see Sam's dark eyes replicated in his father's face. Mrs. MacTorain's eyes were gray-blue, almost-silver. Neither had pointed ears.

"Mom, Dad: this is Fletcher, my boyfriend," Sam said, sounding a little shy and uncertain.

"Red hair, of course; that explains it. You don't know it, but you have the Sight," Mr. MacTorain said after shaking hands. He looked at his wife and she nodded and he turned back, clearing his throat. "We felt the glamour shatter when we were in the Shetlands so we left for home immediately. Without the glamour, Sam is in immediate danger, so this has to be done, and done now."

"Liban, we should have told him long before this. He's eighteen; what'd you expect to happen?" Mrs. MacTorain snapped, clearly furious with her husband. "I knew we should have sent him to the sanctuary in Scotland. It was your brilliant idea to put off changing his glamour to adult strength. So much for this stupid experiment."

"We can argue that another time, Lavy. The experiment was worth trying, you know that. Sam, I'm so sorry, but not him. It's just too dangerous for both of you. Fletcher, you have to go and you must never see my son again."

"Dad, Mom, no, what are you doing—leave Fletcher alone..."

A force, something like a great invisible hand, seized Fletcher, wrapping itself around him, muting his voice, even as he struggled to cry out that this was wrong, wrong, no, please, don't, *I—think—I love him.* He could just hear, muffled, Sam's continuing cries of protest, but he couldn't turn, not even his head. The hand pushed Fletcher away: down the flagstones, onto McGee, and then out into Edgar Alley, dragged him over the gravel. Not until Fletcher was at Carr Street did the hand release him.

He didn't know how he made it into the house, into his room, closed the door behind him and sank into the room's shadows on his bed. Fletcher had been so close, so very close, to what his heart and his body were telling him he wanted. He stared at the ceiling, trying to tell himself it couldn't be real, the time was too short; he didn't really know Sam, let alone this whole crazy magic glowing stuff and pointed ears. That Fletcher could recite passages from Tolkien and Lewis and God knew how many other fantasy novels didn't help. Tolkien's and Lewis's words weren't spells. But, this *was* real. Fletcher knew he was awake. A promise was being made; a future glimmered. They had touched each other. *God, am I ever confused.*

And now Sam's parents had taken everything away.

Fletcher was still lying there, in a half-sleep of exhaustion, when he heard the front door open, voices, footsteps.

His mother and stepfather were home. Were they supposed to be back now? He couldn't remember whatever date Paul had put on the kitchen chalkboard. Fletcher sat up slowly, rubbing his eyes and finger-combing his hair. He looked at his watch, almost too late to make it to English class. *I have to get up, go say hello, eat, make them think everything is okay, not ask me any questions, run to class.*

His mother touched him, very lightly, on the cheek, before going down the hall to unpack. Paul chattered as he gathered food for breakfast in the kitchen: they were exhausted from the trip, came back a day or so early, got everything done in Prague, and loved *loved* the Czech Republic, Fletcher would have loved it, all those castles, what, can't wait to eat, the fresh air did smell good after all those hours on the plane...

Muttering he was going to be late, Fletcher grabbed a can of Coke Zero, a bagel and his book bag, and ran out the front door. Paul was never, ever like that. Did jet lag make people crazy cheerful? Fletcher didn't know. He had to get away from Paul. Still slugging down the Coke, Fletcher eased into the back row of class. More portrait interview presentations—he wouldn't have to say anything, just listen until the very end. He smiled at Dr. Crawford, wishing again that he could tell her, ask her, wondering if she were magical herself, if somehow she could be from wherever Sam's parents were from, some version of Narnia, and she was hiding out here, too—from what? His mind was too tired to imagine what.

"Fuck Western Civ. I need to do *something,*" Fletcher whispered to himself, as he stuffed his English 101 notebook and his copy of *Enrique's Journey* into his book bag, overjoyed that his interview presentation was going to be next week. He glanced over at Dr. Crawford, who was, as always, surrounded by students chattering around her. *Talk to her? What would she tell me to do? Don't be a wimp? Tell the truth?* That had been her main advice about his first *Enrique* essay, in which he had tried to talk about his mother disappearing, the way Enrique's mother had. *Tell the truth. Okay, to whom?*

Sam was waiting for him at the bottom of the front steps of the HHRA Building. He was wearing a dark blue UNCG sweatshirt, the hood pulled over his head, the letters in bright gold on his chest. Light flickered in Sam's face when he saw Fletcher.

"Your dad told me you went to class."

"Stepdad. But—yesterday," Fletcher said, coming down the gray stone steps slowly. "Your parents. Their magic."

"Yeah, I know, I know. They used it on me, too, or I would have come looking for you last night. Locked me in my room. They want to send me to Scotland, to some fey sanctuary there."

"Oh, Sam—I'll never…" and Fletcher's voice trailed off. If he said anything else, he knew his grief would take him down inside it.

"Fletcher," Sam said and pulled Fletcher to him and kissed him right there, in broad daylight, in front of the HHRA Building on Spring Garden Street, while classes were changing, below a flame-colored maple. People were everywhere. "This is real. I had a big fight with them this morning. I got so mad I ran out of the house. Talk about fireworks. I went looking for you. Your dad—stepdad—said you'd gone to class. I came here."

"But what do we do?"

Sam took his hand. Fletcher almost bolted, but Sam held on tight. The public kiss and now this, with all these students and professors milling around them—how could they not notice?

"We go fight them, you and me. I love you. I know, I know: you can't say it yet—but never mind. Come on. I'll tell you what else they told me on the way."

Fletcher was never to forget that walk down Spring Garden, left on Tate, right on Walker, and then down Edgar Alley to McGee. The sky was bright and clear; the air warm; the few clouds far away, like white smears on the blue; more maples on fire; and Sam talking, talking, talking, his words surrounding Fletcher in a golden haze. Everything was so ordinary, and it wasn't. That magic was real was one of the deep wishes of Fletcher's heart, but not like this. This hurt.

"After they *pushed* you away, before we had a fight, they

told me things. For my own good, you had to go—for yours, too. Us together: they think it's dangerous. I was born here, in this world; they weren't. Raising me outside that sanctuary: an experiment—which they think failed. They *are* from inside those pictures you said were Narnia, which they said was just one escaped dream."

"Narnia is an escaped dream?"

"Just let me talk. Dreams were all that could escape from There, the Other Place, your Narnia and Middle-earth, Faerie—they reeled off a long list of names—for a long time. Lewis and that other guy's stories are from the escaped dreams."

"Tolkien."

"Yeah, him. The Queen, Her Divinity, Her Majesty—well, she does have the place in some kind of perpetual winter. They weren't too clear about that. Anyway, the people there have finally figured out how to escape. My parents did, but they have to hide, keep undercover, or stay in the sanctuary. The glamour that was hiding what makes me an Elf, the glowing, broke when we kissed—loved—each other. It wasn't strong enough. They thought you were another fairy passing—that's why they said nothing when they called. And they were afraid someone might hear them. They taught me a little bit how to turn the glowing down—see?" Sam said and pulled back his hood. Light flickered in his face, as if someone were opening and closing venetian blinds. Sam stopped talking in front of his house. He hadn't let Fletcher's hand go ever since kissing him on Spring Garden.

The shadows of the trees, of the other houses around it, seemed to have almost swallowed the house. The white paint looked gray and sickly, the grass wilted, the leaves of the trees had fallen all at once. The pansies and ferns had dried up. The bright morning had disappeared or they had stepped out of it. Fletcher looked behind them: the sky seemed to have lost its color.

"Something's really wrong," Sam finally whispered.

"Let's go check on them," Fletcher said. "Where were they when you left?"

"The dining room."

The front door was ajar, and Fletcher knew from his first step inside that the house was empty. The only thing moving was a slight breeze stirring the half-drawn drapes in the living room. Three plates sat on the dining room table: eggs, toast, three grapefruit halves in white bowls. What had to be Sam's plate had been pushed away from the table's edge; the glass of orange juice beside it was empty. The other two were half and two-thirds empty. English Breakfast tea bags dangled from two cups.

"Look: their shoes, on the floor," Fletcher said, pointing.

"It's like they left between one breath and the next," Sam said, dropping back into a whisper.

"Good. Fletcher, you did well. The parents, now the son."

Both boys jerked around as if someone had yanked them. It was Paul, but Fletcher had never seen the man looking quite this way: it was as if someone had sharpened him, honed his edges, and stained them in black ink. His eyes glittered like hard diamonds, ice in moonlight. He was dressed in black and held a black staff in one hand, blacker than even the night. Fletcher couldn't move; apparently Sam couldn't move either. *Why can't we run? Move, at least say something?*

"It's time, Samuel MacTorain. Her Majesty can't allow people to escape, even their children."

Fletcher finally knew what happened to his next-door neighbor back in Durham.

"No, no, you won't take us," Sam shouted, finding strength Fletcher didn't know the other boy had. He stepped forward at the same time Fletcher stepped back, dropping Sam's hand, shaking, no, no, no.

"Fletcher, come on—Fletcher!"

"Time," Paul repeated and, striking the air with his black staff, cast out a thick, heavy darkness that caught them both.

∞

Fletcher woke up on the floor in the MacTorain dining room. Sam's shoes lay beside him. He felt sore all over, as if every muscle had been used repeatedly and hard. He sat up slowly, and then pulled himself up, using the table's edge.

Three plates. He remembered.

Sam. I have to find him—before—

He knew it was too late, but he still had to find him, find out what his stepfather had done, what he could do, tell Sam he was sorry, so sorry, that Fletcher hadn't meant to pull away, he cared, he really cared, maybe he even loved. Knowing somewhere in his head that he needed energy, that he was hungry, Fletcher first drank the orange juice and wolfed down the now-soggy and cold wheat toast. He went to look in Sam's room, telling himself just maybe, maybe—*you're a coward, a wimp, you know where you have to go*—and stood there a long, long moment. The room still smelled like boy, but the boy was gone.

Before Fletcher left, he put two of Sam's geodes in his pocket: *See, I do care, I just got scared. One for you, one for me.*

At home, Fletcher looked first in his mother and stepfather's bedroom, then the kitchen, the bathroom. He found his mother there, limp on the bathmat by the tub, like a discarded hotel towel, white and crumpled. Fletcher knelt down and touched her bruised face, tenderly traced the hand prints on her skin. Cold. He then pressed his fingers against the veins in her neck. No pulse. Wishing he could cry for her, he held the same fingers under her nose. No breath. Dead. Emptied. He picked up her arm and it flopped as if there were no bones in her elbows. She was wearing her nightgown, as if she had just gotten out of bed. Her robe lay beside her, a pool of dark green terrycloth; her nightgown was torn.

Fletcher knew where to look: behind the locked attic door. The door was unlocked.

"Fletcher. You're awake. I knew you'd come up here," his stepfather said in the same cold and dark voice. He sat at a desk beside a door frame standing in the middle of the attic. Inside the door frame: darkness. Around it, Fletcher could see the rest of the attic: the shelves, the file cabinets, the odd boxes. The skylight was open, mid-day sun streamed in. Even so, the room was cold, a cold that was coming through the door, as if blown by some faraway wind. Paul's black staff leaned against the door frame.

"What did you do with Sam? Where is he? Where are his parents?" Fletcher asked, shivering and hugging himself against the cold.

"Where they belong," Paul said, leaning back in his chair. "The dreams have escaped for millennia—even before Her Majesty came to power—into human minds. Fairy tales, myths, story upon story. A few times, the different peoples and creatures slipped through—what was it your hero said? —'chinks or chasms between worlds'?—yes, I've read all those stories, too; they were useful to me. That was before Her Majesty. So, there are people like you and your mother, fey-touched, gifted with Sight that lets you see through glamour. Very useful to people like me."

Fletcher swallowed the scream in his throat, knowing he had to listen, to understand, not to let this man get to him, break him into tears. "Where is Sam? What kind of a person are you?"

"I told you: There. You can call it Narnia if you like, or what did Tolkien call it? Never mind. The Celts came up with many other names, such as Tir n'Og, the Blessed Isles. Words and sounds can be dreamt, too; echoes can linger. She can't stop the dreams of what once was, of once upon a time—slow them down, but not stop them. But Her Majesty can and must stop those who escape her winter," Paul said, as he sorted what looked like rolls of parchment, stuffing some back into tubes, into different parts of his desk. "Oh, yes, I am a bounty hunter, a tracker, and you, my dear Fletcher, and your mother, are my canaries."

My dreams. I dreamed of the neighbor; I dreamed of Sam.

"They hadn't planned on Sam having falling in love and having sex quite just yet, which shattered the weak child's glamour—and I smelled him on you, his magic," Paul said, his words dripping disdain and scorn.

"She's dead."

"I needed her energy to open the gate—I was running a little low. A few days from now, no problem. You want him back?"

Fletcher slowly and carefully nodded his head.

"You think you're in love. Fletcher! What do you know about love—who have you ever loved or who's loved you? And when he asked for you, at the moment of peril, you pulled back. Don't be a fool: you're not in love."

"My father loved me; I loved him. My mother—before you used her for food. Sam loved me."

"Then go get him. Into Faerie. No happy elves, no dancing fauns, no chatty mice, no heroes with magic swords. No performing Lion, just Her Majesty's winter. No English children. Your boyfriend's there, Fletcher. Or: you could stay here and help me—starting with finding that sanctuary. Do you know how old I am? Her Majesty rewards her faithful: I am two hundred and thirteen of your years old. I have anything I want."

I want Sam. "Live that long, be like you—no. I love Sam."

"You've known him a week and you're in love. That really is a fairy tale. You just think you do," Paul said, dismissing Fletcher's feelings with a flip of his hand. "You can have any boy you want, any way you want—like I said, Her Majesty rewards her faithful. Besides, you're a coward," Paul added, laughing.

Fletcher knew that Paul would never understand, could never understand, that even the uncertainty was enough, that the brightness in his heart, the geodes in his pocket, were enough, even if the week had been just the promise of what would come. Could have come. Might come. Maybe he was a coward. He certainly was afraid, and very good at being afraid. But life had found him, and being afraid didn't mean he couldn't go through that dark gate.

"Find yourself another canary," Fletcher said and before Paul could stop him, ran across the room, through the door frame, into the dark, into the fairy tale.

OUT OF BODY
PATRICIA J. ESPOSITO

Cale spit his favorite peppered burger into his napkin. He couldn't swallow.

Who were these four who had leisurely broken through the pub's heavy wood door, a gust of winter trailing in their wake? Who was he who ambled gypsy-dark through the crooked tables, pulling out a chair to meticulously set his jacket like a cloak across its back?

The man caught Cale's stare, his brown eyes flaring with summer gold.

Penetrated. Quickly, Cale averted his gaze, to the bar where Sanje, a regular, sat sipping scotch as he chatted with pink-lipped Linney. It was winter, nine p.m., and the pub echoed with darkness. Cale shivered and focused his energy again on skinny Sanje.

A light touch on Sanje's shoulders that sagged under the weight of his loss—that's all he wanted to do, project an astral touch of assurance. But it swung back at him as those four, *that man*, entered the pub. The man's *presence* echoed, filling Cale's throat.

No, he couldn't eat.

Across the room were other regulars. Cale scooted left to see beyond those center four, to astrally project his hand onto that fair-haired and freckled boy, who stared at the girl he loved with such tentative longing. In his mind, out-of-body, he envisioned his fingers touching that fair boy's leg. Let him think it was *her* hand; urge him to take the risk. To kiss...

He froze. Under his fingers he felt not the fleecy blue of the freckled boy's sweatpants, but black, coarse heat—that gypsy man's slim leg, restless under the table.

Cale withdrew and risked another glance at him. The man pinched the menu with slender brown fingers that caught in Cale's throat. His cheekbones shone in cinnamon spice; his brown eyes sparkled, gold-flecked and knowing. He passed the menu back to the server, then looked down at his lap, head bent as his black hair rained.

Who was this night-drawn man who sat with regal assurance under the cone of amber light?

Perhaps his projection had unconsciously traveled to this man's leg, Cale thought. Perhaps he was still able to project; he'd just been distracted. He tried again to comfort Sanje, but his ethereal astral self spiraled in. Clouded. Jailed. He sat weighted in the dark chair. His own food went unswallowed as the server brought the four their plates.

Sitting back, Cale glared at the man, who bit heartily into his burger, who stuffed three fries past his full smiling lips. Who ignored Cale's stare.

His shine of hair cascaded over precise black brows, and he swept it back. His full lips spread to a fine white smile, confident the night was his. Cale's throat closed against the pasty burger he forced into his mouth.

Nausea welled in him. Yet, as he watched this man select each fry and place it past those full lips, through that white shine of smile, he wanted his lips bedded there, his hands raking the black sheen of hair. But he sat, hands useless, draping his knees, and mind imprisoned in his corporeal self.

He'd read that some people could never learn to astral project because they were too rooted in the body. Cale lived outside the body more than in it. Yet he now sat trapped. He could only sit and watch until this man moved away.

∞

"You're an hour late," James said. He'd pulled off the headphones as Cale walked in their apartment door, and now swung his legs from his leather recliner to the hardwood floor. "I tried calling…"

Dropping keys in the bluebell dish, Cale shrugged off his coat and met James in the middle of the warm room coated with even light. "Cale?" James ran his hands down Cale's arms. "You're freezing."

"I couldn't move. In the restaurant...Linney's Pub."

"You mean you couldn't project? You know how it is sometimes." No, he didn't know. Unlike James and Margo and Bracie, Cale didn't know how it felt to be unable to project, to send his spirit out, to guide it and watch it move through the world, invisible but tangible. He rarely spent time in one place, in only this body.

"But I wanted to. I wanted to help those kids in love. I wanted to..." *I wanted to touch his hair.* "The simplest moves, but gravity had caved on me."

Smiling, James pulled Cale into the room and guided him to the couch. The afghan wrapped his shoulders and he felt James's hands there as he projected—him standing, his astral self kissing Cale's neck.

The afghan had been Bracie's; Cale had brought it when he moved into James's loft. No one stayed long living among multiple worlds, but their foursome orbited together.

Huddled under the blanket, Cale reached out with his mind and wrapped warm arms around James's waist. He moved in.

"I don't think that was his girl," Cale said, "the one sitting beside him."

James laughed. "Not everyone is looking for a mate. I'd no idea when we first met that you were such a matchmaker. So, who's his lover then?"

Shrugging off the blanket, Cale flushed at the thought of the gypsy man's lips touching another's. "What if I never see him again? No. Worse, what if I do and still can't move?"

Retreating, James collapsed back in his leather recliner and clipped the headphones between thumb and finger. "It's going to be one of those nights?"

Some people didn't question their existence, but rather were simply grateful for their abilities. Some thought of actions as necessary without examining motive. Studying astral projection didn't answer why Cale could be in two places at once, why he could see himself touching someone though he

was a room away. But he wanted it to be for something good.
In the lamplight, he noticed James's taut jaw. From his chair, he reached out to stroke it.

∞

For the next two weeks, Linney's Pub returned to its normal traffic flow. Sanje came in, looking worn, and whispered things to Linney that Cale couldn't hear. Absently turning his scotch glass, he wiped condensation from the bar top over and over again. Sanje had tightly pulled back black hair, and, sitting in the dark corner, breaking slivers of chocolate from his cheesecake dessert, Cale reached out to caress the back of Sanje's head.

"I lost job *and* wife now," he was telling Linney.

Cale whispered in his ear, "It's okay. Everything will be okay." He wouldn't hear the voice, but he'd feel the caress and somehow sense the words. At least this is what Cale wanted to believe.

Removing his cool fingers from the glass, Sanje touched the back of his head, wiping his hair, then glanced behind him. Cale stroked again. Sanje smiled. "You have ghosts in here, Linney?" He drank, still smiling.

∞

On a Thursday, through slanting sleet, the gypsy man returned, no longer bounding in with four, but more quietly, with a male friend. They took the same table, same chairs. He wore no smile this time, offering only a polite twitch of a grin to the server as she brought the menus. In this serious mood, his black brows arced with sharp precision; his burnished eyelids rose and fell, his lashes like a satin cage.

Deadly, Cale thought. As the man glanced up, his gold-flecked eyes seared boldly. Here was direct confrontation—his stare a challenge Cale didn't understand. Averting his eyes, Cale pulled a writing notebook from his sack on the floor. The friend was opposite him in color: fair-skinned, fair-haired, with eager, friendly eyes and a bright smile. Could he project onto the friend? As Cale chanced another look, the fair man whispered conspiratorially to his gypsy friend, but only got a slight twist toward smiling in response.

Cale moved the pen across the page. The cheesecake sat. Could he touch that slim and agile form? Start lower? The calf of his right leg? Before mastering astral skills, some students of projection were taught to write where they wanted to be, to lose themselves by transferring desire into words so that their spirit would more easily transport. Cale had never had to write his desire, but here he was feeling ill again, unable to advance on this man. Apparently, he was moving backward in skill level.

His pants were black, a heavy weave, his leg shadowed under the table. *Touch,* Cale wrote, *the slick slide of my fingers up into the loose cavern, over his shin, around his calf. Skin, satin over shinbone, and warm, the calf muscle taut. And more. His nerves sparking across my palm.*

His body seized. Cale heard himself moan at the table. The pen rolled from his fingers to the floor. He'd drawn back into his body and now his corporeal chest rose and fell as if he'd done more than touch a bare leg. The man was staring. Cale couldn't look. He left the pen on the floor, and both hands tight in his lap where blood pulsed strongest.

A chair scraped the floor, and Cale stared at the puckered cheesecake, the slits from the fork prongs turning into canals. Still he saw the man's slim form sweep around the table, heading his way. Blood rushed Cale's face, the water glass out of reach with his hands clasped useless.

And then he stooped into Cale's downcast view, his lean body a waterfall spilling inside, deep within. "Your pen?" the man said. Cale managed to take it, to look up into eyes that prowled with careful intent. Then the man looked at the notebook and nodded. "Keep writing."

Moving back to his table, the man slid to a casual slouch in the chair, and waited for Cale's further touch.

∞

"Success?" James said. He'd been at the door, opening it as Cale came up the outside hall. "Phew," he laughed, putting his knuckles to Cale's cheek. "You're feverish."

Nodding, Cale slouched out of the wool coat that felt itchy and weighted. "He knew. He knew immediately that it

was me."
 Taking the coat, James draped it over the pine-scented hanger and closed the mirrored closet door. Cale saw himself, cheeks flushed, eyes bright. His body looked tense with adrenaline, sexier than he knew he could be.
 "Of course he didn't. You worry all the time." James grabbed an orange from the counter between kitchen and front room and plopped into his chair. "Did you find his mate, matchmaker?" Juice squirted as he dug thumbnail into rind.
 Cale shook his head. "He's closed. He's controlled. He's used to running the show."
 "Are you going to stand there forever?" James said, glancing over the glasses he'd donned for a closer look at the stubborn peel. Cale felt James's hands imprint on his lower back, nudging him forward. They were a couple made of four people, and still what did they know? They'd resigned themselves years ago to never being one to one, a true couple. It was impossible when every outreaching thought sent them from each other, sent him from himself.
 But who was he tonight, as he ran his hands up the dark mystery of that thieving man?
 Cale's palms still throbbed with the pulse of those muscles tensing in slim, hot legs. He'd felt the man's breathing grow shallow, his cheek on the concave of the man's stomach. And in the dark corner table, Cale had watched those soft lips part to a tongue he wanted inside.

∞

 Cale didn't go back to the pub. On a metal bench at the bus stop, he waited for people to come. Surely, there'd be a man tired and frustrated from a long day at work, someone who would welcome the remembered touch of a father's hand or a brother's spontaneous hug. Or a couple maintaining tense distance that he might prod together by touching one's hand.
 If he had seen those gold-brown eyes shine on the girl, or on the fair-haired man at his side, Cale knew he'd have been able to perform as usual, kiss the friend's cheek with affection as he leaned for a spoon of ice cream, whisper in his ear about love. Set their sights toward a future together. But alone, with

his daring, with his night-deep penetration, black fire over russet canyons, Cale wanted to follow his will. To have no choice.

∞

On the third cold night as Cale sat at the bus stop, the man strode through the pale stream of streetlights, set a small notebook and pen on the bench, and stepped back to lean against the black light post.

Cale tried projecting to move the gypsy man on, imagining a hand to touch his back, a push, a whisper, *you have other destinations.* No luck. Cale's body sat gravity-stricken, his heart raced, and his spirit coiled down through his esophagus, twisting through vacant cavities.

"I can't," he whispered. But the man just crossed one leg over the other, unzipped his jacket, and waited. Taking up the pen, Cale stared at the tiny flakes of snow melting into the green notebook he'd been given—green life amid winter's pale darkness. Where would he begin this time?

He opened the notebook. Where his jacket collar gaped? At the masculine elegance of his smooth, umber neck. He wrote: *One finger under his chin, I tilt his head back. Below his left ear, edging toward the back, I breathe him, mouth hungry, tasting where the Adam's apple swells.* On the park bench, Cale's body drew a deep breath of recovery, and he saw the man's eyes darken, lids flutter and then open to a direct, consuming stare.

Tongue trails to clavicle, the shine of skin over bone, and I stroke his chest, the solid breastplate of male. In the cold he is heat, my hand guided to the source of this fire. Down him, my lips follow the path of my hand.

From the bench, Cale witnessed the response to his invisible touch. The man's slim legs uncrossed as an astral hand threaded under his belt. Cale's tongue ran the width of his narrow waist, and his stomach sucked deep, pelvic bones jutting, leaving another gaping entry to a scent Cale didn't know. He smelled only bitter snow, metallic as it drifted down. *He is the skin of fertile earth.*

When Cale's projection whirled back to his own body,

the man zipped his jacket and grinned. His eyes sparked, warmly amused. Then, shoving hands in his pockets, he nodded thanks, saying politely, "Have a good night." Cale watched the grace of his stride as he walked away, and like a body adrift in lace, winter closed the path behind him.

∞

He didn't go home. Instead Cale followed Clark to Kensington to Balmoral. His paced steps fought against running. Despite the cold, his face remained flushed with the heat of demanding sensuality. Up the three stairs of the greystone, he rang Margo and Bracie's bell. Then, leaning over, he placed his fiery cheek on the snow-wet porch rail.

The buzzer brought him back, and Cale pulled the heavy door, then pushed against heat and the dirty glow of their hallway.

"I just couldn't go home to that polished..." He didn't know how to finish. Bracie had already taken his coat, and Margo, from where she stood pouring his favorite bourbon, had projected a hand on his forehead and brushed sticky hair from Cale's neck.

"Is it James?" Margo said, but before Cale answered, Bracie shook her head. He could see from her eyes that she was with James. Bracie was the only one of them who could, in seconds, astral project beyond the proximity of vision.

"He's relaxed with his book," she said. "No air of a quarrel." Her smile brightened Cale's mood a bit. No, it wasn't James at all. They'd resigned themselves to this condition long ago. He didn't want the sanitized, controlled warmth of their apartment because his body was stirred up, coiled around itself. He needed cold air; he needed release, not comfort.

"I'll take that drink."

"Tell me about him," Margo said, placing the heavy snifter in Cale's hands. He held it with two hands and remembered that timid boy at Linney's that he'd wanted to encourage. He had a purpose; he could do good with this gift.

"This kind of gorgeous doesn't happen often." They both laughed and led Cale to the couch. They sat. Sometimes Bracie's hand met Cale's knee; sometimes one of them projected touch to replace that corporeal hand.

Cale told them about his warm but keen gold-flecked eyes, the black hair that swept recklessly inside him, how he was black fire and copper earth. How he *knew*, how he so nonchalantly knew and took control.

"We all want to relinquish control now and then," Bracie said.

Shaking his head, Cale swallowed the vision of that strong, slender neck sloping to straight shoulders. "No. Think about it…think how we learned to control our thoughts, guide our vision, to be at our destination—"

"And to be removed from where we are?" Margo interrupted. "You didn't go home tonight." Cale held up a hand to protest, but she projected a gentle kiss on his fingers, fiery in this light. "Maybe tonight you didn't want to make that timid boy kiss that girl, or rescue another lonely mother."

But what instead? To feel those plush satin lips on his? To watch those gold-brown eyes haze, the plush, slow eyelids flutter? He had kissed along luminescent skin, soothing and seductive. He'd wanted to live in that body. He had wanted to be stolen.

Margo put her arm around Cale's shoulders, solid and strong, and she tugged him to her. "Your projection is calculated, a means to an end—to help the young couple, to mend a friendship, to make James feel he has a home."

"Because I want purpose, because—"

She put her lips to his temple, and her astral fingers feathered his brow. "Your eyes are wild with captivity. You pace but can't get through the bars."

"Who's my captor then? Him?"

Bracie's projected touch smoothed back Cale's damp hair. "Oh you wish it were him, Cale."

"No," he said, standing, ready to leave. "I could never be owned by anyone."

Bracie followed him to the door. "Could you be owned by passion?"

What did that mean? Cale smiled, wanting to acknowledge their concern, but he needed to breathe outside, run or astral project himself to flight.

"You and James, I see you hug from across the room. It's clean, you know, how you do things. No pillows ruffled. That's why Bracie came to me. Why James came to you."

"And it's better to have a stranger control me? Should I be subject to his whim?"

They shrugged simultaneously and spoke at once. "Maybe. He sounds volcanic."

Cale had to laugh. That was Margo and Bracie—everything was simple. He projected a kiss to the top of each of their heads and set a hand on the doorknob. "I need to walk." Then he set real kisses on each of their cheeks and headed back through the stuffy hall into the wintry air.

∞

For two hours Cale walked the city streets, projecting a hand to secure the tassels on a young girl's hat, an embrace for the suited man who stared at his silent phone. He twirled his bourbon on the slick bar top at the busy Depot, searching for someone in need of assurance. Around him conversation bubbled and bodies stretched back with hearty laughs.

Was he the only one in the fiery glow who was alone tonight? How would it feel if an astral touch smoothed back his hair as he'd done to Sanje? What could he give in return?

Abandoning the burning drink, he returned to the quiet cold. In his sack, Cale had kept the green notebook. Through a dust of frost, his feet made their way to the bus stop. The bench was empty. Though he projected a hand to warm it, he sat on unresponsive metal.

What had that man done to him? Could he find where the gypsy lived? What wood frame, what cement foundation could hold combustible him? Could he shove against the wall that body in its confident ease? Control *him?* Lick down every inch?

Cale wrote. Feverishly, his pen ripped at the page, undressing him, his black hair silk against tongue, his skin sun-baked summer. Did he feel it? Was he now lying on his bed, splayed for the *mouth the tongue the hands* rushing over him?

Cale didn't stop writing until his breath's intake stung

with its force. His chest was heaving, as he sat alone on the bench. Beyond silver clouds the night sky unveiled dim stars. One after another they appeared as he let his head fall back, his legs quivering with the aftershock of climax. So distant, each glinting eye.

He was alone. He hadn't traveled from this bench. How did one find fire that flamed only at its own ignition? Margo and Bracie were wrong; this was no way to live.

∞

Returning home, Cale rushed through the door before James could rise from his chair, before he could project a firm kiss on Cale's cold check. He straddled the leather recliner and slid his tongue between James's lips.

"Here. Now," he demanded. James had solid brown eyes, and this close the color clarified. His lips parted before any touch but skin passed between them.

As the book slid to the floor, place-mark lost, James ran his hands up Cale's back, pulling them closer. Cale kissed back, slow and deep. It was luxurious how mouths converged, and still he felt another set of hands streaming down his legs, and still his own mind went to the fallen book, to replace the bookmark and keep James's world tidy and safe.

Controlled by passion. Cale shifted his astral touch to the back of James's knees, his inner thighs, placed his corporeal hands on James's shoulders. Orchestrated, they traced the places of known arousal. The heated kiss cooled, thoughts wandering to fallen books, to the smell of oranges, to Sanje with his sadness.

Controlled by passion. Projecting to escape. The mind had too many dimensions. Living on multiple planes sometimes felt like living nowhere. This wasn't love.

"James," Cale whispered, all touch frozen in him. He had no single home, a constant traveler, alive in too many lives, none his own. So what was this gypsy man's claim? Why, as Cale kissed James, did he see that mischievous grin?

Why did he see him now though he hadn't projected? Cale's spirit felt wrenched—to *him* pulling off an olive-green shirt. Though his mouth was on James's, Cale felt his tongue circling soft brown nipples, tonguing a harder sternum. For a moment, he tasted a copper bite. Did he hear or imagine a TV faintly playing, though their own apartment carried only the sound of the dishwasher hum?

James closed his eyes, and his astral hands moved in the air. Was he away somewhere, gripping the white tautness of another man's thighs? A shade of darkness slid over, a silk universe, as gypsy hair swept Cale's forehead. He pressed James's shoulders to the recliner, but his hands sank into a white pillow on a strange new bed.

Then, in a gust, the vision was gone. He was back in his sterile home, in a vacant gulf. The gypsy's tease, his taunt—

Cale slid off James. "I need to write. It's him. He wants —" Snatching the green notebook from his pack, he scooted a chair to the kitchen table.

Blankly, James watched him, then his hand stroked the recliner, though Cale felt no astral touch.

Write it. Cale's pen scribbled as if ink could project as well. Who was writing this story? Did the gypsy man control its fate?

"I didn't even know you were a writer," James said, and his eyes closed.

Cale's fingers tightened on the pen to control its wanton rush. And through the words, he saw those knowing eyes, sunlit and night-drenched, seeping deep. His gaze stabbed Cale's throat, took his voice. *Was he here?*

For a moment, he returned his focus to James, imagined his hand rubbing the tension from James's temple, stroking his hair in fond soothing. His lips tilted up with pleasure, as Cale's index finger traced the strained tendon of his neck. But the pen in his hand flooded, blue ink spilling.

Whisper beneath the black silk fringe of hair: what do you own? TV light blinked through an apartment, the sound low as that taut and slender body relinquished to the bed's promised comfort. *Lips feather a cheekbone shining with a low orange moon, the brush of sable lashes, down the slope of nose to pause at soft, cool lips, a sliver of energy between...*

In the recliner, James arched with a low moan.

Cale tried to move his hand to follow James's, but the gypsy owned his pen. *Tongue the Adam's apple, flicker down the sternum, copper skin flushed with core heat, breathe the sun-baked stone of his inner thigh. Hands along the lean-muscled landscape pulsing with fire. Who do you want?*

Cale's body ached with desire. Black silk fluttered against his face, trickled over his arm. He saw James watching him now, saw his own hand gripping the pen, following its trail of letters.

"What are you writing?" James said.

Unthwarted passion, selfish lust, Cale thought. Would it be worse than living on the astral planes? To live only through words, to touch only in the written image of him?

Lips on lips, a flicker of tongue. Astride him, pelvis hovering.

No, not worse. To be slave to this beautiful muse, to be owned by gypsy eyes, his heart and heat demanding, *Write me.*

"A love story," Cale breathed.

James stroked himself. "So you found his love, matchmaker?"

Gypsy lips twisted to a grin. Cale's mind flashed to a black wing on a white pillow, a copper body with the invitation to soar, and his satin lips like a cloud bed, full and foreign, stole his answering words.

AUTHORS

JASON ANDREW lives in Seattle, Washington with his wife Lisa. He is an associate member of the SFWA and member of the International Association of Media Tie-In Writers. By day, he works as a mild-mannered technical writer. By night, he writes stories of the fantastic and occasionally fights crime. As a child, Jason spent his Saturdays watching the Creature Feature classics and furiously scribbling down stories; his first short story, written at age six, titled "The Wolfman Eats Perry Mason" was rejected and caused his Grandmother to watch him very closely for a few years.

THERESE ARKENBERG is the author of short fiction published or forthcoming in *Beneath Ceaseless Skies, M-Brane SF, Crossed Genres*, and *Warrior Wisewoman 3*, and Pink Narcissus Press's anthology *Daughters of Icarus*, as well as a science fiction novella, *Aqua Vitae* from WolfSinger Publications. Her novel *Last of the Lesser Kings* was released as an ebook by Silver Publishing in Janurary 2012 under the name T.L.K. Arkenberg. She also writes erotic romance as T.C. Mill.

BRIAN BOBOWSKI is a hobbyist writer, born in southern Ontario, Canada, currently living in Nova Scotia, planning to join his fiancée in Sweden. An avid reader since childhood, his literary interests include mostly fantasy and science fiction, including the works of Mercedes Lackey, Lois McMaster Bujold, and David Weber, with a smattering of contemporary and historical fiction as well. He has a great fondness for ferrets and other small, oft-misunderstood creatures.

KEYAN BOWES lives in a stream of stories and occasionally grabs one long enough to type it in. A graduate of the 2007 Clarion Workshop for science fiction and fantasy writers, Keyan has had work accepted by *Cabinet des Feés,*

Expanded Horizons, Big Pulp, Strange Horizons, and several anthologies. She is currently rewriting two Young Adult novels in the contemporary fantasy adventure genre. *The Rumpelstiltskin Retellings*, a story in poetry-blog format, was made into an award-winning short film.

GREGORY A. CARTER enjoys reading just about everything, from classics to world literature to anything involving horror—especially tales of zombies and the supernatural. When his nose isn't stuck in a book, he reviews films for *The G.A.S.P. Factor* and zombie-related stories for *The G.O.R.E. Score;* writes short fiction, with stories appearing in several anthologies including *First Time Dead 2, Monster Gallery*, and *Before Plan 9;* and blogs at mrgregoc.blogspot.com. He lives in Long Beach, CA, with his partner of six years.

Author/Artist **JOHN DIMES** is the author of numerous short stories, comics, and books which include: *Intracations* (Mocha Memoirs Press), *The Rites of Pretending Tribe* (Zumaya Publications), *The White Corpse Hustle: A Guide for the Fledgling Vampire* (Publish America), and *There Are No Bad Movies (Only Bad Audiences)* (Lemon Pi).

PATRICIA J. ESPOSITO is a long-time writer and has spent most of her life exploring the intoxicating realms of the imagination and chasing the muse. Her fiction and poetry have appeared in the anthologies *Lights of Love* and *Apparitions,* as well as in various literary and speculative magazines, including *Rose and Thorn, Scarlet Literary Magazine, Clean Sheets, Karamu, Hungur,* and *Midnight Street.* Her first GLBT vampire novel *Beside the Darker Shore* was published in 2011, and she has received honorable mentions in "year's best" anthologies as well as a Pushcart Prize nomination.

WILLOW FAGAN lives in Portland, Oregon. They're genderqueer, which for them means that they feel more like a pirate princess than like a man or a woman. Their fiction has appeared in *Fantasy Magazine, PodCastle,* and *The Year's Best*

Science Fiction and Fantasy 2011.

EDUARDO A. FEBLES, a native of Puerto Rico and resident of Boston, is Associate Professor of French at Simmons College. His research focuses on the intersections between politics and literature, especially in 19th century France. He is the author of *Explosive Narratives: Anarchy and Terrorism in the Works of Emile Zola* (Rodopi Press 2010). He is the author of several short stories, including "The Fury of a Cylopean Cyclone" published in *The Caribbean Writer* (2008) and "Lizards and Butterfly Bats" in *Calabash: A Journal of Caribbean Arts and Letters* (2008).

JEANNELLE FERREIRA spends her days editing, believes in ghosts, and skews the human-to-cat ratio of her household at every opportunity. She is the author of one novel, a two-mom-family children's book, a handful of short stories, and, surprisingly (if you know her from that prosody class in high school), several poems; she has a degree in creative writing from Brandeis University. She lives in Maryland with her wife and daughter. Read more in *Steam-Powered II: More Lesbian Steampunk Stories* (Torquere) and *Stone Telling Magazine* (stonetelling.com).

DAN HART is a systems engineer working, reading, and hiking in Silicon Valley with his boyfriend. He maintains a blog and list of publications at danhartfiction.com.

ZACHARY JERNIGAN lives and sometimes writes in Arizona. His work has appeared in various places, including *Asimov's Science Fiction, Crossed Genres,* and *Escape Pod.* "The Succession of Knoorikios Khnum" was shortlisted for a 2010 Gaylactic Spectrum Award. He blogs about writing and being jealous of other writers at zacharyjernigan.blogspot.com. Information about his first novel, *No Return* (2013, Night Shade Books), can be found at noreturnthenovel.blogspot.com.

J. LANNAN is a writer, poet, artist and costumer that has trouble not taking on any creative project that comes his way. He earned a BA in History from Ohio University, but abandoned the serious study of non-Western history once realizing that his odd sense of humor has no place in research papers about the Iranian justice system.

ROSE MAMBERT has a weakness for dashing swordsmen and a fascination with folktales from all over the world. Although she's never dated a fox spirit, she understands well the dangers of drinking too much sake under the cherry blossoms.

MICHAEL PENKAS has lived in Chicago for eight years. In that time, he has had a dozen short stories published. He spends his spare time writing, patronizing coffee shops and lurking in the background of various open mic events. Like many writers, he is in the process of beginning a novel. If you're honest, you'll admit that you really don't want to hear about his novel-in-progress.

WARREN ROCHELLE lives and works in Fredericksburg, Virginia, where he has taught English at the University of Mary Washington since 2000. Rochelle's short fiction and poetry have appeared in various journals. His short story, "The Golden Boy" (published in *The Silver Gryphon*) was a Finalist for the 2004 Gaylactic Spectrum Award. Rochelle is the author of three novels: *The Wild Boy* (2001), *Harvest of Changelings* (2007), and *The Called* (2010), all published by Golden Gryphon Press. He also published a critical work on Le Guin and academic articles in various journals and essay collections. He is at work on a collection of gay-themed science fiction and fantasy short stories and a novel about a gay werewolf and his godling-boyfriend.

NATHAN SIMS grew up knowing he wanted to be a storyteller. Somewhere along the way his storytelling turned from the written word to the stage and he spent many years acting, directing, and teaching before returning to his first love: writing. He currently lives outside Washington, D.C. with his partner. His fiction can be found in various anthologies from Bold Strokes Books, QueeredFiction Press, Library of the Living Dead, doorQ.com Publishing, and *Collective Fallout*. He is currently at work on his first novel.

J. DANIEL STONE is a 24-year-old writer born and raised in New York City. His stories appear in *Abomination Magazine*, Dopamalovi Books, Blood Bound Books, Pink Narcissus Press, and more. In 2010 *Hellnotes* deemed him "psychologically insightful." You may contact him at: Solitaryspiral@gmail.com or on twitter @SolitarySpiral.

MICHAEL C. THOMPSON is a known murderer. He has a black heart with a delicious creamy center, but do not be fooled. If you see him, turn and head in the other direction. His hideousities have been printed in numerous publications and online, including Volume One of *Queer Fish* and his first short story collection, *The Negatives*. And yes, he finds it amusing to make up words. You don't want to know what else amuses him.

NGHI VO currently lives by an inland sea, and her work has appeared in *Strange Horizons* and *Alien Skin*. Her current interests include old gods, new gods, Tang-dynasty China, glaciers, corsetry and the Ottoman Empire. She can be contacted at bridgeofbirds@gmail.com.

ALSO AVAILABLE FROM PINK NARCISSUS PRESS

QUEER FISH (VOLUME 1)
Our first volume of *Queer Fish!* This eclectic anthology of gay fiction is packed with memorable couples just trying to make it work, whether "it" is as simple as distance or as complicated as figuring out how to date a headless ghost, an insidious incubus, an overworked superhero, or a big stupid Irish guy from South Boston. Whatever challenges these heroes face, there's never a shortage of passion, intrigue and zombie attacks.

ISBN: 978-0-9829913-3-6

FEASTING WITH PANTHERS
A fantasy adventure novel
by Lyle Blake Smythers

We found the first one-eyed man at dawn...
So begins the highly original fantasy tale of warrior poet Catalan, when he and his band stumble upon a handsome acolyte near death in the mountain pass. But when the acolyte reveals his mystical vision, the poet finds himself at the center of a War Game between two mysterious sorcerers. To unravel the mystery, Catalan and the agents of the War Game must seek the missing components of an enchanted chess set in a quest complicated by deceit and treachery, in which nothing is what it seems.

ISBN: 978-0-9829913-7-4

www.ingramcontent.com/pod-product-compliance
Lightning Source LLC
LaVergne TN
LVHW012036110125
800974LV00025B/230